Morning Star Journey

Judy McGrath

Illustrations by Elizabeth Innuso

Judy McGrath

Throughout the book, you will see the below section spacers. The first is the Morning Star petroglyph and the second is the Journey petroglyph.

"Morning Star Journey." ISBN 978-1-62137-756-6 (hardcover); 978-1-62137-757-3 (softcover); 978-1-62137-758-0 (eBook).

Published 2015 by Virtualbookworm.com Publishing Inc., P.O. Box 9949, College Station, TX, 77842, US.

TABLE OF CONTENTS

1

STRIKE ONE

January

IN HINDSIGHT, I SHOULD HAVE WAITED until the mud on the path dried before I tried to climb up to the overlook. "Tuck and roll," I'm told, is the preferred reaction when you fall, and my neck didn't *seem* broken. But, I felt a hundred years old, and probably had some special bruises on my backside, as well.

Thinking these thoughts helped stem a flood of panic over having landed in an immovable tangle of camera and backpack straps, complicated by a stretchy sage green cardigan. Basically, I was immobilized in the middle of the

1

cold, mucky puddle I had carefully stepped around just before my ascent to the summit. Collecting rattled brain cells, I took inventory. The stylish new cardigan was history, I didn't even want to think about the state of my camera, and I was *really* uncomfortable. From my prone position, I could see crisp, blue winter sky. To the left, and up the steeply winding trail, beyond an elderly gnarled manzanita bush, a hint of storm clouds could be seen approaching from the east.

Generally, I liked to build a positive inner image of myself as an elegant, mature woman—fifty last birthday—in complete control of her active, fulfilling life. This helped bolster self-confidence when things went amiss. Though, I was pretty sure that most elegant, mature women weren't normally found imprisoned in a muddy puddle on a chilly day, with a possible cold storm on the way, in a place no one knew they'd gone. A setback.

From early childhood I'd had to deal with more mishaps than the average person. My family—aware that these blips of misfortune didn't usually inconvenience anyone but me—still would have been happier had I ceased sketching trips out in the wilds by myself. At home, I rarely had these problems.

As a wildlife and landscape artist (my canvases are signed J. Gustaffeson, but I go by Janna) staying at home wasn't an option. The southern California wilds were where my sketching and photography subjects were to be found. Even my on-again-off-again arthritis wasn't able to sufficiently restrict my outback ramblings. Theo, my husband and soul mate, worried, but had given up trying to save me from myself some years ago.

The day had begun in sunshine, as I sat astride my horse, Lion, riding along the mountain road on our property that led to this beautiful meadow-like clearing. When I had dismounted to climb to, what I call, the Overlook, the air had been fairly warm. Now, the wind had turned chillier.

Lying in the frigid puddle, I was considering how to rid myself of gear straps and cardigan when a loud snort sounded next to my ear. Lion—golden as his namesake—had become curious about activity that was strange even for me, and had interrupted his munching on the meadow grasses to investigate.

Inquisitively, Lion bumped me rather hard with his head, which had the effect of improving my position such that I was able to roll out of the puddle. Lion had definitely earned himself an extra carrot, whenever we finally arrived back at the pasture where he lived with our other horses, as well as several llamas. "Now, if I could just get unwound from this stupid cardigan," I complained aloud.

"Hold still and I'll help," said a familiar voice. I turned my head to see my friend, Red Thunder—aka Thad Wolfe—walking toward me, shaking his head. A couple minutes later he had me free from the pack and camera straps. After adjusting the ruined cardigan, I stood up. "I'm not even going to ask," said Red Thunder.

"Not sure I could explain, anyhow," I admitted.

"So, did you get any sketches prior to the puddle incident?"

I shook my head. Some days are not favorable outside the studio. Red Thunder was a twenty-nine year old quasi-cop friend and frequent sketching partner. He had been raised by his father's German-American family on the east coast, and had come west a couple years ago, partly to investigate the Navajo-Lakota roots of his mother's family.

He scanned my overall condition, but didn't comment. Instead, he said, "I was over at the pasture and saw you had Lion out. So, I came looking for you."

I smiled at him. "You just think you're going to find me stuck upside-down in a bush again someday." It was a private joke that described how we first became acquainted. In fact, he had saved my hide many times, and mostly kept the details to himself. He didn't talk a lot, and normally could be counted on to not break a person's concentration, qualifying him as an excellent sketching partner.

"I wanted to talk with you." He took a deep breath. "I figured out how to demonstrate my method of sand painting." My friend created beautifully unique sand paintings that were untypical of Navajo art for that medium.

I must have looked over-eager, for he held up his hand. "I'm still not comfortable doing it for an audience. Usually only medicine men do that and, for them, there's a long religious chant involved that often takes several days."

"What happens?" I was curious. My opportunities for this kind of cultural information were rare, since it involved many tribal customs which even Red Thunder was unsure about. His research into his Native American heritage was still quite recent.

"The whole idea of Navajo sand painting is to help a sick or out-of-balance person back to a personal harmony with the natural order of things."

"How would it do that?"

"Not certain. That's what my teacher, Ben Yazzi, told me when I asked. He'd been studying the art for a couple years, and one day took me to participate at a healing ceremony. I was mainly intrigued by the precision needed to direct the sands that formed the painting. The Chant—that's what these healing events are called—took *nine days* to complete."

"Holy cow."

He nodded. "I was there only for the one day. Ben had been teaching me about making jewelry, but sand painting is a quite different thing. A very holy thing to the religious Navajo. I don't know much about the religion, and Ben thought it might help me find more balance as a Navajo if I knew a little about sand painting and its purpose. He explained the process to me as the Chant progressed."

"What did he think about your sand paintings?"

"He was ambivalent when I began to experiment with colored sand, because my compositions weren't traditional paintings. My sands aren't gathered by sacred procedure and the paintings I do aren't part of a Chant. Anyway, the subject matter I use has nothing to do with Navajo deities and religion." He shrugged. "To a Navajo, I am playing in the sand like a child."

He glanced at me. "That sand painting I did for your birthday last summer was the first I'd done with a person in mind. But, now I'm thinking of another individual for the demo. Would this evening after dinner be convenient?" He seemed a little self-conscious.

I was gratified that he would take the trouble to show his art to us. And I was also curious about the "individual" he spoke of. "We'd be honored," I said. "And, of course, you'll have dinner with us. Right?"

He grinned. "Of course." After assisting me back up on Lion, he rode alongside on Fire, his beautiful red and white pinto. We took it slow back to the pasture, because my body was now complaining about how it had been treated that day.

The pasture where our horses lived was part of a fourteen hundred acre parcel of land my husband, Theo, and I had bought and named Cornbread Mesa Ranch the previous year. Most of the ranch was wild, primitive, and mountainous, however we had developed a small corner of it for our horses and llamas, and for ourselves. As a return favor to Red Thunder, following the many times he had helped us, we had offered him pasture and shelter for his horse among our own animals.

Matt Johnson, a college student, stayed in the comfortable cabin we had there and managed the developed part of the property for us. I told him about the return of the horses, then got into my Highlander and headed back toward our house in the Oak Creek Homeowners Association located in the town of Coyote Canyon.

Eleven years prior, when Theo and I first arrived in Coyote Canyon, we were newcomers to California. Theo had been raised in Vermont, and I had grown up in Ohio and Michigan. Our daughter, Rosalie was eight, our son, Christian, was six, and I was pregnant with the twins. The HOA, with its nearby good schools, contractor maintained landscaping, patrolled streets, and volunteer-maintained horse trails, seemed a good place for us. We also appreciated the Oak Creek Club pool, Jacuzzis, tennis courts, and restaurant.

Now the twins were eleven, Rosalie was in college, and Christian a senior in high school. Our house currently burst at the seams with daily living and special projects, making the neighborhood restrictions of the HOA often seemed a little confining. The previous year, we had addressed this problem by seeking a way to expand our activities beyond the HOA. After a property search of several months, the purchase of Cornbread Mesa Ranch had offered us freedom to experiment.

As I turned onto our street, Red Thunder drove his big, black F250 on down the road toward his apartment. Dinner wouldn't happen for several hours and, no doubt, he had cop stuff to do. He was a tall, attractive man with a generally quiet, thoughtful personality. Over the past year he'd become like family, so we encouraged him to feel at home at our table whenever his schedule permitted.

Walking in the door, I could hear Rosalie at work in the kitchen. A few years ago, I had begun a cooking system at our house. Christian and Rosalie cooked dinner and cleaned up at least once every two weeks. They were otherwise responsible for kitchen cleanup two other days a week. The twins, Gwen and John, usually did desserts for Christian's and Rosalie's meals and would, over time, graduate to full meals. The rest of the cooking and clean up I did, except when Theo decided to make breakfast or barbecue dinner. As Christian once commented to Red Thunder, "Mom thinks these are necessary survival skills."

Tonight, Rosalie was preparing her special spaghetti with meatballs, tossed green salad, and garlic bread, one of her standard menus and a family favorite. My youngest son, John had made Jell-O for dessert, to be served with whipped cream. Jell-O didn't take much time and could be made the day before, but sometimes he felt inspired to make a bigger effort, which could result in brownies, cupcakes, or giant cookies.

"Hi, Mom," said Rosalie. Her eyes widened as she saw the condition of my clothes and hair. I had momentarily forgotten the mud puddle. "What happened?"

"You don't want to know." I wasn't keen on discussing specifics. "I'm on my way to the shower, but thought I'd tell you that Red Thunder is coming to dinner." The name "Red Thunder" is on his birth certificate and he uses it as an artist. But, he was called Thaddeus "Thad" Clay Wolfe by his east coast family, and used it in his cop business. Even my family knew him as "Thad," but he'd probably always be "Red Thunder" to me.

I made my way through the bedroom and into the dressing room, shedding icky clothes as I went. The clothes went in a hamper, and I stepped into a nice hot shower. Hot water, soap and shampoo are wonderful antidotes to grossness. And Theo, probably having heard of my condition from Rosalie, was there with a big, fluffy towel. Well aware that I sometimes attracted uncomfortable, possibly dangerous circumstances, Theo considered a routine physical inspection his way of keeping up. But, that wasn't his only interest, and I soon found myself lying on our bed, looking up into slate blue eyes, saying, "I hope you locked the bedroom door."

He smiled. "I always plan ahead, but I got a little side-tracked." He got up to retrieve the first aid kit. A few minutes later he had inspected my bruises and painted an abstract pattern on my scratches with iodine. My twin, Jody, and I had inherited our mother's fair complexion and wavy dark red hair. Thus, injuries tended to appear more dire than expected.

Theo, a year older than I, was in much better shape, due to many years of geological fieldwork. His geological consulting business allowed more time in the field and less time in the office. All of that exercise had kept him lean and fit. I was more rounded, even though I had recently lost most of the extra curves gained during child-bearing years. My five feet, seven inches versus his six feet, two inches was a perfect fit for slow-dancing at the Club. He'd tuck me under his chin and we'd sway romantically to the music, transported back to a more youthful time, twenty plus years ago, when we were dating, and only just considering marriage. The intervening years, while often eventful, had been good to us.

When I walked into the kitchen to see how Rosalie was doing a bit later, I wore a long wine colored velour skirt and matching top with elbow length sleeves. A cozy outfit for a chilly January evening. By supper time, Theo had also showered, changed into jeans, and pulled on a midnight blue sweater. His damp blond hair glinted in the lamplight.

At dinner, Rosalie announced she had decided to take a second job at the Indian Heritage Store, but would still keep designing store windows at the Horse's Tale next door. She had worked at the Horse's Tale, which sold western gear and apparel, since graduating from high school.

Theo was concerned. "How will you have time to do both jobs, and still go to college and do your homework?"

"Well, Amanda wants me to work at the Indian Heritage Store in the mornings. I'm to do her displays, hang paintings, and of course sell stuff when people are in the store. But, she says the store is less busy in the mornings, and I can even do my homework when there's a lull."

"What about your classes?" I asked. "Aren't a lot of them in the morning?"

"Not this semester. Most are in the afternoon or evening now, and a lot can be done online. Matt and I can still carpool a couple days a week, because he has two days of just afternoon classes. "

"So, what about the other three days?" Theo wanted to know.

"There are plenty of other people to carpool with." She had her own Ford Ranger pickup, but, like most students, looked for ways to save on gas.

Red Thunder said, "Amanda will have you selling jewelry, right?" Normally, this would not be a loaded observation, but the owner's recent retail tactics had become of special interest to male customers. Amanda wore low cut knit tops over colorful skirts to model some of the beautiful pieces made by local Indian artists. Displaying jewelry in this way was guaranteed to catch the eye of both male and female tourists visiting the shop. Sales had noticeably risen and creators of the jewelry had subsequently benefitted. Red Thunder was one of those creators, so he had a legitimate interest.

Rosalie blushed as Theo queried, "Is a low cut black top part of the uniform?" Obviously, he felt such business clothing worn by Amanda to be inappropriate for his young daughter.

Rosalie folded her arms modestly in front of her. "It isn't a uniform. I can wear what looks best on me, but shows off the jewelry to customers." Our daughter has that lean look she gets from Theo, but with feminine cushioning to soften her frame. She and her siblings take after their father in their blond coloring. That evening she wore a low slung black skirt and boots, with a violet stretchy knit sweater top that slightly bared her shoulders. Fashionable and attractive, while still modest.

Her boyfriend—also our ranch manager, Matt—wasn't at dinner with us that evening. The previous summer, he had given her a lovely diamond "promise" ring, which was mostly his attempt to warn off other guys. I wasn't sure that Rosalie felt completely "promised." From what I could tell, she was still thinking about the relationship, and hadn't yet decided where it would lead. Theo and I, on the other hand, considered big commitments at nineteen to be premature. There would be plenty of time later for that.

Christian asked, "What does Matt think about your new job?" It was clear he thought the job might cause discomfort for Matt, and he was amused. He didn't dislike Matt, but they were somewhat competitive in guy stuff. Christian didn't mind the thought of Matt being annoyed by his sister's job.

Rosalie colored an even rosier hue. "He doesn't know, since I just got the job this afternoon after talking to Amanda." She turned to Theo, "I'm going to do the display windows for the Horse's Tale on days when I have a free afternoon, or on weekends. So it won't really interfere with other things. Besides, clothing displays change mostly seasonally and at holidays."

Red Thunder looked across the table at Theo, who changed the subject with the observation, "Janna says you've moved your home base from the East Coast to Coyote Canyon. Guess we'll be seeing more of you around here, and so will your horse."

Red Thunder nodded. "I'm looking forward to being here year around. In fact, I was out riding Fire today."

I contributed, "It was a good day for riding. Lion was such a good boy I gave him an extra carrot." Red Thunder glanced at me, but didn't comment further. His policy was to let me choose to tell about my mishaps, using my own timing.

I redirected the conversation. "Did you bring your sand painting gear along?"

"It's in the truck."

Rosalie looked up with anticipation. "Are you going to do a demo for us?"

He nodded again and smiled at her interest. I had noticed that every time our friend spent an evening with us, Rosalie looked at him frequently and asked questions. He was dressed in what he considered his eveningwear—black jeans, silver and turquoise medallion studded belt—otherwise known as a Concho belt—turquoise western-style shirt with an open collar, black hair held back in the usual leather tie. Rosalie was obviously intrigued. My sketching partner had never seemed to encourage her special regard. He was just as kind and considerate to her brothers and sister.

Gwen asked, "What is it going to be about?"

Red Thunder turned to her. "You will have to discover the subject as I create it."

"It sounds like a game," said Gwen, my analytical daughter.

"It should be revealing," he answered, smiling.

John asked, "Why can't you tell us now?" He wasn't big on being patient.

"This painting is to be for a particular person. I want to see if that person recognizes him or herself." While Red Thunder retrieved his pack from his truck and got things arranged for the demo, the rest of us carried supper dishes into the kitchen and helped Rosalie quickly clean up from dinner.

Gathering a few minutes later around my large drawing table in the studio, we allowed the artist plenty of room to move around as he worked. He had positioned the table to be perfectly flat and placed a clear plastic sheet over it to catch errant grains of sand. In the middle of the plastic rested a thin piece of Masonite that hid all but four inches of the table on all sides. As we watched, Red Thunder applied a sticky jell substance called "sand base" with a small trowel in an even layer all over the board.

"Why are you putting that on?" John asked.

"This is what holds the sands in place once it dries," Red thunder replied.

"How long does it take to dry?" Gwen wanted to know.

"It will be mostly solid by tomorrow morning. If I were making a *real* ceremonial sand painting like a Navajo medicine man, I wouldn't use any fixative to set the picture permanently. I'd make the sand painting directly on the floor and it would be much larger than this."

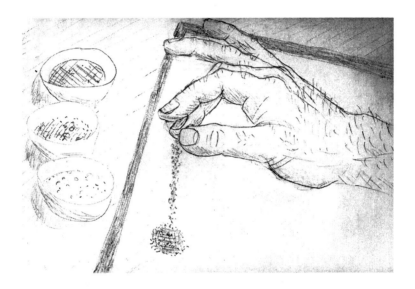

The children looked at the floor and then back at Red Thunder. His lips formed a half-smile.

"Not only that, but when the medicine man completes the picture, the person it is done for *sits* in the middle of it. Next, the medicine man walks on the picture ceremonially sprinkling corn meal on it. By the time a few minutes pass, you can no longer tell what the picture is."

Christian said, "I don't see the point of that."

Red Thunder set out little paper cups filled with various colored sands. He began with black sand, sifting grains through the first three fingers of his right hand to make a fine black line across the center of the painting horizontally.

As he worked, he said, "Sand paintings made during the process of a Navajo Chant are not intended as art. They are to help an individual heal something that's gone wrong in his or her body or life. To help the person set his mind in a harmonious direction, the medicine man has the client sit in a particular place within the painting so that he becomes a *part* of the painting. Navajos believe that the power of thought is much more powerful than western medicine methods. So, they ask a medicine man to make a picture that will help them correct their thinking and therefore their actions."

Tall black lines began rising from the center horizontal line as he skillfully directed the powdery sand through his fingers without ever seeming to err.

He continued speaking, "More powerful even than thought, is the magic believed to be contained in the painting that comes from the gods which are depicted. When the client sits in the painting, it is thought that he takes on the powers of the god on which he sits, receiving absolute protection from all danger of being bothered by his problem ever again."

"What happens if the bad thing comes back?" asked Rosalie, watching his hand move over the painting.

"The responsibility for the success of the Chant lies ultimately with the sick person. According to tradition, if his belief is pure and unwavering, he will reap the benefits given by the gods. Of course, from the time of the Chant and onward, he must consciously live a harmonious life and avoid what are called 'errors' against the natural order of things."

The vertical black lines began to sprout black branches and I realized that these figures were trees.

Theo said, "Belief is pretty heavy medicine in many religions and cultures."

Red Thunder nodded, "The Navajo consider it to be so important that one of the Chants takes nine days to accomplish. The medicine man, the client, and the client's assistants must go through very unusual practices with multitudes of details that must be remembered correctly. Even the large crowd of watching participants must carefully conform in certain ways, such as wearing special clothing and following ritual customs that have been honored with the passage of time. It becomes a community event and memory. All of which helps reinforce belief in the power of the magical help that has been received."

Red and yellow began to appear like flame shapes in the branches of the trees. Then, in the foreground, the distinct lines of a black pickup truck took shape. And as we all watched silently, familiar figures began to appear around the truck. I recognized the pink top I was wearing on the day of the disastrous fire at our ranch early on in the previous fall. The figure—which I gathered was supposed to be me—was opening the door of the passenger side of the truck, while another figure, which looked like Red Thunder, held a woman with short brown hair in his arms, about to place her in the bed of the truck. More flames flashed upwards and around the trees and then the largest figure of all was shown placing a smaller female figure, which seemed to be Aunt Myrtle, in the truck bed.

"That's the green shirt I was wearing, but you've made me look really big," said Christian identifying the scene as the successful rescue of Sandra Gunther, Aunt Myrtle, and me from the devastating fire that swept our land on that grim day. A day, not so long ago, when Red Thunder and Christian had executed a split second operation that took solid courage and quick thinking.

Red Thunder filled in a few more details on the figures and then began to work in the billowing yellow-gray smoke rising into the sky to blanket a glowing orange sun.

Christian asked, "So, is this picture for *me* then?" He looked self-consciously pleased by the idea.

Red Thunder looked up at him. "It is for you. As you noticed, I made you more prominent than the others in order to feature your part in the rescue on that day."

"Thanks, Thad." Christian seemed to be comparing his memories to the sand painting.

I turned to our friend. "It's wonderful to have a good visual record of that occasion." Each detail was depicted to recreate the actions and conditions of that frightening day. The composition came together beautifully. "Does it have any other meaning?"

Red Thunder looked down at his creation with the rest of us. "This painting has no claim to magical power. But, it's a day that should be remembered."

"It's better than a photograph," said Theo, examining the sand details close up. "It must have taken a while to learn to handle sand like that."

Red Thunder gave that half smile again. "There were a lot of attempts that went into the trash before I began keeping a few. Eventually, when someone offered to buy a couple, I decided to display them at the Indian Heritage Store."

I said, "Amanda says they sell very well and that you need to make more of them."

Red Thunder looked pleased, but didn't reply. Soon after, he gathered up his gear, and gave Christian instructions for dealing with the sand painting. We all thanked him several times for the demonstration and Christian repeated his thanks for the gift. When Red Thunder left, everyone cleared out of my studio. I was glad Christian had a permanent reminder of a time when he had performed courageously under challenging circumstances. Everyone needs to be able to recall occasions when they exceeded their own expectations.

A few days later, I sat in a dark vehicle thinking about how much I hated to sit in the dark doing nothing. Bob Taggert, my Coyote Canyon cop buddy, and I were waiting for Stevette Strike to come back to the cottage she had rented with Gudrun Bohn at Lake Mirage, a small desert resort area. We were in Bob's black Explorer with the lights turned off, down the street from Stevette's cottage. Bob told me we were doing it this way so that Stevette wouldn't get nervous.

And why was I—Janna Gustaffeson—on a stakeout with Bob Taggert at nine o'clock at night in a chilly car when I could be home in a comfortable warm chair by the fire? Because, I had known Stevette years before in my twenties, when I lived in an art commune in Ann Arbor. The commune was a period house with many bedrooms originally meant for a large Victorian family. Back then Stevette, a member of the commune, was a statuesque brunette of riveting feminine proportions that had caused particular notice among the resident males. Her six feet of beauty gave me rather inferior feelings for a while, but I had reasoned then that the girl couldn't help being tall and gorgeous.

Nevertheless, the disinclination of several individuals to be regular about the monthly rent caused me to feel a rising disenchantment with communal life. Then, too, there was the general drift of artistic jealousies, and a creeping awareness that risky antics of an intimate nature were growing increasingly common. Mounting concerns about the prevailing situation triggered a decision to move several states away a few months later. Tish Halloran and I, being fellow art commune members, decided after lengthy discussion, that a shared apartment in New York City's East Village would be an improvement over Ann Arbor.

I learned later that the commune folded soon after we left, and with its demise, Stevette and her best female friend, Gudrun Bohn, had struck out for San Francisco. The stated reason Bob was interested in Stevette related to three vaguely suspicious San Francisco suicides in which she had a tenuous connection. Upon arriving on the west coast, Stevette had worked in the movie business, gradually developing a sideline making promotional films and DVDs for young, aspiring actresses, and aging actresses whose careers needed rejuvenation. She had done demos for all three of the deceased women. Within a year of connecting with Stevette they had each committed suicide. To me it seemed a rather feeble connection.

Though the deaths were considered a strange coincidence by investigating police, nothing emerged from official probing to indicate wrongdoing. All evidence pointed to actual suicide, despite the lack of clear motives. A San Francisco detective friend of Bob's noted that Stevette owned a vacation cottage on Lake Mirage. Bob had been asked to quietly check things out.

Somehow—in a way not made clear to me—Bob found out that I had known Stevette when we were both much younger and living in the commune. He quizzed me over what I could recall about her, which wasn't much. She was a noticeable personality, but we hadn't been close, and there had been no contact since those days in Ann Arbor.

Bob worked with that information for a while, but then got word that Stevette would be coming to the cottage for a few days relaxation from work. Bob wanted her to stay relaxed and unaware of continuing police curiosity. The idea was to see if a more solid connection could be made between Stevette and the deaths—or conversely, a clearer indication of her non-involvement—as a way of taking the puzzle a step closer to resolution.

"And what better way for Stevette to relax than to reminisce with an old friend from the commune over fond memories of her youth." Bob thought this argument had a good chance of gaining my assistance. It is worth noting here that using quietly unorthodox methods (sometimes incorporating non-police persons) had been recognized by police authorities in the county. Thus, he enjoyed a certain latitude related to by-the-book procedure. Undoubtedly, this attitude hinged completely on Bob's continued success, involving no embarrassing fallout.

According to Bob, I was to spontaneously drive up to the cottage in my Highlander, after supposedly having heard of Stevette's whereabouts from town gossip, and seek to renew an acquaintance that had never had much sparkle even back in Ann Arbor. When he introduced the idea, it seemed pretty lame to me, and I just looked at him.

I reminded myself that Bob was a good man and a good cop.

"I'll help you," I told him. "But only because it seems important to get this finally resolved for Stevette, and anyone else who has been harmed by the situation. Anyway, I want to ask her if she's heard from Tish Halloran. Tish and I left the commune together, but she and Stevette used to talk sometimes. Maybe Stevette has heard from Tish and has an e-mail address where she can be reached. I haven't been able to find her on Facebook."

"I knew you wouldn't let me down," said Bob, with a grin. Bob and I had a special friendship. I had once probably saved his marriage by reminding him his anniversary was the following day. And Bob had watched over the safety of my family during dicey circumstances that had arisen the preceding year. So, though caving in to his stakeout request was odd, it was not unthinkable. However, before Bob would let me renew my acquaintance with Stevette, he wanted to check out the situation carefully. Thus the stakeout. If everything looked okay when Stevette finally showed up—and if it wasn't too late—then Bob would drive me back to my grandparent's house, where I'd left my Highlander, about a quarter mile down the lake road next to a small county park beach. I was to use my own car so as to arrive at Stevette's door in a more normal fashion—if anything about this expedition could be considered normal.

Anyway, here we were in Bob's black Explorer. Still. I was about to complain about how cold I was and how late it was getting, when headlights appeared on the lake road. A white Lexus SUV made its way slowly around the curve of the lake, lined with gently swaying palms, and pulled into the drive of Stevette's vacation cottage.

Suddenly, whipping around the bend, came an unmarked gray cop car, which then zipped without warning, into the drive right behind the Lexus. Before the gray car even came to a complete stop, the Lexus unexpectedly and rapidly reversed, causing the two vehicles to collide with a resounding crunch.

"Uhn," I said, involuntarily.

Bob put his head in his hands and moaned. "I told him to stay *away* from Stevette Strike. The guy knows it's not his case and he could screw everything up. Now it will be almost impossible to catch that woman unawares. Why me?" As Bob continued to mumble and swear under his breath, I realized that this was going to take time if I just sat there quietly.

"Bob," I said, interrupting his diatribe. "Please explain what just happened."

He groaned again. "The guy driving that gray unmarked is Kyle Krupp. Captain Krupp's nephew, just relocated here from San Francisco. He stepped in something while on the police force there, which I can't really talk about, but, suffice it to say, he made himself unpopular."

He paused to stare down the street. "The guy is thirty three. He's been a cop for ten years, and *still* has no idea what it takes to work a difficult case. He lacks the concepts of timing, of backing out of uncertain situations, and of remaining patient while perpetrators incriminate themselves.

He thinks he knows it all, and that's why he just got the front of his car rammed in the suspect's driveway."

I digested this. "If he's so bad, why was he hired *here*?"

"Aside from the fact that he's the captain's nephew, he isn't that bad all the time. Usually he can follow the rules and be reasonably competent. But, you don't get big promotions by always staying in the background, doing grunt work. He's anxious to make his move, and unfortunately, lacks a clear notion of how to go about it."

I noticed Bob wasn't doing anything about the car crash across the way. "Aren't cops supposed to respond to a collision?"

"*We* aren't going to do anything except sit and observe. Watch." He pointed to a police cruiser making its way down the road. "I figured Krupp would call for assistance over the driveway incident, and now help has arrived."

We watched two women, an angry guy, and a cop in uniform in the cottage driveway. Not much was audible, but everything that could be heard came from the furious guy. I got the impression that he looked younger than his years, because he was losing control. He was mad and waving his arms around. The uniform stood calmly with a clipboard in his hands, while the women just stared at the gesturing man as though he was a specimen of scientific interest. In a few minutes, both the cop cars drove away, and the women went into the cottage.

I said, "Now what?"

"Now I drive you back to your Highlander and you go home. I don't want to risk that those women will associate you with Kyle. If Stevette *has* done anything wrong, they may be extra alert to coincidences concerning the police. I have no idea what that young idiot said to those women, but as you saw for yourself, he isn't subtle. It may be that he's made it unsafe for you to connect with them at all."

He started the Explorer engine and drove me back to my Highlander. "Thanks for coming with me this evening, I'm sorry it didn't work out. I'll get back to you in a day or so and let you know where we stand with Stevette, and our next move. Are you okay with that?"

I nodded. "I'll wait to hear from you."

I had warned Theo that I might be late, and lights in the house were dimmed when I pulled into the driveway back in Coyote Canyon. I noticed our neighbor, Stacy Johnson coming home late, as well. She waved as she drove up the long concrete strip that ran alongside the horse trail and our back yard. Stacy and Bob Johnson were Matt's parents, which is how we came to know Matt well enough to trust him to manage our animals at Cornbread Mesa Ranch. His sister, Christina Johnson, and our daughter, Gwen, were best friends. Even though Matt had given Rosalie a promise ring last summer, the subject hadn't ever come up among the parents for discussion. A wait-and-see attitude seemed to be the unspoken approach to the matter.

I locked the Highlander and walked quickly into our pleasantly warm house. It was well designed for our purposes, having a large kitchen and family room with fireplace, a good-sized dining room, and a step-down living room. The master suite was at one end of the house, and the four children's rooms, sharing two baths were at the other end. Off the center atrium, across from the front door was a guest room and bath.

The interior was a mix of modern furniture with a rustic design and family heirlooms. The walls were covered with paintings and bookcases. Some of the bookshelves had minerals and fossils mingling with the books. An assortment of antique oriental, braided, and American Indian rugs strategically covered some sections of hardwood and tile floors.

My own special space was the studio, which took up much of the garage. Skylights were cut in the roof for lighting. A drawing board, easels, painting racks, and equipment cupboards all shared the studio area of the garage. One corner had carpeting soft with age, and two comfortable chairs separated by a lamp table. This was generally my main thinking and meditation place.

Positioned for easy viewing, was a sand painting Red Thunder made for me last summer. It portrayed a woman standing with a mountain lion at her feet. Various other animals—owls, raccoons, foxes, plus the sun, moon and stars— were arranged esthetically around the borders of the painting. Red Thunder said it was to commemorate something I did last year that he considered courageous. And truthfully, whenever I looked at it, I felt more capable of accomplishing difficult tasks or facing hard situations.

The rest of the garage—about one quarter of the space—was occupied by a washer, dryer, spare refrigerator, general storage racks, Theo's workbench, and a tool rack.

The patio at the front of the house was where we liked to sit and watch the stars at night. At the back, another patio was used mostly for barbecuing. Wild flowers grew beside a flagstone path leading to our horse corral at the far end of the property. On the way to the corral, on the right was a small vegetable garden, and on the left a children's play yard with play equipment. The kids were growing up and seldom used this play yard anymore.

I walked around the house for a nightly check of windows and doors. Next to the back patio were the snug dog houses of Jasper, our old black Lab, and a sweet half-grown yellow Lab puppy, named Bree. I peeked out at them through the kitchen window as I turned out the light.

A few minutes later, I was in bed leaning against toasty Theo. There's nothing quite like a warm husband on a cold night.

2

ONCE UPON A RAINY MORNING

Second Half of January

THEO AND I WERE OUT with our horses early the
next morning, at the ranch, on our way to the
nice cache of white quartz found the previous
summer. I had been familiarizing myself with
some of the characteristics of our newly acquired
land when a deposit of the gleaming white
mineral caught my eye just off one of the main
trails crossing the property. On that day, I had
noticed a largish piece of quartz on the south
side of the trail. When I left the path to
investigate, I realized the boulder it was resting
beside hid behind it a whole cliff of the white

mineral. At the time I immediately thought of Theo, and knew he'd want to photograph this little area and collect samples for our mineral shelves at home.

So, we were riding down the dirt access road that bordered the property. He was on Rusty, a recently purchased brown quarter horse, and I was on Lion. The sun was beginning to burn off the early fog we often get in winter. We were prepared, having layered warm clothes on top of cooler clothes. One always does better with layers in semi-arid southern California. When the winter sun is shining, everything is warm and comfortable, sometimes even hot. But, when clouds cover the sun, or after dark, the air gets chilly very fast.

Theo tugged at the brim of his hat, narrowing his eyes at a distant point on the boundary road that ran alongside Cornbread Mesa Ranch. About a mile away, dust was stirred by a vehicle headed our way. He maneuvered Rusty behind Lion so that the driver would have plenty of room to pass.

When the vehicle got close enough, we could see it was a green Forest Service truck. The driver of the truck pulled over to the side of the road and stopped. A man in khaki got out, and asked, "Are you the folks who own this property?"

Theo dismounted, saying, "I'm Theo Gustaffeson and this is my wife Janna."

The man shook Theo's hand. "Jared Thatcher." He nodded at me. "Nice to meet you, Ma'am." He was probably in his mid-twenties, or so, and looked like he led an outdoor life. About six feet tall, reddish-blond hair, a ruddy complexion and sharp blue eyes. He looked like he didn't miss much, but his smile was friendly.

Theo said, "Yes, we own this property. How can we help you?"

"You've probably heard about the Hunting and Fishing Camp the Forest Service is building not far from your property line on Chain of Lakes." He stated this information as a question. We nodded and waited for him to continue.

"I'm the unofficial liaison to the community, and also help facilitate local area construction progress. Construction is supposed to be finished and the camp open for business sometime this spring."

"That's an aggressive schedule." Theo said, looking at the clouds overhead.

"Yeah, that's what I told them." Jared Thatcher followed Theo's glance at the building thunderheads. "Anyway, we're going to be your near neighbors, which means there'll be a lot of noise and mess for a while. That goes with the job. I'd like to know if any problems come up from what we're doing. Always better to solve things as we go along, than wait 'til a situation arises." He reached into a pocket, pulled out a business card handing it to Theo. "That's all the ways I can be reached day or night. I'm not expecting emergencies, but now you know how to contact me."

Theo thanked him, and gave the Forest Service rep one of his cards in return. Jared Thatcher smiled, then got back in his truck. Theo remounted Rusty and we continued on our way to the quartz deposit. As expected, Theo was quite interested in how extensive the deposit was. It comprised most of the small ridge, where chunks of a boulder had broken off. A cluster of boulders, just off the trail, prevented casual observation of the natural lode of quartz.

Theo spent some time photographing the area and writing notes, then chose a few glistening semi-clear pieces to tuck into his saddlebags. It was late morning by the time we finished. We dropped off the horses in the pasture and then drove back home.

After lunch we went in different directions. He headed toward his office in Rancho Bernardo, and I drove to the Indian Heritage Store in town.

When I arrived at the store, Amanda and Rosalie had their heads together, conferring over a window display design my daughter had sketched. Amanda was the new owner and my good friend. Her uncle had originally opened the store many years ago, and finally sold out to Amanda the previous summer. It was a gallery for local American Indian artists and craftsmen, as well as an art and jewelry-making supply center. Amanda had bright, attractive new ideas to give the store a fresh look. A recent change to dramatic recessed lighting that highlighted paintings hanging along the walls was typical of her design theme. Jewelry was showcased attractively near the front of the store, while pots, sculptures, and artifacts were effectively positioned on softly-lit glass shelving.

When Amanda first took over, she repainted the walls a warm golden white, and accented the woodwork in bright southwestern hues. Rosalie had been hired to make displays that would blend into Amanda's theme, yet distinct enough to catch the eye of a tourist.

Amanda looked up as I entered. "I love your daughter's ideas. Check out the sleek, contemporary shelving. It should be a nice contrast with our traditional pottery."

Rosalie looked pleased at the praise. "I'm glad you like it. A more complex look could be done by adding textiles, but you don't sell those here."

Amanda laughed. "You're thinking of your future crafts store. You should move in next door and sell Native American rugs and textiles along with your yarns and weaving supplies. It would draw many of the same customers who walk in here, and the business would be good for both of us." This was a reference to Rosalie's dream of opening her own crafts business in town.

"Yeah, well," Rosalie shifted her feet self-consciously, "I'm not sure how that is going to come together, yet. But, when the time comes, I'll do your windows and displays if you'll do my books," she said, half joking. "I'm passing my courses, and the creative side of my business plan is good, but the books are not my favorite part." She grimaced.

Amanda shrugged at her, smiling.

I said mildly, "You might feel more confident once you've gotten more courses behind you."

"I suppose," she sighed. "But, *this* is what I love to do." She gestured toward boxes of pottery waiting to be unpacked for display in the window. She began removing pots from their wrappings, carefully setting them to one side as she decided how they would go on the esthetically-arranged shelving in the store's front window.

Amanda and I moved closer to the register and continued to chat. We'd been good friends ever since Amanda had arrived in town to begin working full time for her Uncle Nathan a few years prior. Last year, when Nathan was preparing to retire, Amanda's mother, Mrs. Ruben-Cortez, a jewelry store owner in Queens, New York, had agreed to back the sale of Nathan's gallery to her thirty-year-old daughter. My friend was especially qualified for this venture, having been raised in the jewelry business, interspersed with significant periods spent in the southwest with her Mexican Indian father. During later high school and college summers, her uncle had paid Amanda to help in his store, and learn about tribal artists in the near area. The gallery business was now in her blood, and she had a fine eye for jewelry and art objects.

Privately at home, Amanda kept a potter's wheel in her kitchen, and had a painting easel at the ready. She enjoyed seeing her own work on her walls and liked eating off dishes she had crafted. Most of all, she reveled in her role as the consummate, but not overbearing, saleswoman of Native American crafts and art. Wearing the most original and splendid pieces, such as some of the more elegant squash blossom design necklaces of turquoise and silver, she often sold the jewelry right off her bosom several times a day during the busiest tourist seasons. And since she was constantly on the lookout for the right man, she considered the resulting male attention an advantage.

Today, Amanda wore a salmon and black printed skirt, enhanced by her typical revealing black top. Her dark abundant hair was gathered into a silver and coral clasp on top of her head, allowing a cascade at the back. She wore a silver and coral choker with dangling trails of coral beads from a smooth throat. With matching earrings and bracelets, the effect was stunning.

We stood talking near the back of the store among the art supplies. I was picking up a couple new sketchbooks and some fresh pastels when the front door opened. I recognized Jared Thatcher, the Forest Service rep that Theo and I had spoken with earlier. He glanced toward Rosalie, about to ask a question, and stopped. I could see he was trying to recall what he had been about to say.

Amanda had dressed Rosalie up to sell jewelry, as well. But, with Rosalie's youthful blond appearance, she had opted for an off-white long-sleeved, modest scoop-neck dress. Her throat and slim wrists showed off a necklace and matching bracelets of chunky silver and turquoise. Jared's bemused eyes followed Rosalie's naturally graceful movements as she placed pots in the sunny window.

Rosalie put down the pot she had been holding. "May I help you find something?"

He smiled at her, exuding charm. "Lunch. You can help me find a place to eat in town. I'd enjoy treating you to a sandwich, if you'd keep me company."

Rosalie grinned at him. "Thanks for the offer, but I brought my sandwich with me. There's a lunch café across the street and a burger place if you take a right and go down the next block. Is there anything else you need? Some jewelry or pottery?" She touched the necklace she was wearing and looked at the pots in the window.

He said, "I really do like that necklace you have on. It looks great. But, I don't have anyone to buy jewelry for at the moment. How about you? Is anyone buying you jewelry?"

She showed him the horseshoe shaped diamond promise ring on her left hand, and he shook his head with wistful disappointment. "Well, let me know if you ever decide you're ready for different jewelry. I'll just check in from time to time, and see how you're doing." He straightened himself up. "In the meantime, do you happen to know a guy named Red Thunder?

I heard he sells stuff through this store, and I need to get in touch with him."

Rosalie went to the counter and sorted out one of Red Thunder's cards to hand him. "This has his current contact information."

Jared said thanks, winked at her, and then left the store.

Amanda said, "Next time he comes in, find out if he has a friend. I might be interested."

Rosalie laughed, turning back to her window display. I paid for my supplies and went home.

John and his friend, Travis Lee, came in the back door after school to tell me the news. "Mom, Travis' dad says he can take karate with Gwen and me after school!" The twins went to the Main Street Dojo three days a week for an hour directly after school. It was a good confidence builder and had helped John solve a bully problem he'd had the previous year. Small for his age at the time, he'd been an easy target for a bigger kid to shove around. But, when John began karate, he learned how to block punches and avoid confrontations through his more confident demeanor. The aggressive kids soon stopped testing him. This year John was taller and moved like a boy who could take care of himself. He and Gwen had passed from the white belt of the novice to the purple belt, signifying the next level, during what their teacher, Sensei Jim Kowalski, called the Autumn Challenge. Martial arts training had been good for both kids, but especially for John.

"That's great, Travis. I'm sure you'll like it," I told him.

Travis looked happy. "Yeah, my dad thinks John has been doing really good since he started at the Dojo. So, Dad wants me to learn about it, too."

"So, when do you start?" I asked.

"Dad says I can go with John this week to get my gi and stuff. It's gonna' be cool."

John said, "The Winter Challenge is next week, but I probably won't advance to green belt, yet. I'm going to test anyway, because it'll help me figure out what I need to practice most." He and Travis grabbed cookies and went out to the front patio to climb the Mulberry tree.

That morning, before leaving the house, I had put chunks of browned beef with pieces of potato, carrot, tomato, onion, and herb seasonings in the crockpot with enough broth to make gravy for stew. So, all I had to do was make cornbread and a tossed salad for supper. Rosalie had created a chocolate fudge cake for dessert, which she planned to serve with ice cream.

I was working on the last details for supper, when she came in wearing jeans and a sweatshirt. The dress she had on earlier was strictly for work. The rest of the time she usually wore casual winter clothing. January, even in southern California, was comparatively cold except around noon on sunny days.

About half an hour later the table was set, and we were all sitting down to eat. Travis had joined us, and John was eager to share news of his friend's new membership at the Dojo. After Travis had told everyone his karate plans, and been congratulated, Matt, also at dinner, and sitting next to Rosalie, cleared his throat to announce *his* newest venture. "I just signed up with the Marine Reserves at the college today." He glanced about waiting for a reaction.

"The military is always looking for capable young men to train," said Theo, in his usual mild tones.

"What does this mean for your schooling?" I asked. "Will it be interrupted?"

"No, I have delayed entry for after school ends in June. The good part is that the Marine Reserves will pay seventy-five percent of my schooling. I haven't got all the details, yet. But, I'll have to train for two weeks every summer as part of the bargain, plus, they expect me to show up one weekend per month during the rest of the year. I'll be gone this summer for the thirteen-week boot camp, but then be back in time for school in September." He looked at Theo. "Someone will have to fill in at the Ranch this summer while I'm gone."

Though, this was an inconvenience we'd have to work around at the ranch, I realized, as I glanced at Rosalie, that she was completely surprised by this development. She put her fork down and stared at Matt with great consternation.

She said, "Can we talk?" Then she got up from the table and walked toward the family room.

Matt got a bit red in the face, excused himself, and followed her.

Christian looked amused. "I think someone forgot a communication step."

Theo, tactfully changed the subject, and asked Gwen how things were going with her new pony, Sheherazadhe. Gwen had been given the pony for her birthday in early autumn, and was pleased to be asked. "She's wonderful. Shehri follows me around everywhere when I come to feed and ride her. I wash and brush her about once a week, and she adores the attention."

By the time dessert was served, Rosalie and Matt had returned to the table somewhat subdued, but no one seemed upset now. I was curious how that discussion had gone, but kept such thoughts to myself. Relationships are hard enough without a third party sticking in an oar. Anyway, I was fairly sure Rosalie would get around to talking to me about it. Especially if I didn't push the issue.

The next day I awakened to claps of thunder. It was still dark outside, and raining. I could hear branches rattling against the windows. The kind of day to stay in by the fire with a good book. But this was not an option, due to a promise made to Bob Taggert that I would visit Stevette. He had called a couple days before saying that Kyle Krupp swore he hadn't mentioned my name to Stevette. Krupp had, reportedly, informed her that he had worked in San Francisco and recently transferred to San Diego County. His introduction was to warn Stevette that he was a law enforcement officer who was watching her.

"Doesn't sound very impressive." I recalled Kyle Krupp's over-zealous tailing of Stevette into her own driveway. Though, her response—backing into his car—had seemed a little extreme. Could be it wasn't the first time she'd dealt with Officer Krupp. Maybe he had pestered her in San Francisco, as well.

Bob chuckled. "He didn't exactly come off as a believable threat. The women appeared to throw Kyle off balance rather than the other way around."

"She did get a dent in her bumper," I reminded him.

"But," said Bob, "she won't be paying for the repair. Kyle can't prove she backed into him. Anyway, he pulled into her driveway unannounced. She could easily have been adjusting the position of her car. So, he'll end up paying, just to keep things quiet. He can't afford to draw more negative attention."

"You aren't going to tell anyone that we were there and saw the whole driveway sequence?"

"Nope. He was warned to stay away because he might mess up an investigation. Now he has to pay the price. Everything must be handled with care, because another wrong move could end up costing the taxpayers extra, without the justification of a well-built case against Ms. Strike, or proof of her innocence."

I could see his point. "So, when do we go back to Lake Mirage?"

"Day after tomorrow. We'll work it the same as last time, except there will be no Kyle."

That didn't sound so bad two days ago. But, today it was raining and I hated getting wet. I put on navy cords and matching pullover. Black boots went over woolly socks. I shrugged on a taupe trench coat, grabbed my black shoulder bag, and blue-sky-with-white-clouds umbrella, and went out to face the elements. The gusty wind blew wet drops under the umbrella and into my face.

As I drove down the road, the sky began to lighten and the rain turned to mist. Bob and I planned to meet at my grandparent's house, but I had promised to be a little early to share breakfast with them.

Granddad opened the front door as I arrived, ready to hustle me inside the warm cottage. Lake Mirage stayed a little warmer year around than Coyote Canyon, but was still only ten degrees warmer than miserable. Unfortunately, the rain hadn't turned to mist here at the lake. When I had come down the lake road, the lake was invisible in the downpour, only a general grayness could be seen in that direction.

I ran from car to cottage, wiping my boots on the mat. As I hung my damp coat on a hook, smells of fritters wafted from the kitchen. Not a low-cal breakfast, but soul-satisfying. When Gram made fritters, one never knew what might appear on a plate encased in fritter dough, deep fried to a golden hue. This morning's selection appeared to be apple fritters and bacon fritters. "Lord, save me from high cholesterol," I thought.

Moments later, as rain drummed on the windows, Gram, Granddad, Aunt Myrtle and I sat with plates of fritters drizzled with maple syrup. Big cups of coffee seemed to ease digestion. This was not the sort of food I could eat regularly.

"I was just remembering last night how much you girls liked my fritters when you were with us in Michigan. It's been a while since I made them," said Gram. She was referring to the high school years when my twin, Jody, and I had lived with them.

"You can make them as often as you like, Naomi," my lean, but gnarled grandfather offered, as he neatly demolished the delicacy heaped up on his plate.

"Oh my, yes," said Aunt Myrtle, rapturously. "No one makes fritters like, you, Naomi. I remember how popular they used to be when you did them in the church kitchen for potlucks back in Michigan. Why, there'd be people standing in line just to help themselves to your fritters." She sat there thinking about the past while she ate. "It was a shame about the spilled oil, though."

The oil she referred to was that left over from frying the fritters. To be helpful, Aunt Myrtle had grabbed the fryer containing the cooling oil with the intention of pouring it into a large coffee can for later disposal. Unfortunately, she stepped in front of the swinging kitchen door just as the pastor and his assistant came bursting through to rave about the fritters and compliment the cook. The oil ended up all over the floor. The pastor and his assistant skidded for several feet and wiped out against the massive wrought iron baker's rack, which in the church kitchen was used to store a large assortment of hefty pots and pans. The pastor was treated for double fractures in his left leg, and the assistant pastor somehow ended up with a broken nose and cracked glasses.

As per usual, Aunt Myrtle was physically untouched by the disaster, though she had been horrified that such a terrible thing could happen. After that, Aunt Myrtle was encouraged to keep her distance from the church kitchen. No one exactly blamed her for the chain of events, but it was known in the community that you didn't ask Aunt Myrtle for help if you wanted to live a long and uneventful life. Her intentions were always the best, but being in her near vicinity required caution.

I've always loved Aunt Myrtle. Unfailingly kind, she always had a bright outlook on life. New ideas continue to interest her, even though she had turned eighty-nine her last birthday. Our family dealt with Aunt Myrtle's penchant for disaster by seldom accepting her "help," beyond normal chores.

The doorbell rang, and Granddad got up to let in Bob, who wasn't shy about pulling up a chair to load up a plate. "These are great fritters, Mrs. Takson. I won't tell my wife I had any, though, or she'll never let me have dinner tonight." Katey Taggert was always trying to help Bob return to his slimmer self. I couldn't see that he was fat, but perhaps a little husky.

Not long after that, Bob and I climbed into his Explorer to drive slowly along the lake road past Stevette's cottage. We noticed the Lexus parked in her drive. She was home. Bob kept going on around the lake until we were back again at Gram's house, where I could transfer to my Highlander. Bob wanted everything to look as normal as possible.

I retraced the route in the Highlander—Bob following at a distance—and parked in the street next to Stevette's driveway. The rain had stopped, so my coat and umbrella remained in the car as I stepped on the front stoop. I noticed the front door was ajar, maybe two inches. I punched the bell, anyway, and waited. No sounds of walking feet coming to answer the doorbell. No sounds of voices. Nothing. It was kind of creepy—an open front door, a car in the drive, but no one to answer the door. I guess I was a bit tense.

Bob's black Explorer sat parked down the street. He would be wondering what was going on. I rang the bell again. Nothing. Should I poke my head in the door and shout hello? What could it hurt? Nudging the door open a bit more, I prepared to shout a friendly greeting, but stopped. The idea had been good except for the foot. It wasn't just a misplaced shoe. This shoe had a foot in it, which was attached to a leg, but because the individual in question was blocking the door in such a way that prevented casual investigation, no identification was possible. Bumping the door against the foot had caused no response from the person. Not good.

I backed away down the stoop and rang Bob on my cell. "What?" he answered.

"Come look. The door is ajar, but there's someone lying on the floor just behind it. I can't move the door to tell if they are sick, unconscious, or what." I was worried about the "or what."

Bob sighed, hung up, and I watched him move the Explorer up behind the Highlander. He got out, came up the walk looking beyond me to the partly open cottage door. "Have you heard anything coming from inside the house?"

I shook my head as he leaned over to observe the foot, then went around the side of the cottage to the back. Shortly, I heard footsteps inside the house, and concluded that Bob had found the back door unlocked.

About ten minutes later, Bob returned from around the side of the house. "It's Gudrun Bohn. She's been dead for a few days, looks like. No one else is in the cottage." He wasn't a doctor, but I thought a body dead for more than a day or so must have distinctive characteristics. I decided not to think too much about that.

The whole circumstance was numbing. An effort to visit an acquaintance from the past had turned into a scene of unreality.

"Do you want me to stay, Bob?" I hoped he'd say I could go home. Nausea was threatening to be a problem. Sadness may have been more appropriate, but the dim memories since that brief association with Gudrun precluded anything except an inability to process the unforeseen ending of her life. Definitely a shock.

"You have to stay and make a statement about what you did and what you found, and your history involving the dead woman." Bob, obviously wasn't interested, just then, in any sensitivities I might have.

I nodded. "I'll just go sit in my car until I'm needed." Encapsulating myself in the Highlander and taking sips of cold water from my ever-present water bottle, went a long way toward settling my stomach. Never, never eat fritters prior to a possible murder scene visit, I told myself.

Eventually, I was allowed to return home. Theo and I arrived in our drive at the same time and I moaned to him about the upsetting tragedy. It helped to discuss my discovery of Gudrun with him. Sometimes just defining a bad situation out loud to Theo was enough to re-establish internal calm. A mystery still remained, but it had become less personal. A further aid was to later record the happenings in my Journal. A lot of my life got processed through my Journal.

Following supper, I drove over to Main Street for containers of gesso basecoat for my canvases. After quickly getting what I needed at the Indian Heritage Store, and about to get back in my car, someone tapped me on the shoulder. It was Dillon Cody. For good and sufficient reason, I tended to sidestep contact with Dillon. Prior dealings with the man, due to mostly unavoidable situations, seldom had happy outcomes. When I was polite, he thought I was coming on to him. When I was rude, he thought I was playing hard to get. Nothing was to be gained by an encounter with Dillon Cody.

He said, "Janna, this is a package of work for Stevette Strike. Make sure it gets to her." Then he shoved it into my hands and walked away before I could say no.

I called after him, but he disappeared around the corner, this time apparently, only interested in leaving me with the package. No one had been able to find Stevette, and I certainly had no idea where she was. Anyway, why should I be a messenger service? Still, Bob Taggert would probably welcome more data associated with Stevette about now. I could transfer this smallish, brown paper-wrapped parcel to him. I punched in Bob's number on my cell.

"Hey Bob. It's me, Janna. Where are you right now?"

"Betty's Burgers. What do you need?"

"I'm a block away, in front of the Indian Heritage Store and I have something for you."

I could hear him transacting burger business with a girl in the background. "Be there in a couple," he said into the phone. True to his word, he hauled himself out of his car a short time later with sandwich bag and coffee. "So, what's the big deal?" he asked, getting comfortable in my passenger seat. He took in big gulps of coffee through a slit in the cup lid.

"Something has come up and I'd rather it be your problem than mine." I described the strange meeting with Dillon, and then handed over the package, glad to get rid of it. Anything that came from Dillon was suspect from the start. And considering earlier events of the day, it was more preferable that Bob open the package.

He set his coffee and sandwich aside. I knew what was running through his mind. Dillon Cody was already a "person of interest" after having been injured by a drug dealer under suspicious circumstances several months ago. Now, he was attempting to get a package to

Stevette Strike, a woman closely associated with, the now dead, Gudrun Bohn.

After pulling on the thin latex gloves he kept handy in his pocket, Bob carefully undid the package. Inside was a box, and lifting the lid revealed an X-rated viewing. Dillon—I assumed the photographer was Dillon—had taken about twenty shots of Gudrun Bohn in various intimate postures with other females. The pictures didn't look posed. They looked more like stills from a video. But, whatever, it wasn't my kind of thing.

Bob looked at me. I blushed, saying, "I'm speechless."

"Do you have any idea why he might have taken these photos? Did he explain at all?"

"He said nothing except what I told you." Last year, there was a possibility that Dillon could be involved with blackmail, but it never came to court. Several people had been injured in associated crimes, even killed, but Bob had said the evidence—concerning Dillon's part—wasn't there at the time to get a reasonable certainty of conviction.

"And Cody stated to you that these were to go to Stevette Strike?"

I nodded, wondering what it would take to never have to consider Dillon's actions and concerns again.

"Did he indicate whether Stevette had asked him to do these, or whether the photos are a gift from someone else to Stevette?"

"No. He just said they were for Stevette. I assumed Stevette had paid him for the work, and Dillon didn't know where to find her, so he thought I might." I frowned. "Which is odd. Why would Dillon think I had anything to do with Stevette or know where to find her?"

Bob growled to himself. "I think I have an idea how that might have happened."

I made a not-so-wild stab, "Kyle Krupp?"

Bob looked uncomfortable. "When we did a history check on Stevette Strike, your name came up along with others from the commune. Apparently, Kyle got ahold of that information, somehow." He wasn't saying how, but I sensed frustration with certain communications in official channels.

"But, that was *years* ago," I said. "And why would Kyle talk to Dillon Cody?"

Bob shrugged. "Cody just legalized some of what he's been doing all these years. He recently got his P.I. license."

I gasped. "You mean Dillon's a private investigator now? Why would the State of California license a guy like that?"

Bob lifted his shoulders again. "We may have suspicions about his past activities, but the man has managed to keep clear of anything official."

I was dumbfounded. "I don't know what I'm going to say to Grandma. He lives next door to my grandparent's at Lake Mirage, and has been driving Gram crazy with his snooping for years. She'll have a fit if she knows he now has a *license* to snoop."

Bob assured me. "Cody can't snoop wherever he wants. He has to follow certain rules of conduct, otherwise he can be fined and lose his license. Private investigators have no police privileges. They can only do research. Tell your grandmother to read up on those rules and make sure he's toeing the line. If he isn't, she should tell me, and I'll look into it. Your grandmother is one of my favorite people. I've never tasted fritters like the ones she made this morning."

I didn't want to think about fritters ever again. Changing the subject, I asked, "What do *you* think about those photos, Bob? Do they suggest anything to you?"

He smiled humorously. "These are pretty hot photos, which show a lot of things I've always suspected, but my education was stunted."

I just looked at him.

"Okay," he said. "I haven't had a chance to think about the photos, yet, or relate them to things that may have happened. But, they could be tied to other people and circumstances in both Gudrun's and Stevette's life. I have to spend some time sifting facts."

"When you get done sifting, will you let me know what you think?"

"You may not want to know what I think. You nearly lost your fritters today just looking at a foot." He stared at me intently.

"True. But, I don't want to be left hanging, without any idea what this was all about."

Bob said, "I don't know yet how the Bohn woman died or what Stevette's part in any of this is. But, I promise to tell you anything that's reasonable and not completely confidential. There's some truly bad stuff that comes along sometimes in police work. No reason why you should have pictures like that in your head. I'll try to go easy on your stomach. Deal?"

"Deal." I already knew there were things I could live without knowing.

Bob went to his car and came back with an evidence bag—a Ziploc with a label area. He placed the package in the bag and sealed it. "I have to take this down to homicide." He looked back at me. "I appreciate that you didn't open the package, but just handed it to me. That could make a difference in this case. I'll probably call you in a couple days when I know what we're gonna' do next."

He shut my passenger door, walked to his car, and got in. I started my engine and drove home.

I was smoothing on the white gesso basecoat with a paint knife in my studio the next morning when the doorbell rang. Setting down my knife on the easel tray, I went to let in Red Thunder.

Since Christmas, I had been at work on a nighttime series—begun the previous winter—

which I expected to show at my next exhibit. The series consisted of paintings created from a whole lot of sketches and photos done during forays out into the forest and mountains at night. Night is when many animals search for food. A lot of beauty and drama can be captured in the hours between dusk and dawn. At this point, I was in the finishing-touches stage. Of course, sometimes that part takes longer than the rest, since it depends upon inspiration arriving to give a painting that final, essential zap.

That morning I slapped gesso on canvases for the next two new series that I had decided to work on. The first was of Indian artifacts and ruins. A subject that had come along because of a discovery Red Thunder made out on our land last year. He'd found a very old Indian house built and carved into the interior of a small mesa near the back boundary of Cornbread Mesa Ranch. It had been cunningly contrived to blend into its surroundings so well that no one had ever suspected it was there, until Red Thunder uncovered the entrance by accident.

Within the Mesa House were priceless old pots and tools, mostly still in perfect condition. Theo and I intended to consult an archaeologist friend in the near future. For now, I was planning a series of paintings of what I saw there, from sketches done and photos taken at different times of the day capturing lighting, changes in mood, and clarity of detail.

A section of the ancient site was an intriguing natural cave. One had to pass through the cave, which housed hundreds of bats of assorted varieties, in order to find the Mesa House. A second painting series I'd determined to do focused on the cave and its inhabitants. While not sure how popular the second grouping would be commercially, it was work I enjoyed doing. Reason enough.

My sketching partner and I settled with cups of coffee in the comfy-chair corner of my studio. The skylights let in slanted light from the morning sun.

"Looks like you're working flat-out," he observed, seeing canvases arrayed on easels.

"Looks can be deceiving." I sipped from my cup. "I am languidly winding up the nighttime series. A dab here and there, until each one feels done. Something has to *click* before I can call it finished—not a process I can rush."

He glanced across the studio. "I see a lot of white canvases."

I nodded. "I'm in the thinking stages for two more series. It helps to mull ideas while getting the canvases ready. I've yet to choose specific sketches, photos, and memories for the blank canvases. That's one of the most challenging parts—to decide on the topic for each canvas within the series and the right painting technique for the effect I want." I relaxed back in my chair.

He looked over at me balancing his cup on his knee. "Not something I could do." He seemed to be in an unusually pensive mood.

"No doubt you could if your interests went in that direction. But, your fortes are sand painting and jewelry." His skillful, unique use of Native American techniques to express simple, natural designs sold well at the Indian Heritage Store. Amanda had trouble keeping his work in stock. But, he wrestled with the pull of two cultures.

He shifted uneasily. "I'm not sure where I want to go with it. White, east coast perceptions don't always blend readily with Native American thinking. My art doesn't seem to exactly correspond to either tradition."

I remembered a part of his story. "I'm guessing that your family's investment company in New York still doesn't feel like a good fit for you."

He smiled. "Right. Anyway, my grandfather is probably still furious. He felt I had betrayed him by enlisting in the Army instead of going on to Harvard, and graduating to take a position in the company."

"What you do with your life is your decision, even if it goes against what your grandfather had in mind for you," I said, wanting to be supportive.

He drank more coffee. "Grandfather, who was German born, considered the military to be lower class. I've never been sure if I'm rebelling against Grandfather Wolfe, or whether I'm heading, instinctively, toward my Lakota, Navajo roots. It was partly that confusion which led me west to study with Ben Yazzi. I wanted to visit the reservation, tune into Navajo life and thinking. It seemed I owed it to my mother to at least look into that part of the family."

"Have you *met* your mother's family?"

"Not yet. I haven't wanted to be influenced by relatives, until I took my own measure of Navajo life."

"And what do you think, now that you've seen some of it?"

"Don't know. The Navajo perspective of personal balance with Natural Law could be interesting, if a person put serious effort into it."

"Is that what you'd like to do?"

He gave me his half smile. "It's not clear to me yet what the benefits would be."

"You've taken yourself out of the situations that put pressure on your decision," I said. "Maybe you can relax now and see what seems right."

He studied his feet. "Eventually, I'm going to have to choose a direction and go with it. I don't want to be in the DEA forever, either."

I looked at him thoughtfully. "When I'm in a confusing situation that doesn't seem to have answers, it can be because I've neglected to look in the direction where the answers lie."

He looked up. "Why is that?"

"Sometimes I fear the answer more than the confusion. A familiar rut can be surprisingly comfortable."

He appeared to consider that.

I continued. "But, I've been trying to not get too comfortable with my bad habits. Someday, I expect to see a way past the mishaps I've always coped with. And when that happens, I'll let you know how I did it."

The half-smile again. "I will personally welcome that day. Could be I'll have a better idea about my direction by then, as well."

At the other end of the day, Theo and I were lying in bed drowsily talking about ideas Gwen had proposed at dinner concerning the family campsite at the ranch.

"Her idea of regularly scheduled brush clearing parties at the camp site could work," said Theo. "If we want to build toilets, showers, and a cooking shelter out there, it would be good to have some kind of assurance they won't be leveled by fire. Good maintenance could be key to better fire safety."

"We were fortunate that we hadn't done any building when the fire came through the camp site last summer," I agreed.

"We were fortunate about a *lot* of things last summer."

3

SLIP UPS

February

I ARRIVED LATE ONE FEBRUARY MORNING at my grandparent's house. The sun was shining, and brilliant fuchsia ground cover had begun to bloom like a carpet around many people's homes. Spring was not far off, even though several weeks, perhaps months, of rainy season were still ahead. Temperatures would slowly begin to turn warmer, degree by degree, and inevitably longer periods when the sun shone and the clouds receded. Being essentially a summertime person myself, this was all good.

Grandma met me at the door. "Come in, dear. We're just sitting down to an early lunch. Nice bacon cream of potato soup, with blueberry tarts for dessert." One couldn't expect a diet-conscious meal at Grandma's house.

At the big, round oak table with clawed feet, Granddad and Aunt Myrtle were already busy with their soup. Granddad winked at me, and Aunt Myrtle said, "Oh, I'm glad you're here, Janna. I can hardly eat, I'm so excited." She was about to spend a lengthy visit with an old friend, Violet Bloom, who now lived in Florida. She and Violet had plans to straighten out the problem of salt-water encroachments into Florida's fresh-water supplies. Obviously, a project that could take a while. Having done their scientific homework, the two ladies had decided that these water problems were the fault of big business. Too many hotels, high-rise buildings, and shopping malls being built, and too many people moving in state for the available fresh water aquifer to support. The growing quantities of fresh water—sucked from the water table—had caused salt water from the ocean to flow in to fill the void, even threatening to taint the remaining fresh water. Aunt Myrtle and her friend were incensed about the whole situation and had decided to *do* something about it.

Though a serious problem for Florida, I wasn't sure that Aunt Myrtle and her friend would bring positive energy to the difficulty. However, Florida had to take its chances. My grandparents had dealt with Aunt Myrtle long enough. It was now someone else's turn. Violet understood about my great aunt's tendencies, and had probably calculated that she could use my aunt like a guided missile. That plan hadn't been precisely stated, as such, in her letter to Aunt Myrtle. Yet, on recalling memories of Violet years ago—a ruthless idealist—I could read between the lines. I just hoped Violet would survive her own plotting.

Be that as it may, Aunt Myrtle was all a dither about the upcoming trip two days from now. My part was to drive my aunt a short distance down the road, after lunch, to say farewell to another friend from the local garden club. Accordingly, I packed Aunt Myrtle in the Highlander and ferried her to a little red cottage trimmed in white, located a few doors past Stevette Strike's place. Stevette's Lexus was still in the drive as we passed, but her whereabouts remained a mystery. In the meantime, Gudrun Bohn's death had been determined to likely be a case of too much medication—read a drug overdose. Officially, the investigation hadn't taken any forward leaps despite Dillon's photos.

Aunt Myrtle and I knocked on the door of the little red cottage. Loretta May DuBoise answered the door to let us into her dainty front parlor.

She offered us tea and freshly baked pecan cookies. Loretta May, probably in her early forties, looked much younger. A petite woman with a voluptuous figure, her hips swayed as she moved about on high platform heels. She was a devotee of Dolly Parton and her style, and dressed somewhat like the famous personality, but in more subdued colors.

Loretta May managed to convey to other women that she was a "southern lady" of the first order. Maybe it was the artful makeup worn to define sultry features. Her perfume seemed to be merely an extension of her natural fragrance. The overall impression was as though a Hollywood film-lab's "special effects" department had been consulted on the elements needed to depict a gently maturing southern belle.

Aunt Myrtle considered Loretta May a dear friend, but it was hard to see what they had in common beyond the garden club. True, Loretta May always listened gratifyingly to Aunt Myrtle's concerns about the environment and of those less fortunate. Aunt Myrtle liked to spend her energies for the betterment of the world, and Loretta May seemed to hang on every word my aunt uttered. So I guessed that it must be "causes" they had in common.

After an hour or so of discussion, it got to be Aunt Myrtle's nap time, so she excused herself, thanked Loretta May for the tea and cookies, and promised to keep her informed of activities in Florida. Loretta May said she would *so* look forward to hearing from Aunt Myrtle, then fluttered to the door to let us out.

When we got back to Aunt Myrtle's cottage, I walked her to the door, and after a farewell hug, I turned toward the Highlander to go home. It was then I beheld Kyle Krupp leaning against my car door. Tall with dark, wavy hair, curious brown eyes, a chiseled chin, he had the look of someone who spent time at the gym.

"I'm Kyle Krupp. I don't believe we've met." His smile was charming.

Despite the smile, and due to recent events, I was naturally suspicious of his sudden appearance. "Why are you here?"

The smile continued. "This was the only sure-fire method I had of meeting you."

"Why would that be important?" Probably my tone wasn't very friendly, because I wondered if he expected to siphon information from me.

He turned his palms up in a disarming shrug. "Well, you're already aware of my ridiculous screw-up. You saw what happened in Stevette Strike's driveway."

I looked at him and waited, trying not to be charmed by his manner. A quite different demeanor than he had exhibited in Stevette's driveway.

He looked back at me with sincere eyes. "I was hoping I could tell you some things I know which aren't generally known, and then maybe you'll tell me what you know about this case." His expression was that of a schoolboy desperately wanting to be allowed to play with the big kids.

I'd been told that one strength of his personality was persistence. Maybe not good judgment, but he had tenaciousness down. Best to point him in another direction. "First of all," I told him. "What I know is very little, and even that was long ago and far away. Certainly you realize that Bob would never tell me anything important. We're friends, but he behaves very professionally where police work is concerned." The reference to my relationship with Bob was at least true enough that it didn't make much difference. Bob could be chatty, but he didn't blab privileged police information.

Kyle's expression was angelic. "I'm not interested in what Taggert knows, but I would like to hear what *you* remember about Ms. Strike. May I buy you some coffee at the café down the way? We could talk and you might not mind sharing at least enough to give me a picture of Stevette as a young woman."

There wasn't any harm in telling him, because there really wasn't much to tell. Once I recited my pitiful crumbs of memory, Kyle would realize I had nothing that could be called information, and he'd be on his way.

"Okay," I said. "But, you're wasting your time. The only reason I'm doing this is so you'll understand how limited my information is."

He smiled sweetly. "It's never a waste of time to talk to a lovely lady."

The guy knew how to be pleasant. It made me curious how he could be so inept one moment and skim past difficulties the next.

He followed me to the Lake Mirage Café. It was a quite small, typically informal sandwich shop. Red awnings, polished wooden table tops with red napkins, a cheery owner-waitress. We parked, went inside, and took a booth. He ordered coffee and I settled for tea. As we sat there, I told Kyle about the commune and how I hardly ever even saw Stevette and Gudrun because our schedules were different and we weren't close friends. I was gone everyday teaching art at the high school, and taking college classes at night to fill in the rest of my teaching credential.

"The only thing I noticed about Stevette was that she was tall, dark, and built like an Amazon. She seemed close to Gudrun because, when some guy wasn't making advances on Stevette, she and Gudrun were often together. I didn't have a lot of time to socialize, but, Stevette was definitely a magnet for the guys. The whole commune situation got a bit much for me, so I left when my classes were finally finished. I probably only saw Stevette about once a week during that time."

His eyes had become very alert. "Would you say she was *intimate* with these men at the commune?"

"Well, I wasn't her confidante and I didn't spend much time with her. So, I wouldn't know things of that nature. But, she appeared to enjoy a friendly relationship with various men of the commune."

Kyle sat there quietly drinking his coffee. "Well, I really appreciate that you shared those memories with me. It gives me some perspective to go with."

"Why are you pursuing this case?" I asked. Bob had said Kyle was supposed to keep his distance.

He smiled again. "I need to come up with something good enough to bolster my professional image." A disarming statement, and I could see how Kyle could slip beneath the guard of those he questioned, despite mishaps.

However, I wondered about Kyle's mishaps and whom they affected. Bob seemed certain that Kyle was unlikely to pull himself up from his present reputation; but, not my problem. Having already done what I could to discourage him from thinking I had anything important to say, I thanked him for the tea, and left for home.

It wasn't until I was down the road that I remembered there had been no *trade* of information between us. I had told Kyle what I knew, and he had volunteered nothing. His underdog demeanor had distracted me from asking anything. Maybe I needed to re-evaluate Kyle Krupp. Maybe he was more clever than I thought.

It was mid-afternoon by the time I got home. The sky had clouded over and the breeze picked up. I was chilled. The weatherman predicted snow at three thousand feet by morning, which would affect the ranch, but in Coyote Canyon, we were only at 2,000 feet. I put on sweats and made another cup of hot tea. Arranging myself on the family room sofa in front of a blazing fire with my Journal, I began to feel warmer. Athena curled herself beside me. Jasper lay on my feet.

Last year, Theo and I had developed a very small corner out of a total of the fourteen hundred primitive acres comprising Cornbread Mesa Ranch for our large animals and for recreational use. My favorite spot on the whole property was what we called the Overlook. One could sit on a big boulder up there and look way out to the farthest mountains. On a very clear day one's view reached to the edge of the earth.

Sometimes I went up there to clear my mind or to sort out a problem. The serene vista encompassed an abundance of variations placed there by Mother Nature—ancient oaks, sycamores, pines, manzanita, yucca plants, and many different wild flowers. Underneath all of that were what I thought of as the bones of the earth—the minerals and rocks, hills, mountains, and mesas. Flowing in and around, sometimes seen and sometimes hidden, were springs and streams. Much of the visible water of winter became completely hidden underground or dried up in the dusty, hot summer. Yet, each season brought its own vital contribution to the cumulative whole of a year. And with every winter on the ranch, the whole process began again with the coming of the rain.

I visualized the big rock where I often sat high on the Overlook. Behind it was a narrow path that wound down the precipice to a meadow-like clearing. Within this high clearing were three large oaks whose roots had spread deep into the mountain's soil and rock long before the old house had been built there. The house was now a whisper of the past. Only the fireplace, chimney, and footings remained of what was once a woman's home many years before.

I remembered the first time that I ever saw the property. Our agent, Thelma Zadora, had taken me up the long, tortuous climb in her SUV. It was spring, and wild flowers were everywhere bobbing in the breeze among the old house remains. I was enchanted and found it difficult to take seriously any other properties shown to me that day.

There were many reasons why most property buyers wouldn't have wanted that land. Too big for a housing site, not considered usable land for anything else, since it was mountainous, rocky and, worst of all, had a large area marked "dangerous footing" on the property map. An owner couldn't ever expect to walk across substantial parts of it. Plus it was located half an hour from town, and there were no utilities. No water. No power lines.

Nevertheless, I fell in love with the sheer beauty of the property and felt its primitive majesty. During the period when Thelma showed me the acreage, I was feeling so hemmed in by town life and my own commitments that just looking at that beautiful, unspoiled acreage was like a giant whoosh of fresh air. I could inhale scents of the compelling mix of woodland, rock and wildflower. Thus, when Thelma pointed out electric poles that bordered the large neighboring ranch, mentioning we could probably tie into those for power, I began to see the possibilities.

Ultimately, Theo concurred with me that this particular piece of land seemed to be made for our family, and its challenges have since constituted an absorbing private adventure for all of us. In meeting that adventure, eye to eye, so to speak, each member of our family had benefitted over the past year.

And qualities of the land continued to be uncovered. When we first looked over the clearing at the bottom of the Overlook path, we considered the old fireplace to be convertible for use as a barbecue and picnic area. Theo was even planning to put a flagstone floor between the old footings and bring in a sturdy picnic table. This was the thinking at the end of last summer.

At some point during the fall, I realized Theo's "fall project" wasn't happening. No special rush to get it done, but I was curious what was on his mind. One chilly evening, I found him in the bedroom, looking over plans he had drawn up last August.

He looked up at me. "I've been thinking about maybe building a house there, instead." He paused. "What do you think? Is your heart set on a picnic area there?" Making room for me on the bed, he held the plan so that I could view it with him.

"I wouldn't feel deprived if the plan got changed. Anyway, we have that lovely camp site below the Overlook, which is probably better for a picnic." I looked at the map he was holding. "Tell me what you mean when you say a *house*. Is this a place where you think we would live?"

"I am picturing a stone-faced house incorporating the old stone fireplace which is still standing. It would be about the size of this house." He glanced around our bedroom. "But, tucked into the mountain so as not to take up too much of the meadow." He frowned, thinking. "Probably two stories would be best. We'd have the bedrooms upstairs, and the rest of the house downstairs. That way, when the children are gone, we can just shut off most of the upstairs, and cut heating expenses." He looked at me.

Such a future was strange to think about, since our lives at present were so immersed in the needs of children. But, in reality, only about ten more years of living with our children was a certainty. By then, each child would likely be off living his or her own life, or making plans in that direction. "I suppose we do have to think about the future, and that is a beautiful location. And I agree, closing off bedrooms when not in use, is a very good idea. You're a genius, Theo." I smiled at him. "I'm glad you're figuring these things out."

"So, you like the idea?"

"Yes. My impression is," I said, leaning against him, "that you're thinking of a beautiful, yet practical, family home in that lovely private spot. A place where our gatherings and activities won't disturb any neighbors. Had you planned to give these ideas to an architect?"

"I wanted to work over the details a little more, and I was thinking you might have ideas to make the house more pleasant and comfortable." He scribbled a note on the plan. "As much as we have enjoyed living here, there are things that would be better if they had been built differently—positioning of rooms, efficient use of space, that sort of thing. But, we didn't know all of that until we had lived in the house. Hopefully, those elements can be eliminated in the new house, and you may have a keener understanding of some issues than I do." He squeezed my shoulders. "I'm glad you like the idea, because the meadow has seemed less and less like a picnic area, and more like a place where one would want to build a home."

"Someone, long ago agreed with you." I thought of the lonely chimney up on the mountain. "I'll enjoy adding my suggestions to your plan. Just imagine how nice it will be to take our morning coffee up to the Overlook if we wish."

I thought about that conversation as I sat by the fire, my body finally warm enough to feel relaxed. Theo had drawn up his ideas, getting my input, and we'd presented it all to Todd Jergen, an architect whose office sat next door to Theo's in Rancho Bernardo. Since we weren't in a hurry to build, Todd could take his time working out the best design incorporating our ideas.

A pleasant project for the future, but we were pretty comfortable, for now, in our present home. It wasn't perfect. When is anything ever perfect? But, it had done well for us the past eleven years since setting down roots in Coyote Canyon. The twins had never known any other home, and Christian and Rosalie had become almost adults here.

I looked up at the mantle clock and put my Journal away as I realized that I had better start things happening in the kitchen. In a few minutes the kids would be home from school, and not long after that we'd all be gathering around the supper table. Time to make sure there would be a hot meal for my hungry family.

The next morning I was out at the ranch, dressed in flannel-lined jeans, lined boots, sheepskin lined-denim jacket, deerskin gloves, and a head-hugging knit cap. A thick, fluffy snow had covered the property during the night. Tree branches were heavy with clean white snow. A cold blanket hid the brush, except for last year's occasional brown weed poking through here and there. The boulders all had snowy caps. In fact, I was sitting with my camera on top of a large frosty rock, in the middle of the pasture, trying to get an exact angle for a view of the horses.

All the horses were feeling frisky in the new fallen snow. Lion was strutting around looking regal, his head elevated, taking high steps. Tache, Fire, and Gwen's pony, Shehri, were investigating corners of the pasture, snorting out steamy clouds from their nostrils. I could barely see Whirly and Rusty in a corral, their heads still buried in feeders.

The llamas, although built for weather like this, were, by nature, more circumspect and practical. They kept alert for any horse rowdiness while nosing clumps of grass peeking through snow.

I leaned back to get the right position to frame the composition of the shot. Perfect. Except as I leaned away for best focus, my body slipped backward and the iciness prevented any way to correct my slide. My position deteriorated to the extent that I lost my seat and fell behind the big rock into soft snow. Lion saw my fall and came to investigate.

"Ugh! Stop it, Lion!" Big, damp horse snorts against my ear. I reached around, stroked his cheek, and slowly got up, brushing icy flakes from my clothes.

Satisfied things were okay, Lion lost interest in my doings. He had horse business to take care of. Exposed clumps of grass were to be munched, and Tache's tail needed to be sniffed. A *proud-cut* gelding, Lion was still interested in females, but Tache was in for disappointment if she expected anything to come of it. They were best pals, after spending several years in the same corral and pasture, but Tache would nip Lion if he tried anything funny. This didn't stop the would-be stallion from occasionally pursuing a distant memory. I watched the two horses kicking up snow as Lion trotted after Tache and the llamas scattered to get out of their way. Romance in the snow.

I dug around in the snow next to the boulder looking for my camera. I couldn't see it anywhere. Feeling the cold, I shuffled around the near area, kicking at clumps in case my equipment had gotten lodged in snow-covered weeds. Still no camera.

Matt's dog, Penny, and her now nearly-grown offspring had decided to join me in this fun game. Dog noses ploughed excitedly through the splendid white carpet of fluff, until all memory of its pristine quality was obliterated. I stood hands on hips—adolescent dogs tussling at my feet— and scanned the pasture to detect where my camera could have gotten. I looked up as the sun shot a ray down between the clouds spotlighting the top of the boulder. And there, shining on the boulder in the sun, was my camera. I had evidently let go of it at the last moment before I fell. With the slickness of the rock, there was no certainty I could easily make the climb again. A problem.

Maybe I would go up to Matt's cabin on the shelf above the pasture and think about it while warming up with a hot drink. It was cold. Maybe not cold the way Canadians measure cold, but for San Diego County, it was *cold*.

Walking across the pasture to the road wasn't a simple task. I'd already fallen several times just getting to the boulder. Snow covered small details like holes and bumps so that they looked deceptively smooth, and it was hard to remember just where they were. I felt like a person suddenly blind in a place she thought she knew like the contours of her own body. Odd how one can take things for granted.

I made my way carefully out of the pasture and up the road onto the Shelf. We called it the Shelf because it was a natural, somewhat rectangular flat area cut into the mountain that provided adequate space for a cabin and barn above the pasture. The position allowed our manager to see the entire pasture when he looked out his windows.

The road under the snow was very slippery, making it necessary to consider every step. A ski pole, or even a walking stick would have been useful that day. No sooner did I have this thought than I found myself sliding forward. My feet shot out from under me and I must have landed hard on my back. I lay there a moment, or two, blinking blurrily and thinking about snow. Fluffy snow doesn't really cushion you much from the hard surface beneath it, and the compressed dirt road underneath might as well have been cement.

A big forestry truck chugged up the drive and came to a stop near me. Jared Thatcher climbed out and slid over to help me up. "Hey, are you okay? Did you hit your head?" He stared at my eyes probably to gauge the possibility of concussion.

"Thanks." I was a bit breathless. "I think I'm okay, just a little winded. And cold," I added as an afterthought.

"Let's get you into the cabin. You need to warm up and do a body check." I let him help me up the steps and into the cabin. Though embarrassed, I seemed to have clunked my head pretty good and didn't care. I'd worry about being mortified later.

Matt looking concerned, fixed a chair for me by the fire, and placed a mug of hot cocoa in my hand. While I pulled myself together, Matt got news of the Hunting and Fishing Camp from Jared, who reported that several pads had been poured for the buildings, and lumber had been delivered, but construction was delayed due to weather.

As I warmed up and took inventory of my physical condition, I could feel a small, painful swelling which would probably become a knot on the back of my head. A moment later, Red Thunder came in the door, and I realized that Matt had called him.

Red Thunder saw the consternation on my face. "I was over in the malapi area close by," he said, by way of explanation why Matt would bother him. The *malapi area* was our code name for the archeological find Red Thunder had made on the ranch last year. We weren't disclosing its existence until we had decided what to do about it.

He moved behind me to gently inspect what damage I'd done to my head. "Looks like you knocked yourself a good one, but no broken skin. I would like to drive you down the hill for x-rays, just in case."

Obviously, he had called Theo, who would likely meet us at the emergency room. *Man*, I hated that kind of fussing over a little lump! No one was pushing, precisely, but if I didn't have a medical person look at it, Theo might be up all night worrying and checking on me. It was a good thing no one but the animals had witnessed my fall from the boulder. I definitely would keep *that* to myself.

I let my sketching partner drive me down to Pomerado Hospital for x-rays, so that everyone would relax. I wanted to set Theo's mind at ease, and possibly Red Thunder's, as well. My friend and I had developed a close relationship over the past year somewhat like what I might have with my son, Christian, when he got to be twenty-nine. Red Thunder and I had been through some life-threatening experiences together since we'd met, and had formed a bond beyond our common interests.

Upon arriving at Pomerado, Theo was there as silently predicted. We waited around a couple hours, got x-rays done, and then were informed that I had a bruise and a swollen place on my head, but no broken bones. And no concussion. I was fine. Maybe a little uncomfortable, but no big deal.

At some point, I was going to have to find a balance between other people's expectations and my own self-determination. Was such a thing possible? In the meantime, while I was figuring that out, maybe I could get Red Thunder to retrieve my camera off the boulder. I was pretty sure I'd gotten a great shot of the snowy pasture scene of activity just before I slid off that big chunk of granite.

A few mornings after the bump incident, Bob Taggert showed up at my kitchen door for breakfast. He had called before coming, saying he wanted to talk. I provided the coffee, and he showed up with bagels. I sat opposite him at the kitchen table and waited for him to tell me our next move.

Instead, he asked, "Why did you talk to Kyle?" He didn't look happy.

I raised my eyebrows wondering about his mood. "He waylaid me in my grandparent's driveway, and I was thinking he was going to be a pain in the neck until I said something to him."

"And."

"Well, it seemed the perfect opportunity to discourage him by revealing how non-existent my information about Stevette and Gudrun is. I think I only said about two sentences, which is the sum total of what I know."

He sighed. "I suppose this is my fault."

Now he was really puzzling me. "What gives?"

He sipped coffee pensively. "I was originally thinking that the less you knew about the current version of Stevette Strike, the more you might be able to convince her you hadn't heard anything about her since the commune days."

"So?"

"So, it didn't occur to me that you would talk to Kyle and fill him in on how different Stevette was back then from now."

The mystification must have shone on my face. He said, "I know. It seemed meaningless information to you, but to Kyle it helped him understand that Stevette's personality had gone through a huge shift in the intervening years."

I waited for enlightenment.

"Stevette is no longer a femme fatale for men," said Bob. "She is now, and has been for many years, a lesbian.'"

My eyes opened wide. I couldn't believe he was talking about Stevette.

Bob made it completely clear. "Stevette prefers women."

"When did that happen?" Nothing in my memory had even hinted at this possibility.

"Unknown. It's even possible she's always preferred women. Some lesbians are like that. For whatever reason, some pretend for a long time to prefer men. Stevette never made an announcement about when, or if, her preferences changed. Who knows? Maybe it wasn't a pretense. She just gradually became more and more clearly a lesbian as the years passed."

I didn't know what to say. It wasn't as though her sexuality was any of my business. I don't care to know about intimate activity of anyone, regardless of his or her sexual persuasion. Theo and I were happily active sexually, but we kept it to ourselves. It was a part of our relationship that the world didn't get to know about. Sex was sweet, but private.

"Well, that's certainly surprising," I said. "But, hardly any of my concern."

He looked at me sardonically. "And you're wondering why I should consider it important?"

"Well..." I said.

"Yeah," he nodded. "Whenever someone is in the middle of an investigation for a possibly serious criminal act, cops look for stress indicators that could cause that person to do things an average individual wouldn't normally consider. A hundred and eighty degree turn in sexual preference may be one of those indicators."

"Oh."

"*Any* big change could pin point a stress area that an investigator would want to look at, especially in a case where there are few, if any, clues. If Stevette had always been a lesbian and turned to heterosexual activity, that would cause us to be curious, too."

I was confused. "What does it matter what her sexuality is? Who cares?"

He chewed his bagel thoughtfully. "Normally, it wouldn't matter much. But, in this case, there are threads of evidence that point to something quite not right concerning the subject of sexuality. I have a feeling that, in this case, Stevette's preference—or appearance of a preference—is important."

I could tell he was trying to be delicate. "Just tell me what you think I need to know, Bob."

He said, "I think I just did."

Right. "Okay, so where does that leave us? What's next?"

"First of all, avoid talking to Kyle Krupp. I don't know how, but the guy manages to make women feel sorry for him." Bob looked at me speculatively.

"I admit that I was trying to be kind by telling him not to have false hopes about what I knew."

Bob nodded. "That's how he works. He uses his mistakes to get people's sympathy. I'll bet he offered to tell you some things, but never got around to it."

"Guilty," I said. "It was pretty annoying to realize I had been tricked. He's quite good. I can't imagine why he hasn't improved his career, with such an effective interrogation technique."

"Let me just say that the reason he screws up is due to an unwillingness to wait until he has what he needs," said Bob. "He's impatient because he wants to be the hero and is afraid someone else will steal his glory."

I smiled. "He tries to slice and eat his cake before it's finished baking," I said, by way of goofy *Alice Through the Looking Glass* analogy—a side effect of being a mom.

Bob looked at me. "Something like that. Except what he thinks is cake is more like a dog biscuit. In an investigation he's directionally challenged. He tends to look at the wrong things, and then runs with them."

We sat for a moment drinking coffee, then Bob looked at his watch. "I've got to get moving. Forget Kyle Krupp. He's just a nuisance factor. Concentrate on Stevette instead."

"What about Stevette do you want me to concentrate on?"

"You said you had this friend who knew Stevette that might still be in contact?"

"Yes. Tish Halloran."

"We know that Stevette has a laptop, and we haven't found it in her cottage. So, there's a good chance she has it with her. If so, she can receive email even though we don't know her location. She may even be on Facebook. Possibly we can work something from that angle. If we can get anything like new information, about what she's doing and thinking, it could provide a lead."

He got up from his chair. "Don't *do* anything, but keep thinking about possible routes to Stevette. I'll get back to you."

I had a thought as he was walking out the door. "Would she be answering email or active on Facebook, if she's hiding from the cops?"

"She isn't charged with a crime, and may not know anything about what has happened to Gudrun. Our not being able to find her doesn't have to mean she's in hiding. But, we're using caution." With those words he departed.

The phone rang. Amanda was calling to tell me some art supplies I had ordered were in at the store. I decided to drive over to pick up my order.

When I got to the Indian Heritage Store, Rosalie was putting out artwork in an attractive display, while chatting sociably with another appealing young man. I had seen this individual in the truck with Jared Thatcher the day I clunked my head on the road ice. At some point he had been introduced to me as Dane Munson. The name suited him. He looked like a Viking in a Forest Service uniform. I could see that Rosalie was enjoying his attention. And it was evident that Dane was pleased to have her looking in his direction.

I waved to my daughter as I searched around for Amanda. I found her in the office at the back. When Nathan had this office it was piled nearly to the ceiling with old and broken office equipment, slightly newer equipment he actually used, and boxes of equipment he'd yet to open. Scattered around and on top of all this was a thick layer of papers, Styrofoam coffee cups, paper plates with food still adhering to them, rolls of price tags, markers, pens, and old, empty cookie packages with crumbs and probably ants still lurking inside. On top of all that had been dust. As far as anyone could tell, the room had never been cleaned. Dust thickly obliterated items never used and was less noticeable in high use areas. But, ancient dust bunnies ruled.

Amanda had transformed the room by liberal use of the dumpster, scrub bucket, fresh paint, and clean new furniture and carpeting. She had kept and opened the previously unopened boxes of new office equipment, hung nice curtains on the shiny clean window, and installed a small refrigerator and a microwave in one tidy corner for employee convenience.

The room was once a place to be avoided. Now it was a pleasure to walk into. I sat down in a comfortable chair by the window. Amanda was sitting at her desk with a cup of coffee and a doughnut. She pointed toward the coffeepot.

"No thanks. I just had coffee with Bob at my house. I'm good for the rest of the day."

She was interested. "What's happening with Bob?"

I shrugged my shoulders. "I'm trying to give him a return on help he's given me in the past."

"I don't know what the case is about, but he probably remembers how the pond ripples when you stick your toe in the water." Amanda laughed. "You're so busy sketching and painting and doing mom stuff, that most of the time you don't even notice the ripples."

I looked at her. "Well this time the pond is dry and no ripples to be had."

"Apparently, Bob doesn't agree, or he wouldn't be wasting his time."

I thought about that. "I hope he doesn't expect it to take too long. I have a spring exhibit to get ready for."

Amanda got up from her desk. "That reminds me." She walked into the storage room filled with neat shelves and retrieved a package. "The tubes of oil paint you ordered."

We went out of the office to the cash register. I peered into the glass cases at new jewelry that had just come in, then took my oil paints and went home.

4

THE JOURNEY BEGINS

February into March

IT WAS LUNCHTIME when I came into the kitchen to nuke a bowl of homemade beef barley soup. Sitting at the kitchen table, I wrote notes on the children while I ate.

Last year when things got extra stressful, I helped myself focus on the children's lives by doing regular evaluations and recording my observations in a notebook for that purpose. This wasn't a scholarly tome; it was just me making sure I didn't miss something important.

Every so often I took a few minutes to think carefully about one of the children and write about his or her current problems, solutions, hopes, dreams, and so on. I had discovered last year that I felt more competent as a parent just to know I was consciously keeping track.

Today I was thinking about Rosalie. I knew that legally kids turning eighteen, these days, are considered adults. Yet, it is unreal to think they are completely grownup, no longer needing help or guidance from their parents. Theo and I tried to respect Rosalie's right to make her own decisions, yet, she was still traversing that time of life when waffling between adolescence and adulthood was normal. It was a delicate dance to provide assistance when truly needed, but not give so much help that she didn't do what she must for herself in order to grow into *real* adulthood. The child notebook helped me get a clearer picture of challenges and forks in the road that may lie ahead. Though not foolproof, these musings often kept me from being surprised by circumstances affecting my children.

Even so, there was only so much I could say to Rosalie when I foresaw problems. Advice pushed on her was almost worse than none when it came to Rosalie. She was independent and could be obstinate about such suggestions. Currently, I saw possible relationship hazards ahead. Challenge number one was Matt Johnson, our ranch manager and Rosalie's current steady boyfriend. He had given her a "promise ring" last summer hoping to discourage other suitors. His stated intention was to marry Rosalie after both were finished with college. Rosalie had liked the ring, and had agreed that they should be exclusive in their dating, but she had never committed herself to the degree Matt had.

Other challenges were the interested males visiting Rosalie at the store. She was turning them down, but possibly wondering what it might be like if she weren't wearing Matt's ring.

Lastly, there was the thinly veiled crush she had on Red Thunder. I called it a "crush" because she and I had never discussed the attraction, which meant I had no good picture of what was going on in her head about him.

After noting down these aspects of Rosalie's relationships, the main thing I wanted to say to her, if the right opportunity arose was: "Behave in such a way with others that you keep your self-respect, while respecting the other person. Anything less leads to unnecessary pain for all concerned." Reminders about values that have proven reliable in the past, can stem a lot of confusion for anyone, but particularly for teenagers.

Shortly after dinner, my younger daughter, Gwen, and I drove over to the Community Center for a Girl Scout meeting. Since the previous year the dynamics of the scout troop had changed, somewhat. Mona Henry was still the main leader, and I continued to fill-in as co-leader, but we had added Bob Taggert's wife, Katey, as another co-leader when her daughter, Tiffany, had transferred to our troop in the fall. This was fortunate, because Mona's mother was in and out of the hospital a lot these days, meaning it was often just Katey and me at a meeting and planning events for the girls.

That evening, the troop divided into small groups around particular activity interests. Tiffany passed around a snack of apple juice and pink-frosted sugar cookies in the shape of hearts, in honor of Valentine's Day. While the girls ate cookies and drank juice, they discussed what badges to focus on for the remainder of the year. Some wanted to be involved in sports. Others girls were enticed by home-crafts such as cooking and sewing. Another little group wanted to concentrate on camping and survival skills.

Gwen and Christina Johnson were talking excitedly about a music badge, when Tiffany hesitantly joined them. I noticed Gwen draw Tiffany into the conversation. "Are you interested in music?" she asked. Gwen was often aware of those who could benefit from comfortable, low-key acceptance.

Christina turned a page in the scout manual for Tiffany to see and pointed to the music badge. "Look." Christina was hearing impaired, but able to benefit from a hearing device that widened the range of sounds she could hear. With the addition of this enhancement a few months before, the world of sound had become more available to her, and she had discovered more of the wonder of music. *Hearing* sound, I'm told, is not the same as being able to speak better or sing musical notes, but Christina's confidence had risen and her control seemed to be developing.

When Gwen and Christina's desks at school had been placed side by side the previous year, Gwen had told Christina that she was working on a sign language badge in Girl Scouts, but was having trouble with it. Christina bravely volunteered to help, and in the course of Gwen's mistakes—and a lot of giggles over wrong signs—the two discovered they had other interests in common. Both were curious to explore new directions. While Gwen tended to be methodical in approach, Christina was more creative.

Together they were a formidable force in the troop.

"I wish I knew how to play an instrument," Tiffany complained, looking wistfully at the music badge.

Gwen explained, "I don't know how to play music, either. But, Mom said I could take violin lessons, and Christina has just started learning the electric guitar." Christina struck a pose with an imaginary guitar in her hands.

Tiffany laughed. "We have an electric piano at home my dad wants me to learn to play. Like I'd *ever* be able to do that!"

Gwen nudged her shoulder. "Maybe you could take lessons with us." From across the room I could see an idea take shape in my daughter's mind. "We could even form a band!"

Tiffany's jaw dropped at the thought. "A band? I mean, that would be cool, but how could we do that? None of us even know how to play an instrument, yet." She was obviously not used to Gwen's style of meeting a challenge head on. When Gwen wanted to do something, she could usually find a way to make it happen, and kept working at it until she succeeded. Rather like a mini-bulldozer. I suspected it could be exhausting to be in Gwen's circle of friends, but musical realities would determine the fate of the band idea, one way or another.

Christina had her own brand of determination. "Country," she said, firmly.

Gwen clarified. "Christina and I love country music, especially the love songs. But, we want to play some rock, too." She ignored Tiffany's concern that being musically untrained was an insurmountable obstacle in forming a band.

"Wow," said Tiffany. "You're really serious!"

Gwen laughed at her amazed expression. "We'll all get together to practice and it'll be fun. We could even be a famous all-girl band someday. But, anyway, we'll earn a badge."

Tiffany looked worried. It was clear she wanted to be included, but the idea made her a little anxious. "I hope I can do this."

"Do you like to sing?" asked Gwen.

"Yeah, I love to sing."

"Then you can probably learn to play that electric piano your dad bought you. Christina and I will help you figure it out." Life seemed so simple when you were ten going on eleven.

Christina nodded her enthusiastic assent to this uncertain enterprise, after which followed a flurry of signing and laughter. Christina was still most comfortable with signing for rapid exchanges, and Gwen liked to practice her skills.

Tiffany asked enviously, "Is it hard to do hand signals?"

Christina grabbed Tiffany's hand and arranged her fingers in certain positions to say, "Do you like music?" Gwen answered back, "Music is the best!" For a few minutes they showed Tiffany basic hand signs, which seemed to elevate her mood surprisingly. Being included can be a huge boost.

Toward the end of the meeting, Katey came to stand beside me. "It's nice that Tiffany and Gwen and Christina are so friendly."

"I hope you continue to think so," I commented. "Gwen and Christina just talked Tiffany into taking music lessons for the electric piano. They're planning to start a band." I waited for that last bit to sink in.

But, Katey's face registered the information with pleasure. "Oh, Bob will be so pleased. He's been wanting her to play that electric piano he got her a couple years ago. It looks quite complicated and I think she's worried she won't be able to do it well. But, it's great that the girls are helping her to get past her worries. This will be great!"

Maybe, but simple logic determined that if there were to be band practices, they were bound to end up at the Taggert house. Violins and electric guitars tended to be more portable than pianos. Even electric ones.

I tend to paint in the mornings since I like the light at that time of the day. It is also the time when my mind is fresh and I feel like working with my brush. On this morning, I was doing the last few touches on the nighttime series and eager to be done with it. My inspiration had recently begun to be pulled more by photos taken of the old Mesa House and the stone ruin near the overlook. I had decided that my next double series would concentrate on those impressions.

When planning a new series, I liked to arrange photos and sketch groupings in the order they would be used. Therefore, an area of this sketch and a section of that photo might become part of the final composition when I had blocked in all the components of a painting. All of these pieces of visual information would be later stored in a file folder for each painting, which would allow me to retrace my thinking if I met a similar composition problem in the future. When my mind is feeling blank it helps to have something to kick-start a solution.

By the time Theo arrived home in the mid-afternoon, I had moved sketches and photos around on the board several times. Much of my interest in painting areas of the ranch had to do with discoveries Theo had made while looking into the history of our land, even before we bid on it. What we now call Cornbread Mesa Ranch had once been part of the neighboring twenty thousand acre cattle ranch, which we drove across on an access road leading to our property. The original ranch had been owned by the pioneering Montgomery family. But, in the first half of the twentieth century, all except what we now own, had been sold to a large national cattle company called Emory & Dunn. Emory & Dunn hadn't wanted the portion considered unusable, so that land had stayed with the original family.

We had wondered about the resident of the house, now in ruins by the Overlook. Our agent, Thelma Zadora, said that the house had been used as a sort of vacation cabin for when family members wanted a breather from everyday ranch life. When Clive Montgomery, the family patriarch, passed on, his wife Catherine moved up to the little house as a year-round residence. Her children and grandchildren came regularly bringing supplies, both for necessity and convenience. It was popular to take a day to visit "Grandma."

We didn't know what year Catherine Montgomery passed on, but the house had fallen into ruin many years before Theo and I bought the land. Perhaps, an imagined scene could be painted of that site in 1880, and then again in 1900, and on to 1920, and so on.

Catherine Montgomery intrigued me. A woman who had chosen to leave the home she had known all her married life, which was built on a large, prestigious ranch, as the head of an influential family. What might she have found on the mountain that was lacking on the large profitable ranch? Or, maybe, what was she trying to leave behind her to begin afresh in comparative solitude?

Just standing on the site looking at the ruins, and thinking of the history of the area, had touched me on that day when Thelma first drove me up the mountain. A few minutes later, while sitting on the boulder atop the Overlook, my heart was lost to that endless view of mountains and beyond. Even now, when I am confused, I often find myself climbing the path to the Overlook to confront that endless stretch of primitive land and sky. The view was visual medicine.

The next morning I considered ideas pertaining to the other half of the double painting series. More research was necessary on the old Indian house carved from Cornbread Mesa. For all I knew, it could be hundreds, maybe even thousands, of years old. The pottery and tools found there might have only been from the most *recent* residents. Who could say when the house had first been made?

Perhaps our archeologist friend would have some insight about that. Jed (Jedidiah) Hazard was an archaeologist Theo had run into on a geological consulting job not long after we first came to San Diego County. A man of wide experience in his profession, he specialized in dating artifacts of the original inhabitants of this area and throughout the southwest. Over the intervening years we had found him to be a good friend with considerable common sense.

Today, Theo was taking Jed out to look over the amazing archaeological find on our property. We needed an expert's evaluation of the site, and advice on how we could reasonably keep the property for our own use, but still make it available to legitimate scholarly interests. It was my feeling that the land should not be crowded with professional enthusiasts claiming the area for one purpose or another. So, I was a bit nervous over the outcome of today's discussions, but hoped for a compromise that would leave us with a certain amount of privacy, yet still do our part to preserve an important discovery for study.

While I was thinking these thoughts, Red Thunder showed up to take me out for our weekly sketching foray in the wilds. He always drove and I always brought lunch. As usual, we went out to the ranch because there was so much I hadn't seen of those acres, though we'd owned the property for the better part of a year. Much of the land was difficult to access, having no trails on most of it, other than those that wild animals had made.

Today, however, we decided to follow one of the few well-travelled paths. It lay a few hundred feet down the road from the ranch manager entrance. We suspected the original owners used this path as a route to Wildcat Lake, the northernmost lake in the winding group of lakes called Chain of Lakes. On the eastward shore of Wildcat, where the Cleveland National Forest bordered our land, was the building site for the Hunting and Fishing Camp sponsored by the Forest Service.

Since it was nearly lunchtime when we got on the trail, I suggested that we stop to eat our sandwiches at the spectacular quartz site Theo and I had visited the previous month. We found partially shaded rocks as seats amongst the loose white quartz pieces that had broken off from the main vein. Pleasantly protected from the wind, we ate lunch and enjoyed the winter sun.

I did my best to relax, but Red Thunder, who never misses anything, could see I wasn't at ease. His brow lifted in inquiry, and I turned my palms up in a shrug. "Theo has Jed Hazard out at the Mesa House today." We had told Red Thunder about the archaeologist and our hope for an ideal solution to our dilemma.

"Ah," he said, understanding.

After eating in silence for a few minutes, he said, "I could offer my services as the finder of the site and as a Lakota-Navajo Indian. Those two facts may possibly have some weight among archaeologists."

"We thought of asking you," I confessed. "But, we weren't sure of your plans, or what this site could ultimately demand of you if it worked out."

"My home base is now here. You know I don't want to be a DEA agent forever. If necessary, I can quit sooner rather than later."

"You might find it fairly limiting to be tied to an ancient site," I observed, to be fair, but hoping he wouldn't see it that way.

"I need a break. To be able to roam wherever I want on the ranch and into the National Forest, won't be limiting. And who knows what the year ahead may bring?" He looked up into the sharp blue of the sky as a red-tailed hawk rode the air currents high above.

I could certainly recognize the truth of that. No matter how things appeared to be fixed in any given year, when the next year rolled around, surprising changes might have taken place. Life was predictably unpredictable as far as I could tell. Just when you thought you had it nailed, a tsunami of change could sweep through. Maybe not all the time, and I had no serious complaints, but it was unsafe to make assumptions. Thinking positively was one thing, but being prepared was another.

After lunch we continued down the trail, which was wide enough for two people to walk comfortably side by side. It twisted and turned to follow a fairly level path, avoiding most dips and climbs, making a longer route, due to the mountainous nature of the land. Eventually, we found ourselves approaching the banks of the lake that lapped against our land. Clouds reflected their ethereal shapes in the quiet water. A peaceful scene that turned my thinking toward future painting subjects.

In fact, the ranch bordered Wildcat Lake for a quarter of a mile. Theo and I hadn't realized, at first, how close the lake was, because circumstances of the previous year had prevented a thorough investigation of our far eastern borders. Yet, what we'd been able to view of the property, caused us to go ahead with the purchase, regardless. The view from the Overlook was largely responsible for such a seemingly reckless step. Last fall, after the ranch boundaries had been given a proper survey, it turned out that we actually owned a small portion of the lake, where the ranch enclosed it with an elongated half circle of shoreline. The rest of the lake was part of the National Forest. In the distance the Forestry Camp's main lodge could be seen under construction. Empty concrete pads were waiting for several cabins to be erected. Heavy machinery was active somewhere, evident from the noise, but hidden by trees.

We turned, retracing our steps to the part of the lakeshore a little more distant from the rumble of construction. It wasn't a sandy shore, but had ample silt and small rocks to support both aquatic and mud-dwelling populations of small creatures. Close to the shore the water was shallow and grass-filled, so that it was often difficult to determine where the mud ended and the water began.

Although we had distanced ourselves from the construction din, it wasn't gone. As a consequence, many creatures one might expect to see—water birds, frogs—were not making an appearance. Maybe some of the shyer critters would come out at night when all was quiet. In the meantime, we perched on a fallen tree and sketched a couple turtles on a rock, surrounded by reeds, whose daily sunbath habit could not be interrupted by noisy humans several hundred yards away. After an hour or so, of moving here and there along the lake to catch details of plant and animal, we decided the shadows were beginning to lengthen and darkness would fall quickly if we dallied too long. Packing up our gear, we set off back down the path whence we'd come.

When my sketching buddy had made his generous offer to involve himself, and his name, in our mesa project during lunch, I had called Theo on my cell to tell him. So, my husband was expecting both of us to show up for dinner. Red Thunder was always welcome at our table, but his presence was especially wanted that evening because of the information from Jed Hazard, who would also be joining us for dinner.

At the end of our sketching day, Red Thunder dropped me off at home and went on to his apartment to shower and change. On the trail he'd worn blue jeans, and a tan leather fringed shirt. But, but he didn't consider that garb to be right for evening wear. I looked down at my muddy boots, jeans and flannel shirt, and decided I could stand a shower and change, as well. My sketching pal never got as messy as I did, since he didn't fall around all over things, but it's hard to spend several hours in the wilds and come back looking spotless.

I quietly slipped into the dressing room noting that Theo was in the living room with Jed relaxing over a beer, and Christian was in the kitchen fixing his favorite meatloaf, mashed potatoes, gravy, coleslaw, and basil carrots. Gwen had baked a pineapple upside-down cake as a finishing touch for the meal. While they were thus occupied, I took a shower, dried my hair, and slid a long camel hued knit sheath over my head. Amber earrings harmonized with the dress.

Everyone was just sitting down to dinner as I came into the dining room. Red Thunder was there in his habitual evening black and turquoise. Rosalie still wore her very appealing store "uniform," but had switched to her own jewelry. At her last birthday, Theo had given her lovely tiny amethysts that draped her shoulders in a lace-like necklace. With matching wrap-around bracelets, the effect was elegant on the winter white dress.

Christian's meal was fervently complimented by hungry diners, as was Gwen's cake, and conversation was lively. But, after dinner the children had activities elsewhere. Rosalie would have liked to hang around, but changed into jeans for a night class, then headed off with Matt to the college. Christian went to pick up Michelle to attend a school play. John had stayed at Travis Lee's house for dinner and wouldn't be home until later. Gwen's music lessons had begun, and she had managed to synchronize them with those of her friends. This arrangement allowed them to carpool to their lessons down the hill once a week, and they made it more social by eating out fast food on those nights. That night it was Stacy Johnson's turn to ferry them down and back.

After the departures, Theo, Red Thunder, Jed, and I gathered in the family room around the fire, sipping coffee or spirits, according to taste. I let Theo wait on people for drinks and put in an order for a small glass of Chablis. A little wine took the edge off my nervousness. I noticed that Jed chose cognac, but both Red Thunder and Theo stuck with coffee.

"Well?" I said to whomever was willing to speak first.

"It's not as bad as it might be, but we have to watch our step," Theo answered, looking at me.

I took a big gulp of my wine. "Tell me the good stuff first, and when I've been lulled into a state of security, you can gently let the other shoe drop."

Jed smiled. "It's an awesome discovery, thanks to Red Thunder, and he has a near perfect memory of where each artifact was initially positioned, so we can make a diagram for our records. Those precious pots will be moved around, in any case, during inspection and dating." Red Thunder had moved all the artifacts to one room to avoid damage while he used the ancient house last year for surveillance in his DEA business.

Jed took a sip from his glass. "Red Thunder is only the latest non-original resident. There's evidence of a long series of inhabitants stretching back at least several hundred years. That's as far back as I'm willing to guess without using scientific dating procedures."

"Will you be doing a scientific dating of the Mesa House?" Theo asked, while I wondered what that would entail.

"Undoubtedly. It's a very old site, and very unusual. Its presence will cause a lot of head-scratching in the archaeological community, since this sort of structure is unknown in California. From your point of view this works well. The present school of thinking doesn't like to have unsettling data arise to upset what it considers established evidence and ideas about Native American wanderings and territories. Therefore, though the Mesa House is extremely valuable, very few scientists will be able to come up with funding to do it justice."

"What does that mean?" I wanted to know. Although, I appreciated Jed's professional opinion on the authenticity of the Mesa House, I was more interested in protecting it.

Jed scratched his chin. "Mostly, it means that there won't be a huge rush of professionals wanting to spend time here any time soon. I'd say you'd have to make it available for legitimate academic research, but, it should be by appointment only, and for stated, limited periods of time. I recommend you find a good lawyer who is familiar with your rights under California and federal law, especially pertaining to Native American sacred sites. Your lawyer could write a Use and Fee Contract that you can offer research institutions in order to hold them responsible for any damages and to provide for expert maintenance of the structure over time. It might be useful to find out what other private owners of old Indian sites have done. For example, in New Mexico there are privately owned Anasazi sites, such as the Salmon Ruin, that were made into tax exempt trusts to preserve the grounds for the future."

Theo said, "I've been considering building a boardwalk over the rocky areas and take it straight across to the path. Maybe another section could go directly to the Mesa House."

Jed nodded with approval. "Many of these guys will only be interested in one area which falls within their specialty, so if you make it possible for them to go directly to that place, you won't have them wandering everywhere else."

"If Thad, here, agrees to be our Native American curator and liaison," added Theo, "researchers will have to connect here with him, if they hope to get on the land. And when *he* can't be present, they'll have to apply to his assistant, which will be *me*." Theo grinned at Red Thunder. "Or whoever is available, and can be deputized."

Jed said, "You might want to construct a small artifacts museum, with caretaker's quarters near the mesa. A lot of trouble could be saved by providing better security and a safe area for artifacts to be studied. It's necessary to consider that you and Janna have come into possession of artifacts that would have a huge value on the open market. Also, the Mesa House structure needs inspection by experienced engineers to determine its safety and how to preserve it during use by research teams and after."

Jed's advice was sounding not so bad, and I could see that Theo wasn't surprised by any of it. I asked, "What are you going to be doing during all of this, Jed?"

He smiled, "Well, since you invited me, and I am so honored, I'm going to have a splendid time dating and cataloging all of this stuff. My work will help you keep better control of the artifacts, since a scientist who specializes at one level of history won't have much reason to handle items that have been authenticated for a different time period. Careful planning on your part will make it unnecessary to count on a visiting researcher to have the consideration to look out for your interests."

Jed cupped the snifter in both hands. "I'm grateful for this opportunity, and want to assure you that, until I get your permission, I won't be publishing related papers, or even mentioning the existence of the Mesa House to anyone."

Theo asked, "How much time do you think we will have to put all these safeguards in place?"

"Probably, you'll want to plan for interested academic research, in a year or two. That should give us ample time to do what is needed, physically and legally. The subject should be kept quiet until then or you'll get problems you don't need."

"This is all sounding better than I had hoped," I said. "Thanks so much for taking this on, Jed." After listening to his reasoned comments, the whole thing seemed more manageable.

Jed laughed. "The real gate-keeper will be Red Thunder. No one wants to mess with the rights of American Indians in their sacred areas. There's a likelihood that this *was* a sacred area, although we'll have to do a little research on that." He looked at Red Thunder.

Red Thunder smiled his half smile. "Point me in a direction."

Jed said, "There's no hurry. I'll have to get back to you after I talk to some sources. On an archaeological site nothing happens in a hurry unless an artificial urgency is prompted by information leaks. If we're careful, that won't happen here."

I said, "We haven't mentioned the Mesa House to the children, as yet. It seemed too big a responsibility for them. But, they'll have to know something, because we talked about exploring the mesa with them before Theo and I realized what it held." Some safeguards would need to be in place, before we burdened them with too much responsibility.

"We haven't mentioned it to our manager yet, either," said Theo, looking at me. "But, we'll figure out something."

I felt surprisingly calm and unstressed. Nothing was going to happen tonight, and I was very glad that the future of the mesa area seemed under reasonable control, for now.

At noon on the first Saturday in March, the whole family gathered to watch the raising of the new Cornbread Mesa Ranch sign that Rosalie had designed, and had ordered custom made by a local metal smith. This same craftsman had forged handsome ranch gates and weathervanes that could be seen in use elsewhere around the area. His reputation was deservedly growing.

Christian stood back to look at the completed installation. "This is nice, Rosalie."

We had decided to place the sign at the entrance road to where Matt, our ranch manager lived, overlooking the horse and llama pasture.

Two sturdy poles, twenty feet tall, had been set in the ground on either side of the road. Atop the poles and stretching across the road, rested a roughly squared log, reminiscent of a very long railroad tie. Positioned on the log was the black metal sign shaped like the silhouette of a flat mesa topped with a couple small trees. Cut into the sign was the name *CORNBREAD MESA RANCH*. The design was simple and it fit the look we associated with our land.

Both Granddad and Theo had their cameras at the ready taking shots of the sign and candids of family and friends. It was a good day for a late winter barbecue. Matt had fired up the grill on the deck in front of the manager's cabin. Theo and Christian were the chefs, although Rosalie had prepared biscuits, cowboy beans and coleslaw to go with the barbecued chicken.

All of us ambled slowly in the direction of the good food smells; dragged by our noses beyond the pasture where we kept the animals, and past the corrals where they were fed and sheltered. We walked around and up the Shelf incline that led to the barn, and finally to the broad wooden deck of the cabin.

Rosalie had helped Matt arrange the physical logistics of the party, allowing for flexibility in case the festivities needed to be moved inside. But, looking at the sky, it seemed to me to be one of those deep-blue mostly cloudless days that sometimes blessed a winter day. We had prepared for rain, but the sun smiled on us instead.

Rosalie had set up a table on the deck covered with a red and white checkered vinyl cloth. The table was heaped with tempting food, paper plates, silverware, red paper napkins, and cups for coffee or soda. Rosalie, dressed in jeans and a pink chamois shirt, stood behind the table helping people get what they needed.

I stood in line in front of the table, collecting food on my plate. Red Thunder was in line next to me. I said to Rosalie, "That sign is going to be good for your future business. You may find yourself getting requests from other ranchers to design ranch gate signs."

She smiled and looked pleased. "That would be nice, and it's the kind of thing I'd like to do. Though I don't know how many people will see it. We're not exactly in the center of town here."

Red Thunder looked at her. "You'd be surprised how many people drive down these roads. The sign is well designed. It will be noticed."

Rosalie blushed to the tips of her ears. "Thanks."

Red Thunder smiled and then walked over to Theo to get some hot-off-the-grill barbecued chicken. He was wearing typical Red Thunder daytime winter clothing: tan leather shirt and pants, his black hair tied with a leather strip. He moved like a man able to handle any situation with competence.

I knew he was involved in cleaning up the tail end of the DEA drug bust that had heated up in our area last summer. I supposed it wouldn't be long before he received a new assignment and took off for an indefinite time to an unknown destination.

Although, he was our official Native American curator for the Mesa House site, Theo and Jed had set it up so that Red Thunder could travel if need be. He wasn't chained to the archaeological site. He had talked about resigning from the DEA, but, so far as I knew, that hadn't happened, yet.

A few hours later, when we were home again, I sat in the studio drinking tea, meditating on the day. It had been a happy sign raising. The barbecue had worked out well with the cooperation of the weather. Matt and Theo had led tours for relatives and friends through the barn, down to the corrals to meet the animals at feeding time, and along the road to the family camping area, which still showed the scorched parts left by the fire. We would have to put more labor into the area if we planned to camp there again this next summer.

The following afternoon, I dressed for the showing of my art exhibit which opened that evening. I had to be at the gallery before Jorge opened the doors to the public. Theo came into the dressing room while I was trying to decide what to wear. His taste is pretty good in choosing shades that enhance my natural coloring. So, I let him select a long bias cut dress in an orchid shade. I added beautifully designed silver and amethyst cuff bracelets, and matching earrings, that fit the occasion. Theo wore a nice deep-gray western-cut suit, and silver bolo of Hopi design.

We walked into the gallery together as Jorge was calmly checking the placement of my paintings, price sheets, and stacks of information on the collection. In a distant corner of the gallery, an antique kidney-shaped desk and mahogany chairs were available for the displaying artist to sit and talk with visitors.

Purple irises and white statice were arranged on a nearby table. A thoughtful gesture by Theo.

"Everything seems to be ready," said Jorge, looking at the clock. "We have wine and cheese in the next room, and Maria has included a tray of fruit."

As he spoke, Maria entered in black lace, looking great. "We're going to have people so relaxed and enjoying themselves that your paintings may sell out tonight," she enthused.

Jorge smiled. "Please, leave me enough on the walls to last the length of the showing." They were joking. My paintings move fairly well, but never so fast that Jorge had to worry about his inventory for the month they were on display.

My nighttime paintings were shown with ideal lighting and positioning around the gallery, and included an assortment of several other earlier works I had done awaiting the right buyer. Sometimes I keep a painting for quite a while before it sells. Over time, I get tired of lugging the piece around and start to wonder if there's something not right about it. But then, along comes a buyer who has been looking for just that painting for a particular place in his or her house. The same scene plays over and over, but, for some reason, it always surprises me. Thank God for differences in taste.

While I was musing over the skillful arrangement Jorge had done with the paintings, conversation had changed to the subject of land. Jorge's cousin leased the big Carrington property next to us at Cornbread Mesa Ranch. "Carlos says that the owner is thinking of selling out. He gave Carlos the first chance to buy, but my cousin doesn't want to stay here. He and his wife want to go back to Mexico where there is family land. They want to retire from the everyday work of the ranch." He sighed, and said, "Sometimes Maria and I talk that way, too. But, what would I do without my gallery?"

"What would I do if you retired, Jorge? No one knows how to display my paintings like you do." I smiled appreciatively at him.

"You sure did a bang-up job tonight, Jorge." Theo agreed, scanning the walls with his eyes. "Everything looks great."

"Come have some wine before our guests arrive," said Maria. "Once we open the doors, none of us will probably have a chance for a glass of wine or a bite of cheese."

During the evening we were all kept busy. Maria was right; there was little time to stop and relax.

Grandma and Granddad dropped in to see the collection, and Grandma exclaimed over them. "Oh, I just love the way they all look hanging up. I remember when you did the sketches for that one. Remember those little raccoons, Sven?"

Her favorite was a vaguely impressionistic oil of a family of raccoons under moonlight, in the park next door to my grandparent's home. With line and shadow, I had tried to capture the quiet, chill of the night contrasting with the, sometimes boisterous, business of scavenging for food. Granddad had accompanied me on that occasion and was now examining the composition. A little later I noticed that painting had been replaced by another selection in the series. I wondered if the raccoons would show up on a wall in the Lake Mirage cottage.

Around eight, Christian stopped in with Michelle, a girl he had been friends with for years. They were now formally dating, but no telling what the future held for that friendship. The last I heard, Michelle planned to go away to college next year. But, Christian had decided to stay in San Diego County to further his schooling.

Toward the end of the evening, Red Thunder strolled in the door in his usual Indian chic evening garb, causing many a feminine eye to turn in his direction. He stood beside me and said, "Nice display. I'm surprised there's anything left."

"It's never that easy."

"People like what you do."

"Thanks," I said, and then suggested, "You might talk to Jorge about doing a showing of your beautiful sand paintings. I bet he'd be interested in displaying your stuff."

Red Thunder looked uncomfortable with the idea. "Maybe I'll sign up for a booth at the Coyote Canyon Art Fair this summer, and see what happens with that."

I was thrilled. "That would be great! You could get the booth next to Laurie and me. It's always more fun if you're next to someone you know. You know Laurie, right? She works in the Indian Heritage Store in the afternoons."

He nodded. "She's a good artist and not difficult to talk to." For Red Thunder, this was high praise.

"Laurie always signs me up for a booth at the same time she gets her own. I'll ask her to get one more for you, and you'll be all set."

He shrugged and smiled his half smile.

5

KOLICHIYAW

March–April

A COUPLE AFTERNOONS LATER, I finished blocking in the rest of my ideas for the last canvas in the double-history series. It had taken thought and research, but now I had the basic idea of the direction I wanted to take each painting. Of course, occasionally a painting would take over and go off in a direction I hadn't expected, but one can't plan for that.

I was cleaning up and organizing canvases on the painting racks in the order I wanted to work on them, when Gwen came home with boxes of Girl Scout cookies. Although, I had been Cookie Mom last year, this time I had dodged the bullet and someone else got elected for that honor. Christian had taken Gwen to pick up her order, and now she was geared up to go out and deliver to her cookie customers.

Christian was one of Gwen's major buyers of Thin Mints. He seriously stocked up once a year and stored them in the garage freezer, so he could savor them all year long. From time to time he shared a box with Michelle, who had come home with Christian and Gwen. After hauling in all the cookie cases, he turned to Michelle. "You want to help me change the oil on my truck?"

"Love to." She tossed her red curls and smiled at him. He took a box of Thin Mints, and together they walked out toward his truck. This wasn't quite as bizarre as it may have sounded. Michelle was actually a good mechanic and excelled in shop far ahead of many of the guys. Her hands were small and she could do things to a vehicle that the big-handed lads couldn't. Nevertheless, it wouldn't have been *my* idea of a fun time. To each their own.

As Michelle and Christian went out the back door, John and Travis came in talking about their llama business. They weren't selling llamas. They were selling llama *poop*. Yes, people really did buy llama poop. On a scale of fertilizers, it was right up there with the more desirable bird guanos for enriching a garden.

"I think we could get a few gallon size plastic zip-locks, fill them with llama pellets, and sell them at the farmer's market," John said to Travis, thoughtfully. Both boys looked over at me, and I handed them a box of zip-locks. That was as far as I was willing to go.

"Cool," said Travis. "Let's go out to the ranch and bag pellets. I bet we could sell a lot next weekend at the market." Again, not *my* idea of fun, but one couldn't really complain. It was constructive and they were earning their own money.

Gathering snacks and water bottles, they headed for the ranch on their bikes, a forty-five minute jaunt on dirt trails. I was glad that no one listened in on conversations that took place at our house. A casual eavesdropper might think we were more than a little strange.

Following dinner that evening, Rosalie and I sat in the quiet, comfortable corner of my studio talking about her design ideas. A no-school evening, she was lounging around in gray sweat pants, a red sweatshirt, and fluffy slippers. Her pale blond hair in a long braid down her back, she looked cozy in the chair, curled up, drinking cocoa.

"I'm glad the exhibit opening went so well," she said. "This is the first year you've done an evening opening. Do you think you'll do a repeat next year?"

I shrugged. "It's up to Jorge, of course, since it's his gallery. But it was fun, and we got more local response, because it wasn't held during working hours. Offering wine and cheese didn't hurt, either. Even so, I was surprised at the number of paintings that sold." I thought about people who had come in to socialize, and ended up leaving with a painting. "Next year we could see a repeat."

Rosalie glanced at my loaded easels. "I see you're deep into your next series."

I smiled. "Painting ideas were crowding into my head, and the only exit is through my brush."

"I know what you mean. I have all these design ideas I want to try in textiles. Some are new, but some are interesting twists on old ideas."

"What kind of textiles are you thinking of?"

"Cousin Liz has been trading thoughts with me in email about weaving rugs and blankets. Her art major in college exposed her to a lot of weaving techniques, and now she's looking around for a job. Fortunately, she has an education degree. Her idea is to get a job teaching high school art until she can find her niche."

I remembered my sister's sighs of exasperation over what she thought was my lack of planning when we were in high school. Poor Jody now had to deal with a daughter having many of the same problems as her twin. I well recalled the agony of finally graduating from art school and finding that no one was rushing to hire an artist. Fortunately, at that time school boards in the Midwest were willing to take on anyone who had a degree in their basic subject, provided they registered for evening courses toward a teaching credential. Jody was one who had the presence of mind to get a degree in structural engineering. Of course, it helped that she was naturally smart about things like that, not to mention completely organized. The whole McKenzie family seemed inclined that way.

Except for Liz. At least my niece got her teaching credentials first, before expecting to get a job.

Rosalie continued, "I'm saving up to buy a loom to experiment on. In the meantime, I'm keeping a color sketchbook of ideas with notes on methods to try with each sketch. I've also been buying up beautiful skeins of yarns when I see them.

"How are your business classes going?"

"I'm doing better now. I have a tutor for my accounting course and he's made it all seem very logical for me. So, I think I might do pretty well in the class."

"Where did you find an accounting tutor?" I asked. Once Rosalie got an idea solidly in her mind, she went with it. I was glad to hear that she'd taken the bull by the horns, so to speak.

"Oh," she said, casually. "Well, there's this Forest Service guy, Dane Munson, who usually takes accounting courses during the winter when he's not on call. He's actually some kind of engineer, but he thought it wouldn't hurt to have a degree in accounting, too. Dane's really good at explaining things sensibly."

"You're pretty busy these days. When do you have time to meet with him?" I remembered

Dane as the guy I had thought fit his name because he looked so much like a Viking.

"Dane has a class on the same nights that I do, so we carpool. He told me that whenever I have questions about my classes, I can ask and he'll clarify the material for me. Often we stop at a burger place on the way home and he explains stuff I don't understand."

I observed, "Sounds like you and Matt are having less time together this semester."

"Yeah, we're both pretty busy, and our schedules are a little different this time. He also spends a lot of time practicing team-penning with his friends." She looked thoughtful. "He spends an awful lot of time with animals." She paused, and then went on. "Animals are nice, and I love my horse, and my new puppy, Bree. But, I like other things, too. Like designing things to use in people's homes, and then figuring out how to make them. It's exciting to take an idea I sketch on paper all the way to a beautiful, finished product that someone can use. Matt doesn't seem interested in anything like that."

She sat quietly for a moment. "I want there to be a time when we can talk like we used to. Somehow, I have to make more time to spend with him when we aren't too distracted to communicate."

"Sounds like a sensible plan," I said, giving her a hug. She sighed, and got up to go get ready for bed.

Working in my studio the next morning, I had three canvases from the history series out on easels, and was brushing in the large areas of background color. My paintings often required many layers of color to achieve the depth and detail that I wanted to portray. The background was always the first layer because it helped me think about where I was going to go from there. No matter how well I plan a picture, great amounts of it are decisions that happen as I go along. Finished areas help to indicate a direction for the next layer to follow.

As I was standing, working in sage green with my brush, Christian came and sat on the stool behind me to watch. I said, "What's on your mind?"

"I ordered my graduation stuff. The lady said the robe, cap, and class ring would be delivered in about three weeks."

"Are you pretty excited about graduation?"

"Yeah. I'm *so* ready to be done with high school. Even though I'm already accepted at UCSD for next fall, it's all pretty weird."

"Do you mean it's weird to be finished with high school and beginning a new stage of your life?"

"Yeah. Lots of people at school will be travelling to other states for college next fall, and some guys are going into the military. Even Michelle is going to the University of Arizona. It's just strange that so much is changing. Scary, even."

I said, "Most of them will be back home during vacation times. But, you're right. It's never going to be the same again."

"What if you don't like the changes and want to keep some things the way they are?"

"Life is always evolving from one stage to another, a fact of living. Some of the people who are going away will eventually find that they are really more comfortable in San Diego County. On the other hand, people with plans to go to school locally, may become attracted to other parts of the world. The college years are often full of adjustments while individuals figure out what they *really* want to do."

"I like the freedom," said Christian, thoughtfully. "And it'll be cool not to be treated like a kid in high school, anymore. I'm definitely going to like those parts. The thing that bothers me is I always thought of myself as someone who'd like to travel. But, right now I'm not interested in going out of state to school. I really like it *here*. We just got the ranch last year, and I love being able to go out there to hike and camp." He looked at me purposefully. "I was hoping that since Matt is going to be away all summer, you and Dad might let me stay out there in the cabin while he's gone."

"Maybe. It's a possibility. But, I'd have to talk with your dad to see what he thinks."

"Thanks, Mom."

"Don't thank me, yet. Nothing's been decided." I put down my paintbrush and started walking toward the kitchen. Christian followed.

He said, "I'm hungry. Do we have milk for cereal?" He opened the refrigerator, took out a jug of milk, and offered me some. We ate cereal. A lot of my conversations with Christian have taken place in the morning over cold cereal.

At noon the next day, I pulled into my grandparent's driveway to join them for lunch. I was surprised to find Bob Taggert standing outside talking to Dillon and Loretta May DuBoise.

From what I overheard as I walked up to the house was Bob inquiring into Dillon's new P.I. licensing, and Dillon was proud of his new status and wanting to strut. He was telling Bob that Loretta was "one of my best operatives."

Loretta May fluttered her eyes at his compliment. "I just do my poor best, Dillon." She was dressed in a tight, low cut white sweater dress woven with gold threads. Yet, despite large, sultry blue eyes, she somehow came off as ladylike, even while emanating a come-hither vibration.

Bob smiled at Loretta May. "What kind of research do you do for Cody?"

"Oh, I just check backgrounds of people and verify facts. I also make photographic records when they are needed. I have a lot of local contacts, so it's easy for me to chat with people and do quiet research without stirring anyone up. I always try to be *very* tactful." She smiled into Bob's eyes, and I could see him unconsciously leaning in her direction. Loretta May looked at her watch, gave a little wave, and walked toward her little white Acura parked behind Dillon's red Jeep.

Dillon went on to say, "Loretta May and I have worked together on and off for some time. She had some unfortunate business setbacks in the past, so I was glad to give her some scope with her special skills."

Bob asked him, "Did you ever figure out who took the photos that were in the package you handed to Janna for Stevette Strike?"

"It wasn't me. I've told you that a hundred times. And it wasn't Loretta May. That was an order Stevette placed with someone else. I was just the delivery person." Dillon looked cagey. "As I told your cop friends, it came through the mail to my post office box with a typewritten note attached telling me who to deliver it to. Another envelope had cash in it to pay me for my trouble, so I delivered it. I saw no reason to keep either the note or the envelope."

It sounded fishy to me. I wouldn't have been surprised if Dillon did take the photos, but didn't want to be associated with Stevette after hearing of Gudrun's death. Dillon definitely steered clear of anything he recognized as trouble. Of course, that left all those problems he *didn't* recognize.

"You *didn't* deliver the package to Ms. Strike, though," observed Bob.

"I didn't know where she was, but I thought Janna was in touch with her. I figured Janna would know what to do with the package, and it would not be my problem." Dillon looked a little edgy.

I was flabbergasted. "Why did you think I would be in touch with Stevette?"

Dillon looked sincerely surprised, "I thought you knew. Kyle Krupp suggested the idea to me. It seemed like a good possibility, and when I handed you the package, you took it." He looked at me knowingly, then turned to go back into his house next door.

I had had to stifle any airing of my opinions to Bob about Dillon's remark, because Gram stuck her head out her door to see what was holding me up. She saw Bob and invited him to come in for lunch, as well.

Later that evening, while I was floating in the tingly bubbles and turbulence of the Club Jacuzzi with Theo, he remarked, "I wouldn't worry about anything that comes out of Dillon

Cody's mouth if I were you." He pulled himself out of the warm water to sit on the edge.

"Well, it bothers me that he thinks it, because he goes around and talks to people. And then there's Kyle Krupp. Why would that young man *say* such a thing? Bob said he thought it might be Kyle, but I couldn't believe it."

Theo stood and shrugged on his white terry robe. "Maybe it was a slip on Krupp's part. Or maybe Krupp thinks that you had more contact with Stevette than you're admitting. But, according to Bob, no one pays any attention to what Krupp says, because he's nearly always wrong. I wouldn't lose any sleep over it." Then he helped me out of the hot tub and into my terry robe. We walked to his Ford Ranger through the cold, foggy night, and hurried home before we lost that hot, toasty feel from the Jacuzzi.

On a beautiful springtime day in April, the sun was shining brightly. The air was abuzz with insects and hummingbirds visiting the endless varieties of cultivated and wild flowers in our area. A perfect day to be outside enjoying the warm temperatures that followed after winter. We could still expect rain from time to time, but most of the really damp, chilly days were now in the past.

At least, that was how it was if one were outside in the wonderful spring breezes. However, if one were *inside* in an ancient house with four-foot thick walls carved from the granite of Cornbread Mesa, it was still quite cool. It took a long time for those walls to heat up to the slightly warmer variation in temperature that reached its peak in late August. The internal temperature of the rock-walled rooms were always cooler during the day as they began to warm up from the rising sun. But, by night, the walls would be providing warmth as they began to cool off. The overall effect was a moderation of temperature that was fairly reasonable for habitation, though not completely comfortable. Even with the occasional window to let a little light enter, and the strategically placed square holes to the outside for ventilation, the inside temperatures resembled those one would expect to find in a cave.

A warm sweater needed to be worn in the Mesa House most of the year. On the other hand, the house maintained this moderate warmth with the aid of small vented fires even when the outside froze or snow fell in winter. It wasn't cozy, but it was manageable with a sweater… or two.

My interest in the interior temperature of the mesa stemmed from the work I needed to do there. I had determined that I would make genuine pictorial statements about the history of Cornbread Mesa by sketching very simple scenes, much like a still life. One sketch was of a decorated clay storage pot sitting on a woven fabric pot ring (a woven donut shape that Native American ancestors used to prevent pots from rolling and breaking) by a "T" shaped doorway, which had a wide niche cut on either side at the top. Another sketch was of a metate (a squarish hollowed stone for grinding) placed on a stone floor containing colorful dried corn and a mano (a flat rounded fist-sized stone to rub and grind against the corn). Still another sketch was of the top of a primitive ladder lashed against and sticking out of a dark kiva hole (a place for clan ceremonies and meditation) with a pair of beaded moccasins resting beside it. These were still-life impressions of long ago.

Within the house were many exquisite artifacts from which to choose in setting up these simple scenes. So, on this day, I sat on a folding stool in the center of a room facing a "T-shaped" doorway. These doorways were typical, I'm told by archaeologist, Jed Hazard, of those found in Chaco Canyon, New Mexico and other sacred places where ancestors of Hopi Indians have made buildings throughout the southwest. The unique thing about our Mesa House was that the usual sandstone flakes often used for these ancient buildings were not to be found here. This area of California had an abundance of granite rather than sandstone. But, granite flakes—though often requiring more effort— worked as well, and the builders had added the plentiful granite to the mesa to form the natural-appearing structure found on our ranch.

To emphasize the shape of the doorway, carefully built with rectangular flakes of stone, I placed a perfect jewel of a large round storage pot directly centered on the threshold, resting on a pot ring.

The pot had a background color of white and was decorated with an intricate geometric pattern of black lines. I chose this particular doorway because there was a window slot in the room, casting a mellow light on the pot, giving an interesting effect on the shadowy colors of the doorway and beyond.

I worked with chalk pastels on textured paper, catching all the soft, sometimes unexpected changes of hue. Pastels were an easy preliminary medium to use and didn't require all the messing around that paint did. Very handy for a sketching trip.

At the end of an hour, the sketches for this scene were complete. I was examining details of what I had done, when I felt what, at first, seemed to be my cat, Athena, swishing her tail around my legs under the stool. I was about to automatically reach down to pet her when I recalled my location, and that Athena was several miles away. At about the same time, I became aware of an odd, quite pungent, smell.

Dilemma. On the one hand I wanted to leap off the stool and confront whatever critter was under the stool. Conversely, I knew there were animals it didn't pay to excite by rapid movement. As I was deliberating not too calmly about this, I felt a cold nose touch my ankle. Wonderful. More data. Probably a mammal of some sort. I risked leaning forward a bit to get a view of what was touching my ankle. But, as soon as I moved the stool creaked softly, causing the cold nose to pull away.

So. Here we were; the nameless creature and I trapped in a temporary truce of nervous inaction.

"Ahem," I heard a voice say. "Kolichiyaw won't hurt you, but it would be unwise to frighten her."

"What do you suggest?" I asked, not willing to worry about the incredible presence of a stranger until I had dealt with the critter problem. My adrenaline was hyped, but I could only handle one unknown at a time.

"Slowly put your hand down by your ankle so she can sniff it," the voice instructed.

Great. I should put my hand down next to an animal that I've been told shouldn't be frightened. I carefully let my hand dangle beside my ankle and felt a furry face shove itself into the palm of my hand. If the action hadn't reminded me of Athena's methods of getting attention, I might have had an embarrassing accident.

I could feel soft little ears, whiskers, and considerable silky fur. Hmm. I risked a look to the side and down into a beautiful black pointed face sporting a double white stripe on its head and, in all probability, along its back and tail.

I said, "Tell me that this is a tame skunk that has been de-scented."

I heard a dry sound of mirthful laughter behind me. "That would not be factual. However, I've found that she never sprays unless she is threatened."

"Have we established that she isn't feeling threatened, at the moment? Is it safe for me to turn around?" I asked.

"Probably so," said the voice.

I slowly pivoted on the stool bringing my hand up into my lap. However, Kolichiyaw wasn't finished being petted, so she followed my hand and climbed into my lap. It was reasonable to conclude that I didn't frighten her, but now I was stuck with a somewhat odorous skunk in my lap. To say I was stunned didn't begin to describe my feelings.

My human visitor must have realized my dismay. "Kolichiyaw means 'skunk' in your language. I'm afraid she's become more presumptuous and domesticated than I ever intended."

I looked up into the angular and craggy, brown face of a man who was probably at least seventy years old. He had gray hair with a long gray ponytail. His nose was hawk-like and he had deepset, intense, but curious, black eyes. He was clad in very worn cowboy-style clothing with tan, boot-like moccasins. He said, "I regret that our resident skunk frightened you."

I asked, "Can I put her down without dangerously offending her?"

He nodded. "Support her abdomen and set her down while you stand up. If you don't stand up, she may return to your lap." He had an amused look on his face.

I meticulously followed his instructions. Kolichiyaw was okay with it, but she rubbed around my ankles like a cat, her long extremely fluffy tail brushing my shins.

Now that the skunk problem was temporarily under control I could turn my attention to other considerations. "Who are you? And what are you doing here?"

My visitor replied, "I was about to ask you the same questions. I am Micah Sekaquaptewa and I am the caretaker of this place, sacred to the Hopis." He waited for me to respond in kind.

Wow, I thought. Now what? "I am Janna Gustaffeson and this building is on my husband's and my land. It is a part of Cornbread Mesa Ranch. I am an artist and I am making studies of the artifacts here."

Micah Sekaquaptewa looked thoughtful. "We knew this place might eventually be found." He paused, and then asked, "What is its status here?"

I knew what he was asking even though his words were cryptic. This house was so well hidden that, as far as we knew, it had never been known by anyone but Indian occupants over the centuries. It might never have been discovered by Theo and me, but we had the good fortune to have Red Thunder as a friend. He had stumbled across it last year, while eluding the drug dealers who used to cross our land, and he had shown its secrets to us.

I told Mr. Sekaquaptewa about the circumstances of our buying the land. As I talked, Mr. Sekaquaptewa suggested I call him Micah. I was grateful because his Hopi last name was difficult for me. Then I explained the problem of the drug dealers and Red Thunder's discovery of the cave, and thus the path which led to the Mesa House. When I finished, I waited while Micah thought about what I had told him. Normally, I wouldn't have been so free with information to a complete stranger, but I recalled the reputation Hopis have for being polite and very humble in demeanor. Somehow, he reminded me of Granddad. He even had similar expressions and body language. Of course, Granddad didn't make friends with skunks, but you can't have everything.

At last Micah looked at me, and said, "Correct me if I'm wrong. You and your husband bought this fourteen hundred acres mostly in order to preserve it?"

I nodded.

He continued. "And it's your intention to leave this sacred house unchanged?"

I nodded again. "There is one thing, though. We have consulted a very reasonable archaeologist friend, Jed Hazard, who thinks we can get our legal rights documented as a trust. Eventually the academic community will hear of it, and we will need to protect this area, but Jed thinks we may have a couple years before that happens. Much depends on which Native Americans have legal rights here under California law, and the gravity of their claims. But, seeing you causes me to hope that maybe *you* may have the necessary traditional rights to protect the site. Is that possible?

He looked at me. "These things are in the hands of the Higher Beings, but I will do what I can to keep this sacred place from violation and misuse. It seems we have a little time to work on the problem. Your friend, Jed Hazard, said as much as two years before a serious challenge might occur. We will talk. We will pray. We will prepare." He started to turn away.

"Wait! I need information from you. Have you always been here and I just didn't notice, or did you just arrive from somewhere?"

He replied, "My wife and I arrived last week. We have an obligation to visit this sacred site each year and attend to its maintenance."

"Do you come at the same time each year?" I asked.

"Normally. But this year we were delayed by illness in our family. In a normal year we will be here in December and stay through January. It is more pleasant here in April," he said with a glimmer of humor. He was built lean and wiry. I could see he was accustomed to a demanding life out of doors. He was only my height, but had undeniable presence.

I looked around me. "You said this site is sacred to Hopis. You are Hopi, then? Are you staying in this house? Is this where you normally live during your visits?"

"Yes, we are Hopi, but we are not staying here. My wife is more comfortable in our RV. We are parked by Wildcat Lake and I make a daily visit here. This dwelling is one of many sacred places left over from when Hopis were a very large tribe long ago. On some days my wife comes with me. I fear, however, that we are guests on your land." I could see he was trying to gauge my reaction to his presence on our land. "It is where we usually park because of the available water and privacy. From your story, my wife and I can be happy we weren't here for the drug people and the fire."

"You must have left last year before the drug lab began operating back there. I'm glad you avoided those problems. I will speak to Theo, my husband, but I'm certain we have no objection to your camping by the lake."

He nodded his appreciation and appeared to be relieved. "It seems that all is still not serene even now with the drug people banished."

"Oh," I remembered the sounds of heavy equipment emanating from the camp area. "Do you mean the construction of the Forest Service Hunting and Fishing Camp?"

"Ah," he said with understanding. "We wondered. But naturally that would be an ideal location. I have fished there, also."

I wondered if he hunted, too. I had wondered a lot of things since mingling with various Native Americans, but my experience was limited to Indian artist friends. Of first importance now, however, was the presence of the skunk.

I asked, "Does Kolichiyaw always follow you when you come here?" I looked at the animal that was now investigating a dark corner of the room.

Micah looked at me with dawning comprehension. "Kolichiyaw in not my pet. I meet her from time to time and we have a friendly co-existence. But, I am not responsible for where she goes. My wife tolerates her visits to our camp, but probably considers Kolichiyaw a nuisance."

I was at a loss. "How does she get in here?"

"I would guess the same way I do," he said. "Through the back door."

I was puzzled. "Back door?" I stooped to pack gear into my backpack.

"Come, I'll show you." Micah Sekaquaptewa turned and walked out of the room. I followed. We walked through several rooms to what looked like a storage room. Micah went up to an uneven part in the corner of the room, stepped down into a shallow hole and seemed to disappear. This was reminiscent of when Red Thunder had first taken me to the entrance of the cave in another section of the secret area. He had seemed to disappear, as well.

I peered around the corner, discovering an almost hidden architectural slot through which a fairly lean person could pass. Leaving caution aside, I stepped down and through the slot where Micah waited to guide me to the outside. We crept down the side of the mesa along a tortuous path hidden from any curious eyes by boulders. At the bottom of the path was a dense thicket of live oak, which covered a fair amount of area. It grew right up against the boulders and along the rock wall of the mesa. Micah carefully lifted branches brushing the wall and indicated that we could walk along the cliff wall in this way until we reached a game trail that led to the wide path, which ultimately skirted Wildcat Lake.

I accompanied him to the wide path, but told him I'd have to come and meet his wife on another day since I was due at home soon. I gave him our address in Coyote Canyon and telephone number, and I invited him and his wife to visit. Micah gave me his cell phone number, and thanked me for allowing him and his wife to continue to use the lakeside site, and then went on down the path in the that direction.

When I walked in the door at home, Theo was just coming out of the bedroom after cleaning himself up following a day with Matt and the building crew. They were working on Theo's boardwalk idea that stretched across the bad-walking area—*malapai*—from the wide lake path to the secret area. His idea was to take the boardwalk near, but not quite up to, the secret area. At the end of the boardwalk was to be a wide deck where we would place a couple picnic tables. It was shaded by large sycamores and seemed reason enough to end the boardwalk there for those who wondered. Later, if we felt it was timely, we could extend the boardwalk the rest of the way without too much trouble. But, we didn't want to jump the gun, so to speak. There were still many unknowns.

I told Theo about meeting Micah Sekaquaptewa and extending our permission for him to continue camping on our land beside Wildcat Lake. He thought the appearance of a traditional Hopi Indian caretaker of sacred sites was a fascinating development. Shaking his head, he said, "Just when I think I've got everything down, a new situation arises. I should know better than to think I've heard the last about anything."

I continued, "I should also mention Kolichiyaw, and the presence of a back door in the Mesa House."

Theo looked at me, his eyebrows raised.

"Micah showed me another way into the Mesa House which he called the 'back door.'" I told Theo where it was located and how to find it.

He nodded, seeming to visualize the place. "It makes sense that the original inhabitants would want more than one exit. Especially as it was supposed to be kept hidden." He paused, thinking about it. "What is this Kolichiyaw you mentioned?"

I described my meeting with the skunk and Micah's explanation of his nominal relationship with the animal.

Silence.

I went on. "I have no idea what Micah means when he says he 'maintains' the Mesa House if he thinks it's okay having skunks—and I suppose other creatures—coming and going at will."

Theo said, "We'll probably learn a lot about what he does and about his ideas if he intends to help us keep the Mesa House secure. I wonder what he thinks is a violation of its sacred status? You said they are Hopis?"

"Yes. Micah said the house is left over from a time when Hopi lands extended much further than now."

Theo rubbed his chin. "We should probably see about protecting those precious artifacts from Kolichiyaw and her cousins."

I nodded. "Those pots have lasted this long without our protection, but now I feel responsible as a land owner."

"I'll mention the care and preserving of the ancient artifacts when I meet Micah," said Theo. "Maybe he'll have some ideas. We're going to have to come to some agreements."

"We will have to be careful, Theo," I said. "The Hopis may look at those pots as their property, still being used for household chores. They may be very valuable, but it is likely these things *belong* to the Hopis."

Who would have ever thought we'd end up negotiating with an itinerant Indian caretaker and a skunk about the maintenance of our property? As Theo says, you can't ever take anything for granted.

The next day after lunch, Bob Taggert stopped by to ask questions about Dillon Cody. As far as I could tell—though Bob wasn't saying anything—the search for Stevette hadn't uncovered anything further. But, Dillon had been allegedly misbehaving. Not to the extent that Bob was ready to haul him into the station, but the man was decidedly skating on thin ice.

Bob took a sip of the coffee I handed him, and asked if Dillon had made any remarks to me alluding to rumors of people's sexual preferences and who they sleep with. "Even in this day of sexual openness, people's personal lives can be damaged if the wrong things get said," he remarked.

I assured Bob that I'd had no communication with Dillon since the day we stood talking in his driveway at Lake Mirage. "Last year he spread rumors to the drug people about me taking pictures of their illegal operations; while, in reality, I was just doing my regular wildlife photography. He really put me at risk for a while. But, what you're talking about sounds like a different kind of thing."

Bob remembered last year and nodded. "A nerve-racking time. It was good that Thad finally got the evidence to send Horton away."

"Did you ever find out anything pertaining to that package of photos?" I asked, thinking about the wrapped package Dillon had shoved at me.

"So far we haven't been able to positively identify any of the women except Gudrun Bohn."

"And I suppose it's fairly difficult to ID naked people." It seemed to me that a lot of how we recognize others is by how they dress and by their body language. "I guess no one had tattoos or anything like that?"

Bob smiled. "There was this one woman who had the cutest little ladybug tattooed on her backside. She was actually in a couple of the shots, but it was impossible to see anything that would indicate who she was." He grinned. "It isn't as though we can go around checking ladies' behinds for ladybug tattoos." He seemed amused by the idea.

"You said her death was ruled as a suicide due to overdose, but why would Gudrun die at the front door of the cottage? Wouldn't a suicide prefer to die in a more comfortable place? It was almost as if the event took her by surprise."

Bob sighed. "Suicides do sometimes occur in odd places. You have to remember that a person committing suicide isn't normally in a balanced state of mind. But, we are keeping our eyes open in case more evidence turns up to raise questions."

He changed the subject. "In the meantime, I wanted to consult with you on an idea I had. Suppose your friend, Tish Halloran, had actually been in contact with Stevette all these years. How would you go about finding her without going through Strike?"

"Hmm. Interesting idea. From the way you've phrased the question, I gather you've already tried searching for the name Tish Halloran, Facebook and other obvious search programs."

He nodded, watching my face carefully now.

"You've tried all the art avenues and so forth, I suppose." I thought about Tish, remembering the last time I saw her.

Bob sat up straight. "What was the thought that just crossed your mind?"

"What?"

"You were thinking something. What was it?" He stared at me.

"I was thinking of the last time I was with Tish, just before I moved to Vermont. We had shared an apartment in New York, located in the East Village. It was really only intended for one person or an intimate couple, because there was only one bedroom. The living room had a sleeper sofa and we made do."

Bob looked intent. "And?"

"Well, I went to Vermont in the autumn for a water-color seminar and fell in love with the town of Greenwood. I later met Theo there," I reminisced fondly.

"Come on, Janna." Bob was a bloodhound on the scent. He *knew* I had something for him.

I continued. "Anyway, while I was spending time in Vermont, enjoying the autumn, I found a teaching job and decided to move. So, when I returned to the New York apartment to collect my stuff, I was afraid Tish would be hurt and angry."

Bob pushed my story along, saying, "And she wasn't upset because...."

"Because she had a boyfriend she wanted to invite to live with her, and my presence in the apartment would have made that awkward. She was *elated* when I moved out. We both promised to keep in touch, but you know how that is."

"The boyfriend's name," Bob said. "She introduced you, right? What was his name?" He had his notebook out poised to type in information.

"You're in luck. Normally I wouldn't have remembered if his name hadn't been unusual. He was Big Bobby Bruiser, a fighter, and everyone called him 'Big Bobby.' I suppose Bruiser wasn't really his last name. But maybe he's traceable, since he was quite a public figure locally."

Bob was entering data into the notebook. "This may be important, Janna. I won't know until I work on it to see where it goes. But, thanks for your gold-plated memory." He got up to go. "I'll check back with you in a couple days to bring you up to speed." And he left.

One minute Bob and I were having an interesting conversation, and the next I was sitting by myself in the kitchen looking at empty coffee cups. I cleared away the cups and went out to the Highlander to go to the Indian Heritage Store. I wanted to talk to Amanda. She always had her ear to the ground and was in an excellent position to pick up all the latest local news from customers.

As soon as I came in the door of the store, Amanda saw me and pulled me to the side. She was angry and upset. Her voice low and intense. "Do you know what that jerk, Dillon Cody, has been saying about me and Laurie?"

I shook my head no. But, I could guess given my discussion with Bob.

"He said we're having an affair! One of my customers just came in to report the rumor. Of course no one who knows me believes it," she crossed her arms and whispered harshly, "and it wouldn't hurt my business, anyhow. But can you *believe* he has spreading lies about my sex life? The nerve of that guy!"

I stayed quiet.

"Okay," she conceded. "Maybe I'm over-reacting. But Laurie isn't going to like it, either, when she hears. In fact, she may even quit working for me. She has a steady guy she's dating now."

"If he can't tell she's not a lesbian based on his own relationship with her, I'd say she's not losing much. But, that's not the point. Nothing has been lost so far. Get a grip, Amanda." I gestured toward her office and we went in and sat.

Amanda began to relax and her uptight expression morphed to thoughtfulness. "Dillon generally wants to profit from the rumors he spreads, and not everyone can afford to pay for his silence. He could really hurt some people, Janna. I'm upset, but some people could suffer *injury* if a rumor gets to the wrong person. People's reputations are *important.*"

She had simmered down and begun to think more calmly about the problem. Once Amanda dialed back her emotions and turned her considerable intelligence to an issue, it was only a matter of time before a solution seemed to appear. If I had liked Dillon, I would have felt sorry for him. As it was, I just marveled that he thought he could get away with stuff like this.

"Janna?" Amanda asked. "What is the name of that attractive and charming new cop that works with Bob?"

I told her Kyle's name and said I'd direct him to *her* next time I ran into him. But I couldn't get her to reveal her plan. She said it was still in creative flux and she didn't want to disturb the delicate threads of the idea by talking about it. So, I left her to her plotting.

I glanced toward my Highlander as I was leaving the store, and spotted the gentleman in question leaning against my car. Again. He smiled and did a little wave.

I walked over and gave Kyle a cool stare.

He looked a little ill at ease. "I guess you're still mad at me, huh? I'm really sorry about slipping away that day when we had coffee in

Lake Mirage. I was desperate to find out what you knew, but had nothing to trade."

"And you're telling me this now, because...?"

He ran fingers nervously through his hair. "Look, I know you don't trust me. I guess I wouldn't either. But, I'm in a real bind, because I didn't realize what kind of reputation Dillon Cody has. People see him as a low life, and because I've been associating with him in order to find out more about Stevette Strike and company, his reputation is beginning to rub off on me. I can't take additional hits to my professional standing." He did look a little desperate. A clean-cut, good-looking guy, with apparently no discernable judgment. Possibly.

"What are you hoping I'll do for you? I asked. I was truly curious.

"I don't expect you to give me any information. Anyway, you probably wouldn't." He glanced at me and then looked away with embarrassment.

I waited.

"Okay." He took a deep breath. "I know you're friends with Taggert. He talks with you all the time and trusts you. I was hoping that you might let me take you out for coffee every so often so I could run ideas past you. I'd like your opinion. I need a disinterested perspective. Maybe you might consider taking me on as a charity case." He met my eyes with a hopeful puppy dog look on his face.

My jaw dropped open. Bob would laugh hysterically picturing *me* as Kyle's "mentor." It was hard to see where he had gotten that impression of Bob's and my relationship. Probably he'd listened to Dillon.

Kyle said, "If you have a little time now, I would really be grateful if you would hear what I've been digging up associated with recent events."

I held up my hand to forestall any confidences. "I have no special interest or aptitude for police work. The times Bob has talked me into helping him are related to circumstances when I was directly affected, or thought I owed him for the help and consideration he has given my family."

"Well then it's hopeless," said Kyle, looking even more deflated. "You don't owe me anything, and I don't suppose I have anything you want in trade." His shoulders slumped and I felt like a killjoy.

Recalling my promise to Amanda, I said, "Okay. There is one thing you *could* do."

His eyes blinked, probably amazed that the door had reopened a tiny crack. "Tell me. Whatever it is. Just tell me."

"Amanda Ruben-Cortez was just talking to me about rumors Dillon is spreading about people in town. She has come up with some sort of plan and she asked me your name. Maybe you could talk to her and offer your assistance."

Kyle smiled. "I'm on it." He wheeled about and walked into the Indian Heritage Store.

I wasn't sure what would come of my suggestion. Even though Amanda was angry, I'd seen her angry before, and she had never compromised her ethics over it. She was good at evaluating people, too. She'd take one look at Kyle, realize his limitations, and take them into consideration for any action she took. I would just wait and see what happened.

6

TWOITSIE STEW

April-May

WHEN I GOT HOME Gwen and John had already returned from school and were rooting around in the refrigerator for a snack. They settled on apples, cheese, milk and cookies. The twins were definitely growing and needing more fuel, these days. Their pant legs were showing quite a bit of ankle. A shopping trip for more school clothes would be coming up soon.

I went into the studio to paint, carrying a cup of tea. Later when I returned to the kitchen to refill my cup, Christian had begun barbequing chicken for supper on the back patio. Theo sat in a chair near the barbeque, a canned drink in his hand. The kitchen window was open a crack and I could hear their conversation.

"What do you think about me volunteering for the Search and Rescue team, Dad?"

"I know they have a training program for young people to try it out," said his dad. "I hear it's demanding, both physically and emotionally. But, maybe you're one of those who can cope calmly with such emergency situations, and just concentrate on what needs to be done."

Christian turned over chicken pieces with long-handled barbecue tongs. "I'd like to learn things like that. About how to help people in trouble. I've been thinking about that a lot since the fire storm came across our land last year." He paused to add more wood chips to the fire. "We knew Mom and Aunt Mrytle were somewhere around the campsite when the fire started. Thad didn't waste *any* time trying to figure out what to do. He was primed. It's like he has a set of different responses that he can automatically call up in his brain whenever there's a crisis. As if he knows he can't take time to think about. Anyway, I could tell he was on top of things, and I just did what he told me to do."

"Thad is very competent," Theo agreed. "But, he was also impressed by your response in an emergency."

Theo stood with his empty can. "Look into it, son. It could come in handy even if you don't join the S&R team. Any experience you gain that could save your own, or someone else's life, is valuable."

I stood at the window drinking tea as Theo came into the kitchen. He came over and wrapped his arms around me for a long hug. I understood his mood. What he hadn't mentioned to Christian was that search and rescue can be dangerous for the rescuers, as well. It is normal for parents to have stabs of anxiety whenever their children confront potentially dangerous situations. The later teenage and early-adulthood years can be crammed with challenges like that. Often, a parent just has to stand back and hope that the training they've given their children, thus far, will help them make wise decisions. Parenting isn't for wimps.

Later in the evening, the twins were taking showers before bed, Theo was tapping away on his laptop in the bedroom, and I was in my comfy studio chair jotting down notes of recent observations concerning Gwen and John in the notebook I keep on the children.

Gwen is my child executive, who faces life's problems head-on and will quite often make fairly unemotional decisions. Things that affect only Gwen are easier for her to manage. She revs up her engine of methodical operations and moves forward.

During recent observations of my youngest daughter, I had noticed three major draws on her time and energies: Jezebel, her parrot, and Shehri, her pony, and other responsibilities at the ranch; her martial arts studies, karate and judo; and her music lessons and band involvement. She had other interests such as Girl Scouts and camping, but these didn't take up the regular hours each week that the above mentioned interests did.

From an outside assessment, her schedule was beginning to be unwieldy and I guessed that she would soon decide to shed something in order to concentrate on things most important to her. Reasonably sure what would be cut, I decided to wait until she came up with the idea herself. There had been times when the feelings and well-being of others appeared to be at stake and caused her to take on too much responsibility. At the moment, however, I was basically pleased with her problem-solving. So, hands off.

And things were going well for her twin, too. John was moving ahead in his martial arts training—working toward a green belt in karate. He was being responsible about the daily care of his llamas. He and Travis had begun a small cottage industry of selling bags of llama pellets and sacks of soft llama wool for stuffing hypoallergenic pillows. These two pursuits seemed to keep both boys occupied. Add to that their involvement in the local 4-H group and they were busy, indeed.

John was now reading normally for his age, and his grades were showing a recent upswing in reading skills. For many years he had struggled with learning disabilities, which hadn't completely disappeared. But, of late, things seemed to be under control. Unlike last year, he was having no problem with schoolyard bullies. The confidence built by taking karate, and the additional inches gained in height, had probably put that problem behind him. At least for now.

I put the children's notebook away and got out my Journal. Every so often I needed to record events or write about stressful challenges. That evening I wanted to make a note about meeting Micah Sekaquaptewa—the Hopi caretaker of sacred places. It seemed odd that there would be any Hopi Indian sites around Coyote Canyon. Archaeological research and tradition had all of Hopi land located in

Arizona. But, I had noted from time to time that what we know must sometimes be re-evaluated. I had seen Micah since our first meeting, and he had mentioned that as a medicine man, he had a responsibility to "maintain" certain sites in the southwest. Our Mesa House was one of them. He called it Taalawsohu Waynumto, and said it means: Morning Star Journey.

I wrote: *Taalawsohu Waynumto = Morning Star Journey, in Hopi.*

A more beautiful name than Cornbread Mesa. At present the mesa lived an outward life as Cornbread Mesa, with a hidden existence as Morning Star Journey. I wondered what the future would bring.

As I wrote, the thought occurred that I hadn't mentioned the arrival of our ancient caretaker to Red Thunder. I picked up my cell and punched his number.

"Wolfe here."

"Hi. I have news," I informed him.

"News?"

"You know how we've been worrying about Cornbread Mesa House and the history of its origins?"

"Yeah," he said, waiting.

"Well, it turns out that an old Hopi medicine man—a caretaker and his wife—have been coming by quietly every year to maintain it as a sacred site."

Dead silence.

I told Red Thunder about my adventure with the skunk while sketching in the Mesa House and of meeting Micah.

"I should know better than to grow complacent around you," said my friend. "So am I off the hook? Do you still need a curator?"

"I'm afraid so. Micah doesn't spend more than a month each year here. His knowledge of the mesa history and its continuing use by Hopi Indians down the centuries should help, but you're the Native American guy who established its existence, plus you live here. Besides, you are more likely to be able to deal with the strange ways of lawyers, local government, and whoever else might come along."

"I knew there would be a catch." I could tell he was pleased to be needed even though it was a sacrifice of his time and freedom.

I went on, "We still want you to hang around to whatever extent you can. Anyway, I'm hoping you'll be available to join us when we have Micah and his wife, Sonya, over for dinner."

He said he was always interested in dinner, and was looking forward to meeting Micah and Sonya.

A little later, Theo and I sat in the HOA Club's Jacuzzi. During the cool mid-spring evenings, we didn't use the pool much, but enjoyed soaking up warmth in the swirling bubbles of the hot tub.

I sat in the almost-too-warm froth, my toes floating up in front of me. Theo, across the tub, was doing the same as we talked over happenings of the day. I told him of Kyle Krupp's request.

Theo looked at me shaking his head. "That guy is nothing but trouble. I thought you told Bob you weren't going to talk to Krupp anymore."

"Actually, it was Bob who told *me* not to talk to Kyle. I didn't promise anything. But," I sighed, "I would really rather Kyle be Amanda's problem. She'll probably keep him plenty busy." Another interesting thought struck me. "I wonder if he's married? Amanda thinks he's charming and good looking."

Theo laughed. "Good luck to them. I hope she can help him straighten out. A good woman can make a big difference in a man's life." He stood up and helped me into a cozy white terry robe before we drove the short distance home in his Ranger.

Soon it was May, a month I love in Coyote Canyon. The weather was warm, as one would expect in late spring, but the daytime temperatures were still in the reasonable zone somewhere between 75 to 90 degrees. There was usually no rain. Just blue skies, with big puffy clouds. The grasses on the mountainsides were still green, showing abundant new growth from earlier rains. Best of all, the days were progressively longer, and would eventually push back the dark to only a third of the 24 hour day.

I walked into the Indian Heritage Store late one May morning full of exuberance, a result of sniffing glorious roses blooming their little hearts out in our yard, and hearing the morning chorus of birds chirping from every tree and bush.

Regardless, not everyone is affected thus by the coming of long sunny days and the delightful scents and sounds of burgeoning springtime. Right off I could see that Amanda was not enchanted. She stood by the front counter, in her usual jewelry-selling costume, a frown pinching her eyebrows together over cheeks flushed with annoyance.

She looked up at me. "Black Snake has been complaining about my commission again. I only take fifty percent, and that's *after* I price his stuff high enough so that he gets back what he initially wanted. Plus, he has the gall to object to my sales technique."

I checked her ears for steam, but she must have been calmer than she looked. "I'm certain you've mentioned he could take his jewelry elsewhere."

"Countless times," she answered. "But he complains that it'll cost him more gas to drive down to San Diego or up to Julian. Anyway, he knows he won't do as well with another gallery. I'm tempted to just let his product sit on the shelf and let him see how fast it sells that way."

I shrugged. "Maybe you need one of those signs that says: *"We refuse to do business with you if you are rude."* Then point to the sign and let him make his own decision to go or stay."

"Don't be surprised if I follow your suggestion. I really hate being whined and crabbed at by people when I'm working my tail off to sell their stuff." But, she said it less emotionally, and I could see she was getting past her snit.

I looked into the jewelry case in front of us, noticing a collection of new silver pieces done in intricate polished silver designs. "These are nice. Especially this beautiful bracelet that is crafted to look like a feather."

Amanda looked where I was pointing. "That artist brings me stuff about once a year. He doesn't live around here, but I really like his work. He's an old guy who's been working silver all his life." She shuffled through a stack of cards and pulled one out. "Micah Sekaquaptewa. He lives on a reservation called the Colorado River Indian Territory—CRIT. It's kind of unusual, he says, because members of several different tribes live there. His jewelry is characteristic of Hopi silversmiths. They prefer to work with just the silver itself and seldom use stones in their jewelry."

"I like his designs," I said neutrally. I wondered if our Hopi caretaker had been coming into the Indian Heritage Store year after year and I had never noticed. Probably.

Amanda handed me a package of supplies I'd ordered, and then turned to serve another customer who was interested in the jewels displayed around Amanda's neck and wrists. As I left the store, she was unclasping her necklace for the customer to try on.

I was about to pull the Highlander out into traffic when my cell phone played tones at me. "Janna," said Gram. "Would you like to come for lunch today. I just fried up a batch of lake perch your Granddad caught this morning."

I told her I'd love to help them eat fresh perch, and drove down the road toward Lake Mirage. Forty-five minutes later, I could see lake waters sparkling beyond the swaying palm trees. This was the picture of Lake Mirage that always came to mind when I thought about this peaceful place, away from the world of business and crowded lives. A vacation spot often visited by people whose families had rented cottages there for generations.

When I peeked into her kitchen, Gram was just sliding grilled onions and lake perch fillets onto a heated platter to serve for lunch. As she carried the fish through to the dining table, overlooking the lake, she said, "Janna, please bring in the tartar sauce and coleslaw."

I placed the additional dishes in the center of the table just as Granddad was settling into his chair. He smiled, saying, "It's a pleasure to enjoy your company for lunch, Janna. Seems like we haven't seen much of you lately."

"I've been working pretty hard on my new painting series, both in the studio and out at Cornbread Mesa Ranch." Theo and I had let the grandparents in on the hidden aspects of our land just after realizing that Micah and Sonya were actively involved in the mesa house maintenance.

We had especially wanted to get Granddad's view of how the matter should be handled. It had been gratifying to hear that he had generally agreed with our responses in safekeeping the ancient Mesa House. Theo and I were still awaiting the right moment to inform the children. We wanted to tell them at a point when the knowledge would be fun and interesting, rather than stressful—a time when the tension had damped down from the issue.

In the meantime, it was enjoyable to taste the delicious fish Granddad had lured out of the lake that morning, and to hear of lake community doings.

As I left Gram's house after lunch, Dillon walked out of his cottage next door to have a word with me. While I braced myself to deal with Dillon, Kyle Krupp's red Dodge pickup slid into the drive behind me. The two men arrived at my side at about the same moment. Judging from their expectant expressions, I concluded they both wanted something from me. I was wrong.

Kyle, a fraction ahead of Dillon, said, "I want to thank you for sending me to Amanda. I think we're going to work well together in solving her problem." He seemed very pleased. I didn't know whether he was pleased that a town business owner was taking him seriously, or whether he was just pleased to spend time with Amanda. Either way, I was seeing less of him, so I looked on that as a plus.

Dillon overheard and his upper lip lifted in a sneer. "She's got problems, that for sure. I wouldn't go in her store too often, Janna, or people may start to think funny things about you, too." He had a self-satisfied smirk on his face.

I opened my mouth to reply, but Kyle jumped in first. "Be careful about what you say, Cody," he warned in a gravelly voice. "People who slander, play with fire. I'm thinking it wouldn't take much to trace those rumors back to you."

"Don't threaten *me*, boy." Dillon, sneered at Kyle. "I'd hate to have to mention to your superiors you've been consorting with immoral women. You're shaving it pretty close as it is."

Kyle started toward Dillon, but I intervened. "Hold it! This sort of fuss should not be taking place on my grandparent's property!"

Dillon started to make another comment when his eye was caught by something behind me. I could see his face turn instantly pasty. He shut his mouth, and abruptly walked back to his cottage, and we could hear the click of his front door lock.

I turned around to see what had spooked Dillon, but whatever had bothered him didn't seem to be there now. It was puzzling.

Kyle apologized. "I didn't mean to lose my temper. But, it annoys me that he mouths off about perfectly nice women like you and Amanda." He kept glancing at Dillon's door, but it stayed locked.

I observed, "When I last talked to Amanda she appeared more *mad* than worried. Dillon may regret trying to squeeze Amanda." There was local suspicion that some percentage of Dillon's income was paid to buy silence from him. A sad thing to think about.

Kyle seemed to relax, and surprised me with a chuckle. "I wouldn't want to get that woman mad at *me*! She doesn't mind turning the tables on Dillon. But, I better not say anymore." He thanked me again for connecting him with Amanda, then got in his Dodge truck and drove back down the road. At which point, I was able to return to Coyote Canyon in peace.

Later that day, just before supper, John came into the kitchen to tell me that his female llama, Topaz, had delivered two babies—twins! A rare event, since normally a mother llama will have only one cria (a baby llama). We were equipped to help Topaz raise her babies, so they would probably both survive. Twins are a demanding circumstance for a new mother, and the stronger twin will often be favored, making survival of the weaker twin not a sure thing where there is no assistance via well-timed bottle feeding.

John was excited, but knew he needed to give Topaz and her offspring space in their specially-sheltered pen. Even in keeping a proper distance as bonding took place, he could observe how everything was proceeding, and able to step in with help as needed. Between the new births, and discussions about planning a summer 4-H llama-packing trip across our land to Wildcat Lake, it was a pretty exciting evening for the kids.

While that was going on, Christian needed to discuss something with me as I fixed a supper of macaroni n' cheese with ham, and a side of Italian green beans. Gwen had made strawberry shortcake for dessert. As I sprinkled herb flavored bread crumbs on top of the macaroni, Christian explained, "For my birthday this weekend, I'd like to take Michelle out to dinner and dancing at the Club, then come back here to watch an action movie. She likes thrillers. Can I do that?"

"Sure. Go ahead and reserve a table for dinner tomorrow. The dance floor is available to anyone who wants to dance, although I don't know if you'll hear the kind of music you like." He was a fan of rock and blues.

"Michelle likes country music bands, so that'll work out okay."

I reached out to give my, almost, eighteen-year-old a hug. Another milestone passing.

At noon the next day, I rode Lion to Wildcat Lake on the long, winding road that traversed our land. Micah had issued an invitation to me from Sonya that I should come for lunch. It was to be just Sonya and me getting to know each other. Micah would be gone on his own business.

Coming into view of the lake, I could see an ancient Winnebago RV parked in a little clearing just off the path near the boat ramp that sloped down to the water. A small boat was tied to a tree beside the ramp, and in the clearing Micah and Sonya had set up an outdoor kitchen with an overhead tarp canopy.

She was a short, slender woman about sixty to seventy years of age with tan skin and long graying black hair gathered back in a silver barrette. Clad in blue jeans and an attractive tunic style top with bright turquoise designs, she met me as I dismounted. I handed her a little bag of blueberry muffins Rosalie had sent along, as I said, "It is so nice to visit you, Sonya. I've been wanting to welcome you."

Sonya's dark weathered eyes crinkled at the corners in a smile. "I should have invited you before, but I am a little shy with people I don't know. Please come sit with me." She pointed to a fold-up style picnic table that sat under the tarp in the outdoor kitchen.

We sat across from each other at the table, and she handed me a spoon, a bowl, an empty plate and a cup of coffee. On the table was a meal she had prepared for my visit. "Please, help yourself to the food and make your coffee the way you like it."

I sniffed the air. "It looks and smells delicious."

Between us on the table was a pot of what Sonya called *Twoitsie*, a traditional scorched corn stew with dried beans, dried corn, and mutton, to which she had added onion, colorful mild peppers and seasoning. As an accompaniment, a plate of *Someviki*, a sweet cornbread cooked in cornhusks, sat steaming hot and smelling gloriously fragrant. I filled my bowl from the pot, and then Sonya showed me how to eat the *Someviki*. One removed the husks, then sank one's teeth into the moist cornbread. The combination of stew and cornbread, Hopi style, was flavorful and satisfying.

After eating, we fixed our coffees and Sonya opened the bag of muffins. She smiled and said, "Thank you. We will enjoy these. Did you make them?"

"My daughter, Rosalie, made them. She asked me to bring them to you."

"Micah very much likes blueberries," said Sonya. Then she asked how many children I had, and we traded information of our children and her many grandchildren. She also told me a little of the Colorado River Indian Tribes Reservation—which straddled the border between California and Arizona—their home when they weren't travelling. She told me about her aunts, uncles, cousins, brothers, and sisters until every known relative had at least been mentioned. I reciprocated in proper fashion with my and Theo's relatives. It is part of Indian protocol in many tribes to trade family relationship information to establish one's identity, or place in society. Family and tribe is first and foremost. What one does for a living, or where one resides are mere details to most traditional Native Americans. As we talked, our identities were soon truly established. I couldn't even remember the last time I had trotted out so many facts about my family.

I complimented the camp set up, and asked, "Is it difficult to cook and keep house here by the lake?" Camping wasn't my best thing. I enjoyed it occasionally, but I never tried to do anything fancy. Keeping everything simple had been challenge, enough.

Sonya looked thoughtful. "It's not like being in your own house. We are more comfortable at home, but not so bad when you get used to it. Micah and I have been doing this for many years now, and we have practiced ways."

I could relate to that. People can do almost anything once they develop a method that works.

She continued. "The children have grown, so we no longer bring them."

I smiled and looked around at the campsite—no running water and no electricity. I couldn't imagine caring for little children for months on end in locations such as this. Sonya was a more accomplished woman than I was. I asked, "How do you do laundry?"

She laughed. "We go to a Coyote Canyon Laundromat whenever we collect enough laundry. This is much easier than before there were laundromats. But, important that Micah maintains the sacred sites."

"What does he do to maintain them?" I asked. "Does he clean them out and stuff like that?"

She laughed, again. "No. My daughters and I—now I alone—maintain the floors, walls and roofs of the rooms here. Micah trims trees and removes fallen rock to keep clear the sacred viewing points for the sun, moon and stars. Also traditional points in the hills are watched on special days of our calendar. You would have to talk to Micah to get details. I go into the sites to sweep and remove things that blow in with the wind, and the leavings of animals. Hopi women take care of everything inside the house. It is an honor to care for Taalawasohu Waynumto."

I thought about the debris that must collect from one year to the next. "I met Kolichiyaw while I was in the Mesa House last month."

"Tcha." Sonya wrinkled her nose. "I don't know what to do about Kolichiyaw. She follows us around. Micah should never have fed her. He has a weakness for animals."

"She's very friendly. It may be she visits the Forestry people, as well. The people who are building the hunting and fishing camp across the lake," I explained.

"Ah. You must be right. She has a path she travels each day. Often she comes from there." Sonya pointed down the road that went around the shore to where the Forestry Camp was being built.

As my eye followed her finger, I noticed a work table off to the side holding jewelry making equipment. "I was in the Indian Heritage Store yesterday, and saw that Micah had placed some nice silver jewelry with Amanda in the store. She has it on display in her front case."

Sonya smiled. "Yes. We work silver while we travel. We both draw designs. Micah cuts and shapes the silver. I finish and polish."

"You do beautiful, intricate work," I said.

"Thank you. We've worked many years on our craft. Always there is something new to try. But the old designs sell best."

Sonya began to gather empty plates as I stood up, getting ready to go home.

I said, "Can you and Micah come to our house for dinner tomorrow evening?"

She looked a little wary. "Would it be your family?"

I smiled. "Theo and me, the children, plus our good friend, Red Thunder, who is like family.

There is plenty of room at our table, and we'd like to include you and Micah."

She smiled, a little uncertain. "I will talk to Micah, but I think we will come."

I drew her a picture of the route to our house on paper. I thanked her again for the tasty food, and friendly company, and then called Lion.

The next evening we were sitting at our dining room table feasting on Christian's barbecued chicken, red potato salad, and coleslaw. We had ten people, including ourselves, at the table. Along with Micah and Sonya, there was Red Thunder and Matt. Both Theo and Red Thunder had gone out of their way to put the Hopi couple at ease.

Micah and Sonya had arrived about an hour before dinner. Since our Hopi friends didn't use alcoholic beverages, Theo took Micah into the living room with sodas, for some quiet discussion about the Mesa House and its future. There were questions about what "maintenance" meant to the Hopi medicine man and his wife and what Micah's ideas were on preservation of the sacred site, Taalawsohu Waynumto. These discussions eventually veered off to Micah's fishing methods in Wildcat Lake.

Sonya came into the kitchen with Christian and me. She was a little shocked that a nearly grown male would be doing "inside work." But, I explained our system as a way to make sure all of our children could care for themselves when they left home. She thought the idea had merit, but might be dangerous. Her concern was that a man might not think he needed to get married if he could do everything for himself.

"They might want to have children," I reminded her. "A man can't do that by himself."

She nodded, thoughtfully. "Yes, but times are changing, and some have children without marriage. The old ways aren't always followed these days."

Rosalie came in to take her deep-dish apple pie with crumb topping out of the oven. Sonya took the opportunity to thank Rosalie for the gift of blueberry muffins. "Micah had two for breakfast today," she confided.

"I'm glad he liked them," Rosalie said, her eyes captured by the simple design of Sonya's long teal knit dress and silver necklace, earrings and bracelets. The Hopi woman's shiny hair fell in a single braid midway down her back. "I love your dress and jewelry. Mom says you and Micah make this jewelry yourselves."

Sonya smiled, thanking her for the compliment. "Yes. It is how we make our living."

Then Rosalie invited Sonya down the hall to show the older woman some of her own textile crafts, while the kitchen crew finished making dinner.

By the time we all sat down at the table, Red Thunder had arrived early enough to have spent a few minutes in the living room with Theo and Micah, getting an update on the Mesa House. Everything was quite congenial as we passed around extra barbecue sauce. It came to my mind that at some point, even though the Mesa House was a stressful situation, it was becoming more awkward to keep the children apart from the information.

Micah was appreciative of our efforts to keep the Mesa House hidden from general knowledge, and therefore, when asked by John about why he happened to be camping on our land by the lake, he answered, "It is a tradition that began with my family many many years ago. Each year we come back to enjoy the lake and the tasty fish we catch there." Adult business had clear definitions among the Hopi, and this rather narrow description of his business was that which he felt able to share with young ones. His eyes twinkled when they looked at John. John could understand motives like that. But, I figured that Theo and I were going to have to have a private conference with Rosalie and Christian, soon.

After dinner, all the kids disappeared on their own missions. Gwen went to her room to practice her fiddle, eager to gain enough proficiency to accompany Christina's electric guitar. Matt had promised John he could stay at the ranch overnight to be there for the special cria feedings. Rosalie was going with them for a few hours and would return later. Christian had a study date with Michelle at her house. Reportedly, the birthday evening had been a huge success.

The rest of us had settled ourselves comfortably on the front patio to enjoy the sunset fading to stars. We could hear the wild chorus of yapping coyotes calling to each other. It was the normal evening serenade.

Red Thunder, Micah, Sonya, Theo and I spent a relaxing hour trading past histories and getting to know each other better. This was necessary because it looked like the Mesa House would cause us all to be close friends and companions for many years, if all went well. As the sliver of moon began its climb heavenward,

Red Thunder thanked us for dinner and said he had to be up early in the morning. As he left, Micah and Sonya also said their thanks and goodbyes, for they had to find their way back to the lakeside camp.

A few minutes after our guests were gone, Theo and I went for a twilight walk up the hill that wound up above our house, giving a lovely view of Coyote Canyon. Windows were lit with lamplight in the homes below. This also gave us a chance to discuss our concerns about cluing in our oldest offspring about the Mesa House. After coming to the same conclusion that basic parts of the information could be entrusted to them, we stood for a while just enjoying the night time scene before us.

Theo moved on to another subject, "I've been thinking about turning the guest room next to the atrium into an office for my work. How would you feel about that?" He looked over at me to assess my reaction.

"Not a problem. My family mostly lives nearby, and your family rarely visits. And if they do, they usually prefer a hotel." Theo hadn't heard from his mother, Regina, for several months. But, in any case, she wasn't the sort of woman who wanted to stay in a house with children and animals in residence. Grandmother Regina was not a *cuddly* grandma.

"That's what I thought," said Theo. "I'm also thinking that I spend a lot of time driving to and from Rancho Bernardo through the mountains for no good reason. I've made many business contacts in the years we've been out here, and I'd like to try running the consulting business from the house. The front door is right across the hall from the atrium, so clients needn't be in the rest of the house."

We paused beside a low rock wall bordering the upper boundary of a property. "It could work out nicely for your business, and I'd have you home more often for lunch. I could live with that." I made myself comfortable on the wall.

He sat beside me, and seemed to remember something. "Bob Taggert talked to me today, and mentioned that something strange is going on with Dillon Cody. Cody's been complaining about threatening phone calls he gets late at night warning him to leave *you* alone." Theo looked at me quizzically.

I raised my eyebrows. "Me? He's been warned away from *me*? What is that about?"

"Don't know. Bob says Cody doesn't have a clue who it is, but it's making him mad, and probably nervous, too."

Thinking back, I said, "Dillon came out of his house a few days ago when I went to visit Gram.

He was talking to Kyle Krupp and me in the driveway, when I noticed he saw something behind me. He turned almost ashen, and ran back inside his house, locking the door. I tried to see what upset him, but couldn't figure it out. Neither could Kyle."

"What was Kyle doing there?"

"He just wanted to tell me how pleased he was to be working with Amanda. Things deteriorated a bit when Dillon joined the conversation. So, it was a relief when he left. But I had no idea he was being harassed."

Theo said, "It's hard to feel too sorry for him."

Amen. Our conversation drifted in another direction. "While I remember, Christian said he was going to go over to the Sheriff Station to find out about Search and Rescue training for teens tomorrow morning."

Theo put an arm around me. It was getting cooler as the sky became blacker, though flecked with starlight. "It's evidently something he wants to try out."

I leaned into his warmth. "We'll just pray that things go well for him, as normally happens."

Theo agreed. "It's a good thing he's a kid that can take things in stride. If he just avoids hurting himself, we'll be good."

7

THE PROTECTOR

May – June

THE NEXT MORNING I WAS TOO RESTLESS to paint. Theo's story about Dillon being warned away from me by someone making threatening late-night phone calls bothered me. Whom did I know that would do something like that? I mean, they weren't threatening *me*, but it was strange that I wouldn't know who was taking so much interest in my life. It just felt weird, and I didn't like it.

Instead of painting, I drove out to the ranch and on down the dirt road to our family camp site. I wanted to see what the winter rains had done to the burned area left over from last summer's fire. It's surprising and reassuring to see how fast the green growth will come back, and slowly hide most evidence of a burn. New trees begin and old, semi-burned trees seem to find inner strength to send out new branches. No matter how devastating a fire may have been, it's only a short pause in Mother Nature's program.

I drove on to the end of the campsite to look over the worst of the fire damage. The winter rains had done fine work. Although there was some erosion on cliff sides, where earth-retaining brush and trees had burned away, there was still the winter watering had encouraged new growth. There weren't as many birds as usual, and probably some yearly nesting sites had been destroyed. But, many animals automatically move into a new place and start over again when such a thing happens.

Having satisfied myself of nature's rampant renewal, I turned and started back toward the manager's cabin by the pasture. Red Thunder was there and wanted to ask me a few questions concerning Dillon before I drove back to town. "Taggert told me about the threats Cody's been getting," he began. "Do you know anything about that?"

"The first I heard about it was last night when Theo mentioned it. Neither of us understand where this is coming from."

He nodded his head. "Is that why you came out here today?" He knew how I reacted to situations and had figured out within certain bounds what I was likely to do when I had a problem.

"I couldn't paint," I admitted. "I think it's strange that someone is trying to protect me, but wants to keep his identity a secret. By the way, do we know the person is a male?"

"Cody says the voice is deep and masculine sounding."

I asked, "Should I be doing something about this? I wouldn't like to think Dillon's in danger because of me."

"You could do some thinking about your friends and acquaintances. Go back in your memory for anything said that might make us want to investigate."

I didn't like the sound of that. I knew Bob and Red Thunder could be very crafty in their investigations. People never had a clue they were being analyzed when he and Bob were on the job, unless they wanted to make someone nervous enough to betray themselves. But I didn't think my loyalty to old friends would permit a police investigation. I hated being in a position where either side I took looked like a bad idea.

Red Thunder decided I needed a reality check. "It may come down to the fact that your information could save a life if you help us. Anyone who makes strange threats in that way, could be prepared to take it all a step further."

I looked at him and knew I'd cooperate, but I wanted to know something first. "Why are you involved in this? You're DEA."

He glanced at me and considered. "There is a possibility that these threats fall in the DEA's province."

My eyes opened wide. "Dillon involved with drugs? And why would anyone connect me to Dillon in that case?"

My friend held up his hand. "Slow down. There isn't anything actionable that we know, as yet. And you, for sure, are aware that one doesn't have to be connected with drugs to run afoul of drug people. We are attempting to check into the situation quietly and determine what kind of problem we're looking at."

"Okay, I'll try to see if I can remember anything," I said reluctantly.

"In the meantime, just live your normal life, and Bob, or I, will check back with you in a couple days."

A few days later, in the early afternoon, I was sorting through photos in my studio, when Bob rang my doorbell.

I poured him some coffee, and we sat at my kitchen table to talk.

"So," he looked at me carefully, "have you come up with anything that would give us a place to begin looking?"

I shook my head. "Nothing unusual. No one I know actually *likes* Dillon, so you have to take that into account. Just because people say they'd like to strangle him, doesn't mean they'd really do it."

Bob looked at me. "We're not talking strangling here. This is about threatening phone calls."

"Okay. I guess the whole idea stresses me a bit." I sat and thought. "I've really tried to sift through things people have said in the last month, and I haven't come up with anything that they haven't been saying for years."

Bob tapped his pencil on his chin and considered. "Let's look at this from another angle. What has Cody been doing around you lately that might cause someone to feel especially protective?"

"He's always a pain to be around, and he just got his P.I. license, and that's stressful for my grandmother because he's always been such a snoop, anyway. And to have him living next door as a professional P.I. is a problem for her. But, those aren't things that would set anyone off in a dangerous way, probably."

Bob waited as I ruminated.

"He has been spreading intimate and untrue rumors about some of my friends. That upsets me, but no one would think *I* needed protection because of that." I paused. "Although Dillon did hint that I shouldn't go in Amanda's store or the same rumors might float around about me. Kyle was there and heard him say this, too."

Bob frowned. "Kyle? Why was Kyle there? I thought you were gonna stay away from him."

This sort of thing made me exasperated. "*He* doesn't stay away from me. Awhile back he wanted to talk to me about his ideas, and I told him to go talk to Amanda. That worked pretty well, but he still considers me a friend. The day he heard Dillon spouting negativity, Kyle had come by to thank me for directing him to Amanda."

Bob shook his head, but said nothing more about Kyle Krupp. "So Dillon did actually threaten you?"

"That's the way it sounded," I said. "But, a funny thing happened as he started to get really nasty." I told Bob about Dillon being frightened by something I couldn't see, and locking himself in his house.

Bob made notations in his notebook. I asked him about the status of the cases pertaining to Stevette Strike and Gudrun Bohn.

"We're still working on it, but it's slow going. Nothing new. We found that Big Bobby Bruiser died about ten years ago related to complications from brain injuries. It's one of those things that happens to boxers. We couldn't find anyone from his background who remembered Tish Halloran."

I was pouring more coffee, when the phone rang. I picked it up and heard Christian's voice say, "Mom! I'm on 67 and there's been a horrible accident—Michelle's car went over the cliff and she's in bad shape. They've got a Life Flight helicopter coming for her."

"Are you okay? Were you in the car?" I could feel my heart nearly burst with anxiety, but by sheer act of will I made my voice calm.

"No, I'm okay. I was following behind in my truck when this big semi coming from the other direction went over the yellow line and forced her off the road. I barely avoided going over the side, too."

I heard sounds that told me he was crying. "Christian, just stay where you are and I will come and get you, and we'll go to the hospital wherever they take Michelle."

Bob looked concerned as I hung up. So I rapidly explained while grabbing my purse and heading for the door. He said, "Get in my cruiser. We'll make better time. You'll never get through without my police flasher, anyway."

Bob was easily able to get to the accident location and past the barricades. It was really upsetting to see what had happened to Michelle, and realize how close Christian had come to suffering the same, or worse. Bob had talked briefly with the paramedics and reported that Michelle was alive and currently stable—that she had a fair chance of survival from what could be assessed at that location.

Christian was, of course, still horrified by the accident, but no longer crying. Instead, he was tense, pale, determined to go to the hospital where Life Flight had taken Michelle.

Many hours later at home, I reported to Theo about Christian's close call. "He kept his head and was able to pull off on the other side of the road, fortunately. But, it must have been awful for him to witness Michelle's crashing through the guardrail. She's at Pomerado Hospital in the ICU with a punctured lung, broken ribs, and a bad concussion. Actually, it could have been a lot worse."

Theo squeezed me against him. We both needed the comfort of being close. "Where is Christian now?" He asked.

"He wanted to stay down at the hospital until he hears news. Apparently, she's in the operating room right now. Red Thunder and Rosalie drove down there to stay with him. When they arrived, I came back home so Gwen and John wouldn't be alone in the house."

Theo said, "I'll go down and join them. Christian might like me to be there."

I said, "I'm sure he would. I don't think he's ever faced anything quite this awful. We'll keep the home fires burning. Call when there's news or when everyone is ready to come home, and I'll have food ready."

At suppertime the following day, a bedraggled crew arrived home. While they were scarfing down sloppy Joes, and coleslaw, they reported that Michelle's prognosis was good, but she'd have a long recovery period.

Christian looked like he'd been, "dragged backwards through a knothole"—as the saying goes. But my son is a determined survivor and I knew he would weather this.

At the beginning of June, I started to get deeply into painting compositions of my visions of the history surrounding our land. My research had been done concerning the sort of scenes one might expect to see on our acres down through the years—horses and carriages, Model T Fords, and other evidences of the era being depicted. And I had blocked in the views I wanted to paint. Now, the real work began of making it all come together via paint on canvas. It was exciting, but tricky. In one way it was great to get these ideas into paint and on a canvas, but serious concentration was necessary to make sure it moved in a direction that showed the story I wanted to tell. In some cases I wasn't completely sure of my bearings. I would just have to trust to my instincts as an artist on those paintings.

To give myself a break from painting, as needed, I interspersed it with cooking and writing in my Journal, and Child Notebook. Currently, I sat in the studio in my blue chair writing down notes about Christian, while the painting I had worked on earlier (involving a wringer washer and clothes being pinned to an clothesline flapping in the breeze) simmered in the back of my mind.

Christian was about to graduate from Coyote Canyon High School in a little more than a week. He had managed a solid A average for the last two years by moving a little closer to maturity and becoming more responsible. Not bad for a guy who would prefer to ignore English and history. But, he was better able to face unpleasant realities now—learning to make "lemonade out of lemons"—than when he first entered high school.

His laid-back approach to life had suffered a severe jolt when Michelle had her disastrous accident. But, she was on the mend. True, it would be months before she could live a completely normal life again, yet she was alive and had a future ahead of her. Christian made time to visit her in the hospital almost every day and brought back reports of her progress.

I would guess that Michelle's recovery was quite positively affected by Christian's interest and daily attention. After he became certain she would survive, he looked upon Michelle's recovery as a challenge. Christian definitely liked being a "rescuer." During this same period, he formally enrolled in the Search and Rescue program for teens, which was given locally, and began attending their evening classes.

Once regular school was finished, he would begin to get opportunities for supervised search and rescue operations that didn't involve high levels of risk. He was excited by the whole concept of being "on call" at a moment's notice to scour the countryside with his team to find and help missing individuals. I just hoped he could keep his enthusiasm going when the inevitable sad cases arose that no one could make right again. Hopefully, he would have plenty of positive episodes that would help him ride over rough parts.

I wrote: *Be available for Christian to talk out his experiences however they work out.* I foresaw a lot more conversations with Christian over cold cereal and milk.

I put the notebook away and went into the kitchen to take a lemon pudding cake out of the oven. I was planning to serve it for supper following bowls of a northern-style chili, based on a remembered recipe of my mother's. I gave the chili a stir on the stovetop.

An hour later, my family helped themselves to chili and took their places at the table. The weather was cool for June, so the thick chili made a satisfying meal. Theo picked up his napkin and asked Gwen, "How are your violin lessons going?"

Gwen tilted her head considering the question. "Okay. My teacher has me play classical stuff. But, I'm learning how to make the violin sound good. And I've got some music for country songs I can now play, if it isn't too complicated."

"When are we going to hear you play?" asked Rosalie.

Gwen laughed. "You can hear me every night when I practice. Christina and I have been trying to play together, but we don't sound very good, yet."

I asked, "What about Tiffany? I thought you girls were starting a band."

"It takes a while to learn our instruments. We have to get sort of good at it, before we can all play together. It gets too confusing, otherwise."

I got out the lemon pudding cake and began to dish it up. This was one of John's favorite desserts. He asked for a large serving, and then observed, "A lot of times there's a band that plays at the Farmer's Market on Tuesdays after school. Travis and I've heard several bands play there while we were selling our llama pellets and pillow stuffing. I bet you could do that someday, Gwen."

Rosalie said, "There are bands that play at the Coyote Canyon Fair, too. While Dad and I were over at the fairgrounds entering our exhibits yesterday, we heard a couple of the fair planners talking about local groups who were going to play in the evenings." Theo always entered a part of his mineral collection in the town fair, and Rosalie had submitted one of her exquisite textile crafts, as well.

Theo added, "They seem to be new groups just wanting to get a chance to have people hear them play."

"No one would want to hear us, yet," Gwen laughed. "But, maybe someday we might be really good."

In the middle of June our house was a scene of non-stop activity. Outdoor temperatures often read between 95 and 100 degrees; fairly typical for the second half of June in these parts.

Christian had graduated with gusto and had his diploma in hand. Michelle had also received a diploma in her hospital bed with her family standing proudly all around. A big accomplishment in two young lives. The future lay out ahead. Fortunately, it was still full of promise despite recent horrible close calls.

Matt left to go check in at Marine Boot Camp for the summer in the Navy-Marine facility in San Diego. He wouldn't be far away, but there could be no contact with his family and friends—other than letters and certain sanctioned phone calls—until the end of training in September. Rosalie wasn't pleased about this, but she was resigned. I had noticed faint-hearted symptoms from Matt, possibly due to worries about Rosalie. Maybe it had hit him that it wasn't the smartest move to leave Rosalie alone all summer in constant contact with other interested guys. But, too late now. He now belonged to the Corps. He would find out how good or bad his timing had been in September.

Meanwhile, Gwen's Girl Scout troop spent four days camping out at our ranch in the family campsite. I stayed at home during the night time, opting to join activities at the site each afternoon, starting at lunchtime. Sleeping in a tent is not my favorite thing, and I needed to be available to John. He had a busy summer activity schedule, but he would be home for many meals and at night.

There was also the fact that Christian was in process of moving into the ranch manager's cabin while Matt was gone. His buddy, Don Schneider, would be joining him the next week, but this week Theo was staying out there to help Christian get settled and answer questions about animal care. We had five llamas, five horses, one pony, and three dogs living out there. They all needed some kind of attention and feeding. There was also general maintenance and the duties of representing the ranch when the Forest Service reps or local business people came to call. It wouldn't be a complete vacation for the boys, but they would enjoy a decided change of lifestyle in the mountain cabin from what they'd been used to in town. Besides, they were being paid as stand-ins for Matt.

The morning after Gwen's troop set up their tents out at the ranch, I was up early. A lot of errands had to be taken care of before meeting the troop for lunch at the campsite. I threw on jeans and a tee shirt, and clipped my hair in a barrette off my neck. The day was going to be hot, and I wouldn't be spending much time in air-conditioned surroundings.

I got in the Highlander and reached for the ignition, when I saw Kyle in the rearview mirror getting out of his red Chevy pickup behind me. Probably, this was his day off. I powered down the window as he came alongside my car.

"I have to talk to you." He looked uncomfortable.

"What's happening?" I wondered about his nervousness.

"It's about those phone calls Cody's been getting." He looked at me intently. "I want you to know that Amanda hasn't had anything to do with that."

I stared at him.

He ran his hand through his hair, looking disturbed. "I know I said that Amanda was out to 'turn the tables on Cody'. But, she'd never have anything to do with something like those phone calls."

I waited for him to continue.

"She only hired Loretta May to surreptitiously take pictures of Cody going about his questionable activities. Amanda only intended to give him the photos and then tell him he was just as vulnerable as anyone else. Actually more vulnerable, because most of the rumors he's spread are probably false."

I said, "It's fun to know what she was up to, but I never suspected Amanda of making those phone calls, Kyle. I know that's not how she operates. Amanda isn't underhanded. She's basically a straight-shooter when she has a grievance." Though it was interesting to know that Loretta May didn't mind betraying, Dillon, her boss. I wondered if it was money or annoyance with Dillon that had caused her to help undermine his disreputable business affairs.

"Yeah," said Kyle. "Well, I just didn't want you to get the wrong idea after what I said that day."

"Have you talked to Bob about this?" I knew my pal, Bob, would love to add this bit of info to his notes.

"No. I didn't want him suspecting her of anything."

I considered the man standing in front of me. He had a somewhat appealing, though boyish, personality, but, couldn't seem to figure out some important things. "Kyle, have you ever noticed how Bob *does* things? He doesn't instantly assign guilt. I've observed him over a long period of time and noticed he takes down everything he hears in his notebook. And then he thinks about what he sees and hears, long and hard."

"That notebook drives me crazy," muttered Kyle.

I ignored that and went on. "Next, he quietly investigates everything he collects in a way that doesn't cause notice or repercussions. Little by little, he finds out what needs more scrutiny, and also, what can be placed on the back burner along with other ideas that are probably dead ends. He doesn't leap ahead to do *anything*. All his work is slow, but sure. You don't have to worry about him jumping to conclusions about Amanda, or anybody else, for that matter." I knew this to be true, even though I had had my own hysterical moments when Bob was investigating something. And Bob did seem to have certain prejudices against anything involving Kyle. However, it didn't seem the time to mention these things to Kyle.

Kyle didn't say anything. He looked stressed. His cop poker face wasn't working for him that morning.

"Is Amanda worried about this?"

He shook his head. "No. She's too nice to think bad things about Taggert."

"She's known Bob for a long time, Kyle. Since she's innocent, she would know she has nothing to be concerned about with Bob. You needn't worry, either."

He shook his head again. "I just don't know what I'd do if anything happened to her." He got a little red faced and walked back to his truck.

I started my car and backed out of the driveway. My first stop was the Indian Heritage Store. Amanda was, as ever, bedecked with the creations of various Indian silversmiths.

"So," I said to her. "How is Kyle Krupp doing?"

She beamed at me, a pleased expression on her face. "He's doing all the rights things for me.

That man is definitely good material. He just needs a little career guidance."

I smiled at her. "And you're just the woman to help. Kyle came to my house this morning as I was leaving." I told her of his concerns.

"Poor man. He just doesn't get how things happen around here. But, I'm going to give him the benefit of my experience." She happily arranged some items in the front jewelry case. "Of course, I have to be careful. It wouldn't do to wound his pride."

I looked at her. "You know that man is in love with you."

"Yes!" She glowed. "Isn't it wonderful!"

"I'm really happy for you." I felt a wide smile of pleasure spread across my face. "And I wish you both the best possible future, whatever that is."

"Thanks," she sighed. "Everything seems to be better these days."

I hesitated. "If you and Kyle are harmoniously together, are you still intent on your scheme to get photos of Dillon's misdoings?"

She considered. "I haven't decided, yet. There's a lot of people he could hurt and I don't want to just stand by and let that happen. But, Dillon appears to have his own problems at the moment, which might put a damper on his rumor mill." She looked at me. "So, who's your secret protector?"

"Haven't a clue. He hasn't shown himself, and the whole thing makes me uneasy."

"I wouldn't like that, either." She put an arm around my shoulders. Apparently, she wasn't worried about her reputation now. "Let me know if there's anything I can do to help, Janna."

"Thanks." I gathered the tubes of paint I'd come in to buy and smiled at Rosalie, working on a display on the other side of the store as I left. I noted in passing, that there was yet another attractive male standing by to keep her company.

Outside the store, my cell phone chimed. Gram said, "Janna, dear. Your Aunt Myrtle just sent a package here for you all the way from Florida. I wondered if you'd like to come by to pick it up?"

"Thanks for letting me know, Gram. I'll come get it, but can't stay long. I'm expected at Gwen's campout for lunch."

While driving to Lake Mirage, I thought about Amanda and Kyle. Amanda was thirty now and in all the time she had been in Coyote Canyon she had never met a man she would consider seriously. The males that had flocked around her had only been attracted by her looks. But, while Amanda's solutions might not always be what I'd choose, her capacity for logical reasoning and problem-solving left most people in the dust. Not that she went around with a sign proclaiming how smart she was.

My mind didn't often operate like flash fire as hers did, but Amanda and I had a warm friendship. I just hoped that Kyle was in love with the *real* Amanda as he seemed to be.

I pulled into my grandparent's drive in the late morning. The air felt steamy. It was somewhat hotter here than at home, and moisture from the lake made everything relatively humid. But, if you're in your swimsuit splashing in the water, you don't care about things like that. Looking in the direction of the rippling palms decorating the park beach next door, I could see that many people had declared a holiday and were taking advantage of the sparkling blue water. A snack stand set up by the parking lot was doing brisk business in sno-cones and other treats.

I knocked on the front door and Gram opened it. "I'm glad you came right away for the package. Myrtle called and was quite anxious that you should have it as soon as possible." She picked up a long, brown package sitting on the table in the entryway and handed it to me.

"I wonder what it is." It was really two packages wrapped together. One was small and boxy and the other was long and narrow. The small package had a note attached that read:

Janna, dear. Perhaps you wouldn't mind delivering this to Loretta May. It seemed just perfect for her and I wanted her to know I'm thinking of her and the good things we've been doing in San Diego County. Unfortunately, I have temporarily misplaced my address book. I hope you enjoy this walking stick I received from a Seminole medicine man living deep in the Everglades. He was difficult to find, but I heard that he sells several very helpful herbs. He also has these wonderful carved walking sticks. I know how much time you spend sketching out in the mountains, so it seemed the perfect companion. I think of you often, dear, but the important work Violet and I are doing in Florida is very time-consuming and I am needed here. Love, Aunt Myrtle.

I handed the note to Gram so she could read it, too. "I wondered why she had sent your package here. I should have guessed that she couldn't find her address book." She looked worried. "I hope she's being careful when she goes back in those swampy Everglades. I've heard that alligators and water moccasins and probably other dangerous animals live there."

I gave Gram a hug. "I'm sure she'll be all right, Gram. Aunt Myrtle is pretty good at avoiding injury to herself; and remember, she *always* manages to take her afternoon nap." Privately, I thought that it was the alligators and other swamp creatures that should be taking care. With Aunt Myrtle in the near vicinity, things could get downright dangerous for them. I hoped that the Seminole medicine man didn't suffer a sad fate from my aunt's visit. But, one can't worry about every person and creature that my aunt passes by. Sometimes the world just had to look out for itself.

Slipping the wrappings off the walking stick, I examined it. It appeared to have been made from the branch or root of a tree. Its graceful curved top was carved into a sitting frog shape, and winding around the long stem was a snake with red, yellow, and black stripes. I recognized the colors of the reclusive, but deadly coral snake. It was smoothly crafted and had a sturdy, good feel in my hand. The frog top actually fitted to my fingers so that it was easy to grip. Aunt Myrtle was such a thoughtful person.

I kissed Gram on the cheek. "Thanks for keeping it for me, Gram. I'll just quickly run this other package down to Loretta May, and then I have to get out to the ranch."

I parked in Loretta May's drive a couple minutes later and rang her bell. She came to the door in a frilly apron, wiping flour from her hands with an embroidered tea towel. "Oh," she said. She looked a bit startled to see me, but smiled warmly. "How *nice* to see you again."

The plan had been to hand her the package and quickly be on my way. Instead, she grabbed my hand, pulled me into the cottage, and sat me at the little table Aunt Myrtle and I had sat at a few months prior.

"I have been experimenting with a new recipe," said Loretta May. "And you just *have* to test it for me." She brought me what looked like a piece of peach cobbler with pecans tucked in among the peaches. She handed me a fork and I took a bite. It was heavenly. The dough was flaky and buttery, and, with the hint of cinnamon, flavoring the peaches and pecans were perfection.

"Oh, my *goodness*." I closed my eyes to concentrate on the tastes of Loretta May's creation. "It's delicious!"

Loretta May's eyes glowed with pleasure. "This is a variation I thought up for one of Momma's old recipes."

"Wow. You should enter this in the County Fair baking section. This is certain to get the blue ribbon for something." I stood up, suddenly realizing the time was passing by, and that I'd better get on with the business at hand. I gave her the package Aunt Myrtle had sent. "My aunt sent this for you from Florida."

"This is for *me*? You are both so *sweet!*" She unwrapped it to reveal a little white box. Lifting the lid uncovered a small piece of costume jewelry. It was an attractive gold, red, and black ladybug pin. Loretta May immediately pinned it on her dress. Today she was wearing a tan jersey-knit wrap-around style that highlighted her feminine shape. The frilly apron added to the picture of an alluring, but domestic woman.

"This is *perfect* for me. I'll have to write a special note to Myrtle to thank her. She's always been so thoughtful, and such a powerful personality. I just *so* admire her."

I started toward the door. "I'm glad you were home today so that you could enjoy it right away, and thanks for letting me test your spectacular cobbler."

Loretta May was so touched she gave me a floury, and enthusiastic, hug before I left.

Driving back to town I thought more about Loretta May. Today she was happily creating in her kitchen, but she broadcast a peculiar vibration that I just couldn't put my finger on. Maybe it had something to do with the mystique of being an investigator, or at least a person who does research for private investigations. Maybe it was just that she worked for Dillon.

I barely made it in time for lunch with the scout troop. Katey Taggert and another co-leader, Mellissa Scott, had things well in hand. Katey handed me a hotdog as I walked into the canopied cooking area of the campsite. "Mustard, ketchup and pickle relish are on the table." She pointed to the picnic table where several girls were already eating lunch.

Gwen was in conference with Christina and Tiffany, but was happy to give me a big hug nearly causing the demise of my hotdog. "You missed the best part," she informed me. "Last night while we were in our tents, a momma raccoon and her babies came into our camp looking for food. It was really neat, Mom."

"That's all right. You just save up all those good memories and tell me about them. Maybe it would be fun to keep a diary while you're here." I took a bite of my hotdog.

"That's a good idea." I could see her mulling over the concept of recording thoughts and ideas for later reference. Another executive tool.

Katey sat down on the bench across from me with her own hotdog. "This afternoon we plan to do a nature hike to identify wild plants and flowers, and observe signs of animals living in this area. Then we'll bring back leaves, petals, and things like that to preserve and press for the craft we plan to do tomorrow." The whole troop was working on a couple badges that dealt with identifying woodland surroundings and gaining woodland skills.

"Sounds great," I said. "What would you like me to do?"

Hours later, I kissed Gwen goodbye for the day, dragged my sweaty, dirty, scratched body into the Highlander, and drove home. Diving directly into the shower at home, I stood there until my hair was clean and my skin felt human again. Combing my wet hair into a knot at the back of my head, I dressed in faded-blue jeans topped with a lime green tee.

In the kitchen, I put together a tasty shrimp and crab salad served over romaine lettuce with a previously marinated cucumber and onion salad to accompany the meal.

Rosalie, John and I were the only diners this evening. It was strange to have everyone else gone. After we ate, I cleaned up while Rosalie and John discussed evening plans. They were going to make banana splits and popcorn and watch old adventure movies. I felt a little wistful, and would have liked to join them, but had agreed to meet Bob at Belvedere Park in the upper parking lot in an hour. Normally, I wouldn't have been invited on such an expedition, but it was a place I could often be found at any hour of the day or night, anyway. Plus I knew details about the site that Bob didn't know.

When I arrived at the unlit park, it was twilight. Close to the edge of the parking lot was a nearly sheer drop of many hundred feet to the desert floor. Not far away was located a primo spot that hang-gliders favored for weekend jumps. In the far distance, dark mesas and mountains rose, a spellbinding scene in the cool light of the rising moon.

I pulled in beside Bob's black Explorer. He was standing beside the SUV waiting for me. I got out and stood next to him. "What's happening?"

"I heard a car squeal in and out of the lower parking lot earlier. Teenagers, probably." He scanned the lot where we were. Nothing. The upper lot never seemed to get all the activity drawn to the lower one. "Where is this path you said you walked along with Amanda last summer?"

"Over this way." I pointed a flashlight toward an edge of the lot several yards distant. We walked to where a narrow path went through the brush and trees for a short way, and then opened into a small clearing with a concrete picnic table at its center. On the other side of the clearing the path continued descending down a slight grade. The trees and brush were dense on either side and the path was dark. At the end was a large juniper splitting the path in two as it emptied into the lower parking lot. I was probably safer here at night with a cop beside me, than when it was just me and Amanda—or me alone—finding our way around in the dark.

Standing behind the juniper peering cautiously around its trunk, we could see Dillon's Jeep parked fifty feet away. It was Friday evening, a time Dillon often met like-minded individuals here to make what, he thought were, secret deals. Amanda and I had accidentally witnessed such a meeting last year. Later the person had ended up dead. Remembering that incident and the recent disturbing phone calls Dillon had been receiving, Bob wanted to find out just what Dillon was doing with himself at night. Bob wasn't talking about what he suspected.

Another car was parked alongside Dillon's, but impossible to see its make from the angle we were observing. We heard low voices and I made out two people standing between the vehicles. Dillon's face was captured by moonlight, but the other person—it looked like a man—had his back to us. Bob whispered for me to return to my car, and he crept forward to get a better view. When Bob was about twenty-five feet away, some items changed hands between the men in the parking lot.

Just as I was about to follow Bob's direction to go back to the car—because, actually, I had nearly *no* interest in Dillon's exploits—a hard hand came from behind me to cover my mouth, and a steel arm wrapped around my waist, pulling me further behind the tree.

"You must not put yourself in danger this way, Ms. Janna," a low masculine voice told me. "Please do not do anymore favors for the police, and stay away from Dillon Cody. It's my job to protect you. I will make sure that he causes you no more problems."

Staggering, when I was suddenly released, I turned to identify my "rescuer", but he was already gone. My heart was pumping, and I felt a shortness of breath as I retraced my steps to the Highlander. I heard Bob come running after me.

He caught up with me and asked, "Are you okay? What happened?"

After listening to my explanation, Bob told me to stay in the Highlander and lock the door. Briefly, he checked out the surrounding area, but didn't find anything to help identify my "protector," or indicate where he had gone. And when he checked the lower lot again, Dillon and company had already fled to other destinations.

Bob appeared back beside my window. "I didn't find anything, but in the daylight tomorrow, something may show up that isn't visible now." He looked unhappy. "In the meantime, I'll follow you home in my car."

Rosalie and John were still up watching a movie, nibbling popcorn in the family room when we got there. Bob and I went into the dining room with tea and coffee. It felt good to be at home, and as I took a sip of tea, most of the tension fell away.

Bob was chagrined. "First, I want to say that I am sorry this happened. I'll never ask you to do anything like that again, and I never should have left you standing there by yourself."

"I go out there by myself frequently." I was now able to smile. "And how much danger would I normally have been in with you only a few feet away? The problem is that this guy is *stalking* me. He doesn't appear to mean me any harm, but he seems willing to do whatever it takes to keep me from 'endangering' myself. I about had a heart attack when he showed up tonight, but he obviously doesn't consider things like that."

"Repeat what he said, again."

I repeated the message fairly accurately, remarking, "It was a deep masculine voice."

Hearing footsteps, I turned to see Theo and Red Thunder. Theo pulled me close then looked me over to see that I was alright. Bob had, undoubtedly, called them as we drove back to Coyote Canyon.

While I drank tea, Bob told Theo and Red Thunder what had transpired. Theo's assessment of the situation agreed with mine. The guy was stalking me, making everything different from normal. However, he felt I should go along with the stalker's demands, until we understood things better. So, no more outings with Bob.

Bob nodded. "I agree. And I also want to put a police watch on your house. Maybe we can spot this guy."

Not much later, I was in bed lying against Theo's side. "How are you feeling?" he asked.

"Tired. It's been a full day, and the events of the evening pretty much used up any energy reserves." I must have fallen asleep after saying that.

8

DEVELOPMENTS

July

EVEN THOUGH CHRISTIAN was now staying out at the ranch with his buddy, Don Schneider, he still visited Michelle Frost every day for at least half an hour. She had been released from the hospital and continued to heal at the Frost home in Coyote Canyon.

Christian shoveled horse manure into a pile as he talked. "I've been getting her to walk around a little with me. She's really slow and doesn't go very far, but I can tell she's trying hard." He leaned his tall, sturdy frame against the side of the horse corral, wiping his forehead with a muscular arm. "I'd hate to feel like she does, and then have to build myself up again just to do normal stuff."

"Does she still have a lot of pain?" Missing my son's regular presence, I had driven out to the ranch to see how Christian and Don were fairing on their own.

"She has some pain, but she says it's more a feeling of weakness and having no energy." He leaned the shovel against the rail and jammed his gloves in a pocket. "Come up to the cabin and have lunch with us, Mom. I've got sandwich stuff in the fridge."

"Let me just get the chocolate cream pie Rosalie sent." I walked toward the Highlander parked by the pasture gate, and glanced down the road at the ranch entrance. That same truck that I often saw in my rearview mirror while running errands around town, now paused by our ranch sign. As I watched, the truck turned around and drove back down the country road.

I didn't have time just then to worry about mysterious trucks, but I filed the incident away for later consideration. Picking up the pie, I handed it to Christian before driving us around the end of the pasture, and up the incline to park in front of the cabin.

Don Schneider was in the kitchen making a sandwich from the fixings spread all over the counter. Christian grabbed a couple plates from the cupboard and began constructing his own idea of a sandwich, consisting of a little of everything within reach. He made three of these. Two for himself, and one for me.

Don said, looking at the chocolate cream pie, "Nice to see you, Janna. Can I cut you a piece?"

Don was a friendly boy, mostly considerate, but nutritionally challenged. He would eat healthy things set in front of him, but naturally turned toward greasy pizza and sweets like a compass points to north. One would never know this by looking at him. He was long and lean, with dark hair that fell over dark eyes. His clear, tanned skin had nary a blemish to mar teenage perfection. Christian told me that Don was a "chick magnet." But Christian said he liked Don anyway because he was good in science, didn't spend all his time around girls, and was a paintball demon. The girls liked him, but Don wasn't sure about the girls. He was having enough trouble just trying to figure out his ditzy, earth-mother mom.

Rene Schneider, Don's mom, had been one of my volunteer art docents for an art program I ran in the grade school each year. She had another younger son who had been in Gwen's class for several years in a row. Divorced now, she found it difficult, as a disorganized, suddenly single woman, to keep a schedule of healthy summer activities going for both kids, and work at the same time. With Don at the ranch for the summer, she felt she had half as much to worry about.

Don was delighted to be out of the house and earning his own money working with animals. His dad had paid tuition and was providing college expenses starting in the fall, so Don merely had to get through the summer and he was good. Christian said Don's little brother, George, had already been allowed to stay overnight a couple times at the ranch. Christian liked little kids, so he was fine with it.

Christian watched Don ogle the pie. "You're going to have to control yourself, Dude. Rosalie made that pie for me. You can have *half* the pie, after Mom gets a slice."

"That's okay," I assured them. "The sandwich will be plenty." It was huge, and anyway I wasn't that much of a chocolate fan. Chocolate was good, but I didn't go crazy for it.

"Cool," said Don. "I haven't had my chocolate requirement for the day. Wouldn't want to be malnourished." He made himself a plateful of food combinations one might not want to examine too closely.

"So," said Christian, after swallowing a gigantic bite of sandwich. "I went out on my first assignment with Search and Rescue a couple days ago. This woman lost track of her mom who has Alzheimer's. She just unexpectedly disappeared out the backdoor when no one was looking. The woman's daughter, Mrs. Craig, called the Sheriff's Station for help. She was really frightened."

"They called you in to help look?" I hoped this story had a happy ending.

"Yeah," he set down his sandwich to intake several gulps of milk. "My crew chief called me on my cell and I drove to the station. It took us four hours to find her. She was dehydrated, but not enough to hospitalize her."

"I'm glad. What a difficult responsibility for Mrs. Craig." As the story lacked tragedy, my appetite returned and I ate some of my sandwich.

Christian started on his second sandwich. "Mrs. Craig was really relieved that we found her mom, although her mom was very confused. She didn't even recognize her own daughter. She kept struggling, saying we were kidnapping her, and that she would call the police. When we got her home she was still shouting for help and trying to hit her fists at us."

"I'm glad you were able to find her in time, even though she didn't seem to understand you were trying to help."

After marking a center line in the pie with a knife to indicate the halves, Christian cut himself a humongous piece. "It must be hard taking care of a person like that. Mrs. Craig said that she was going to look for a professional home for her mother. But, I could tell it made her sad to think of doing that." He ate a bite. "I guess, sometimes, people's problems get to be too much for their families to take care of them. I mean, that woman could have *died* if we hadn't found her. It was a hot day and she had no water with her." Such a thing was unimaginable to Christian, a boy who had been raised in a time and place where water was a priority to be considered whenever leaving home.

"It's a good thing that there are people who know how to care for people in that condition," said Don, who had been listening closely to Christian's story while he demolished his lunch. "I wonder what the symptoms for Alzheimer's are?" He looked thoughtful as he chewed.

"My crew chief said the main things are an unusual kind of memory loss, and inability to manage daily life. But, he said that there are medical tests they run on people for a diagnosis." Christian drank another tall glass of milk.

Don looked up from his reloaded plate. "My mom is sort of like that. I wonder if I should suggest that she get a checkup?"

"Stress can cause those symptoms, too, Don," I said. "She's having some tough things to deal with these days."

Christian assured his friend. "Rene isn't *anything* like that woman we rescued."

I left a little later, on the whole pleased by what I had seen. The boys weren't completely tidy, but the cabin hadn't been trashed. They seemed happy to be on their own, but aware of what it would take to get their paychecks. It was good to have leverage.

I ran a few errands, checking my rearview mirror every so often, but saw no mystery truck behind me. Maybe it was just coincidence. Might be good to pay more attention to my rearview mirror, though.

At home, Gwen told me about preparations for the summer scout fund raiser. Last year the troop sold homemade strawberry pies at a Fourth of July fireworks booth. During that event, held at the Community Playing Fields, we had sold all of our thirty gorgeous, tasty pies. It hadn't hurt being placed next to the ice cream concession. This year the troop had the same booth and the girls were excited. They had received lots of gratifying compliments on last year's pies and were eager to do it all again.

The biggest change this year was that the pie baking wasn't to be done in my kitchen. This year a different co-leader would keep track of sixteen girls while they cut up strawberries and rolled out pie dough. Despite last year's success, I didn't feel at all deprived when Melissa Scott volunteered to host the pie marathon this time. She had a gourmet kitchen with lots of areas conveniently set up for work stations. Melissa was definitely a better woman than I for the job. No contest.

"We made forty pies today, Mom. Do you think we'll be able to sell that many?" Gwen looked concerned.

"Why not?" I asked. "We sold thirty last summer and no one even knew we'd be there with our pies. Just imagine what it'll be like now that people know."

Her eyes grew huge. "Gosh. Maybe we should bake *more* pies." I could see her mentally totaling up the profits of an even bigger pie inventory.

I cautioned. "The troop should go with what they've got, and refigure again for next year if that seems like a good idea."

Gwen frowned. She didn't want to worry about what to do with a problem of overstock, either. "Right. Maybe next year we should offer two kinds of pie. Strawberry, because we know people really like that. And something else, like, maybe, peach." She turned and walked down the hall to her bedroom, probably to check the dessert cookbook she'd gotten for Christmas.

Rosalie came in the door from work looking out-of-sorts. Her classes were over for the summer. She had opted for a summer break from school in order to work more hours and save up money for her yarn collection and a loom. This was in aid of furthering her business ideas.

She opened the refrigerator door, scowling, and took out a pitcher of lemonade. I opened the cupboard and got out two glasses. She filled them up with the lemonade, then took a long drink from her glass.

I sat at the kitchen table and sipped. Rosalie got some cookies and sat across from me.

"So," I said, "How was your day?"

"Two. Count them." She held up two fingers. "Two impossibly hot guys asked me out for the Fourth of July, and I had to turn them *down* because I have *this*." She held up her ring finger displaying the promise ring Matt had given her.

I didn't say anything.

"And where is Matt when I need him?" She gestured at the ceiling. "Gone! Boot Camp for the whole summer!"

I remained silent.

"I know, I know. I should never have accepted this dumb ring." Last year she had been entranced with her fascinating new boyfriend and the pretty diamond promise ring. It had been intended to warn-off other interested males, since it was a sign of possible commitment between two people. However, such did not seem to be the case now.

She continued. "How could he sign up for a whole summer away without ever *consulting* me about how I might feel about that? How can he spend endless hours with his buddies and animals even when he's *here*? Especially since our schedules are so different and we have so little time together? I am feeling *seriously* taken for granted. I am *so* going to give his ring back when he returns." She twisted the ring on her finger as though she wanted to throw it across the room.

She looked at me. "I know. I can't just take off the ring and date whoever I want to. I wouldn't feel right about that until I've talked to Matt and explained how things are. But come September, when he gets back home, he's going to find things have *changed*. I'm done with this no communication thing!" Tears of frustration began to trail down her cheeks. I stood up and came around to the other side of the table to hug her.

I said, "I take it that you haven't heard from him since he went off to Boot Camp." She nodded. "Romantic relationships involve some of the most difficult decisions we ever have to face in life. Some of these relationships are worth working hard on and some are not. A major lesson is in learning to tell the difference and then doing the right thing. That's where giving oneself time to experience a little more of life, before making relationship promises, can help."

"What's the right thing now, Mom?"

"When I was a young person, Granddad gave me a good tool that helped a lot in sorting through this kind of thing. He suggested that I write out a list of pluses and minuses toward what I was trying to achieve with a relationship. For example, was I at a similar level of maturity as the young man I was befriending? Did we share similar values and have enough in common to *stay* interested? Were we respectful of each other? Were our goals similar, or at least compatible? And so on. Then I was to pretend I was looking from a distance at someone else's relationship to try to see it non-emotionally. This helped a lot, but it wasn't necessarily easy, because I had to be very *honest* about whether I'd done what was necessary to fill in my part of the relationship. As a result of this, sometimes I would choose to give the relationship a bit more, and other times I realized I had already given it too much. But no one except me could make that decision. And the same applies to you. You have to decide what's right for you."

I pulled back and looked at her. Her eyes were red, but she looked calmer. "I have something in the studio that might be of help." She followed me to the sitting corner of my studio. I picked up a new blank page book and handed it to her. "You might want to start by writing down all the characteristics you consider absolutely necessary in your ideal of a balanced relationship. Then think about what it might take for you and Matt to achieve that ideal. We can't expect our men to be perfect—neither are we—but you both should be able to meet *basic* needs of a relationship without a serious problem, otherwise the future will be an unrelieved uphill climb. After you determine what you consider are basic needs in a relationship, anything beyond that is gravy." I smiled at her.

Rosalie smiled back. "I can consume a lot of gravy. But I know what you're saying, Mom. Thanks." She looked at the bound blank book she held in her hands. "I guess I've been needing to do something like this. I've been feeling so frustrated, and I'm sorry for taking it out on you." She took the book to her room and closed the door.

After Rosalie left the studio, I painted for several hours. This happened to be one of those rare, informal summer evenings when everyone just grabbed something to eat on his, or her, own. The reason this could work was that John was having dinner at Travis Lee's house, and Theo was in Imperial County on a consulting job and wouldn't be back until late.

The next day, needing to pull back from current painting projects, I drove to Belvedere Park during the daylight hours to sketch. The view there was magnificent. The landscape stretched out to the edge of the earth, and the sky encompassed infinity. It was warm and breezy. Big puffy clouds arranged themselves overhead. The sun lit the distant mountains and mesas many miles away, creating blue shadows and golden sweeps of desert in-between. Here and there the desert was spotted with the green of brush and cactus.

In summer it rarely rains even when there are clouds. After years of expecting rain when I saw summer clouds form in southern California, I finally came to realize that these clouds were merely artistic statements by Mother Nature. I could understand that. One could get tired of just unrelieved blue sky.

I sat on a granite boulder that was fairly comfortable seating, and recorded the views before me with pastels on paper. I was having a good time and didn't notice the dark clouds moving in from behind until the wind whipped up and snatched a perfectly good blank piece of sketching paper out of my hands. I watched, surprised, as it sailed far away toward the valley floor hundreds of feet below. Then I felt something cold drop on my neck.

I turned to see the dark gray of a storm swooping in and felt more icy drops on my face. Knowing I didn't have much time, I gathered my stuff, ran for the Highlander, and got quickly inside, closing the windows. It would have been nice to move the car under the oak tree across the parking lot to avoid hailstones from hitting my car, but a lone tree is the likeliest place for lightning to strike.

Moments later, I watched, covering my ears, as ice balls thundered on the roof of the Highlander and bounced forming high arcs on the ground. They weren't golf ball sized hail that some places get, but they could sting against your skin. Probably it wouldn't be bad enough to damage my car. I'd seen vehicles that had suffered small dimples over every upper surface after exposure to super-sized hail. This wasn't like that.

Presently, the stormy dark clouds blew further on and the sun came out again. Piles of melting ice balls had collected. An interesting addition to the landscape, but I was ready to go home. I had some good sketches of big landscape and sky, and would look for more sites like this for times when my mind needed a rest from current work.

Putting the Highlander in gear, I rolled across the parking lot to the entrance. Across the road under a tree I saw what looked very much like the mystery truck, sitting silent. Waiting. I would have bet anything that my unknown protector had been watching to make sure I didn't fall off the mountain. Jeez. I was tempted, but not quite courageous enough to drive up to his window and complain.

Oh well. I pulled out onto the road and drove home. Later, I called Bob and described the truck.

A couple weeks after my visit with Christian and Don, they came to join us for dinner in town one evening, and reported progress at our family campsite. A construction crew had come and gone. Now there were two toilets with sinks—one for men and one for women—all hooked up to the well and septic tank. An additional utility-size sink was located on the outside wall of the toilets. The place where we had placed our picnic tables last year, was now a cooking shelter which had a stone wall on one end that included a large fireplace, a barbecue, and a wood storage rack. No showers yet, but space had been made available for them, and a water heater planned. That would be another year's project. Compared with the non-amenities of last year's family camp, we'd be very comfortable.

The next day I took Gwen out to the ranch to look over the campsite improvements. This was her special area of interest, and Theo encouraged her to take responsibility for thinking up good ideas for its maintenance and improvement. Our philosophy to involve the children at the ranch helped them feel they had a stake in its future. Whenever Gwen reported to Theo that maintenance needed to be done on the campsite, he listened and then sat with her to make a plan that would work.

As we drove on the access road to the ranch, Gwen confessed that she was probably not able to keep up with everything in her schedule.

I replied, "Well, everyone has to re-evaluate every so often. We can't just keep adding things to do without occasionally removing things that crowd the schedule."

"That's what's worrying me, Mom. I couldn't see how I could do everything. I have lots more to do now than last year."

"Have you figured out something that you don't want on your schedule anymore?"

"Yes," she said hesitantly. "I don't want to do martial arts anymore. I know it's good for me to learn, and maybe I'll go back to it someday. But, right now it doesn't interest me as much as music, my animals, scouting, and planning for family camp. All those things take up a lot of time, and karate classes are two or three times each week. I'm glad I got the purple belt, because now I know some basic moves to take care of myself, but I want to concentrate on other things now." She looked at me carefully to detect whether this was something I could understand.

I smiled. "I've been thinking that you were going to have to let something go. Your music is becoming more important to you now and will probably take up more and more time. Your pony needs to be exercised regularly, so that needs to continue. You still seem to be gaining a lot from Girl Scouts, and, naturally, you need to spend time on your ranch project."

She let out a relieved sigh. "I'm glad you don't mind about the martial arts, Mom."

I said, "I want you to honor your real responsibilities, but not every activity is a responsibility."

As we drove into the camp site, I was struck by how comfortable it all looked with its reassuring concrete block building housing the toilets, and the beautiful stone wall for the redwood shelter over a concrete floor.

"Look Mom, they've put the picnic tables in the shelter."

I stopped the Highlander next to the shelter and we got out to inspect. "Notice the roll-down canvas sides." I pointed to the sturdy sail-weight canvas that could be let down in bad weather.

"Yeah. And Christian didn't mention they put ovens in the wall." She opened one of the two heavy ovens that contained fire boxes beneath. "I wonder if we could do our Thanksgiving turkey in one of these?"

"Don't know. We'll have to talk to your father and Christian. They've discussed smoking a turkey that way. Maybe that's what they had in mind for these ovens."

"You know, Mom, I think this is a lot like the chimney wall at the old house ruin up on the mountain. I bet Dad and Christian decided they wanted all those things here for family camp." Gwen continued to investigate various features of the wall.

We next checked out the new toilets. They looked comfortable, clean, and easy to maintain. The sinks had running water piped from the well, but no hot water tap. It was a reasonable solution for camping. One didn't expect the comforts of home. But, I resolved that if showers were eventually put in, there would be hot water available for those. I was unwilling to rough it to the point of cold showers.

"Wow. This is great!" We both looked at the outside utility sink. Perfect for rinsing and scrubbing dishes, an immense improvement over a filled bucket.

By the time we had looked at all the new stuff, checked out the fire circle to make sure all was as it should be, and looked over the burned areas to gauge regrowth of brush and regreening of charred—but not dead—trees, it was time to go back home. Gwen had a music lesson that night, and we both needed supper.

The following evening I was in my studio again working on my history of the ranch series when the phone rang. It was Dillon Cody and he wanted me to know that he hadn't had any threatening phone calls for a while.

"I just wanted to call and say thanks for calling off the dogs, Janna. You *know* you never have anything to fear from me." His voice sounded a little slurred.

"What are you talking about, Dillon? I didn't have anything to do with those calls you've been getting."

"Whatever you say, Janna. Why don't you come over some evening by yourself and we'll talk. I think I could guarantee that if you come talk things over with me, you'll *never* have to worry about unpleasant rumors."

"You have a problem, Dillon, and it has nothing to do with me. Don't call again."

That conversation put me completely out of the mood to paint. After all this time, I should have learned to not let Dillon upset me.

The next morning Bob came by with breakfast, his usual bagels. I supplied the coffee and told him about Dillon's call.

"It's a coincidence that you should be telling me this." He paused to take a bite of his bagel. "Cody opened his front door last night, preparing to go out to get something from his car at about ten o'clock. He swears he didn't see anyone around, but some person had rigged up a contraption over his door allowing a large bucket of fresh horse manure to dump when the door was opened. He called the station and when we arrived at his cottage, there was still a mess all over his front step. He had cleaned himself off, but he showed us his discarded clothes. They were pretty bad."

I laughed. It wasn't as though horse manure was a huge deal, being that it is really only decomposed hay. As anyone who spends time cleaning up after horses realizes, getting slimed by manure may be odorous, but it's not that much different from mud.

Bob smiled slightly. "If I didn't know you were home last night, I might have considered the idea that you rigged that bucket. But doesn't seem like your style." He took a sip of coffee. "It's probably safe to assume your 'mysterious protector', as you call him, was responsible. Maybe he was listening outside the window while Cody was on the phone threatening you."

"Maybe," I said. "Unless it's a delayed reaction from someone he's done something bad to. It isn't something I would have done, but I sure can appreciate the temptation." I chuckled some more.

"Well, this brings us to my next question," said Bob. "Did you *tell* anyone that Cody called you and what he said?"

I shook my head. "No. I didn't even mention it to Theo. It's an unpleasant subject and not anything he could do about it."

"In any case, it's not a major crime to dirty Cody's clothes. Though that's not how *he* looks at it. Unfortunately, his personality tends to attract this sort of thing."

"What I don't understand is why Dillon made that phone call to me in the first place. If he's so worried about phone calls in the night, why would he *make* that idiotic suggestion? Especially if he thought I was causing his scary phone calls."

"It's just a guess," said Bob. "But, I think he had started drinking beer a bit earlier in the evening. Probably he began having fond thoughts about you and decided to try his luck."

I shuddered and shook my head.

"I'm not implying intelligence on his part." Bob drained his cup and got up to leave. I walked out with him, since I needed to go to the Indian Heritage Store.

A few minutes later, I saw Amanda by the front register. As soon as she saw me walk in the door, she started to laugh. I guess I didn't need to ask if the word had gotten around about Dillon's mishap the previous night.

Eventually the hoots dampened to chuckles when she got a stitch in her side. "God," she said. "That was so funny. It couldn't have happened to a more deserving person. I vote that we take up a collection for the individual who slimed Dillon. That person is a hero and deserves a reward!"

"It was kind of humorous," I admitted.

"Well, maybe Dillon will be more circumspect about throwing dirt around after this. He's found out these things can backfire," Amanda said, as Laurie Wilson strolled up to the counter from where she had been working in the back.

"Hey, Janna. Heard a certain scummy person got his just desserts." Laurie grinned at me and I smiled back. Laurie smiled a lot these days, because two weeks before, she and her boyfriend had gone off and gotten married. Laurie was peeling back her hours at the Indian Heritage Store to part time to accommodate her new situation at home. I was glad for her. It's never easy to be a single woman with a child to raise. But, according to Laurie, her new husband's relationship with her son, Jerome—a year younger than Christian—was excellent. It seemed a happy ending all around.

I got my supplies, congratulated Laurie again, and then left to go home.

Later that day, while looking over unfinished paintings of the Mesa House, I thought of the Hopi couple that we had come to feel so much affection for. They had stayed much longer by the lake than was normal in order to talk with us and make plans about Taalawsohu Waynumto, as they called it. But, when June was nearing its end, they confessed that they had business that couldn't wait at home. They would be gone until December, at which time we would see them again.

I would like to have finished my current series of Mesa House paintings by the time they returned. That would mean, of course, that I would have to get busy in my studio again. That was okay. At least it would be different from my ranch history series. There was something about working with the Mesa House compositions that gave me a special sense of satisfaction.

At supper, John reminded us that the Summer Challenge was coming up at the Main Street Dojo. John was going to attempt a move up to green belt skill level. He wasn't certain if he was up to the required level of skill, but he was going to try. He would just do his best and see what happened.

Toward the end of July, Theo took me out to dinner to celebrate my fifty-first birthday. We went to the Chinese place in town that we both enjoyed. But, it was a quiet celebration compared to the previous year, because Gram wasn't well. She didn't seem to have any specific symptoms except that she was very tired and felt weak. The last couple weeks she had actually let Granddad do all the housework that her regular cleaning woman didn't normally do.

A few years ago, Gram had re-evaluated how she was doing things and decided that she didn't have the energy anymore to clean two cottages and still feel good at the end of the day. So she hired a woman to clean with her once a week. Gram had also replaced everything cotton that must be starched and ironed, with wrinkle-free fabrics. She was an old-fashioned woman, but practical.

However, just recently Gram didn't seem to be able to do much more than sit in her chair by the window looking out over the lake. It was a worrying time for her family. But, she didn't appear to be concerned beyond an annoyance that she didn't seem to have "enough steam" to go about and do normal things.

Granddad had taken her to have tests done, and her doctor was still waiting on some of the results. Going through the tests wore her out even more. On some days, she stayed in bed and didn't even get dressed.

It made me anxious. I wanted her to go back to being her old self. Of course, I knew that she wasn't going to live forever, and being ninety that year was a quite respectable age for an active woman. Nevertheless, I couldn't believe that we would lose her now. Maybe it was just a virus.

Whatever it was, it distracted me enough that I didn't want much made of my birthday. Anyway, it wasn't a big deal birthday like last year. Turning fifty-one a person can do standing on her head. No giant psychological wallop was attached. Just another year.

Accordingly, a quiet dinner with Theo felt just right. I had a special breakfast with the children and Theo, and they had all given me gifts—I was wearing a lovely silver chain with wide links and turquoise stones set in-between as Theo's gift—and now he and I were relaxing with our usual delicious dinner at this comfortable restaurant. It was good.

Theo said, "At least we don't have Aunt Myrtle dining across the room tonight like that time she set the restaurant on fire." He smiled over the memory. It was easy to smile about things like that when Aunt Myrtle was safely in Florida, on the other side of the country.

"You're right about that," I agreed. "But, Granddad said that she's called a few times since Gram's been sick and is making noises like she's thinking of coming back to Lake Mirage to 'help' until Gram gets better."

Theo looked horrified. "Someone has to stop her. Sven has enough on his hands without Myrtle causing mayhem all around."

"Well, it isn't a sure thing, as yet. Anyway, I'm not certain what would stop Aunt Myrtle returning, except perhaps a national disaster in Florida that she felt only *she* could clear up. And we don't happen to have one of those readily available."

As the family gathered for supper the next evening, I had to break the news that Granddad had since called to let me know that Aunt Myrtle was definitely on her way. It was an uncomfortable moment, because while we all knew Aunt Myrtle was a very sweet lady, we also were aware of how disruptive she could be. Even the twins weren't sure how to respond to the news.

Red Thunder was with us for dinner and understood our hesitation. He had seen my aunt in action in the past.

But, Rosalie was ready to ride in and save the day. "I'll go and stay in the guest cottage with Aunt Myrtle while she's there, and do the cleaning and cooking, which will leave Aunt Myrtle free to sit and visit with Gram, as usual. It should make it easier on everyone."

Red Thunder hadn't previously seen this aspect of Rosalie. He hadn't been around in years past when Rosalie's inner heroine had emerged—like the time when I broke my leg and Rosalie volunteered to take over all my household responsibilities at the age of sixteen. That was a long stretch that caused her to decline most social occasions in order to be available to the needs of our household. Both Theo and I had been impressed with her sacrifice at the time of my fracture.

Red Thunder looked over at Theo. But, Theo remembered Rosalie's heroine side, too. "Offer accepted, Rosalie," he said. "Naturally, you have to check with your grandparents first, but I'm guessing they'll be pleased. Your grandfather would have to figure out something, anyway, and Naomi will love having you around. I'll make sure you don't lose out financially at work. But, yell for assistance when needed," he warned her.

Red Thunder wasn't exactly shaking his head as he left, but I could tell that he was making some realignments in his mind about Rosalie.

Theo and I later sat with glasses of wine on the front patio looking at the stars and listening to the hoots of a Great Horned Owl that roosted in our next-door neighbor's oak tree.

Theo asked, "How long do you think Myrtle will be here?"

"No way of knowing. She probably feels she has to stay as long as Gram is sick."

Theo grunted and sipped his wine.

"Maybe we'll have a better idea of timing once Gram's doctor has all the test results." I didn't want to think about too many possibilities at that point. Procrastinate. Someone once said that lots of things that look bad coming down the pike, never quite arrive. Definitely hold off on thinking.

9

CAMPING UNDER THE STARS

August

ONE DAY IN AUGUST, soon after Aunt Myrtle had returned to Lake Mirage from Florida, I took her down the lake road again to see her friend, Loretta May DuBoise. As a small contribution to the tea party to which we had been invited, Aunt Myrtle brought a pecan log with its own little knife that had been purchased in Florida.

Loretta May was delighted to see Aunt Myrtle and thank her in person for the *lovely* Ladybug pin she had sent. Loretta May said that she had been so *inspired* by Aunt Myrtle's crusading

277

example that she had joined the Save Our Environment Committee of California.

Aunt Myrtle blushed. "You are most welcome for the pin. It looks lovely on you, my dear." She gestured at the gleaming insect that decorated Loretta May's low-cut beige silk dress. "And I am so pleased that you are finding such wonderful ways to help with our environmental problems. Violet and I are having to be very patient in Florida with our work there. So many businessmen and women need to be re-educated in how to live in that delicate environment without endangering the fresh water supply." She shook her head over the apparent ignorance that she believed abounded among real estate developers.

The whole subject made me nervous merely listening to her and recalling unorthodox methods of persuasion she'd used in the past. I didn't want to hear about the "re-education" program for developers. I presumed that Violet wouldn't actually risk their going to jail over the issue, but one couldn't take anything for granted. Fortunately, the conversation got interrupted by the ringing of the doorbell.

"My goodness," said Loretta May opening the door to let in Dillon Cody. He appeared frazzled, and began to glower when he saw me. "You're a lot of trouble, Janna. Women always take everything personally."

I could make nothing of his words, and was determined not to comment. No reason to get into a pointless conversation with Dillon.

Behaving as a boss, he turned to Loretta May. "I want you to put everything else on hold and concentrate on who is persecuting me." His glance flickered over me momentarily. "I realize Janna is behind it all, but someone else is doing the dirty work for her. Find out who." He frowned even more heavily at me, but, I wasn't taking the bait. People sometimes leave no option, but to figure out things for themselves.

Loretta May looked at me wonderingly, but said, "You know I always do my poor best to assist you, Dillon. Tell me the facts you have and I'll see what I can do."

"Someone has released thousands of *crickets* in my cottage. That's a fact!" He flung his arm out in a wide, angry gesture, and managed to stab his hand on the point of the sharp little knife Aunt Myrtle had been about to hand to Loretta May with the pecan log.

"Aah!" Dillon yelled. "Even her *aunt* is working against me!"

Aunt Myrtle became alarmed and stepped toward him. "Oh dear! You mustn't think these things about dear Janna."

Her forward movement, knife still in hand, caused Dillon to jump back, trip over the throw rug under his feet, and somehow end up on the floor, bleeding all over himself, yelling, "Assault!"

Loretta May gingerly helped him off the floor and into a chair. Confused, Aunt Myrtle suggested, "Perhaps we should come back another time." She set aside the pecan log and knife on the table.

Loretta looked embarrassed, but escorted us to the door. "I'm so *sorry!* This just isn't a good day for him."

Having made our exit, I drove my aunt back to the guest cottage for her nap, then phoned from the Highlander to give Bob a heads up before Dillon called with a complaint.

Bob thanked me. "Your aunt is a nice lady, but she can sure stir things up. I'm certain I'll get an earful from Cody. Added to that, someone—we don't know who—actually *did* leave a large box of crickets open in the middle of Cody's living room floor last night. They're the kind that pet shop owners buy to feed lizards. Anyway, he woke up this morning with them crawling all over him, and didn't take it well."

"Yikes!" I could understand that part of Dillon's problem.

"Cody thinks, naturally, that it's somehow your fault."

"As though that's how I would enjoy spending my time."

"It makes sense if you're Cody. At least these stunts haven't been life-threatening. They are more the kind of prank a kid would pull. Maybe I should check out your son, Christian."

"He doesn't know anything about my Dillon problems, and he's been occupied out at the ranch this summer filling in for our ranch manager, Matt Johnson. You remember that Matt is off at Marine Boot Camp for the summer?"

"I heard about that," said Bob. "I'm not really thinking about Christian, anyway. He doesn't seem the type. Usually it's kids with too much time on their hands that do stuff like this."

"So you've ruled out the mysterious protector?" I asked, wondering what was going through Bob's thoughts.

"He's still the best guess. I'm keeping an open mind."

After Bob hung up, I went into my grandparent's cottage to chat with them a while. Gram seemed better from the last time I saw her, and Granddad was looking more relaxed. I didn't know whether it was Rosalie's presence that was making the situation easier, but I hoped Gram was regaining her health, as well. I planned to stop by again in a couple days.

A few days after the Dillon incident, Aunt Myrtle began packing again to return to Florida. Gram's tests came back inconclusive, but now anyone could see that she was doing better. Every day she was getting up and dressed. Rosalie reported that Gram came into the kitchen regularly to help with the cooking. Rosalie thought Gram might do even better with the kitchen to herself. She vacated the kitchen, but stayed close by doing normal cleaning jobs.

A week after Aunt Myrtle had gone, Rosalie returned home, and just in time for family camp. Rosalie had been especially looking forward to family camp that summer. With Matt gone her social life had collapsed, so family camp was one of the few diversions she could expect until his return. I wasn't sure what status Matt held in her life at this point, but maybe spending some time out at the ranch would provide a chance to contemplate.

To prepare for our camping weekend, Gwen consulted Rosalie about cooking in the new ovens at our campsite shelter. Michelle Frost would be joining us as a special guest this year, and Gwen wanted things to be relaxed. Michelle wasn't fully recovered from her accident wounds, but was coming along well. The doctor said that as long as she took things easy, there was no reason why she couldn't spend a few days enjoying the outdoors. So, the girls were dreaming up a menu to allow experimentation with the new ovens, while tempting the taste buds of those who stayed at the campsite.

It seemed a short time before we were all sitting around the picnic tables in the camp shelter enjoying the first supper of the weekend. There were more of us in attendance this year, and two tables had been set up for eating. Besides Gustaffesons and Michelle, there were Travis and Christina—friends of the twins—and Red Thunder. Don Schneider would be joining us during the day when he didn't have to be attending to animals. Eleven of us.

Instead of last year's tent arrangement of one for Theo and me, and two more split between girls and boys, this year we had a second tent for Red Thunder and Christian, a third for John and Travis, a fourth for Rosalie and Michelle, and a fifth for Gwen and Christina. That way if the younger members of the campsite wanted to talk and giggle all night they wouldn't disturb the rest of us as much. Such an arrangement seemed to work better all around. Don slept in the manager's cabin, as usual.

For supper that evening, we had Theo's barbecued chicken, Rosalie's coleslaw and potato salad, and Gwen's Amazing Chocolate Cake. Gwen had a secret ingredient she wasn't divulging. It was a rich dark chocolate cake with milk chocolate frosting, and she served it with vanilla ice cream. We were spoiled this time because Don had no problem carting all the leftover food back to the manager's cabin refrigerator when we were done. So, we could eat almost any menu that appealed to the cooks to make. Last year no manager's cabin had been available, and we'd had to pack extra food in coolers with ice packs and store them in our vehicles to discourage foraging raccoons.

The tables naturally divided between young kids and adults. After everyone had eaten and we were sitting around drinking various hot drinks in the cool of the evening, Theo announced that we didn't have plans for site improvement that weekend since so much had been done in July—a big change from the primitive conditions of the previous year. Everyone had inspected the recent additions upon arriving and loudly approved.

"But," continued Theo, "If anyone has an idea we'd be glad to listen to it, and put it on the list for future consideration. Other than that the agenda for tomorrow is to cook and eat, wash dishes and clean up. Chop a little firewood, exercise the horses, and relax." He glanced at Michelle. "We do want everyone to relax." He looked at John. "Did you want to talk about Sunday's plan?"

John stood up. "The 4-H Club is coming for lunch on Sunday, and then we're all going to do a llama packing hike down that main trail that goes from the access road all the way to Wildcat Lake on the other side of the ranch. We'll hike the lake trail around to the new Hunting and Fishing Camp. Mr. Thatcher, from the Forest Service, said he'd show us around. After that we'll come back here, but the 4-H Club isn't staying for supper. They have to take their animals home. After supper we're having a campfire."

After that announcement, tables were cleaned off, dishes washed, food hauled back to the cabin to discourage midnight critter visits, and everyone settled down in their tents.

Following a long night of trying to get comfortable on my cot while listening to Theo's soft snores and animal noises, finally falling into a sleep interrupted twice by needing to get up, hunt for my robe, slippers, and flashlight to visit the new toilets, I decided to get up early and make myself some tea. The sun shone in our tent, and I never sleep well while camping, anyway. We might have a more comfortable campsite this year, but I rested best in my own bed.

Red Thunder sat at a table drinking coffee when I entered the shelter. He looked up and smiled. "Camping isn't your thing, is it?"

"Sad, but true. I love being out here on this beautiful land, but my living out-of-doors skills stink."

He chuckled. "You don't seem to have passed that on to your daughters. Both Gwen and Rosalie slept all night and are still in their sleeping bags."

"Well, Gwen is able to adjust to nearly any situation, and Rosalie wouldn't wake up before her usual time except, possibly, for an earthquake. Even that isn't guaranteed."

On another subject, he asked, "Does Rosalie's return from Lake Mirage mean your grandmother is doing better?" Being almost a family member, Red Thunder was often aware of family dynamics not noticed by others.

"She's getting up and doing things, so that's a good sign. Improvement seems to be happening. Maybe it was one of those strange viruses that people get sometimes with no special symptoms except fatigue. But, it was great that Rosalie was available and willing during this time."

"That surprised me," he admitted.

I laughed. "That side of her doesn't emerge often, but an important family emergency can give rise to a sense of family duty in her that's surprisingly strong. A couple times she's been very helpful."

"I might have realized there'd be something hidden like that." He shook his head with a half smile curving his lips. "She's your daughter."

Theo came into the shelter, and the conversation turned to the Forestry Camp. "I heard that they managed to get everything done by July," he commented, picking up a cup to pour coffee.

Red Thunder nodded. "The original schedule was for an April completion."

Theo smiled. "We knew *that* wasn't going to happen. Yet, all things considered, July isn't so bad. Deer hunting season doesn't start until fall. I'm just glad to have them as neighbors." The other option, the previous year, had been a hidden illegal drug lab drawing in drug dealers from all over the county. It had been a boon to the whole area when the Forest Service announced the building of the Hunting and Fishing Camp.

"Jared tells me that some odd characters wander back there sometimes, but since the drug lab is gone they don't return." Red Thunder poured himself another cup.

Theo looked at him speculatively. "I would have thought your DEA job in these parts would be mostly done by this time."

"There's a detail or two remaining." Red Thunder sipped at his coffee.

Rosalie, Christian and Michelle entered the shelter to make hot cocoa. While they were getting cups, I started to put out milk, cereal, bagels, cream cheese, jam, oranges, sweet rolls, bananas, bowls, plates, silverware, and napkins. Before I had finished, Christian found a frying pan and began frying bacon, and Rosalie worked on a pan of scrambled eggs.

Just as the cooked food was ready, the twins and their friends appeared with camp-sized appetites. Soon the shelter was a sociable breakfast scene, and food disappeared at a remarkable rate.

John and Travis had plans to exercise and groom the llamas, and gather more sun-dried llama pellets into the one-pound ziplocks for market. Gwen and Christina intended to gather kindling for the next day's campfire, and then groom Gwen's pony. Christian and Michelle volunteered to do dishes, after which they would sit in the sun and play Scrabble. Theo and Red Thunder had quietly told me they were going over to the *malapi* area near the Mesa House, to talk about erecting a caretaker's cabin and small museum. Theo and I had waited until Matt had gone off to Boot Camp to explain to the older children about the hidden facts of Cornbread Mesa, but we still didn't speak openly about the area.

Don would be delivering lunch ingredients soon, but would then return to the manager's cabin area to catch up on some chores. Keeping Don on the job part of the time allowed Christian to be Michelle's companion during the campout, and Don would, as compensation, get the following weekend off.

Rosalie and I were the lunch and supper cooks for the day. We decided to pool our efforts for both meals, because there's something very pleasant about cooking outdoors if you can take your time and chat as you go. While Christian and Michelle cleaned up and did dishes (Michelle was taking it slow, but enjoying herself) Rosalie and I scoped out the food Don delivered, and figured out how we would use the ovens for the next two meals. There were two large pot roasts that, together with potatoes, onions, and carrots, would make a good stew for our evening meal. We would also have an applesauce upside-down cake. These recipes would test both ovens with different types of food. To go with the meal we would slice tomatoes and cucumbers. At lunch we would have chili dogs, tortilla chips, fresh fruit salad, and the chocolate chip cookies Rosalie had made at home before we left. Simple meals that would satisfy hungry campers.

After lunch, Michelle decided to nap in the hammock we had tied between two eucalyptus trees, while Christian helped Don take leftover food back to the cabin. The twins and their friends finished up activities of the morning, and Theo and Red Thunder went back to the *malapi* area.

Rosalie and I made the stew and set it on a low heat soon after lunch. Midway through the afternoon, Rosalie put the applesauce upside-down cake together. In-between cooking chores, we talked and enjoyed the comings and goings of the camp. An hour before supper we walked over to the pasture to see how the animal grooming was going.

Approaching the corral closest to the road, we could see everyone at work with buckets of water, brushes and combs. The animals had been exercised earlier in the day. Now their coats were being attended to.

"John! Watch where you're splashing that water!" yelled Gwen. She looked down at her wet clothes, then looked up just in time to get a geyser in the face.

If I hadn't been standing there, I would never have believed her next move. Gwen picked up the bucket of dirty grooming water and dumped it over John's head. He gasped and turned around to look at her. They were both dripping wet looking at each other. Their friends were standing a little ways away looking uncertain.

John wiped the water dripping off his nose, shook his wet hair, and then burst out laughing. "Gwen," he said. "You've never done anything like that before!"

At first Gwen looked stricken by her own action, but now she joined in the laughter. They both laughed so hard they fell on the muddy ground and pointed at each other. "You look ridiculous, John!"

The animals had moved away from the strange-acting humans. John and Gwen looked around and then got up to brush each other off. That proved impossible, so they handed the hose to Christina for a rinse off.

I was astonished and looked over at Rosalie who was still guffawing over the scene. "Who would have ever thought?" she laughed.

I knew Gwen was capable of explosive emotion because she had punched someone out last year for hurting John. But dumping water on John's head seemed to be in a different class. And, of course, there were so many witnesses that the story spread. Gwen got teased a lot at supper. Nevertheless, due to other mishap stories—Christian had dropped sticky leftover fruit salad all over the cabin floor involving serious cleanup—Gwen's episode didn't stand out as much as it might have. Life goes on, but it would be good to find out what was going on in Gwen's thinking of late. Always good to keep track.

The next day, we all slept a little later, and then hurried around getting ready for the 4H Club's visit. John and Travis were members of the Club, and they wanted everything to be right. Yesterday, among other chores, they had gotten out their tack and made sure all the leather and metal pieces were clean, buffed up, and ready to go.

We served everyone—campers and 4H Club people—hamburgers and big slices of watermelon for lunch. And we handed out bottles of water to take along on the hike. Christian and Michelle stayed behind to clean up while the rest of us walked down the road with our pack-laden llamas.

It was partly a training walk for the animals to get used to carrying a load. One didn't usually have to worry about overburdening a llama, because it would sit down on the ground and refuse to move if that happened. But, we had put specially prepared packs on the llamas, filled with twenty pound bags of rice, to give them a light load. Since it was just an afternoon walking trip, we didn't really need them to carry anything. But you have to start them off somewhere.

We hiked along the broad path that Sonya and Micah travelled to their campsite beside Wildcat Lake. Few of the hikers had ever been down this way before, but they appreciated the mostly level, winding trail that was an easy walk for animals and people alike. When we got to the lake we followed the lake path all the way around to the Forest Service Hunting and Fishing Camp.

Jared Thatcher, the Forest Service rep, was there to meet us as promised. He was quite pleased to show off all that had been accomplished. I'm certain the job had been bigger and more difficult than he had anticipated. But, now the area was finished, and he was leading the way, pointing out the spacious stone-fronted lodge with a full-length, log-timbered porch at the entrance of the building. Since we had to remain with our animals, we didn't go inside—that would be for another day—but we approved of its rustic, sturdy appearance. Classic Forest Service architectural style.

Jared led us on, past utility buildings and separate cabins, all with architecture and colors that blended into the landscape. There was a tiny "village" of stores where gifts and equipment could be purchased, laundry could be done, ATMs used, and internet accessed. In the same building was a seasonal restaurant that served three meals a day for lodgers and visitors.

It was getting late in the afternoon and time to turn the llamas around to go back the other way. Back at the pasture, we dropped off our animals, while the 4H Club members loaded their llamas into vans to take home. We waved goodbye and walked down the road to the campsite just in time for supper.

Christian had made a simple, but tasty meal of shredded barbecued beef in barbecue sauce on buns, and cucumber salad. We all helped clean up and then joined Gwen and Christina, who had gotten the campfire going in the fire pit within the circle of log seats. While those who cared to toasted marshmallows, we began an outrageous storytelling game. Red Thunder made up the beginning of a story, which the person next to him had to take a few sentences further, and the individual beside him added his part, and it went around the circle with additions becoming more amazing and difficult to factor into the storyline. By the time all the improbable plot twists had been added, we were all laughing and gasping for air. When it got back to Red Thunder, he ended with satisfyingly ridiculous flourish that amused us all. Everyone got a turn to start and end one of these fantastic improvisations.

When things wound down at the end of the evening, and people were heading off toward their tents, Theo and I stayed behind to make sure the fire was thoroughly doused with water. After Theo brought back a refilled bucket, we sat for a few minutes looking at the stars in the clear open space above us.

Out here at Cornbread Mesa Ranch, the sky seemed vaster and deeper. The stars appeared brighter and more numerous. Details of the night were visible that couldn't be seen in town, even though there were no streetlights on our street.

"I think everyone enjoyed themselves this weekend," said Theo. We sat leaning against each other, his arm around me.

"We were all impressed with the improvements. And, naturally, when everyone pitches in, the camp work is more fun, and they become more than just visitors." I yawned.

Theo stood, pulling me up from the log. "We'd better get to bed. We're breaking camp tomorrow."

The next morning, following breakfast and camp clean up, we caravanned back to town. As pleasant as it was out at the ranch, it was nice to get home to my familiar bed, indoor kitchen, and an actual shower.

But, I wasn't as glad to return as Rosalie. When we walked up to the door a flower delivery van pulled into our drive and a man got out with a beautiful arrangement of roses for Rosalie. Accompanying the roses was a sealed letter, which the man handed to her. Though we were curious, we all wanted to get into the house and unload our belongings. Rosalie placed the roses in the center of the dining room table and then disappeared into her room with the letter.

I looked at the card attached to the arrangement. It said, *"To my forever love Rosalie. Love, Matt."* Whew! He was using the heavy artillery. I wondered what effect this would have on our daughter.

A little later I was doing laundry when Rosalie floated out to the garage with another basket of dirty clothes. Her eyes were dreamy and her lips curved into a smile, as she figuratively floated above the plane of ordinary mortals.

I knew she'd come down to earth eventually, without any help from me. So, all I said was, "Nice flowers."

A wide grin appeared on her face. "Aren't they wonderful! Matt sent them and he wrote a long letter about how he's realized that we need to talk more and how much he loves me. He says that I'm the most important thing in his life, and he can't *wait* to see me in September." Spinning around on her toes, she dumped her laundry in the washing machine, then went out the door, saying, "I have to write a letter to Matt."

This began a period, lasting until Matt returned, of love letters flying back and forth through the mailbox. Since in Marine Boot

Camp all personal high tech equipment—(cells phones, computers, and other communication devices)—were confiscated, and only returned *after* graduation, snail-mail was the main avenue of communication available. Therefore, all personal communication was confined to the U.S. mail delivery system. Flowers arrived at least once per week. And one day, even a box of expensive chocolates arrived with the flowers.

For a comeback effort, it was fairly admirable. I just wondered how Matt was going to follow up on this act when he got home. I had nothing against him, and he was a good ranch manager for us, but I wondered if he realized how different his goals were from hers. However, communication is a good thing. The more communication they had, the better they would know what the other wanted. And that was what would make, or break, the relationship.

I had to go into the Horse's Tale the following morning to stock up on fall clothes for myself. They had a sale, and the cooler months would be here before we knew it. Already we were halfway through August and evenings were beginning to come a little earlier.

When I was done shopping I had a couple bags of corduroy jeans, matching pullovers, and turtlenecks that I liked to wear in cooler months. As I was loading the stuff in my Highlander, Loretta May appeared beside me looking pleased at the chance meeting.

"It was so *nice* to see you that day when you and Myrtle came to my cottage. I know that dear Myrtle has returned to Florida on her important work, now that her sister is feeling better, but I *hope* you know that *you* are always welcome, too. It was such a shame that day when Dillon got all upset and *ruined* everything, but he won't be doing that again, I'm sure."

"Well, no one but Dillon is responsible for how he behaves. You can't be blamed for the things he does," I told her. This seemed to be very important to her. Undoubtedly, working for Dillon had its embarrassing moments.

"I really don't much *enjoy* working for him anymore. But a girl does what a girl has to do." She sighed, gave a little wave, and walked to her own car. It had always seemed to me that there must be other options than being Dillon Cody's employee. But, then I didn't know what pressures were present in Loretta May's life. I didn't know the woman well at all.

Meeting Loretta May made me remember Dillon's problems and I wondered whether Bob had discovered the identity of the person harassing Dillon. When I got home I punched the button for Bob's cell. He answered and I asked my question.

"No. We have nothing that tells us anything new about this dude. What's up?"

"As you know, I think it's the same guy who keeps following me and is supposedly protecting me. So, naturally I'm interested."

"Okay. You don't have to get grumpy with me."

I was puzzled. "Has someone been stepping on your feelings today, Bob?"

"Us rough, tough policemen don't have feelings." He was sounding a bit cynical. "Maybe I need to get away from my desk. I'll call you when I have something." He hung up.

Next, I called Red Thunder thinking maybe he had heard something, or thought something about Dillon's persecutor. He answered, "Wolfe here."

When I put my question, he said, "I don't have any information for you, as yet. But, I'll let you know when I do." Then he interrupted himself to say he had another call coming in and hung up.

I looked at the phone. What was with these guys today? It was almost as if they were trying to avoid talking to me. I felt frustrated.

When Theo came home, I complained about the state of affairs and he suggested that we go into the bedroom and discuss the problem. We ended up sharing a shower which put me in a much better mood.

After that I felt good enough to work in my studio for a few hours. The Art Fair was coming up again soon, and there were things I needed to finish up. Several of my Mesa House still-life paintings were nearly complete. A final touch was needed that said "done." And, they all needed to be framed. My ranch history series was in pretty much the same condition. I had to get moving or I'd have nothing to show in my booth at the Art Fair.

The next few days were spent in a frenzy of walking from painting to painting, putting a touch here and a dab there. Little by little the number of finished paintings grew, until one morning—unlike some previous years— I carted the whole lot off to Jorge Morales to frame. For, although I mostly dealt with him as an exhibitor in his gallery, his main business was framing. I think this was true of most galleries around the area. Selling paintings was fun and could be lucrative, but the bread and butter was framing.

As I began hauling paintings in through his door, he came out to help. "Go and sit. I will do this. Go have a cool drink with Maria, and then we will set your paintings around and talk about how to present them."

So I went in back where Maria kept a pitcher of the special fruit punch she makes. She poured me a tall glass over ice. I sat in a chair and relaxed for a few minutes chatting with her. Even though I wasn't going to sell my paintings through the gallery this time, they were still pleased because I would have a sign up at the fair that told buyers my work had been framed by the Morales' gallery. Jorge gave me a very nice price for his work, and it was a good deal for both of us.

He squinted at a painting. "I think we will go with a silver frame for that one." Turning to another, "And this one will be magnificent in stark black." He went through each of my thirty paintings and pronounced colors and framing styles that he thought would show them off to best advantage. His judgment in these matters was excellent, and saved me a lot of time. Occasionally Maria would demur and bring out another possibility, and they would discuss the pros and cons of each choice. It was nice to just turn it over to them at this point, and drink frosty cold punch.

When the framing decisions had been made, we sat chatting. I asked, "Has anyone bought the Carrington Ranch that your cousin manages, yet?"

Jorge shook his head. "There is no rush. They haven't advertised. Just waiting for word to get around, and to see if anyone in the local area is interested."

Maria, added, "Carlos and Juanita aren't in a hurry to leave. They don't want to buy the ranch, but they aren't quite ready to pack up all their furniture and move back to Mexico, either."

Jorge began putting my paintings on racks to store them prior to framing. "It's a hard decision to change a lifestyle of forty years. Carlos has been the manager through the last two owners. He has had to adjust to the ideas of each owner. But, to move from the ranch is a much bigger change."

"We will miss them when they return to their family's land in Mexico," said Maria. "We like having them near, and it has been enjoyable to go out to the Big Ranch at fiesta times. They always like to put on a traditional fiesta."

We talked for a while longer and then, after making arrangements for delivery of the paintings, I went home.

A few days later, I was sitting on a folding lawn chair at the Art Fair with Laurie and Red Thunder. Laurie's paintings were arranged in the middle booth, Red Thunder's sand painting were to the right, and my paintings were to the left. We had put two large white canopies over all.

Laurie was shaking her head. "I just can't believe it."

"Now you know how I felt last year," I said, patting her shoulder, although she really didn't need consoling. She had just won the Purchase Award for thirty thousand dollars, and was rightfully stunned. It is just not an ordinary thing that happens in one's life. It takes getting used to.

Red Thunder got up to inspect the painting—*Sunset Over the Range*—which had a big blue ribbon attached to its lower left hand corner. It was a magnificent, large watercolor done at sunset featuring cowboys gathered around a cooking fire by a wagon to get their supper. Cattle could be seen in the near distance, and further back brilliant pink and orange mountains reflected the waning light of the sky. In the foreground were details of the meager comforts of cowboy life—saddlebags, rolled blankets, a spare pair of boots. On one side, a weary cowboy was adjusting a feedbag on his horse before he sat down to his own supper next to the fire.

The painting fully deserved the prize. Laurie had done an inspired job on the work, and I was glad that she had asked a high price for it. A trio of out-of-town judges had agreed that *Sunset Over the Range* was worth the Education Foundation's purchase award, and had posted the blue ribbon accordingly. The painting would go to our local library for a couple months, and then would travel with a group of other paintings chosen under similar circumstances, until it eventually ended up in a children's museum in the state capitol, Sacramento.

This had turned out to be a blue ribbon year for Laurie. First she met, eventually became engaged to, and then married the love of her life.

She and her son, Jeremy, had a happy family life with the new husband and dad, Rafe Poston. And now this. Laurie was speechless with delight.

As had happened the previous year when it had been me in that spot, the nearby paintings—meaning Red Thunder's and mine, this time—got lots of attention from buyers. People who buy prize-winning works often are looking for other name artists to add to their collection. Just having one's booth in the proximity of a winning painting can make one's own paintings more interesting. Although, the most amazing sales were coming from Laurie's exhibit, Red Thunder and I were doing very well, indeed.

Red Thunder hadn't said much about his own paintings sales, but I could tell that he was mystified by the attention his work was receiving. He had put together a collection of twenty beautiful sand paintings in his own unique style and with his own approach to content. His careful depictions of nature and its many manifestations were superb. Merely to look at his work and realize it was all achieved by shaking smidgens of sand from his fingers, made one wonder how he had managed such control. The colors were intensely rich, and the shaping of his subject matter—eagles, mesas, and mountain lions—seemed perfectly right. It was my guess that other Indian artists would agree with me, at least in part, due to his growing reputation among non-Native American buyers, which tended to commercially benefit all Indian artists.

It was the second day of the Art Fair, and we had been slowly folding up empty easels and display racks as paintings had sold, and inventory depleted. Laurie would have nearly nothing to cart home, and Red Thunder and I had sold the greater part of our offerings, as well. It was very pleasant all around.

We were sitting enjoying Laurie's faithful lemonade, each with our own thoughts, when Red Thunder announced, "I think I'll do this again next year."

His statement struck me as funny and I began to laugh. Laurie turned to him with a big grin. He looked at us as though we'd both gone nuts. But, then realized that his words were so deadpan obvious, that it was hysterically amusing to two weary women who had been working a booth with him all weekend. Red Thunder joined in our laughter just as Theo walked up to the booth, and wanted to know what the joke was.

I said, "Laurie just won the purchase award, and Red Thunder has sold nearly all of his sand paintings. We're just overjoyed at how well things have gone this weekend. We're nearly cleaned out!"

"Well," said Theo, "that calls for a celebration. And as it happens there is a birthday party for the twins about to take place this evening. Rosalie sent me to tell you that we're ready to rock, and to help you transport stuff, if needed."

We quickly packed up Red Thunder's and my remaining stuff into our vehicles. Laurie had her own celebration to go to with her family. As we waved adios to Laurie, we saw the officials coming to collect the winning painting in exchange for her nice big check.

At home Theo and I transferred my last few paintings to the racks in the studio, and then I went into the kitchen to see what was transpiring.

Rosalie had created a cake from one of Gram's famous recipes—a splendid light lemon cake with coconut icing. It was a wonderful success and Gram was as proud of it as though she had baked it herself. I was so pleased that Gram felt well enough to attend Gwen and John's eleventh birthday party. She still didn't look completely herself, but she was doing well. Rosalie had sat her in a chair and let her direct the proceedings so that she could be a part of the preparations.

The party was fun. The twins received many much-appreciated gifts; and they both made wishes and blew out their candles. The cake was truly delicious and went well with homemade strawberry ice cream. Soon Granddad decided it was time to get Grandma back home. She was looking tired, so she got hugs and kisses from all of us before Granddad packed her into his comfortable Chrysler sedan for the trip back to Lake Mirage.

Tents had been set up in the backyard again this year—one for Gwen and Christina, and the other for John and Travis. It was quite late before the giggling stopped. In the meantime, Theo and I sat out on the front patio with glasses of wine. It felt good to unwind under the stars after a crazy successful weekend at the Art Fair.

"Naomi was looking far better than I've seen her for quite some time," noted Theo.

"She was delighted that Rosalie made the special cake from her recipe." I sipped my wine. "Gram and Rosalie have become very close since Rosalie stayed there during her illness."

"Rosalie is a good person," said Theo, leaning back with his glass and looking up at the half moon. "I hope she's making the right decisions for herself."

I knew he was referring to Matt. "It'll be September in a couple days and Matt will be coming home soon. When that happens she'll get a clearer picture of how things are going to go."

"Well, however it goes, Rosalie will have thought it completely through. I'll say that for her. She always takes her time making decisions," said Theo.

"She'll be turning twenty this next month, Theo."

He shook his head. "You never think the time is going to come when your children are all grown up. It's amazing enough that they get born."

"She isn't our baby, anymore." I was half sad about this, and half happy for Rosalie for the things she had accomplished for herself. She was jogging right along toward her goal of owning a crafts business.

Theo said, "She'll always be our baby." I guess by that he meant we'd always have that special feeling for her no matter how many years went by.

Judy McGrath

10

UNEXPECTED CHANCE

September

I WAS OUT SKETCHING at Cornbread Mesa Ranch in an area I hadn't been in before. Thus far we had stayed in the areas of the ranch we had become familiar with over the past year. But, there wasn't any reason to do that now, since we no longer had to be extra careful. As far as I knew, there were no longer any criminals lurking back there, and besides, I was looking for new sketching areas. It seemed reasonable to further investigate the ranch, since there was a lot I'd never seen.

So, I had gotten out early and driven much further down the boundary road than usual. At a little more than half a mile from our Cornbread Mesa Ranch sign, I noticed a pretty area of rocks and boulders. I pulled over and parked. Lifting my pack out of the Highlander, I slung it over my shoulder and began to follow a barely visible game trail, threading my way through the rocks and brush lit by the sun rising slowly into a clear blue sky.

The rocks I touched seemed to have already shed the chill of night. It would be a very warm day. I was walking along looking intently at striations in the boulders shining in the sunlight beside the path, when a large, heavy, dark shape slammed into me and knocked me off to the other side of the trail into the brush.

I sat up, pulled weeds out of my mouth, and looked to see what had attacked me. But, instead, I observed a large coiled-up snake sunning itself on the path just ahead of where I had been walking. A Diamond Back Rattlesnake, apparently asleep. Probably, it had eaten a good meal the night before and was enjoying the sun as it continued to digest whatever it had dined on. I shuddered to think of what might have happened if I had stepped on it. Even sleepy rattlers bite.

I could feel my heart thumping, and clutched my arms across my chest. Everything was fine, I told myself. I was okay. I hadn't stepped on the snake, no thanks to me. Though, too stunned to look beyond the snake, at first, now that my heart rate was descending, I glanced around. I could see no one else in the area. My savior had fled. I was pretty sure there was only one savior, and he was the guy I'd been calling my "mysterious protector."

I got up gingerly, backing away from the area where the snake continued to sun itself, undisturbed. Retracing my footsteps all the way back to the Highlander, I sat in the driver's seat to catch my breath. As I sipped from a bottle of water from my pack, I considered my situation.

First of all, I hadn't been careful. I knew better than to not look where I was going first thing in the morning when snakes were gliding out from under rocks to warm up in the sun. I was going to have to tighten up my safety precautions a bit more. Even though I had stuff on my mind, it wouldn't improve my thinking to be bitten by a rattlesnake. I *had* to be more careful.

Okay. That was good for problem number one. Next. What was this... this nearly annihilating me in order to save me? I needed to identify my protector, and soon. We needed to talk. It wasn't that I didn't appreciate being saved from a rattlesnake bite. I truly did appreciate it. But, couldn't he have just grabbed my arm and pulled me back? Did he have to ram into me like a commando and bruise my whole right arm and right side? Jeez. With this guy protecting me, I might not live to see my fifty-second birthday! I had to find that guy and set him straight.

I called Red Thunder and asked him to meet me at my house for lunch.

At home, I moved carefully to avoid jarring my body too much as I got together beef tacos and put on a pot of coffee. No matter what, Red Thunder always needed coffee.

He knocked at the backdoor, and I let him in. Immediately, after looking at me, he said, "You're in pain. What happened?"

I reported the incident, recalling as many details as I could. "You're right," said Red Thunder. "This 'protector' guy needs a lighter touch." He looked at the developing bruises on my arm and winced.

"I'm glad you understand about the problem," I said. "I can't deal with that kind of help. It's only a bit better than coping with the snake. This scaring me to death or knocking me around and bruising me can't continue."

He nodded agreement and picked up his cell phone to call Bob Taggert. In a little while I had two law enforcement men consuming tacos.

"Let me get this straight," said Bob. "This guy did a running tackle like hitting a quarterback in football?"

I nodded and ate some taco of my own. "I didn't even know he was there, and suddenly this dark shape appears out of the corner of my eye. Before I can react I'm flying through the air into the brush."

"Definitely overkill," agreed Bob. "I'm still of the opinion that his intention is to help, otherwise you would have other kinds of complaints about him. But, since he has no contract with you for protection, and I'm guessing no license, he is operating illegally. This rough stuff could be explained by stupidity or just bad judgment. Not every guy understands how easy it is to hurt a woman or a child without meaning to."

"Still," I said.

"Yeah," said Bob. "This can't go on or you'll be a hospital case."

"What do you recommend?" I asked.

Bob and Red Thunder looked at each other. "Actually," said Bob. "We've been working on the problem from another angle, but didn't want to mention it to you, prematurely."

"I thought it was something like that when neither of you would talk to me."

Bob held up his hand. "You don't like secrets, but you might like knowing the information even less."

"What do you mean?"

Red Thunder said, "He means we think your pal, Jake Horton, is behind your mystery protector."

I could feel the blood leaving my face. "How *could* he be? He's in prison. And he's *not* my pal," I added.

Red Thunder leaned forward. "Remember how I said it might be difficult to shake him even if he was in prison?"

I thought back to the day when meth lab owner, Jake Horton, decided that I was "okay" and that he was going to take care of me like he did his little sister, Jane. I stubbornly repeated, "He's in prison."

"Being in prison merely means he's not here. But, he's still very powerful," said Bob. "Criminals who have a strong network of associates at the time they get put in prison, sometimes are able to have all kinds of things done for them outside of prison. And everyone in the criminal world knows Horton is rich. All Horton might have to do is get a message out, or in some cases he might only have to drop a hint about what he wants done. It could even be that this protector guy is doing it on his own, thinking that Horton would be grateful, and would reward him. But, in a lot of cases like that, thinking is not what they're best at, and without specific orders mistakes can happen."

"So, that's what you think is happening here? A mistake?" I asked.

Red Thunder said, "We think it's possible. We have to find this guy and question him to be sure."

Bob added, "And to do that, we're changing our method to plan B instead of plan A."

"I'm afraid to ask." The whole thing was making me nervous.

"Up to now, we had thought we'd be able to catch him in the act, because he's been doing some weird things to Dillon Cody's house. But, it hasn't worked out that way," said Red Thunder. "So, now we're going to follow you during times when we think he's most likely to be watching you. He has to sleep, so we don't need to be on the job 24/7, but we need to cover the main hours when you've seen him."

Bob pulled out his notebook, and I gave him a list of all the times I could remember when I thought I'd seen the mysterious dude behind me. It turned out that he tended to show up when I was awake, and when I was asleep he probably wasn't around. Great.

"Realistically," Bob said, "we can't follow you around all day. It would drive you crazy, and we have other things to do. So, I am going to give you a special cell phone that is programmed with just our numbers. If you think you see him, or the mystery truck, all you have to do is punch the button and it will show up on both our cells. We will respond by calling back or showing up to chase him down. This phone has a small GPS device that tracks your location and reports it directly to us. We'll always know where you are if you have it with you."

They both looked at me and smiled. I smiled back. "Okay, I guess this will probably work. Right?"

Bob got up to leave, patted me on the shoulder, and went out the door.

Red Thunder stood up. "Make sure you keep that cell turned on and in your possession all the time. It could make a difference to your health." And then he left, too.

I looked over the new phone carefully. It looked just like other cell phones. In fact, it looked like the phone I carried in my purse.

I sat in my chair, drank lemonade, and thought. After a while, I realized that what I actually needed to do was to follow my original plan. I needed to talk to this guy without any interference from my team of interested protectors. Granted he had been a bit rough, but he may have saved my life. I thought I owed him a little consideration just because of that.

And there was another thing that seemed important. My mystery dude tried to avoid any use of violence. I thought of the things he had done to Dillon. If he were a violent guy, he could have saved himself a lot of trouble just by killing Dillon and not having to think about him again. End of problem. But, he wasn't doing that. He was also watching Dillon for misbehavior toward me—when Dillon tried to do some wretched thing to me, Mystery Dude punished him, but didn't maim or kill him.

The next time I had a good opportunity, I wasn't going to be a wuss. I was going to pull up to his car window and find out what the heck was going on.

Not long after I had this private talk with myself, Red Thunder called me again. "Hey," he said. "I forgot to tell you that I met this girl who is some kind of cousin of mine. She saw my paintings at the Art Fair, picked up one of my business cards, and called me at home."

"How wonderful," I said. "Is she one of your Navajo relatives?"

"Yeah. I was wondering if I could bring her by to meet you." There was a little hesitancy in his voice.

"Of course. We'd love to meet her. Bring her to dinner tomorrow night. Are you excited about meeting her?"

"Yes," he said uncertainly. "I'm just not sure what's expected of me."

"Ah yes," I said. "If you follow what you think of as ethical conduct, you will probably be just fine. But, it wouldn't hurt to do a little research." I could tell he was worried about Navajo dating and marriage customs. Probably didn't want to compromise himself.

"I was hoping you'd say something like that." I could hear relief in his voice.

That evening, I was clearly bruised and sore. Red Thunder had talked to Theo and told him of my adventure before he got home, knowing I was going to need help. Theo gently smeared MSM cream on areas I couldn't reach to stop the swelling. I lay in bed with ice packs along my side for much of the evening.

The next day I didn't go out at all. I just creaked around the house and groaned like an old hag. By dinner time, after I had taken a really good nap, I was in reasonable shape to be conversational. Christian made dinner—one of his favorites with meatloaf, mashed potatoes and gravy, basil carrots, and salad. And Rosalie made chocolate ice cream pie.

Rosalie wasn't quite sure what to think about her relationship with Matt these days. The "love of her life" had finally come home, and she was very excited and happy about that. They had talked and talked and talked just the way they had planned to do. And things were good. Mostly. It turned out that Matt had a different picture of what life would be like once he and Rosalie got married. He expected her to stay home, and raise children, and help him with the ranch he planned to have. Maybe when the children were in college she might want to open a little business, as long as it didn't interfere with family things. Meaning she should be there all the time when he needed her there. None of this was outrageous according to many traditional views of marriage, but clearly it wasn't what Rosalie had planned for herself. She was mulling it over and looking happy that he was home. It wasn't as if she had to make up her mind in the next moment. She could do her regular Rosalie thing, and think things through. Over time.

In the meantime, Rosalie wasn't sure what to make of Red Thunder bringing home a girl cousin. Red Thunder had reported her name was Julia Begay, with the nickname, "Spotted Fawn." His cousin was twenty two years old, and in her first year of teaching on the Trepasoti Reservation.

When Rosalie heard Spotted Fawn would be joining us for dinner, she said, "I hope Thad doesn't feel he has to *date* her or anything like that. I'm not up on Native American marriage customs, but some cultures put pressure on cousins, that aren't too close, to marry."

"I'm not sure he *could* date a cousin," I commented. "I seem to remember that traditional Navajo Indians cannot marry within their own clan. Any cousin would certainly be in his clan. In any case, I think Red Thunder can probably look after himself."

My daughter looked at me as though I was hopelessly naive, and then hurried away to change her clothes. I could tell she was feeling protective of Red Thunder. It was also possible she was confusing herself with unexpected feelings of jealousy. On the one side of the question, she had this imperfect relationship with Matt, a guy her own age. On the other side, I had observed a long-standing attraction to Red Thunder, a very interesting, but much older man. Probably Rosalie had never seriously visualized herself dating him because of the age difference. Girls of Rosalie's age normally didn't think about men ten years older than themselves. Particularly, when there were plenty of men near her own age that were interested. And as far as I could see, my sketching partner had never behaved differently with Rosalie than he had with her brothers and sister. However, Rosalie appeared to be struggling with her feelings. Male and female relationships can be difficult.

When Rosalie came out of her bedroom, she wore a blue off-the-shoulder knit dress that fit perfectly, and a silver choker with matching bracelets. Her hair was in the flowing style she liked to wear for special evenings. Matt didn't take his eyes off her all evening. He looked quite handsome in his Marine uniform; however, Red Thunder was always an eye catcher in his Indian-style black and turquoise evening attire. Spotted Fawn turned out to be an elegant, dark-eyed girl with a simple shiny black braid down her back. Her traditional Navajo dress was very feminine, a long dark green skirt with a lovely sage over-blouse. With this she wore turquoise Concho style earrings, a matching belt, and a large, but delicate, silver and turquoise squash-blossom necklace.

Spotted Fawn was a shy, but enchanting, guest. She sat gracefully beside Red Thunder at dinner, quietly eating. I asked her how she was enjoying her teaching job.

"I have kindergarten children, an age I like very much." Her face was serious, her voice soft. "They are sweet and eager to learn."

Red Thunder commented, "Spotted Fawn told me the education facilities are quite good on the reservation due to tourist attractions that bring income for the Trepasoti Band. Having a Navajo father and Trepasoti mother makes her able to live and teach on our local Trepasoti Reservation. This means we'll get to see a lot more of her than if she was on the Navajo reservation in Arizona." He smiled down at her and she shyly smiled back.

Although Matt was right there beside her—and apparently oblivious to her feelings—Rosalie couldn't stop looking at Red Thunder and Spotted Fawn.

A little before Red Thunder took Spotted Fawn home, he asked me to talk with him for a moment in the studio. He looked at me seriously. "I have to go away for a while on DEA business. I had hoped that I would be able to be here and help with your stalker, but I am needed elsewhere. I don't know when I'll be back, and I won't be able to communicate with you while I'm gone. But, I *will* be back. Please take care of my horse, Fire. And please keep yourself safe!" He gave me a hug. "If things go very wrong, I've asked the agency that you be notified."

He must have seen the shock on my face, and added, "I'm fully expecting to come back and sketch with you again. But, until then, *don't* do anything dangerous. I expect you to be here when I get back, too."

"I'll be good, if you will." I wiped my eyes and gave him another hug. Then he left the studio, found Spotted Fawn, said thank you and goodnight to everyone, and left.

I told Theo about Red Thunder's trip for the DEA while we were getting ready for bed that evening. He didn't seem too surprised. "Either you quit doing that stuff, or you're always on call. There is no in-between. I figured that since he hadn't quit, it was just a matter of time."

"I guess I knew it, too. But I hoped that maybe he would find a way to remain here. He isn't one of my children, but sometimes I feel that way."

Theo hugged me close as tears prickled pooled in my eyes. I knew he was worried about

Red Thunder, as well, and felt a special bond with him. "We have to think positively. You did say that he's expecting to come back, didn't you?"

The following day school began again for John and Gwen at Coyote Canyon Middle School. No longer in elementary school, they had moved up in the world. Of course, that meant they started again at the bottom of the heap. They were the sixth-grade newbies, and in a new school to boot. It was a humbling experience, but not intimidating. During the previous year they had both grown taller, and John had learned to stand up for himself. Now there would be new challenges to face: multiple teachers instead of just one, different subject matter, changing social patterns. It would take a period of adjustment, but they both looked excited rather than apprehensive about the prospect.

Christian had begun his college classes at UCSD the week before. He was taking a basic course of study with one science class just to make it more interesting. Now that Matt was back at the ranch doing his regular duties,

Christian was living in town with us again. Don Schneider had gone off to a veterinary school in northern California. He was hoping to spend some vacations from school at the ranch with our animals.

Rosalie was back in school, too, taking most of her courses at night. A couple classes were during the day when she could carpool with Matt. They seemed to be a happy couple again. But there was no talk of anything in the future, as yet. Rosalie was still working hard toward honing her business expertise and saving toward her loom. And as far as I knew, she was still planning to open her own crafts business when the time was right.

One bright morning in September, after the children were all in school, I was on my way to Lake Mirage. It had been a while since I had seen Grandma and Granddad, and I had been invited to have lunch with them. I drove down the hill toward the lake and, again, enjoyed that view of the water sparkling beyond the trees. There was something idyllic about that approach road that never failed to relax me. I felt fortunate to have such a beautiful place to come to.

As always, Gram was leaning out the door as I pulled into the drive calling to me, "Hurry up, Janna. We're just sitting down to eat."

I got out of the Highlander and went into the house. The aromas were of wonderful, hot roast beef sandwiches with gravy, and green beans from Gram's garden on the side. I sat down across from Granddad and loaded up a plate.

Granddad asked, "What are you doing with your art these days?"

I finished a bite of roast beef. "I'm working on dramatic landscape scenes. In fact, I was just noticing that the approach road to the lake might make a great painting. I'll have to do some sketches and see what I think."

Gram was pleased to think of me working so close by. "What a good idea! You'll be able to come here for lunch on those days." She looked around the table. "Oh dear, I seem to have forgotten the salt." She put her hands on the table to help lift herself up, but it was as though one of her hands wasn't working, and she began to lean sideways. She kept leaning sideways until I realized that she was falling and moved quickly to catch her. We ended up with me on the floor and Gram with her head in my lap.

Granddad was already calling 911 while I sat there on the floor smoothing Gram's hair and telling her not to worry. Help was coming soon.

It seemed a very long time, but was probably only minutes when an ambulance drove up close to the front door, and Granddad ushered in the paramedics. They immediately lifted her onto a stretcher and into the ambulance. Granddad rode along, holding her hand, while I followed behind in the Highlander. Before leaving I had called Theo, and when we got to the Pomerado Hospital emergency entrance, he was there to meet us. I sat at a desk and answered questions for insurance from cards Granddad had given me. Theo went with Granddad to the little room where they were working on Gram.

When I finished the long form and answered questions for the admissions people, I searched until I found Theo and Granddad talking to a doctor. "We won't know for a few days how bad it is, but she's had a stroke. Fortunately, you were right there when it happened and got her into emergency right away. This will make a big difference in how much functioning she is able to recover. But, we won't know exactly how much can be expected for a while." The doctor looked sympathetic. He had the demeanor of a man who had experience with crises where nothing could be offered except the care that keeps a condition from getting worse. And he had patience. Lots of patience.

Theo and I took Granddad down the hall while the medical staff started arranging things to move her to a room in the Intensive Care Unit. As we approached some chairs, Rosalie—whom Theo had called earlier—rushed in and threw her arms around Granddad. He softly patted her back, helping her to regain composure. Then he led her to nearby chairs and they sat down. Granddad was always able to consider the needs of others, first. It was like second nature to him, a part of his character.

"Granddad," said Rosalie, "I want you to know that I'll move back to the cottage as soon as we get Gram home from the hospital. I'll bring my dog, Bree, with me this time, and I'll take care of everything just like before."

"I'm sure you will, Rosalie," said Granddad. "And I'm sure it will please your grandmother to see you by her side. She's always appreciated having you around."

Theo said, "We'll work it the same way we did before, Rosalie. But you have school this time. Will you be able to do that, as well?"

Rosalie smiled now. "No problem. We can have Home Help come if necessary on the afternoons when I'll be in class. But most of my classes are in the evening when Gram will probably be sleeping. There won't be any days when I'll be gone the whole day."

I said, "Thank you for your generous offer, Rosalie. You know we appreciate it." A little later I left for home to be there for Gwen and John. Christian's schedule was erratic these days, and I had no idea when he would be home.

That evening I sat in the studio writing in my Journal. I knew at least one of the reasons why Rosalie was so eager to volunteer her help to her great grandparents. She had always had a close relationship with them. She and Gram loved to pour over recipes together from the time she was a tiny girl. Naturally, she wanted to help in times of trouble.

Another reason could be that she wanted to put some distance between herself and Matt. She had hinted that she needed some thinking time when she didn't see him as often for a while. They had had a time to talk out what was on their minds. Perhaps Rosalie now needed to stand back and think about where Matt's plans fit into her idea of the future.

And then there was the fact that Rosalie's being gone over a family emergency would test Matt's understanding of Rosalie and what she saw as her duty. Matt had gone away for the summer on what he had considered important business, and had expected Rosalie to deal with that calmly. Now Rosalie would be gone for her own important reasons. Would Matt be able to accept this sort of thing without grumbling? It would be interesting to see what developed. I imagined that Rosalie would watch, too.

A week later, Gram came home from the hospital, and Rosalie, bringing her yellow lab, Bree, for company, moved into the guest cottage. Matt hadn't immediately understood why Rosalie needed to be the one to move into the cottage, but he told her that he was willing to be patient about it.

A few days after Rosalie moved to Lake Mirage, she celebrated her twentieth birthday. Matt had wanted to give her an engagement ring, but Rosalie wanted to wait until she was back in Coyote Canyon to talk about that. Rosalie and Matt still saw each other on the days when they carpooled for afternoon classes. Rosalie would drive in from Lake Mirage and meet Matt at our house, and they would go from there together. Then they would do the same thing in reverse order when they returned. But, there were apparently no dates, and no visits by Rosalie to the ranch. She was a busy woman and Matt had to be patient with that. It wouldn't always be that way, but a man had to, "be able to be flexible," said Rosalie.

One of the things that touched me during this time was a visit from my sister, Jody. She drove to our house from Ramona, and then we went in my Highlander to Lake Mirage. Jody and I never got enough time together. She was a very active structural engineer with a doting husband, and several grandchildren to keep her busy. She also spent a lot of time in her garden. Her daughter, Liz—the child closest to Rosalie's age—had graduated from college and was teaching high school art. Liz now had her own apartment in Ramona and was enjoying the freedom of having her own space.

As mentioned, Jody's and my lives were busy and it was hard to get uninterrupted time together. However, about twice a year—spring and fall—we made an effort by going on a picnic just by ourselves, or visiting the Quail Botanical Gardens over by the ocean, or some other escape from family and commitments. In this way we could spend a few hours just talking and enjoying each other's company.

Today wasn't one of those golden days of relaxation. It was a day of family responsibility and togetherness. "I remember how we used to talk about making our parents proud of us after they passed on, and we had to go live with the grandparents," said Jody. "We were so lucky to have them when we lost Mom and Dad."

"I'm sure it was a tough adjustment for them, too." I remembered the pain of that first year as it very slowly receded. "Imagine losing your daughter and son-in-law and then having to care for their twin teenage daughters after you'd just retired and made things comfortable for yourself."

"I wouldn't want to even think about that," said Jody. "I can't imagine how they did it. I don't even recall that they made a big deal about us coming to stay with them. They just seemed to absorb us into their comfortable home, and we didn't think about it at all, or what it might be costing them. Teenagers often aren't able to consider things like that."

"I'm pretty proud of Rosalie right now," I said. "I don't know that I would have stepped up at her age the way she has. But then she knows how to cook, and when I was her age I had no clue about things like that. And she knows how to clean. You remember, I'm sure, how unsuccessful I was at cleaning and being tidy when we were young."

Jody laughed. "It used to drive me crazy, because of our shared room when we moved to Michigan. I was always a neatnik and felt I had to tidy up for both of us."

"It probably would have worked better if you'd only tidied up your own half and let me be embarrassed by the contrast to mine. Although, I admit, I wasn't always reasonable about that sort of thing. I've since made it a point to teach all my kids how to cook and clean. Life is a whole lot easier with basic survival skills." I sighed as we turned off on the road that led to the lake.

"The doctors are pretty sure she's stable now, right?" Jody asked. "I mean, is she at a point where no more damage is going to happen and she can begin working to improve her functioning?"

"The doctors said that another stroke is always a possibility. But, yes, she's stable. She has a therapist that comes and works with her three days per week, and in-between Rosalie and Granddad help her do her exercises. But, no one knows, yet, how much of her abilities she will be able to recover. The doctors say that only time, and Gram's determination, will tell."

Jody said, "I'm sure that Rosalie won't be able to stay at Lake Mirage forever. She has her own life to live. What is the plan if Rosalie has to leave and Gram isn't ready to take over?"

"We'll cross that bridge when we come to it. A lot will depend on how active Gram becomes. It may be that consistent professional help will be needed."

We pulled into the cottage driveway and parked. Jody and I looked at each other and she said, "It's just another stage of life, Janna. We'll survive this one, too."

11

REVELATIONS

October

DILLON MADE A STRANGE PHONE CALL to me early one morning about some photos he said he had of Loretta May. He wanted me to know that Loretta May was a slut and I shouldn't have anything to do with her. He was planning on giving the photos to the police and letting her explain some things to *them*. He was mad, by golly, and wouldn't be taken advantage of like that! It was odd to picture Dillon as a victim. He fell more naturally into the abuser role instead of the other way around. It was also possible that he was missing a few of his cylinders.

Possibly drunk as well. Which, come to think of it, wasn't normal for him that early in the morning. His drinking habits were offensive, but regular. This was a departure from the norm.

I didn't want to bother my grandparents, so instead called Loretta May to see if she might knock on his door. He was her boss and she lived just down the street. The phone rang, but I got no answer. Sighing, I decided I might as well drive to my grandparent's house to see how they were doing, and take a moment to scope out Dillon's cottage next door, just to make sure there was no medical emergency.

I got in the Highlander and drove down the road toward Lake Mirage. As I was making the turn that put me on the Lake road, I noticed a familiar truck behind me. Okay; be calm, I told myself. I pulled over and waited. Sure enough, the truck parked a ways behind me.

The truck wasn't a great truck. It was an older Chevy. Dark blue, tinted windows that were dirty, and some chrome was missing. Maybe not a great truck, but it certainly got around. It had been following me for months. I was tired of having a faceless truck behind me. Time to clear the air.

I sat in the Highlander and patiently waited. After about twenty minutes, the mystery dude must have decided he needed to check on me in case something was wrong. In the rearview mirror I saw the driver's side door open and then a very large young man emerged. He was dressed in black saggy pants and a huge black and red shirt. He wore his dark brown hair long, and he had a gold chain around his neck. If one could see underneath that mound of baggy clothes, he was probably built a good deal like Christian.

The large young man looked in my direction and closed his truck door. He pocketed his keys, ambled over to my window, and stared at me. I powered down the window and said, "It puts a crick in my neck to talk like this. Come around to the passenger side." I unclicked the lock as he walked around the car to get in. It may seem like I was taking unnecessary risks, but I knew he wasn't there to hurt me. He might, in fact, have saved my life at least once. Anyway, an at-ease situation has to be set-up if you need a guy to relax and talk. And we definitely needed to talk.

He opened the door and swung into the passenger seat with the grace of a young man probably in his early twenties. He had a good-looking tan face with dark brown eyes. At the moment he wasn't smiling, but I could see smile lines and thought that he probably laughed often. However, right now he was all business. Right, must get down to business.

I asked, "Why have you been following me for all these months?"

He said, in the husky voice I remembered from Belvedere Park, "You know why I've been following you. I've been trying to keep you safe. And I gotta' tell you it's not an easy job." He adjusted his weight in the seat.

"Why do you feel the need to keep me safe? You don't even know me."

"Let's just say there's someone I know who cares a lot about your safety and I've volunteered for the job." He looked at me. No expression. Tough guy.

I looked back at him. "If you are trying to keep me safe you need to work on your technique." I pushed up my sleeve and showed him the remains of the bruises I had received when he had prevented my stepping on the rattlesnake by slamming into me. "This is what I still have left after two weeks of healing."

He looked at my arm and then back up to my face. He looked puzzled.

I explained. "When you pushed me away from the snake, you did it with such force that I not only got these bruises on my arm, but my whole side was bruised, as well. Next to you, I'm a small person, and it isn't that hard to cause bruises and injury. My husband wanted to take me in for x-rays for possible broken ribs. But, I was pretty sure you hadn't broken my ribs. Anyway, I hate fussing around in hospitals." I looked at him to see if he was understanding what I was saying. He was just sitting there, apparently thinking.

I said, "The problem is I can't go on like this. If you do things like this, I'm going to end up in the hospital from your rescue attempts."

"Look, I'm real sorry." His voice was uneven, as though he were trying to contain emotion. "I never intended to hurt you. But, you scared me and I just reacted. I haven't been around that many women. There are only guys in my family. I guess we get a little rough sometimes."

"How about your mom?" I asked. "I'll bet you're careful with her."

He nodded his head. "Yeah. But she never does none of the things you do." He looked at me with a wondering expression on his face. "Why do you do those things? You could be killed. I've never seen *anyone* do all the things you do."

I thought about some of my more recent moments while scouting the countryside for sketch-worthy sites. "Well," I said, "I have a problem."

He grunted and I said, "Do you want to hear this or not?"

He said, "Yeah. I want to hear it."

"I have always been a little accident prone. It's just a thing I've had to deal with whenever I go out into the countryside to take photos and go sketching. I'm a wildlife artist, so I have to go out into wild country. And I love what I do for a living, but sometimes there are these accidents." I shrugged my shoulders.

He just stared at me. I guess he didn't know what to say.

"Look," I explained. "It's a matter of focus. I go out sketching, I see something I want to sketch, and I forget about everything else around me. It's as simple as that. Over the years, I've tried to make my life safer. I bring all kinds of safety and survival gear with me whenever I go out into the wilds. I even have survival stuff I keep in my pack with my art supplies. Although, that doesn't help much if my backpack slides away and I'm stuck somewhere." I didn't want to complicate things with too many details.

"Can't you just be careful?"

"Well, ever since you slammed into me by the rattlesnake, I've done more thinking about that.

First of all, I realize that I should never have been walking along at that time of day without looking to see what was on the path ahead of me. But, I'd never been to that part of the ranch before and was very distracted by the beautiful rock formations." I shook my head thinking about how careless I'd been. "So, I've determined that I have to do a safety check whenever I go to a new place."

He nodded. "That would be good."

I sighed again. "But, you have to realize that there are odd things that happen to me that have nothing to do with making mistakes." As a case in point, I told him about the time a Red Tailed Hawk just flew through my windshield and shattered glass all over the front seat, leaving me with a large unconscious bird to deal with and cuts on my face.

He looked aghast. "You mean that you just have bad luck following you around?"

I considered the idea and rejected it. "I wouldn't quite put it that way. My luck isn't really bad. I think that God is just trying to teach me something—through many lessons—that I haven't learned yet. But, you'll be happy to know that no one else is ever hurt by the things that happen to me." I smiled at him. "I only inconvenience myself."

He looked like he disagreed with that. I could tell that he felt like he had been very inconvenienced by how I lived my life.

I said, "I can't help it that you've chosen to involve yourself in my world. It may make you feel better to know that I have at least three other important men in my life that try very hard to see that I don't come to harm, and they are only somewhat successful. Even so, I'm hoping that they'll eventually back off and just let me figure this out. So, maybe you should rethink this mission of keeping me safe. It might not be something that you can do."

He sat slumped in his seat thinking, a frown on his face. Obviously he'd never come up against a problem like this. He was probably used to simple solutions. This job was taking on odd dimensions he hadn't counted on.

He said, "At least I don't have to hide anymore. You know who I am, so I can just hang around and make sure nothing bad happens."

"I don't think that's how it works," I said. "Why are you doing this job? You say 'someone' wants to make sure that I'm safe. Why are you the person that needs to do this?"

He didn't know how to answer that. He said, "Just because. I can't tell you why."

I took a deep breath and asked, "Does this have anything to do with Jake Horton?"

He whipped his head toward me, appearing shocked that I would say Horton's name.

"Don't worry," I said. "Jake Horton and I are acquaintances. He had a drug lab next to our property last year before he got busted and sent to prison. For some reason—I'm not sure why—he wants to make sure my life goes smoother. But, really, I would rather that he didn't do anything for me at all. I don't wish him ill, but, I don't want his help. Actually, I have enough problems in my life without Jake Horton's help."

My visitor nodded. He could understand that.

"What involvement do you have with Mr. Horton?" I put up a hand. "I don't want to know about anything criminal. I just want to understand why you've taken this job."

He looked affronted. "I'm *not* a criminal!"

"Then you're dancing on the edge by hanging around criminals," I pointed out.

"I don't hang around criminals."

I just looked at him.

"Okay. Maybe I see them from time to time, but not all the time."

I continued to look at him.

He sighed. "I have a friend who maybe knows Jake Horton. He said that Horton might be grateful if I kept you safe and if he came to hear about it."

I shook my head at him. "That is not a smart idea. Mr. Horton's gratitude is trouble, and once you get that kind of attention, you can't just make it go away if you don't want it anymore."

"But, I need the money!"

"What money? Have you been promised any money?"

He shook his head. "But, my friend says that this kind of favor always pays off."

I looked at him. He looked depressed. Probably at his inability to control what he felt should have been a simple situation.

"You know my name," I said. "What is *your* name?"

"Hernando."

"Hernando what?"

"Valdez."

"Okay Hernando Valdez. Are you saying that you haven't been able to get a job and have resorted to doing favors for criminals?"

He shrugged.

"How have you been feeding yourself if you don't have a real job?"

He realized I wasn't going to stop asking questions and gave up trying to stonewall. He told me that he came from a family of legal immigrants. His parents had become citizens a few years ago. His family was in reasonably good circumstances in Los Angeles. Hernando showed me his California driver's license with his parent's address on it, and his student ID card. I noticed that his age was twenty.

He had been in college for a while in a two-year program for x-ray technicians, and thought he'd suffocate. He hated living in the crowded city, and he didn't want to work inside. He said that he'd always wanted to live and work on a ranch. He wanted to own land and have animals. He had come to the San Diego area to look around at property and figure out how to accomplish his dream. While he was thinking about how to earn enough money to do that, he was sleeping in his truck and washing dishes late at night in a local restaurant for food and gas. This allowed him the daylight hours to look for a better job. One day, he had met a guy who turned him on to the possibility of becoming a good friend of Jake Horton. So he began to spend his days saving me. Go figure.

"First of all," I said. "You don't want to have anything to do with people who are 'friends' of Jake Horton. They are probably all drug dealers, and the police keep constant watch on those guys. You don't want to be a person that the police are interested in. Although, just what you've been doing to Dillon has made them a little nervous."

He snickered and leaned back in his seat. "That Cody is true crud. You wouldn't believe some of the stuff he does. I haven't hurt him a bit. Just made sure that he knows if he messes with you, he's gonna pay." He grinned. "I loved the deal with the crickets. You could hear him screaming all the way down the street."

I said, "Much as I don't mind Dillon suffering from his own bad ideas from time to time, you've *got* to stop harassing him, or you'll end up in jail. And trust me, he's not worth it. You're hovering on the edge of doing jail time."

"I wouldn't like that," he agreed.

"So," I said. "I have a better idea. Do you have any experience working around horses?"

"Yeah. My dad's cousin has a small ranch with horses above L.A. Me and my brothers used to go spend summers with him, and ride around on the horses. We'd feed them and clean the pens. That's how I decided I'd like to have a ranch. I like being around animals and taking care of them. But, I didn't like my dad's cousin, so I didn't want to ask for his help."

"Well, you know about Cornbread Mesa Ranch and the horses and llamas we have there. Right?"

He nodded. "You have beautiful animals."

"How would you like to work with them and be paid a regular wage, while you gain experience? I'd have to okay it with my husband first, but I think he'll agree with me."

His eyes lit up. "Would you really let me do this?"

I nodded, smiling at his excitement. "Okay. Here's the deal. I have to go to Lake Mirage to check on Dillon Cody and stop by my grandparent's cottage briefly."

Hernando looked incredulous. "Why do you have to check on Cody?"

"He called this morning, and didn't sound right. It's a matter of seeing if 911 should be called."

"This is a man who is scum, Ms Janna. You do not need to help him."

"Nevertheless, it would bother me if I later found out that he was badly hurt or had died when I realized something was wrong and didn't act on it. I can't help it. It's just my conscience."

Hernando wasn't buying it.

"If it makes you feel any better, I wasn't planning on going into his house. I was only going to peek in the side window to check out the situation. You can even come with me. In fact, that would probably be a good thing."

"Okay," he conceded, "I'll follow along behind you." He opened the passenger door, swung out and ambled back to his truck. He got in, started the engine, and waited for me to pull out on the road.

We got to Dillon's place and parked in front. I walked quickly up to his handy side window and peeked in. With Hernando there I didn't need to be so sneaky, but there was still the problem of dealing with Dillon, which I didn't want to do. Looking in the window, I couldn't see Dillon or anyone else. And, actually, his car wasn't in the drive, so maybe he wasn't even home.

I stopped briefly at Gram's to see how everything was and ask if they needed anything. Granddad said that Rosalie was at school, but that they were fine. Then I drove back to Coyote Canyon with Hernando behind me. I called Theo on the way to explain the situation. After a moment of shocked silence, he said, "This is the guy who tackled you? And you want to give him a *job?*"

"He saved my life, Theo. Admittedly, he didn't do it with finesse, but he's just a kid. He will remind you of Christian, I think. He's made a couple of mistakes, but he seems to be a decent person from what I can tell. And if he isn't what he seems, we don't have to keep him on. He's had lots of opportunities to do us harm and hasn't taken them. In fact, it's been just the reverse, all things considered. I think the kid needs a break."

Theo said, "I'll meet you at the ranch and see what I think. We do have enough room to house another hand, and I wouldn't mind having a fill-in for Matt when he's not there. But, I'm not making up my mind until I see him."

"Well," I said. "We'll definitely want to stake him to some new clothes. Right now he's in L.A.

street clothes so he'll need some jeans, boots, and shirts. You're going to have to be a little understanding about that. Anyway, it can come out of his wages."

"Hmmph," said Theo and hung up.

Forty-five minutes later we were all pulling up beside the pasture. Hernando got out of his truck and came over to stand beside me. He looked uncertain of himself as Theo climbed out of the Ranger and then stood to take his measure of Hernando.

I said, "Theo this is Hernando Valdez. He's told me he would like to work with our horses and other animals. He says he's had experience during the summers working at his father's cousin's ranch north of L.A. I think it's worth giving him a fair trial."

The two men shook hands, and Theo asked for more details of Hernando's past ranch experience. My husband seemed to relax as he listened to the young man's ranch work history, heard the note of intense interest in his voice, and observed his body language.

Hernando said, "I appreciate getting this chance. I didn't know how to get a job like this." He looked at our horses in the pasture. "They are beautiful animals, and well cared-for."

Apparently coming to a decision, Theo said, "Your job would be to do pasture and corral maintenance, plus any other work that Matt needs you to do. He is our ranch manager and would be your boss."

"I can do that," Hernando said eagerly. "And I am good at grooming horses."

"You will have to talk about grooming with the owner of each animal. But, it's good to know you enjoy working with them," said Theo. "Can you move into the cabin today?"

Hernando nodded. "I have all my things in my truck."

"Come up to the cabin and I'll show you where you're going to sleep. But before you move in, you and I are going to take a trip to town and get you some clothes you can work in." Theo looked askance at Hernando's street duds.

Hernando said, "I would be more comfortable in ranch clothes. This," he looked down at his baggy clothing, "is what I wear in LA. I haven't had money to get anything else." He smiled and looked happy. "It will be much better working here on the ranch."

I was amused. I could see that Theo liked Hernando. Hernando really was a lot like Christian, in many ways. But Theo didn't want to seem like he was too easily won over. He had a gruff, abrupt way of speaking when he didn't want to look soft. Yet, I could see that things were going to be okay.

What a relief! This morning I had started out with the same tough, mysterious Protector Dude hanging out in my rearview mirror. And now we had Hernando Valdez helping out at the ranch. No more getting slammed by surprise. No more crickets or horse glop at Dillon's house. Not that Dillon didn't deserve it; however, it was turning out to be a problem for me, since Dillon was misunderstanding the situation and becoming more difficult. So, no more of that. And no more Jake Horton interference from a distance. More than likely, Horton didn't even know that he had hired a protector for me. At least we'd hope so for Hernando's sake. But life was good. It was all good! Well, mostly.

I went home. In the kitchen I noticed the message light flashing on the phone. I pressed the button. It was Dillon, "Janna, thanks for messing up my life. Now I've lost those photos I was going to take to the cops. My life is crap!" I heard some scrabbling in the background and then the message cut off. Dillon Cody spent a good portion of his life being incomprehensible to other people.

A few days later, it was mid-afternoon, and I was on my way to visit my grandparents again. I really love the month of October. The skies are usually clear and though not all trees in southern California change color in the fall, the portion that do are about midway through the process by that time. The fall-blooming Eucalyptus are bursting out all over. The roses are giving us another color show as the long days of summer weather are past. And the holidays haven't started yet. It is one of the months with relatively few demands. Halloween comes at the end, but it's practically November by then, so it doesn't really count.

Aside from the pleasure of seeing and chatting with Granddad and Gram, I hoped to get hints of their idea of the future. Rosalie's time with them was limited, but I was pretty certain that, if at all possible, they wanted to remain in their cottage at the lake. Were they up to that? And could they handle Aunt Myrtle's visits?

As I parked in the drive, Granddad opened the cottage door. I stepped inside, noticing fresh autumn flowers in vases and shining windows.

Rosalie's fine hand was evident. She loved the details.

Gram was sitting in her usual chair by the window overlooking the lake, and Granddad had a chair he liked to sit in across from her. He pulled up another chair for me and poured me a cup of tea. I could see that Gram was using her left hand to lift her cup. The stroke had affected her right side, but her left side was still functioning normally. When she smiled at me only the left side of her mouth curved up. It was a little odd to see after being used to the way she looked when she smiled for so many years. But she was still Gram, and still with us.

I took a sip of tea, and Granddad, suspecting that I had some concerns, said, "I know you've been worried, Janna, about how we are doing here." He smiled at Gram. "But, I think you can rest assured that we'll do just fine when Rosalie has to get back to her own life. We know that she has other obligations, and, anyway, we're used to being independent."

"Lord, ... yes," said Gram, the words coming slowly. "We ... want to do our own thing for ... as many ... years as we can." She slurred her words a little, but I understood her.

"I'm glad to hear that," I said. "I expect you'll be happier keeping things as much the same as possible." Gram formed words slowly, but it was a joy that she could speak at all.

Granddad said, "You've probably been worried about Myrtle, too. But, I've talked to her on the phone and told her she doesn't need to rush home."

Gram looked down at her tea. "Myrtle ... really wants ... to be in Florida now. Probably ... just as well ... we don't know ... just what ... she's doing there."

I noticed Granddad didn't add anything to that. My guess was that a lot of what they said was bravado, but much of success is often due to a good attitude. So, I felt calmer about their situation. And when Rosalie decided to return to Coyote Canyon, we'd watch to see how things went.

After leaving the cottage, I decided to go to the ranch and take Lion for a ride. We couldn't stay out too long, because the sun was starting to dip, but we could go for a quick canter along the broad path to Wildcat Lake, let Lion take a drink, sniff around, and then canter back. It had been a while since we'd done that, Lion and I.

Lion was rip-snorting ready to gallop, so I let him set his own pace. The trail to the lake was somewhat flat and well travelled. If one had to gallop, that trail was a good place to do it. He covered ground rapidly until we got near where the Lake Path turns and goes parallel to the water. Then he slowed down to a walk, sniffing the air. Clearly, something up ahead must need investigation. Nothing Lion considered dangerous, or he wouldn't continue. I was curious now to see what was by the lake.

When we came around the bend, a parked RV and a pickup truck came into view. Our friends, Sonya and Micah Sekaquaptewa were setting up camp. I was surprised to see them in the fall. They had said that they usually didn't come until winter. As I rode up, Lion snorted and Micah turned to wave.

I dismounted and let Lion wander down the lake ramp to take a drink. Sonya came up to me and I gave her a welcome back hug. "It's so nice to see you! I didn't know you would be coming or I'd have brought some blueberry muffins."

Sonya explained, "We started thinking about the worries with Taalawsohu Waynumto and we decided we needed to come a little earlier to make sure all is well. We will stay until the end of January."

"I'm so glad you're here. Red Thunder has been called away by the DEA. There will probably be no difficulty, because our news of finding the Mesa House still hasn't gotten around, and we intend to say nothing as long as we can. But, we don't know when we'll see Red Thunder again, which could be a problem if we should need a Native American spokesperson."

It was very fortuitous to have these friends present. Theo had tried to reach them by cell phone in the past few months, but communication by cell can be chancy on the far reaches of Indian reservations, and often no land lines available, as well. An Indian reservation can be a quite isolated place.

Micah came up to us and greeted me as Sonya told him the news about Red Thunder. Micah nodded. "I expect that all will go well, but we wanted to be near."

"Theo will be very interested to talk with you, Micah. I know you probably don't want to be bothered tonight. But, can the two of you come to our house for dinner tomorrow? We'd love to have you share our table."

Micah looked at Sonya. "I'm sure we would enjoy that. Thank you, Janna."

"I'll leave you to your unpacking and setting up," I said. "Tomorrow at five would be good. That'll give you time to speak with Theo before dinner. See you then."

I remounted Lion and we cantered back down the trail, and then down the road to the pasture. It has been a good ride for both of us, and nice to have discovered Sonya and Micah back at their campsite beside the lake.

I mentioned the return of the Hopi couple to Theo later that evening, while we were enjoying an evening walk around our neighborhood in the cooler night air of the autumn. He was surprised and pleased that he would be able to talk to Micah the next evening. "That's great. Now the plans and ideas Thad and I talked about for a museum and caretaker's quarters, can be passed under Micah's sharp eye."

"What are your plans about the museum?" I had chosen to stay out of the deliberations.

"After talking with Jed Hazard, and getting his thoughts about the kind of space we'd need to exhibit the pots and artifacts collection from the Mesa House, Thad and I came up with some possible ideas. We rounded a cul-de-sac and went past a few lots that were sitting empty, but maintained. "We're thinking that a building about the size of our house here in town would be a reasonable space for display and also allow a small amount of room for an office, a storage-maintenance area, and restrooms."

"What about the caretaker's quarters?"

"We aren't sure whether to add those onto the back of the museum, or put them in a separate building. We're still talking about what would be the best solution, yet most cost-effective for our purposes."

"Have you talked to Todd Jergen about this?" I was sure that our architect would have done some thinking about problems of this sort in the past.

"I plan to run it by Todd after I've heard Micah's thoughts on the subject. We'd like the structure and design to be generally aligned with Hopi thinking, while being comfortable and convenient to use."

I pulled my sweater closer around me. "It would be nice if there could be a plaza area in front of the museum with benches and attractive plantings."

As we walked back toward home, Theo said, "We've considered that. When we extend the boardwalk that we built last March, and connect it to the museum site, I was thinking of creating an open area in front of the building for people to gather and relax. But, we'll have to get Micah's thoughts on this."

The next few weeks saw Gwen, Christina and Tiffany all practicing together at the Taggert's house. As I had foreseen, it was much easier not to have to move the piano. So Gwen brought her fiddle and Christina brought her electric guitar. It wasn't long before they were starting to write their own words to existing music. At some point, Christina began making new music to go with their words. None of it was in the expert category, but it was experience you couldn't buy. So much was learned during that time of tolerance for each other's mistakes. The trio was learning to recognize what sounded good, and figuring out how to put ideas and feelings into fewer words. All the while, their instruments began to blend. Learning to blend into the music together was a big work in progress. Yet, as they practiced individually and then at Tiffany's house a few days each week after school, they improved.

Bob was very pleased. He had always wanted Tiffany to learn to play the electric piano he had bought for her when she was seven. He had been afraid it was never going to happen, but now he was happy. And a good thing, too. Because there were a lot of sounds that came out of those practices, particularly in the beginning, which were not musical.

As the girls became a little more competent with their instruments, got a bit smoother with their delivery, and more confident of their abilities, they began to offer to play at the family gatherings of each girl. Informal gigs. They presented a small repertoire of romantic ballads, old rock, and country-style music. The families enjoyed these occasions. I know Theo and I looked forward to them, and it made a good opportunity to gauge improvement from one performance to the next. Plus, it was fun to watch the obvious pleasure the girls had in creating their own sound together.

Another thing that happened during this time was Christian's return to martial arts. He had gone to the Dojo to talk with Sensei Jim about benefits Michelle might receive from becoming involved with the various arts. Although to earn specific belts she would have to conform to standards, Sensei Jim had been very encouraging. He said that a special approach could be tailored to Michelle's difficulties and weaknesses for her own strength development. He was especially pleased that Christian would be joining her as an incentive. Sensei Jim always believed that it was a mistake to let one's martial arts training lapse. To him it was a lifestyle that evoked self-discipline and personal fulfillment.

Christian was surprised how quickly he remembered the old skills.

In the meantime, I spent a lot of time sketching and taking photos of breathtaking landscapes, and then going home to paint them. I was so taken with the dynamic landscape idea that, for a time, I didn't want to paint anything else when I was in the studio. I thought this series would be a grouping with impact for my spring exhibit. Still, I needed to take pauses to ponder what I was creating, which meant that laundry and cooking went on as well. I made apple-crisp and beef stroganoff one day. On another day I made macaroni and cheese. The veggies coming out of the garden were great and we used them in salads, as well as cut up raw to eat as finger food.

One evening toward the end of the month after supper, Theo and I were at the Club soaking in the Jacuzzi, alternating with laps in the pool. I asked him how Hernando was doing.

"He's doing okay." Theo dipped himself down into the warm water of the Jacuzzi.

"I figured he must be, because you haven't fired him," I said. "I meant, is he good? And do you think he's going to be someone we could eventually teach to do other things?"

"He's pretty good with horses. Has a nice gentle touch with them, but lets them know who's boss. He's good. He likes the llamas and thinks they're comical. But, he thinks Gwen's pony is stubborn, which she is. Gwen is the only person who can get that animal to cooperate every time."

"So you're happy with Hernando?"

"Yeah. I'm happy with him. Why?"

"Just wondered. I was hoping we could someday train him for a better position. At some point he's going to get tired of just doing horse grunt work. I was thinking that he might be intelligent enough for a more managerial job." I got up on the side of the Jacuzzi to cool off.

"We'll have to see how it goes. I'll think about it," said Theo. "I'm just glad he's not following you around anymore trying to 'protect' you. I can't believe we went through all that time with that kid pulling those stunts and we never caught him."

I said, "That's what makes me think he's smart. That, and the well-engineered tricks he pulled on Dillon."

Theo chuckled. "That *was* funny. I never laughed so hard as when I heard about that bucket of manure propped above his door and then those crickets crawling in his bed. The boy is a genius when it comes to non-lethal deterrents. I'll give him that."

He pulled himself out of the hot water and handed me my robe, then put on his own. The evenings were cool again, so we drove home in the Ranger.

12

EVENTS LURCH FORWARD

November

AUNT MYRTLE WAS BACK AGAIN in the cottage staying with Rosalie in Lake Mirage. She had decided that she wanted to be with the family for the holidays; and anyway she needed a break from retraining all of Florida's real estate developers, who were a balky lot at best. She thought it might take the rest of her life, as it was, there were so *many* of those wayward developers.

Parking my Highlander in my grandparent's driveway, just before lunch one day in early November, I noticed that the lake air had turned chillier than usual. The cooler fall weather was here, and winter wasn't far behind. Naturally, there would be no snow or ice, or anything like that—well, maybe rarely in the dark of night— because even winter daytime temperatures at Lake Mirage wouldn't get lower than around forty degrees. It was the desert, after all, and the lake was only about a thousand feet above sea level. When I drove to my grandparent's cottage from Coyote Canyon, I went down altitude about a thousand feet. This made a difference in the kind of weather and temperatures we got. At the ranch the altitude could be anywhere from twenty-five hundred to almost four thousand feet on the peaks. That's why the ranch occasionally got snow in winter. But, that day the air seemed just a bit crisp for Lake Mirage in the fall, and the wind coming off the lake was cold.

As I walked up to my grandparent's door, Granddad swung the door back for me and took my jacket. Good smells were coming from the kitchen, and my stomach rumbled. Peeking into the kitchen I saw Gram stirring a pot on the stove. A wonderful sight. There was a period when I wasn't sure if we'd ever see her cooking at her stove again. We were truly blessed to have her in her apron shaking pepper into the pot, just like always.

I came up behind her and gave her a hug. "Lordy, Janna. You ... gave me ... a start," said Gram, her speech still not fluid, but improving. "I've been ... trying this white bean chili ... you make." She sighed. "Never thought ... I'd learn new ... cooking ideas ... at my age."

The doctor had been quite stern in telling her that she couldn't continue to serve and eat the foods she was used to eating. She was going to kill herself and everyone who ate at her table regularly if she did. She was horrified that she might have been hurting Granddad all these years. Granddad told her he was just fine, and that he didn't have any problems. But, he thought Naomi's body seemed to suffer from that style of cooking, so maybe she should listen to the doctor and try out some new recipes. Soon after that she started paying close attention to the kind of meals Rosalie was serving them.

At our house, in recent years, we might have meals offering a fat heavy choice. But, the whole meal isn't that way. A while back when I started to seriously get back to my normal size —and stay that way—I insisted that our approach to cooking at home had to be re-evaluated. We could still make our favorites, but try to take out unnecessary fats and carbohydrates, and always have a leaner choice available, if needed. Naturally, Rosalie had been cooking that sort of meal for Granddad and Gram. And they seemed to like them, so Gram wanted to see the recipes.

That day we sat down to bowls of white bean chili, which was a tasty thick soup containing white beans, pieces of chicken breast, diced mild green chilies, onions, pimentos, chicken broth and various seasonings.

"Good chili, Naomi," said Granddad as he tried a spoonful. "Just right for this time of year. It was cold on the lake early this morning. Had to put on a jacket when I took the boat out."

Rosalie said, "I think I've lost my job in your kitchen, Gram. This is really good!" She had no classes that day, so we had the rare pleasure of her company at noon.

Grandma said, "I'm getting ... the hang of it. This chili is ... quite good. "

Aunt Myrtle, busy with her own bowl, said, "I think everything you make is just excellent, Naomi. I've always been of the opinion that if my sister made it, it has to be good." She beamed at Gram and continued eating her chili.

Granddad looked at Aunt Myrtle with approval. "I agree. Don't know why you're so worried about a cooking change, Naomi. Nothing you ever made was bad. Why would some small changes make any difference?"

Gram looked at me and shook her head, but I could see that she was pleased. The compliments on her cooking had caused her to relax. Maybe the changes would just slide into her life with no ripples. One could hope.

After lunch, I packed Aunt Myrtle into the Highlander for a visit to Loretta May's cottage. Loretta May had, again, invited us for tea. So Aunt Myrtle and I had not eaten the tasty lemon pecan cookies Rosalie had baked, knowing that we would probably get more than enough sweets at the tea.

Loretta May was excited to see us. She showed us into her cottage and fluttered around, getting chairs into just the right position around her little table. The table was mounded with baked offerings of all sorts. Lemon meringue tarts, little sparkling cherry squares, chocolate mint roll cake, and her special peach and pecan cobbler. Loretta May had been a very busy bee.

"Now I want you both to have some of everything," she said as she set delicate china tea plates around. "I'll just pour this tea and you can tell me what you think of my recipe changes." She looked at me. "You remember that I've been modifying some of Mama's recipes?"

"I'll never forget your incredible cobbler, Loretta May." I smiled at her.

Aunt Myrtle said, "You should have been a pastry chef, my dear. You always do such delicious and creative things with desserts."

Loretta May actually blushed. "Well, I always *try* to do my poor best." She was wearing a crisp pale pink voile apron atop a low-cut ivory knit dress with a tight skirt. Prominently placed on her shoulder was the little lady bug pin Aunt Myrtle had sent her from Florida.

Aunt Myrtle noticed the pin, and said, "My dear Lady Bug—if I may call you by that cute nickname you have—you certainly have a lovely array of treats."

Loretta May blushed even more, practically melting at our feet. "Let me serve you." She placed a portion of each kind of pastry on our little plates. I could see that this was going to be like another meal. And not low calorie, either. "This is wonderful," I said, licking lemon filling off a spoon. "Aunt Myrtle is right. Have you ever considered doing this professionally?"

"Well, I have always been *interested* in pastry. But, I didn't know if I had what it *takes* to be a chef." Loretta May helped herself to a cherry square. She loved to bake, but she didn't seem to partake much herself. It was as though she would rather watch other people enjoying her art.

"You could probably sell your splendid desserts to local lunchrooms, my dear," Aunt Myrtle said, and then looked flustered. "But, I don't mean to tell you what you should do, dear. It's just that you're so talented."

"Oh no, dear Myrtle," Loretta May rushed to assure her. "I *want* you to tell me what you think. And I'm so *happy* that you think I might have a *future* in pastry." She rearranged the tarts more artistically. "I haven't been very *content* working for Dillon Cody, and it *reassures* me to hear your encouragement toward my *heartfelt* vocation of pastry." She gazed off in the distance as though seeing a vision.

Not long after that I could see that Aunt Myrtle was wanting her afternoon nap. So, we thanked Loretta May for the delightful tea, and I ferried Aunt Myrtle back to her cottage.

As I saw her up the walk to her door, Aunt Myrtle said, "Such a talented woman our little Lady Bug is—we always call her Lady Bug in the garden club because of her ideas about how helpful ladybugs are for gardens. So glad she liked that little pin I sent her." She went into her cottage, and I got back in the Highlander and began the drive back home.

Something was troubling the back of my mind. Something I had seen in the past had clicked with something I had seen or heard today. But, I couldn't remember what it was. Something about a ladybug. I strained my brain to remember, but all I got was brain strain.

Reaching home, I thought Aunt Myrtle's idea of a nap wasn't so bad. I would just go lie on my bed for a while.

An hour later, I suddenly awoke and realized what I had been trying to recall. I called Bob and asked him to come to breakfast the next morning, after the children had gone to school.

When Bob arrived, I handed him a cup of coffee and a plate of toasted bagels as he sat down at the kitchen table. He sipped coffee and looked at me, waiting.

"I think I may have happened upon a clue," I said, not quite sure of myself.

"A clue for what?"

"Do you recall last winter when you were trying to get a lead on Stevette Strike, and then Gudrun Bohn died, and you couldn't locate Stevette?"

Bob became alert. "I remember. Tell me what you've got."

"I don't *have* anything. But, yesterday Aunt Myrtle casually mentioned a tiny fact that bothered me for hours until I realized what the connection might be."

"The fact," said Bob. "What's the fact?"

I took a deep breath. "Loretta May DuBoise's nickname is *Lady Bug*." I felt stupid. "That's my fact."

Bob looked at me. "That's your fact?"

I hated this. "Remember the pictures that Dillon passed to me after Stevette disappeared and he couldn't locate her to deliver them?"

Bob slapped himself in the forehead. "*Lady Bug*. You're thinking about that little lady bug I told you about that was tattooed on the bare seat of one of the photographed ladies."

"Yes." I sipped my tea while Bob chewed a bagel and thought.

379

"Okay," he said. "You're right. There may be something there. Loretta May lives just a couple of cottages down from Stevette's place." He looked a little dazed. "She's probably interested in men, also. I know I've picked up vibes coming from her that were absolutely hetero."

I said, "Personally, I've found her to be one of the most confusing people I've ever run across. I've never known quite what to make of her. She seems pleasant and Aunt Myrtle likes her. And she's a great pastry chef. But, I think her 'vibes'—as you call them—conflict. I've never been at ease around her."

Bob was musing over possible scenarios. "Maybe Loretta May fell for Gudrun and played around with her behind Stevette's back. And maybe Stevette found out. The only problem is that we can't find Stevette. We haven't stopped looking for her, but she isn't in any of the places we've looked."

I said, "You also don't have any way of knowing if Loretta May has a lady bug tattoo. This might easily be just a silly coincidence. That's why I wanted to tell you privately over breakfast. I didn't feel right keeping the fact to myself. But, it's a pretty measly fact. I'm not sure what you can do with it."

Bob sipped more coffee. "The interesting thing about facts is that they tend to generate more facts. Now that we have a possible direction in which to look, quietly of course, it can be surprising what might be found. People who think they are hidden often aren't careful about evidence of their doings. And there's nothing criminal about having an affair, even if it makes the original lover insane with murderous rage. So, if Loretta May is the lady in a couple of those photos, she probably is only concerned about being embarrassed if she were identified in them."

That made me think about something else. "A few weeks ago, Dillon called me early in the morning. He was drunk and carrying on about how I had messed up his life and how I shouldn't hang around Loretta May because she was a 'slut.' He said something about bringing some photos to the police, but then it turned out that he lost them. Did you ever hear anything about that?"

Bob shook his head. "Not about photos. We've heard more than enough from Cody the last few months to last us for a long time. Haven't heard from him lately, though. I guess he isn't being harassed at the moment." Bob looked at me appraisingly. "How about you? We gave you that special cell phone, but as far as I know you haven't used it. Are you still being followed?"

I looked at him innocently. "No. I guess my mysterious protector must have lost interest. Maybe you scared him off."

Bob looked at me intently. "Just because one guy is gone, doesn't mean you won't have that problem again. Jake Horton thinks of himself as a fixture in your life. Don't make the mistake of thinking you're finished dealing with him. If he or his cohorts aren't giving you the benefit of his expertise at the moment, he likely will sometime in the future."

I didn't want to think about more of Horton's minions showing up to "help" me out. There's only so much reforming of delinquents that I was willing to do, and there were only just so many ranch jobs I could give out. Anyway, Hernando could hardly be called one of Horton's minions. He was just a nice kid who didn't have a clue.

Bob stood up preparing to go. "Thanks for passing along your fact. I may let you know what came of it someday, if that seems like a good idea."

"I'd love to know what happens."

"Well, the problem with facts are that you can never tell where they might lead." He thanked me for breakfast and left.

Now that I had done my duty by Bob, I was free to do whatever else I wanted to do with the day. I got ready to go out wearing sage green cords and a matching turtleneck top. I had my sneakers on and carried a tan blanket jacket with a subtle American Indian design. Picking up my pack, I was ready to go.

The plan was to stop at the Indian Heritage Store to get a set of new sketching pens. As I paid Laurie at the front counter, Kyle Krupp came in the door and asked to talk to me, privately. We walked out of the store and got into the Highlander.

I waited for him to tell me what he had on his mind.

He said, "Amanda heard through the grapevine that Stevette Strike was seeing a guy."

I stared at him for a moment. "A guy? As in a *man?*"

"Yeah," said Kyle. "It's weird, isn't it? Anyway, I was thinking that if Stevette was getting it on with a guy, then what was her relationship with Gudrun?"

And here I thought I'd cleared the air earlier this morning. And why was Kyle consulting *me* about it?

Kyle went on. "I don't know who this guy was, but I think it would be a good direction to take the investigation."

I cleared my throat and held up my hand. "I happen to know that Bob just got new information this morning. Maybe there could be a friendly trade of information between the two of you."

Kyle didn't like it, but he thought about it. "Amanda said the same thing to me this morning."

"Well then. Amanda is a smart woman, and you know she has your best interests at heart."

He smiled, and I could see he was crumbling. "Yeah. She's a wonderful woman. Okay, I'll go talk to Taggert."

I smiled back. "I'm sure you won't regret it." I just hoped that Bob would realize Kyle was serious about trying to get things straightened out in his life. Bob was pretty smart and would probably work with Kyle, if he didn't stray from regular procedure.

By the time I finished my errands, it was time to go back home and pack a lunch. I had asked Rosalie the previous day, while at my grandparent's cottage, if she'd like to take the next afternoon off and we'd picnic at the ranch on Table Rock as we had done a few times the year before. She was glad of an excuse to get away for a couple hours.

When Rosalie arrived, I had made chicken breast sandwiches with salsa on whole wheat and included water bottles. Once in the Highlander, we headed out to the ranch. It was a beautiful blue-sky day, and all the Liquid Amber trees had turned crimson and gold. When the sun shone behind them, they glowed a fiery color that took one's breath away. The air was chilly in the shadows, but pleasantly warm in the sun.

Arriving at the top of the mountain in the old ruin clearing, I parked in the usual spot. We took our lunches and sat upon Table Rock. "More coyote droppings," observed Rosalie.

"I'm beginning to think of them as a part of the ambience," I said, taking a bite out of my sandwich.

"Something you can count on," agreed Rosalie. "Like this mountain. Everything around might change, but the mountain will still be here."

We ate and stared out from our high seat overlooking the landscape of the neighboring ranch. Rosalie said, "Gram's doing really well. She's doing all the cooking now. I'm still cleaning anything not covered by the woman they hired to come in. But, I think Granddad is planning to talk to Grandma about having the woman come in more often, at least until she is able to do normal stuff." She folded up the sandwich bag and put it back in the cooler pack. "My plan is to move back home when it seems the right moment. The Horses Tale has been calling me to ask when I can begin the holiday windows, and Amanda has new merchandise that needs to be displayed for good sales."

"Sounds like you're in demand," I was glad she was going to pick up her normal life again. "Have you been able to keep up with school while you've been at Lake Mirage?"

"Yes. Actually, I've had more study time in Lake Mirage than I have at Coyote Canyon."

"You've been carpooling with Matt, right?"

"Right. But he's more distant with me. It's as though he's mad at me for going to Lake Mirage to help my grandparents. He doesn't understand when I try to explain. I think the problem is that he doesn't have any grandparents that old. His are all quite young and healthy, compared to Grandma and Granddad. So he hasn't had experience with that kind of family problem."

"It can be hard to put yourself in someone else's place. It takes a little extra compassion and imagination, I think."

"Mom, I don't think Matt has a lot of imagination for some things." A crease formed between her brows. "He knows what he likes and knows what he wants. But, the divorce his parents went through when he was young was hard on him. He thinks his dad wandered away because his mother worked." She took a sip from her water bottle. "He's loads of fun when he's on familiar ground. And he has big plans for the future that involve taking care of me, and starting a family right away after we get married. But for all of that to work, I have to fit in with *his* picture. I'm not allowed to have a picture of my own."

"Sounds as though you may have a tough decision to make." I sipped my tea and looked at her.

She said, "I'm not going to make *any* decision. I'm going to go on being the person I am, and *he* has to decide if that's enough. I haven't hidden anything about myself from Matt. He knew I was interested in my own business and even recommended that I go to college."

I said, "Maybe when he saw you riding Tache, and watched the care you take with your animals, he thought that you were kindred spirits in that way."

"Well, we are, and I'm sure that's part of it. And I've never said I don't want him or his way of life. I just want him to be able to include what I want, too. The two ideas aren't really incompatible if he was willing to be flexible. I can learn more about ranch life, and would even enjoy living on a ranch. But, I'm still going to be me when all is said and done."

As we cleaned up lunch leavings, she said, "Matt and I are going to keep talking, and spending time together. But, I'm not planning to be engaged until there is a willingness to compromise on our plans for the future."

I told her I sympathized with how difficult this was for both of them, and suggested we walk up to the Overlook to sit on the big bench-like boulder there, which had often been a refuge for me when troubled. It was like an open-roof temple that took in the whole sky and land spreading out into the misty distance. Merely sitting on that rock often produced calm.

A few days later, I was looking appreciatively at the Carrington Ranch, that twenty thousand acre cattle ranch beside ours, comprised of beautiful rolling hills and grassland. In the winter it turned green all over. In the summertime the hills became an amazing golden color, and in the autumn it all turned a soft brown, as though patiently awaiting the return of the rains. The Big Ranch actually rested in a wide hilly valley between mountains. Our mountains of Cornbread Mesa Ranch were at the southern end of the valley, but the range of mountains continued, curving to the east around this broad, grassy valley, perfect for grazing cattle.

Having been occupied in sketching different parts of our own land, I hadn't thought of investigating what might be worthy to sketch on the neighboring ranch. We had walking and riding privileges on all the old trails of this adjoining ranch, just as our neighbors were free to walk or ride on our trails when they felt the urge. These trails were so old and well-used by everyone around here, that I thought Micah and Sonya's distant ancestors would have recognized most of them.

I drove under our ranch sign and parked the Highlander at our ranch down by the corrals, then walked back down the drive to study the land across the road. I'd brought my pack along in case of a good sketching or photo opportunity.

The grasslands across the road seemed to be cattle-free just now. Fairly flat for a short distance, the land became two hills gently rising up to a small cleft that separated them. At the point where the uppermost parts of the hills were joined, was a boulder and a few small Live Oaks. Live Oaks never get very big around cattle. The cattle think they are a tasty change from grass, so a natural kind of topiary action occurs. The trees remain as big rounded bushes. They never get completely eaten up, but they don't become giants, either. Unless they are protected by lots of boulders and have reliable water.

What I wanted to do was to get up to the top of one of those hills, and see what the landscape looked like on the other side. I was still doing my large landscapes, and this site looked like a good possibility for the series.

I threw my pack over the fence and carefully parted the barbed wire, only slightly snagging my clothes as I slipped through. Slinging my pack over my shoulder, I started across the grasses toward the hill.

As I got closer, the gradual-seeming incline became quite steep. It wasn't a huge hill, but having passed the fifty year mark constantly reminded me of things I'd left behind with youth. A big one was youthful energy. I used to have a nearly limitless reservoir of energy. That reservoir had shrunk considerably with the passage of time. It took more oomph to walk up an incline these days. No one was *making* me drag myself up this hill, but it was a big relief to finally reach the top. I wobbled a little at the crest and tripped into a large boulder there, bumping my head hard enough to cause a headache.

However, reaching the top gave access to the extraordinary vista now displayed before me. Maybe like viewing God's personal web site on the Big Screen showing His idea of what the perfect California valley should look like.

Early morning fog had been the norm for the previous several weeks, so the grasses were beginning to perk up again from the moisture. Here and there the softly rolling landscape was dotted with Live Oaks manicured by the cattle to look like dark green fluffy balls on thick stems. At the lowest part of the valley was a vernal type pool. Grasses grew out of the water, and mud around its sides showed hoof impressions. Lying in bunches near the pool, were variously brown, white, and black cows chewing their cud—a peaceful, idyllic scene.

Feeling a little bit dizzy after bumping my head, I stood between the boulder and a Live Oak tree, taking in the serene vision of the valley, when I heard a rumble off to my left and slightly behind. Turning, I saw the hugest cow I had ever seen in my life. It had an enormous head, which was lowered in a not friendly manner, and framed by a respectable set of horns. Its chest was the broadest I'd ever seen on a cow—although I was no expert on the question. This animal began to paw the ground with its hooves, and snorts commenced as an accompaniment to the deep chest rumbles.

All of the above evaluation, which is lengthy to describe, flickered through my headachy mind in a nerve-rattling instant. My brain added up the data, concluding that this wasn't a cow. This was a *bull*. Somehow I had managed to threaten his territory and he was planning to remedy the situation.

This seemed to me a basically unfair situation. I had carefully scoped out the territory with safety in mind, prior to making this foray onto our neighboring ranch. Everything had seemed "all clear." More was apparently needed.

However, having scrambled my brains against the boulder, I wasn't in my best problem-solving mode. Which might explain why I dropped my pack and leaped into the small, but handy, Live Oak tree. A quick solution, but in some ways meeting the bull could have been preferable. The bull was possible instant death, while, on the other hand, the little tree—might as well call it a bush—was a dense, prickly, unaccommodating piece of greenery. I had several gashes in my skin just from trying to reach its interior. My clothes were in a shape I can't even describe. Pointy, brittle leaves were in my mouth, my hair, my ears—the only reason they weren't in my eyes was that I'd protected them with one arm. Best not to discuss that arm.

On the plus side, the bull could no longer see me. He knew I was there, probably by scent. However, I was in the bush, and didn't pose a visual threat. His instinct was to charge a threatening target, but a bush probably didn't fit that definition.

Instead, he took out his annoyance on my backpack, which had my cell phone, camera, and all my art supplies in it. That backpack wasn't going to make a fool of him! No way, no how! He tromped on, pawed, and gored my backpack until it was only a sorry looking rag. Little pieces of my equipment would fall out from time to time, get investigated, and then stomped.

All the while, the cows down by the pool were contentedly chewing their cud as though everything was just the way it should be. And no rescue would happen, because I hadn't told anyone where I was going. When Matt or my family saw the Highlander parked by the corral, they would naturally think I was somewhere on our own acres. It would never occur to them I would be at the Carrington Ranch across the road, because I hadn't ever done that before. I was on my own. Obviously, a good addition to my safety check-off list would be to leave a note as to where I had gone and when, with estimated return time included.

Stuck in the Live Oak, I contemplated that my whitening skeleton might be found years from now as a warning to others about pastures and bulls. I was deep in thought—or maybe I was in shock, due to the wide variety of ills that had occurred in the last ten minutes—when a voice on the other side of the bush, next to the boulder, said, "Ms. Janna. Are you okay?"

My first thought was, "Of course, I'm not okay! I'm almost dead!" But, then I recognized the voice of Hernando.

"Ms. Janna. Can you talk? Can you move?" He sounded really worried.

I croaked, "Is that you Hernando?"

"Yes!" He sounded very relieved. "Are you injured?"

Now there was a question. I hadn't given the bull a chance to hurt me, but I sure had done a job on myself. I answered, "I'm not hurt." That was mostly true. If I got back to civilization, I wouldn't die of shock, infection, or any of the other things that had passed through my mind.

Hernando said, "If I distract the bull, can you climb out of the bush and go behind the boulder and down the hill?"

"Don't put yourself in danger, Hernando."

Hernando snorted almost like the bull. "I will not be in danger. I'm used to taunting bulls. My father's cousin had cattle and sometimes my brothers and I had to separate the bulls from the cows. The quickest way is to get them to run after you toward the place where you want them to go. I am *good* at this, Ms. Janna."

This was scary. "Are you sure you want to do that?"

"Yes!" he hissed. "As soon as I start running down the hill toward the cows, the bull will run after me to protect his cows. When you see me running, jump out of the bush and run around behind the boulder and down the hill to the fence. I will follow after I've given you a little time to get away and through the fence."

Jump? Run? Was he talking about me? Through the leaves I saw Hernando start to run past me yelling. The bull, who had just begun to calm down and lose interest, was quickly aroused when this horrible, screaming threat zoomed past him. That was all it took to rev up the bull's aggressive rage. The ground shook as he slammed down the hill after Hernando.

As soon as Hernando started to yell, all my nerve ends seemed to sizzle and I actually leaped out of the Live Oak, gashing myself again on the way out. I didn't have much time to get to the fence. As I hobbled around the boulder, I was so unsteady on my feet that I tripped at the top of the hill and proceeded to roll all the way down until I reached a somewhat flat place not far from the fence.

Out of the corner of my eye I could see Hernando start down the hill with the bull after him. I lurched to my feet, practically levitated over the remaining ground, and dove over the fence landing in a heap in the dusty dirt road. Hernando dove over just a few seconds after me. He jumped up immediately—what would it be like to have such an unused body again?—picked me up, slung me over his shoulder and jogged down the road out of sight of the bull.

The bull, who had been considering bashing on through the fence, turned around and slowly started back up the hill when he couldn't see us anymore. His programming must have been, if you can't see it or smell it, it isn't there.

Hernando put me down and helped me limp my way to the manager's cabin, where I washed my wounds and investigated the amount of damage I had done to myself. It wasn't long before Theo was there taking over the first aid process, and thanking Hernando profusely for thinking to follow me when I went across the road.

Hernando said, "I knew she wasn't safe over there alone. Anyway, I've followed Ms. Janna enough times to know what she might do."

Theo clasped Hernando's shoulder and nodded. Theo knew just how Hernando felt. Heck, I scared myself sometimes. But, I had actually followed my new safety rules. I had looked around carefully before I went through the fence. There had been no cows and no bulls. There had been no moving thing but me. And when I saw the cows from the top of the hill, I stayed where I was. I didn't go down among them, or even approach them. I left a big space between them and me, and I also had an avenue of retreat directly behind me. The problem was that I hadn't counted on having to outrun a bull that would lay siege to me next to the Live Oak bush while I went into shock. The boulder had been too tall to climb up on, and I hadn't thought about whether I could beat the bull to the fence. At that point, my best bet was the bush.

I had done mostly all the right things. I was going to have to think about this problem some more. One thing that entered my mind—not for the first time—was whether being "rescued" was always a good thing. In reality, I might have been able to sneak away following the bull's loss of interest. Apart from clocking my head on the boulder, I hadn't been injured except for bruises and some deep scratches. Painful and nasty-looking, but not life-threatening.

I was thinking that, while I needed to communicate better, maybe I also needed to dampen some of that protective male instinct toward me that seemed to be interfering with my ability to find my own way out of situations. Not an easy thing to define, but I could feel a shift taking place in my mind. More thinking needed.

Before we got into our vehicles to return home, I said to Hernando, "Thanks for helping me out again, Hernando. I'm glad the bull didn't get you. It scared me to see the bull running after you. I thought we were both goners."

He laughed, "Nah, I am faster and smarter than the bull. I've had a lot of practice. But, I wasn't sure you would be fast enough going down the hill. It was a good thing you thought to roll."

"Yeah," I said. "That worked out pretty well, didn't it."

Theo just looked at me, but didn't comment. That man knows me too well. He herded me out to the Highlander. And when we got home he squeezed antibiotic cream into gashes I could feel but couldn't see.

When Theo was finally satisfied with his first aid, we sat in the family room in front of the fireplace enjoying the crackle of the fire. We sipped a little wine, and nibbled at crackers and cheese. Fortunately, the children were all occupied elsewhere that evening, so I didn't have to immediately explain my battle-worn state. Anyway, it wasn't as though my kids were ignorant about some of the challenges I had in dealing with the wilds. I could sit in my pajamas with a wonderful, tolerant husband, and warm my feet by the fire while the wine dulled various aches.

"So, did you get any good photos or sketches?" Theo wanted to know.

I shook my head, sadly. "No. I was just admiring the view thinking about how I wanted to record it, when El Toro appeared. After that I spent every moment in the bush watching him gore my back pack, destroying everything in it. My camera, cell phone, art supplies. All gone. Even if I had taken photos or made sketches, I wouldn't have them now. When I go back, I plan to take Hernando as my lookout."

Theo choked on his wine. "Go back? I would have thought today would sour you on the idea of returning."

"I just love that beautiful rolling land, Theo. That area is really special. I know it's for sale, but I desperately hope it doesn't get sold to some company that wants to develop it into a bedroom community, or something."

My husband looked alarmed at the idea. Clearly, he hadn't thought of that possibility. It would be a tragedy to mar the current splendor of that land. Also, a personal tragedy for the Gustaffesons, because the character of our own ranch would be changed due to its proximity. Our privacy and quiet would be fondly remembered treasures that had been lost if that ranch were to be developed into thousands of lots, built up with closely packed houses. Of course, that wasn't necessarily going to be the cattle ranch's fate, but one couldn't know for sure what would happen.

Theo rubbed his chin. "Maybe we should drive by our neighbor's ranch tomorrow and look it over. It never hurts to have more information about land adjoining ours."

I smiled at him and sipped my wine. I knew exactly what he was thinking, but said nothing.

13

THE HORIZON EXPANDS

2nd half of November

WHEN I WOKE THE NEXT MORNING, Theo was still there beside me. He had decided not to drive down to his, not quite vacated, office that day. I groaned, and his arm snaked out to pull me against him.

"Do you feel really bad?" He sounded concerned.

I opened my eyes. "I'm probably not going to die."

His face cleared. "Good. I want to drive by the Carrington Ranch this morning. Get dressed and I'll take you out for breakfast after the kids have gone to school."

I moaned while putting on my clothes, but it was surprising how greatly lessened were my hurts of the day before, so mostly I was pleased and exhilarated. I looked forward to viewing land that might someday become Gustaffeson land. Which was what I thought Theo had in mind. There was still that greater part of the hefty trust fund remaining from his grandmother, intended for land purchases and improvement. If the Carrington Ranch could be had for the right price, who knew what might happen today?

A couple hours later, we turned onto the main road of the Carrington Ranch. This turnoff was just before the diagonal road that cut across and led to Cornbread Mesa Ranch. We drove along, looking at the rippling flow of grasslands all around. A long row of tall eucalyptus lined either side of the approach to the main house. It was a large Spanish ranch house—an old style mansion. A gate prevented vehicles from driving right up to the house. We sat in front of it and discussed our next move, as a white Dodge truck drove down the drive from the house. We waited. Perhaps this person would know whom we should talk to.

When the truck got within a few feet, the gate slid open on a track. The Dodge drove out, then stopped next to Theo's rolled down window. The driver asked, "Can I help you Senor?"

"Yes, sir," said Theo. He told him our names and that we owned the neighboring Cornbread Mesa Ranch. "We heard this ranch might be for sale, and if so, we were interested in viewing the property, if someone has time to show us around."

"Oh, si, Senor," the man smiled broadly. "I will take you to the assistant manager. If you will please follow, Senor."

We drove behind the white truck and parked when it stopped at a smaller house, slightly to the rear of the main house. Leaving the Ranger, we followed the man up to the door of the smaller house. He rang the bell and another man answered the door.

After a few words in Spanish, the man in the doorway turned to us. "I'm Raoul Gomez, and I will gladly take you around the property, Mr. and Mrs. Gustaffeson." He shook Theo's hand, then indicated a stone walkway. At the end of the walkway, we went through a wrought iron gate. Crossing the courtyard beyond, Mr. Gomez opened the door of the house for us. We stepped into a foyer which had a dramatic double staircase of heavy, dark stained wood. Matching waist-high paneling followed the curves of the staircase, which came around and down either side of the room. Between the two arms of cascading steps, a massive chandelier made of black wrought iron hung from ceiling-mounted black chains. Beneath our feet the floor was of richly colored, intricately designed Spanish tiles.

The foyer foretold what we would find in the rest of the house. Everywhere was dark, dramatic Spanish styling from long ago. Lots of built-in cupboards and glass-fronted shelving. Much massive, carved furniture, and heavy, brocaded draperies. Most of the downstairs common rooms were enormous with high ceilings. Many of the upstairs rooms were large, as well. It was a big, old-fashioned Spanish colonial house.

Moving through the large rooms, I began to see at least one possible reason to cause the original matriarch, after the passing of her husband, to take up residence in the little rustic house on the mountain top, leaving the prestigious home to her daughters-in-law. There was nothing light and airy about this house. It was dramatic, but to some it may have seemed oppressive. That aura might have been dispelled with redecorating, but from my point of view, the house would need to be nearly gutted to make it livable. Granted, not everyone shared my taste.

Anyway, it would have obliterated the incredible historical details of the house. It was in a class all its own.

Mr. Gomez led us next to the summer kitchen, a stone building that housed all cooking activities during the hot months of the year, and was a year-round kitchen and eating area for the hired help. We next were shown the bunk houses, and the foreman's house. We saw the barns for equipment and feed. We were shown the cattle barns and pens. And then there were the horse barns and pens, followed by the garages with cooks' and servants' quarters built above. All very aged structures that would need varying amounts of maintenance and repairs.

Finally, Mr. Gomez drove us out to the land, itself, in an Expedition SUV. We went from one end of the wide valley to the other, swallowed up by the waving grasses, studded here and there by granite boulders. The herds of cattle were huge. Raoul Gomez said that some of the cattle were being selectively bred to fulfill different commercial purposes. I noticed an area with black cattle, and another herd of red cattle with white faces. These were immense areas. Much bigger than Cornbread Mesa Ranch. One could fit fourteen ranches the size of ours into Carrington Ranch. It was twenty thousand acres, which was approximately thirty-two square miles, nearly a township in size. It was a really big place.

At last we thanked our patient guide for taking the time to show us over the ranch. We told him to tell the Morales family that we would be in touch with them. Then we climbed back in the Ranger and drove through the gate, as it automatically opened. We continued down the road for a bit, until Theo pulled over and parked. We both stared out over the land and thought for a while.

Theo turned to me. "What are your impressions of the place?"

"It's hard to put it all into words." Suddenly it seemed like a monumental responsibility to even consider owning that much land. When I was thinking the day before of the land needing rescue from the possibly inevitable developers, I hadn't understood how big the "rescue" task might be. The whole thing seemed overwhelming now, and I wanted to know Theo's take on it. "I love the land. It's beautiful. But, if we bought this property, what would we have to do to keep it? I mean, do we have enough money to just pay for it?"

"Maybe. I'd rather not just dump the total assets of the trust into this property, because we may have other circumstances arise that will need funding. We don't know what the asking price is, and, undoubtedly, what will be acceptable is a bit lower. But, there are a number of things that can be done to ease the finances. For instance, we know that the Morales' aren't quite ready to leave the ranch. So, we could let them run their cattle and pay us rent, just as they have been doing all these years with the Carringtons. And I don't know about you, but when they do decide to leave, I couldn't live in that house." He glanced sideways at me to gauge my reaction.

"That would be a deal breaker for me," I agreed. "It's beautifully made, though. One can almost envision Zorro, the eighteen century swordsman, descending the grand staircase."

"Good. Because, I have a better idea. The Morales aren't living in the house. They have a house in town, and only use the Spanish house for fiestas. We could turn that house into a museum of the old southwest and charge admission. There could be tours of the house and out-buildings. Maybe a gift shop that sells Spanish and western books and doodads. Tourists love that stuff, and it might help to pay the taxes. The place looks like it has its original trappings. There are even bunk houses for staff to run the place. If you remember, I learned a lot of this sort of thing at my grandmother's knee. She used to buy properties like this at bargain prices, and turn them into profitable enterprises. It was a lucrative hobby that she enjoyed."

I did remember his Grandmother Althea lecturing us shortly after we married, about the importance of owning property. Of course, having been born in Europe, she was interested in the security from poverty that only owning property could bring. Not long after she became a United States citizen, Althea had started with a small grocery delivery service, and invested her profits back into the business, and also into land. When she died sixty years later, she was reckoned to be one of the bigger landowners in Vermont. On her passing, she had arranged that her land holdings go to various favored relatives. But, since Theo was the only grandchild she had personally raised, for him she set up a trust that he might select land that appealed to him. She would have been excited by the opportunity before us now.

Even though Althea had encouraged us to become substantial landowners, for most of our marriage we didn't touch the trust, because we were busy with our careers and raising a family. We had moved several times due to Theo's need for practical and varied experience in his passionate interest, geology. During the years when he was establishing his reputation as a water geologist, we didn't want the responsibility that came with owning land. For a long time we didn't even own a house. Renting seemed so much easier when we had to pull up stakes to travel to another part of the country to answer the call of geology, and geological work opportunities.

But, now we were well and truly rooted in San Diego County. After the purchase of our present home, it might have been a long time before we delved into the trust again, if it hadn't been for the HOA restrictions that eventually became too confining for several family projects. This caused us to seek the new-found freedom we now so enjoyed on Cornbread Mesa Ranch. Thus, we had initially ignored the rumors that Carrington Ranch was up for sale, since we weren't in the habit of acquiring land simply because it was available. Yet, it was a big gamble to assume that the next buyer would choose to keep it as grazing land. No ranch families had leapt forward to buy the acreage, and current reality being what it is, we knew what the likelihoods were.

So, here we were, thinking about how to make all of this work to our benefit. I said, "How about if we donate a small portion to the agricultural college and allow them to lease parts of the pasture for breeding experiments?"

He nodded. "We could do that. And we could also consider running buffalo. Get a knowledgeable foreman with buffalo experience to manage the herd. This would have tourist appeal and the meat is very popular commercially." He leaned back in his seat. "We have time while the Morales' are here to do some research, pull out some of my grandmother's ingenious profit-making schemes, and create a plan that will work for us. I like the idea of making the ranch a place that other people can visit, see the history here and view herds of buffalo. Of course, best of all, these plans would help keep things relatively sane for Cornbread Mesa."

"We have to decide pretty soon, don't we," I said. "Some developer could be putting in a bid right now." I looked at Theo. "The thing is, I don't want to change our lifestyle. I like living in a normal house, and—except for land improvement—keeping our budget to what we earn from our businesses. Our life is good the way it is."

"Amen!" Theo gave me an exuberant kiss, then put the truck in gear, and began driving down the road again.

"Where are we going?"

"To see Mike Raines, our lawyer. The ranch hasn't been put out to real estate agencies, yet, so we don't need to deal with them. However, we do want our lawyer to handle the legalities of the sale and make sure everything happens as it should. We'll get him to contact the Carringtons this evening."

By the time we returned home that evening, we had met with Mike and he had connected with the Carrington's lawyer. We had heard the particulars of the sale, and asked Mike to put our bid for the land in proper form to present to the Carrington's.

And then it was done. Theo and I looked at each other as we sat that evening after dinner in front of the fireplace, again. The house was full of our children. Homework was in progress in the bedrooms and at the dining room table. Rosalie was in the process of bringing her stuff back home from the cottage to her bedroom. And Bree was back in her doghouse next to Jasper's—a happy reunion.

"Well," said Theo, smiling quietly. "A toast. May we always be glad of the decision we made today. And may it be of benefit to everyone whose life it touches." We clinked our glasses. We hadn't shared the news with the children, as yet. The plan was to keep it to ourselves until our bid was accepted. If it was accepted. We had offered less than had been asked, but then no real estate commissions were to be paid. We'd just have to wait and see.

We weren't really celebrating the land yet. Rather, we were toasting our own courage. It took a lot of guts to take responsibility for that much land. Obviously, there were many ranches in the United States that were many times more vast than the Carrington Ranch. Nevertheless, the bid we put in a few hours earlier was a huge deal to me. I realized that this land bid would cause a lot of words to get written in my Journal just to keep me sane while we waited to hear if we were the new owners. And, if we actually *got* the land, I figured I'd have to buy a whole *new* Journal.

A few days went by, and on one morning, while I was stretching canvases for my dramatic landscape series—a good way to release nervous energy—Christian came into the studio with a bowl of cold cereal, sat on a stool, and said, "Why do you go to the trouble of stretching your own canvases?"

"Because it's part of the art process I practice."

"But," he pointed out. "If you bought the canvases already stretched, you wouldn't have to spend that time and could be doing something else." He slurped up cheerios with a spoon.

"Actually, I enjoy stretching the canvases. It's a time when I'm thinking about the paintings. The sketching is mostly done for this series. So now, while I stretch canvas, I think about the size needed for each landscape to make the best picture. Already, I'm making painting decisions before I've even begun to apply paint."

He changed the subject. I suppose he thought if I wanted to be a fanatic that was my business. "I did good on my midterms."

I put down a finished canvas and Christian followed me into the kitchen to eat his cereal at the table. I told him I was pleased that his classes were going well. "Are you liking college?" I got out a bowl and poured cereal and milk into it.

"It's okay. I'd like to just take science courses, but I realize that isn't possible. So, I'm getting several of the basic courses behind me this semester." He finished his cereal bowl and poured in more.

"How are your teachers?" I took a bite of cereal.

"My chemistry teacher, Mr. Hart, is great. He knows his subject and makes it interesting."

"What about your English teacher?"

"We have to read these ridiculous books about people having personal problems that are weird and beyond boring." He exhaled his annoyance. "Anyway I got a B+ for that midterm. I think that's good."

"When I was in college having to read horrible books, I would mentally change the character's names to something funny that helped me remember their part in the action. It entertained me and served as a memory aid. I also bought Cliff Notes, but just as a pre-read so that I could understand what the heck they were saying when I skimmed the real book."

"That's not a bad idea. I'll have to tell Michelle about that. She hates those books, too."

"What's she planning to major in?" I knew she was enrolled for the spring semester at University of Arizona.

"Engineering. She wants to be an electrical engineer. She was always interested in the electrical problems in shop. It's kind of a natural course for her to follow. She'll probably like it."

"How about you? You have a general science major. Have you thought more about what direction you want that to take?" He talked about several options, but I could tell that nothing had quite jelled in his mind just yet.

Later that day, Theo and I were back again in Mike Raines' office. He was talking to us about the next thirty days. Our bid for the enormous parcel of land had been accepted, and I was clutching my chest, trying to breathe. Theo looked almost as blown away as I was. It was going to take a little digesting.

Mike was saying, "For the next month, you need to look everything over thoroughly. Find out if there are any physical problems that should be fixed by the Carringtons before you take over. Discuss things with your accountant. You need to talk to a local surveyor about the exact boundaries of the ranch and where the corner monuments are. Find out what all your property is being used for in the lease. The long term lease is up for renewal soon. You may want to consider other options for the land. You've mentioned a few, and I'll look into the legalities of these." He paused and then grinned. "Congratulations. You've bitten off a big chunk."

He wasn't kidding. On the way home, Theo and I stopped for sandwiches and more talk at a local burger joint. We ate sitting in the Ranger for greater privacy.

"What do we do now?" Somehow, I didn't feel like racing home and telling the kids. I needed an adjustment period.

"I think we should let it rest for a couple days before we talk about it with the kids," he said, holding his sandwich over a wrapper balanced on his lap. "We need to work out a plan of action for the next month, also a general plan for what we think might be done with the land."

"I feel the same, and agree about the need for a plan." I nibbled at my sandwich and sipped coke.

"Do you mind if we close ourselves in the studio this evening and use your drawing board?"

"Not at all. Anything that moves us in a direction of more control is good."

He laughed. "I know this makes you nervous, and it's a giant step. But, for years I watched my grandmother do stuff like this without blinking an eye. If we use her practical approach we should be able to come up with a good result, as well."

That was true. Theo's grandmother would have been drooling over an opportunity like this. And it would have been one of *many* projects she had on the fire. I should stop being such a wuss and involve myself in the process of making this land ours. Yes. I squared my shoulders. I *can* do this.

"I'm ready," I said. "Let's do it. We want to, at least, have some of our plans penciled in by the time we show the new ranch to the children."

He smiled at me. "That's one of the things I love about you. You don't throw cold water on my ideas. We work as a team until we're both satisfied." He leaned over to me for a kiss, then turned on the ignition and started for home.

We spent the whole evening in the studio working out ideas on paper. Theo had gotten all the topographical maps of the Carrington Ranch and the San Diego County Tax Maps even before our bid was accepted. He had wanted to be prepared, with several extra copies to scribble over.

Finally, after midnight, he leaned back and stretched. "I think we're good to go. We have a fairly thorough inspection schedule for the month. Carlos Morales said that he would like to keep his cattle operation on the ranch at least a couple more years, which means we don't have to commit ourselves about any tentative plans for a while. It gives us considerable time to evaluate what would be our best moves."

"We should probably tell the kids tomorrow." I was starting to be more enthusiastic now that I understood a little more of how we were going to manage things, and that we weren't going to rush into action.

Theo said, "Let's spend tomorrow morning at the new property checking out a few details, then, after school is out, we can gather up the kids and take them out to our new ranch." He grinned. "They won't believe it. I can just *see* their faces."

"I'm still not sure I believe it," I said, but I was smiling. It was the biggest, scariest adventure we'd shared to date. But, we were in it together, and that made a lot of difference. Althea had coached her grandson in how to work with land deals, and showed him methods of managing and maintaining large properties from the time he was a small boy. Yet, he hadn't picked up her need to always be looking for more land. Theo had been perfectly happy with what we had until the moment a need was shown to him. When that happened, he made the necessary adjustments without fuss. He loved land. He was a geologist. But, he wasn't interested in the responsibility of additional acreage without an important reason. Concern about what could happen to the land in the hands of developers became that reason. And in thirty days, if all went well, we would own the Carrington Ranch. Gasp.

The following afternoon, shortly after the twins got home from school, giving no explanation, we packed everyone in the Highlander. Rosalie, who had moved back home, went with us, and so did Christian. The drive had a lot of similarities to that day when Theo and I had first shown the children Cornbread Mesa Ranch. Except that Rosalie had known about that purchase ahead of time. This time she didn't. She looked at me oddly, but got into the Highlander.

John asked, "Where are we going, Dad?"

I was driving, and Theo looked over his shoulder from the front passenger seat. "It's a surprise."

Christian looked at Theo. "The last time this happened, you bought our ranch." Christian was no dummy.

Gwen asked, "Are we going to see more land, Dad?"

Theo smiled, but didn't say anything.

Christian said, "Yes, Gwen, we're going to see land, but Dad doesn't want to talk about it until we get there."

"Oh." She looked out the window, trying to figure where we were going. All of the kids were straining their eyes ahead to see what we had bought this time.

When we drove under the Carrington Ranch sign, all the children's eyes got very big. And when Theo pulled down the remote that clicks the gate open just before the main house, Christian started to laugh, Rosalie gasped, and Gwen's eyes got even bigger. John was practically bouncing off the ceiling.

"What?" said Rosalie. She looked like she was in shock. I could relate.

As I drove up to the house and parked in the circular drive in front, I said, "Come into the courtyard and we'll sit down and talk to you about what's going on."

When we were all seated on the cushioned wrought iron furniture, Theo told them about our bid on this ranch, and that it had been accepted. He explained that we had decided to buy the ranch because no other ranching family stepped forward to buy it, and we were concerned that it might be acquired by a development company.

Christian straightened up and looked interested. Rosalie just sat, absorbing her father's words. The twins were looking all around while they listened.

Theo said, "I don't know if you know what that could mean. But, development companies often make large housing tracts when they get ranch land such as this." Theo paused. "We wouldn't have wanted that, because it would destroy many features of Cornbread Mesa Ranch that we value. Plus, we thought it was a chance to preserve most of this beautiful cattle ranch as it is. We can't afford to only be ranchers just now, but some things can be done with this land that we hope will benefit the people who live in this county and still not change it too much."

"What were you thinking of doing, Dad?" asked Rosalie. She seemed to be taking all of this very seriously.

Theo gestured at the house surrounding the courtyard and talked about the possibility of turning the large house into a museum for tourists, and local residents, to visit and see a piece of California history. He explained that it was "one of the oldest, intact ranches in southern California, with a very interesting Spanish flavor, and," he pointed out, "with nearly all of the original furnishings and tools for organizing daily life from the past still here."

I added the possibility of bringing in or developing a buffalo herd. A good tourist lure and the meat brought a good price. Theo said, "Conceivably, we could even sell buffalo robes and such in our museum store and gift shop."

This was something that resonated with John's thinking. "Wow. I could sell my llama pellets and pillow stuffing here."

I didn't want to get too far ahead into specifics. "That would certainly be something we could discuss, John. In any case, as when we bought Cornbread Mesa Ranch, we have only a month to decide what we think of this place. And there's a much greater area to cover this time."

"On that note," said Theo, "let's go in and look over the house, keeping in mind the idea of using it as a museum."

An hour later, we were back in the courtyard, and Christian was saying, "This place is *perfect* for a museum. Do the owners actually live here?"

"The Morales', the people leasing the ranch, prefer their house in town. It's only twenty-five minutes away, and they find that location more convenient. But, they like to hold fiesta's here during holidays. The historical setting here creates a good Mexican fiesta mood." Theo looked around. "Especially in this large courtyard." We were surrounded by arrangements of heavy, well-crafted wrought iron furniture in groupings amidst colorful potted flowers, and southwestern succulent ground covers and plantings. All of this encircled a lovely pool with koi fish and a fountain.

Rosalie said, "I was thinking about the gift shop idea. What a great way to sell local crafts to go along with the Spanish theme of this place."

Gwen said, "Maybe when Christina, Tiffany and I get really, really good, we can play music here. It would be a great place to have a music fest."

"We'll consider all of these ideas when the time is right," I said, drawing things to a close. "At the moment, we have the real work of going over the property before the month is finished."

There was a subject we did bring up later back home at the supper table. "We don't want to mention this purchase to anyone just now," said Theo. "The news will get around, and anyone can look up property tax records, but it'll make our lives easier if we don't make a big thing of it. We are normal people and we don't plan to change that. In a real sense, we are only stewards of this land, and we need to keep that in mind all the time."

"We'll be moving on with our regular daily lives, just as always," I said. "The only difference is that we have a little more responsibility now."

It was a busy month, as might be expected given the task of inspecting twenty thousand acres. And before we could blink it was already Thanksgiving.

Since it was a sunny, pleasant day on Thanksgiving, we went ahead with plans to smoke a couple turkeys in the camp shelter ovens out at Cornbread Mesa Ranch. Theo and Christian went out to the shelter early to get ready for the turkey-smoking process. This was to be Theo's project, and Christian was his assistant.

Sixteen people, including Gustaffesons, were expected for dinner. Hernando would be with us. Matt and his family would be there. And our Hopi friends, Micah and Sonya would come for the feast.

I was a little sad that Red Thunder couldn't be with us. A lot had happened since he'd been gone, and I hoped that he was okay. I also hoped it wouldn't be too much longer before we saw him again.

Gwen and John had conspired together to make a dazzling layered Jell-O mold for the meal. It had many colors and flavors. They planned to serve it with whipped cream. We also had traditional pumpkin pies created by Rosalie, and I had made Rosemary Onion Bread. Those foods had been prepared ahead. In the morning of the day itself, while Rosalie and I worked to produce mashed potatoes, green beans, turkey dressing, and candied yams, the twins put together tasty relish trays—carrot and celery sticks, radish roses, olives of several kinds, artichoke hearts, pepper rings, and various pickles. Theo and Christian were already out at the ranch tending the turkey-roasting process in the shelter ovens.

In the early afternoon, the home kitchen crew packed everything up and carted it out to the camp shelter in the Highlander. Hot things were put in the warming oven, and then tables were set with autumn colors and decorations. Traditional serving platters were present, and attractive, yet substantial, paper plates and foam cups were ready for use when serving began.

Guests began to arrive. Sonya and Micah came first bringing a special Hopi lamb stew with gorgeous sweet red peppers and onions. Rosalie exclaimed over its beauty and took it away to keep warm in the oven. Sonya looked over the decorated tables, and said, "So pretty, but many places."

I remembered her shyness among strangers. "These will all be family and a couple close friends."

Micah moved over to the center of the men's activities right away. Theo had bought two twenty-five pound turkeys, making sure that there would be plenty for everyone. An air-flow contraption built into the ovens allowed smoke from the firebox underneath to impart that special smoky flavor. Theo used pre-soaked mesquite, adding to the coals as needed to keep the smoke circling around the tender birds.

Micah approved of the oven, saying that he had smoked fish by the lake. "It keeps longer than fresh fish. I learned to smoke fish and meat long ago, but Hopi see this as women's work. Among your people, barbeque and smoking is men's work. Sonya likes the Hopi way, but prefers her fish the way I smoke it." He and Theo laughed together.

Christian asked, "Is this almost done, Dad?"

Theo peered in at one of the birds, poked it with a long fork, then shut the oven door again. "A few more minutes."

Hernando arrived with Matt and his family. Gwen went to greet her friend, Christina, while Stacy took a covered bowl from her husband, Bob, which allowed him to join the cluster of men next to the ovens. When allowed to take a look, Bob thought the bird looked "done."

I lifted the cover of Stacy's dish and realized she had made a large mincemeat pie. "My goodness, Stacy. This smells and looks heavenly! And still warm. Did you just take it out of the oven?"

She smiled. "I always make mincemeat on Thanksgiving. An old family tradition. "

Gram came up behind her. "Glad to see.... a mincemeat pie. Thought ... no one made them ... anymore." She looked approvingly at Stacy.

I gave hugs to my grandparents and Aunt Myrtle, and suggested that they make themselves comfortable at a table. Granddad decided to wander over to the turkey smoking and roasting consultation group. Aunt Myrtle exclaimed over the table decorations. "What a handsome display of gourds and leaves!" She clasped her hands together in delight, then sat down to sample some of the relishes from a tray in front of her.

It was getting close to serving time, so I rapped a spoon on a ceramic bowl for attention. "We don't want your food to get cold once you're served, so we thought we'd take this moment to sing a favorite old scouting grace for the occasion. Anyone who knows the words is welcome to join in." I nodded at Gwen who began to sing in clear tones, and as she sang, many voices joined her.

"Back of the bread is the flour,

And back of the flour is the mill,

And back of the mill is the wind and the rain,

And the Father's will."

After that, the hot food was arranged buffet style on one of the tables set aside for the turkey carver, Theo, to ply his craft. Everyone grabbed a plate and got in line to fill it from the various dishes until they reached Theo, who was carving off white and dark meat according to each person's taste. Matt helped Hernando get drink orders from the cooler. And we also had a fire going with hot water boiling for anyone who wanted a hot drink.

Finally, we were all sitting down eating, talking, laughing, and telling stories and jokes. Micah and Granddad were sitting side by side telling fish stories. I head Granddad say, "Maybe I'll have to come to your camp one day by Wildcat Lake and try one of your poles."

Micah returned, "You would be welcome, Sven."

I sat across the table from Gram and Stacy, who were deep into a discussion on mincemeat ingredients. At the other end of the table Sonya said to Rosalie, "Did you or your mother make this bread? This is very good bread."

Gradually, plates were emptied and refilled again. We got to the dessert portion of the day, and people groaned that they couldn't eat anymore. But dessert is a funny thing. Everyone can usually make some sort of room for dessert, and many were impressed with Gwen and John's colorful, layered Jell-O. It was at least light. But, there were those of us who went big time. We had pumpkin *and* mincemeat pie, *with* whipped cream!

There was a point when it began to get quite cool, and night was drawing in fast. We wrapped up individual packages of leftover turkey and fixings, so everyone could take some home. The cleanup wasn't bad, since a lot of it—disposable plates, cups, etc.—went directly into the covered trash or recycle barrels. This was the kind of Thanksgiving celebration I liked. Fun, plenty of space, and limited clean up.

Later that evening at home, it was just Theo and I once more in front of the fire talking about the success of the day. Rosalie had stayed behind at the cabin to talk with Matt. Gwen and Christina had promised to show up at the Taggert's house to play and sing their music for a family gathering there. John went over to Travis Lee's to consult with Travis' many sisters about how to make llama fleece-filled pillows for Christmas, and Christian took Michelle out to a holiday movie.

Much later still, after Theo had gone off to bed, Jasper, Bree, and Athena were still unconscious beside the last hot coals in the fireplace. I shooed the dogs out to their snug doghouses, then checked to see who was home before I locked up. Rosalie had come home a little earlier, taking Athena into her bedroom with her. Athena slept at the foot of Rosalie's bed nearly every night. Gwen and John were both asleep in their rooms. I peeked in to see if Christian was in bed. No Christian. Still out with Michelle.

As I turned to go back to my bedroom, I heard Christian coming in the door. He turned, saw me, and smiled. "Happy Thanksgiving, Mom."

I smiled back, "Happy Thanksgiving, Christian."

14

CHRISTMAS

December

THE SECOND DAY IN DECEMBER it was raining. Cold, uncomfortable rain. When I'm inside feeling cozy, I can look outside and be glad the plants and trees are getting a drink. But, when I have to go someplace and we've got dreary, slanting rain, I can hardly wait to get back home to a hot cup of tea in front of the fire.

That day it was inevitable I would have to brave the elements for a trip to the Indian Heritage Store. I had run out of vermillion and no other color would do for the composition in front of me. I had squeezed the very last pigment molecule that I could out of that tube. Bundling up in woolly pullover, fleece-lined rubber boots, lined jeans, yellow rain slicker with tie-shut hood, I headed out the door before I could talk myself out of it. Dashing to the Highlander, I put the windshield wipers on high, and felt the car water-ski all the way to the store.

I parked in front of the Indian Heritage Store with no problem, because there were literally no other cars. Getting out on the passenger side, I didn't have to slosh through the water-swollen street to the sidewalk. But, the wind fought me as I opened the door to the store. Amanda stared at me from the front register. "You must be desperate to come out on a day like this."

I blew water off the tip of my nose. "I needed a tube of vermillion."

"That would explain it. You're probably the only customer I'll have all day. Come back to the office and have some cocoa. You can buy your paint just before you leave." She led the way to the back of the store.

That sounded good. I was always willing to listen to a reason not to go out in the rain. I hung up my dripping slicker and collapsed into the comfy chair by the back window. Rain was running in an unbroken sheet down the panes of glass. Amanda handed me a steamy hot mug of cocoa that felt good just to hold.

I commented, "Kyle came by a while back to tell me of your revelation, via the grapevine, that Stevette Strike was hanging out with a guy." I carefully tested the cocoa. "I told him to go consult Bob Taggert about it. Do you happen to know if anything came of that? Did he talk to Bob?"

"Apparently, with the combined weight of our suggestions that they talk things out, Kyle talked to Bob and they are now working together."

"Do you know if they've gotten anywhere with it?"

"Kyle said something about a guy named Hank Rhodes." Amanda shrugged. "But, they can't seem to locate him."

"And Hank Rhodes is...?"

"The guy Stevette was seeing." Amanda was sitting at her desk, elbows resting on the top, a mug of cocoa cradled in her hands. She wasn't dressed to exhibit jewelry that day. Instead, she wore a red sweatshirt over a black turtleneck, black lined sports slacks, and hot pink fluffy slippers. Her rubber boots were sitting not far from where my wet slicker was hanging on a hook.

We chatted about the puzzling aspects of the still unsolved Gudrun Bohn case. A lot of months had gone by since Gudrun's death, and although the newspaper tried to keep things stirred up, as far as Amanda and I knew, there had been no big breaks. Most of the facts of the case were common knowledge now. All except my "lady bug" clue. I didn't mention that.

We had more mugs of cocoa and the subject changed back to Kyle. Amanda said, "He's doing a lot better now." Kyle's romantic feelings toward Amanda had made him more willing to listen to her practical suggestions about his career. As unlikely as it might seem, according to Amanda, his job was benefitting from this romance.

She continued, "Being willing to work with Bob was the turning point. He knows that Bob has earned a platinum reputation in his police work. Everyone knows how competent Bob is. So, when Bob was willing to start working a case with Kyle—I happened to be able to give Kyle a bit of information Bob didn't have yet—Kyle's reputation was boosted."

She set her mug down. "Things are still in a delicate stage, but if he keeps his head, and consults with Bob, his past will gradually fade.

Folks are mostly interested in what a person's done lately, and that attitude will be what saves Kyle's career." She smiled, "Plus, I've been making sure he knows how much I appreciate him."

I rose up reluctantly from the comfortable chair. "I'm glad things are looking up for Kyle. It always seemed that he had potential. I'm glad for you, too. It's nice to see you looking so happy these days."

"Life is good right now," she agreed. We were standing at the front counter, and I was just putting the paint tube in my slicker pocket, when the door blew open and in stumbled Dillon Cody. He was in rain gear, and he was sopping wet. Water was running off him as though he had been swimming in the engorged, turbulent nearby creek.

He bent over to hack and cough for a moment, then slowly straightened. "Someone pushed me in the *creek!*" His face contorted in a painful grimace as he coughed hard. I got a chair for him to sit on, while Amanda called Kyle. Moments later, Kyle and Bob burst through the wind-buffeted door, shutting it behind them with some difficulty. They had been a block away having coffee.

"Someone pushed me in the creek," Dillon said again.

"Start at the beginning, Cody." Bob slipped his notebook out of a zippered pocket in his raingear.

"I parked next to that little bridge that runs over the creek, because I had to deliver a package next door to the real estate office. As I was getting out of the car I didn't have a real good grip on the package, and the wind pulled it out of my hands." He stopped and coughed some more.

"Go on," said Bob.

"The wind got underneath the package, because it was so light, and I was afraid it was going to be blown right into the creek. So I leaped forward to grab it just before it would have dumped into the water. It was right then that I felt someone *push* me. Someone pushed me in the creek! I could have *drowned!* I was just lucky that there's a big tree limb that sticks out low right there or I'd have been pulled downstream." He ran a hand through his wet hair. "The package is lost. I had photos for a lady who had me tailing her husband in a divorce case. Now I have to reprint those photos. I'll probably get pneumonia and God knows what else from that disgusting water." He looked like the proverbial drowned rat.

I didn't like the idea of anyone suffering such an underhanded attack. Drowning in freezing, filthy water wasn't one of the better ways to die. Fortunately, he had been able to pull himself out.

Kyle asked, "Did you see anyone nearby when you parked, or when you got out of your car?"

"There was no one. Anyway, I was dealing with that package. I wasn't looking at anything else." Dillon looked as though he felt very ill-used, sitting there and dripping into a puddle while he answered questions.

"Did you get any kind of a glimpse of the person who pushed you?" asked Bob. "Such as the color of a coat sleeve, or other impressions like that?"

"No. I told you. I was looking at the package and trying to keep it from going into the creek. Anyway," he looked up at me annoyed. "It was probably Janna's fault. She had that guy harassing me for a long time. And he's probably back doing stuff like this!"

I kept quiet, and Kyle said, "You have to be more careful when you accuse people, Mr. Cody. There are laws against slander."

Bob said, "The police have found no connection between Mrs. Gustaffeson and your unknown harasser. Furthermore, the attack you experienced today doesn't sound anything like what has happened in the past. Everything you called in to the police before was in the non-violent, non-lethal category. What you've reported today is quite different. You were fortunate, because what you've just told us could have been fatal."

I privately wondered what Dillon had done to someone to finally cause them to want him dead. He could always be counted on to be annoying. What had changed to make Dillon's life intolerable to someone? Or was it more like the final straw? I hadn't any idea.

Dillon sat dejectedly in the chair. "Let us know if you think of anything else," Bob told Dillon. "In the meantime, drive over to the station and fill out a statement of what happened today. We're going to look around by the creek to see if we can spot anything that could help us identify your attacker."

Bob and Kyle ushered Dillon out the door and left to go about the soggy business of inspecting a probable crime scene. It seemed likely that Dillon was telling the truth. He had looked pretty miserable and he was upset about losing that package. It didn't seem a time when he'd be amusing himself by trying to stir something up.

Amanda and I looked at each other when they had gone. I said, "And you thought you wouldn't see anyone in the store today. Girl, you have no faith in the quirks of fortune."

She replied, "I have plenty of faith in quirks, and you be careful when you're driving home." She waved as I tugged open the door and went out into the deluge.

Several days later, Christian dragged into the house after an hours long hunt for an older man who had gone for a hike in the desert. The man hadn't returned to his family at the expected time, and still hadn't come back by the next day. The desert wasn't very hot during the day in winter, but the nights got quite cold and people had died of exposure when there was no warm place to huddle during those frosty hours.

Fortunately, the man had told his family where he was going. He had gotten turned around and then tripped over an uneven place in the trail, badly breaking his ankle. Christian's team had found him on a rarely traveled path off the main hiking trail. He was chilled and in pain, but immensely grateful to be rescued. It was a feel-good kind of a day for Christian.

"Except for the bones, Mom. That was awful and gross." Christian helped himself to a big bowl of beef barley soup.

"What bones?"

"There were human bones out near where the man was. We called the sheriff right away when we saw that."

"Whose bones were they?" I checked on the status of a spinach, tomato, egg and ricotta cheese casserole I had in the oven for supper.

"I guess there were two skeletons, and the cops weren't saying what they thought. But, I overheard one of them mention the name, Strike. One of the officers said they ran the plates of some car while we were there. Maybe we'll read about it in the paper tomorrow." He ate some soup. "It's like that in sports, too. Have you ever noticed that there's a lot of stuff you don't hear or see when you go to a game, but later when it's being picked apart on television, you find out all kinds of details about what the players did?"

A couple days later, Bob invited himself for breakfast. He brought onion bagels and I made the coffee. He sat down at the kitchen table, and said, "We found Stevette Strike."

"Christian said that some bones had been found by his Search and Rescue crew when they were looking for someone else," I contributed. I cupped my hands around a cup of tea feeling chilled by the confirmation of what Christian had mentioned, and the conclusion to which my thoughts had leapt.

"That's right, and when the bones were brought in to the medical examiner, his people were able to check dental records. We were already fairly sure who they were by the surrounding evidence." He sipped some coffee.

"What happened?"

"By the evidence, it looks as though they drove out in the desert in a Jeep. They were investigating a seldom traveled canyon when the Jeep got badly stuck in soft sand. Probably they would have needed some help getting it out. They must have tried to walk out and couldn't, for some reason. We found only a couple small, empty water bottles by the Jeep, and there didn't seem to be any blankets or anything else that might have helped them last long enough to get assistance."

"Why would they let themselves get in that kind of predicament?" I asked. "Stevette has been in California for enough years to know how dangerous the desert is."

Bob chewed some bagel. "Probably the same thing that's been happening to other folks the last few years. There's all kinds of people heading out into the wild desert regions without proper precautions these days, thinking that all they need to do if they get in a jam is get on their fully charged cell phone and call for assistance. We found cell phones among the remains."

I knew what he was saying. There were a lot of people who should know better, but didn't stop to think about the fact that cell phones often—maybe *usually* is a better word—don't work in wild areas and far out in the desert. Cell phone companies arrange good service in high use areas, fair service in lower use areas, and poor or no service in places where people go infrequently. In the future we might have reliable communication even deep in a mountain tunnel, but the infrastructure wasn't there yet. I guess a lot of people don't think of that—and a few of them die.

I asked, "Who was the other person?" I was pretty sure I already knew.

"Guy named, Hank Rhodes. His friends say he had been seeing Stevette off and on for about a year. She had kept it all quiet from Gudrun Bohn. According to sources, she hadn't been happy for some time and thought maybe she needed a change."

I sipped some tea. "So now what happens?"

"Well, the Strike and Rhodes deaths have been determined to be accidental due to exposure." He drank coffee. "Gudrun Bohn's death is still considered suicide. And so are those deaths up in San Francisco. I've given up on those. Probably, they were actual suicides.

Could be the evidence collection was bad. Who knows? It seems like a lot of dead bodies, somehow, but I have to be moving along with other cases." I knew he hated to give up when there was uncertainty.

"Did you find anything the other day when Dillon got attacked?"

"No. But, I think he actually got attacked. He's a terrible liar, and he didn't look like he was trying to put anything over. I'm reasonably sure it wasn't the practical joker who'd been entertaining everyone at Cody's expense for several months. Some of that was really funny stuff. But the joker guy had a lot of opportunity and never did anything that was harmful. So, he isn't a contender for pushing Cody in the creek, as far as I'm concerned."

I was inwardly pleased to know that Bob didn't have Hernando on his list as a suspect.

Bob looked at me intently. "Which leads to my next question. Do you have anything you'd like to share with me about what happened to your mysterious protector?"

Blindsided! His question was completely unexpected. I had thought since my mysterious protector had stopped drawing attention to himself, people would stop worrying about it and the whole thing would fade into the past. I should have known that nothing was ever that simple with Bob. He doesn't like unanswered questions. He was always looking to fill in the blanks no matter how much time had gone by. Not having had time to prepare myself, my expression must have looked guilty.

"Come on Janna," he said, an amused look on his face. "I *know* you know something about your mystery protector."

"How could you know that?" I demanded, outraged that he suspected me of not coming clean. Of course, I hadn't. Come clean with him, I mean. I suppose maybe he deserved to know a *little* something. But what could I say? I didn't want to cause problems for my friend and employee, Hernando.

"I'm not dumb," he said, in the understatement of the year. "Shortly after you were all upset following your rough rattlesnake rescue, and after Thad and I gave you your special cell phone, you suddenly appeared to have no more worries. You were looking happy and content." He looked at me in that focused way he has that must make anyone hiding anything, nervous. "That's not the behavior of a woman concerned about her safety. You *did* something to the guy, didn't you? What was it?"

I looked at him uncertainly. "I didn't hurt him."

Bob laughed, snorting through his nose. "I'm not concerned that I'll find his bones somewhere, and I'm pretty sure you haven't committed a criminal act. I just want to satisfy my curiosity.

Oh. Well, if that was the case. "I started thinking about how quick he is and how he could mangle me unintentionally before I even got out my cell phone. So I decided to have a little chat with him. Just to clear the air."

"A Chat," he repeated, and started on another bagel looking at me with faintly horrified fascination.

"Yeah. There was also the problem of not wanting a person who had saved my life taken into the station and maybe detained. I just felt I owed him a little consideration."

"A little consideration." Bob smiled, shaking his head. "So what did you talk this guy into?"

"Well, we discussed his rescue technique and while we were talking, I realized he reminded me of Christian." Bob had stopped the bagel halfway to his mouth, waiting for the next part. I continued. "So, I gave him a job on the ranch."

Bob nearly fell off his chair laughing. "You gave your *stalker* a job? And what did Theo have to say about this?" He knew Theo wasn't a bit backward explaining about things he didn't like, and that he wasn't going to do.

"He balked a little at first," I admitted. Bob laughed some more, probably thinking about Theo's reaction. "But, when I told him my reasons and after he met Hernando, he agreed that the kid should be given a chance. And Hernando has already proven to be an excellent employee. Plus, he's saved my life again since then without hospitalizing me." That was true. All the damage was what I had done to myself.

"The whole story," said Bob, still laughing. "Out with it, I want the whole story."

So I told him everything from the moment I saw Hernando in my rearview mirror and decided to set him straight, up to Thanksgiving Day when Hernando was part of our family gathering.

Bob said, "Not many people invite their stalkers for Thanksgiving dinner, Janna," he chuckled. "I think you're right about keeping his history quiet. It sounds like he's a decent guy that got pointed in the wrong direction. I agree that he should get a break. I'll run his name through our system, and if he hasn't committed any felonies, I can't see any reason for us to bother him so long as he minds his manners. He's in a good place, a citizen doing a man's work. That's enough for me." And then added, "Anyway, Valdez now has a specific address where I can find him, if that should turn out to be necessary."

"Thanks," I said. "I appreciate this, Bob."

"No problem." He got up from his chair and walked to the front door. "Now, I have to see what I can do to find this person who attacked Dillon Cody. That guy isn't a prankster. He's the real thing, if he intended to kill Cody. And you watch yourself, okay?"

Not long after that, the lawyers did their magic, money went from our trust to the seller's account, and we became the new owners of the Carrington Ranch. We arranged with Carlos Morales to continue their lease, because we were in no hurry to do anything with the ranch. We had ideas for the future, but no rush. The main thing was that it would remain a working ranch. No concerns about an enormous construction project next door ruining the quality of life at Cornbread Mesa Ranch. And even more important, we would be saving open space in a county that was being rapidly built up.

A few mornings after the land changed hands, I noticed that the sliding door to the back patio was not completely shut, letting in chilly air. Someone had probably been in a hurry letting the dogs out, and didn't wait for the latch to click. I went into my bedroom for a sweater. On my way across the room, I noticed Athena on the bed. Sitting. Staring down at something on the bed. Cautiously, I approached the bed and observed a small furry object resting next to my pillow. The object yawned and stretched its tiny paws into space, then collapsed into itself again. Leaning closer, I could see there were actually *two* of these objects, apparently just-weaned Siamese kittens, about eight weeks or so old. Both had tan colored sides with deep brown faces, legs and tails. One was a little darker than the other. Obviously, they couldn't be Athena's offspring, because she had been spayed long ago. She now alertly watched to see what I would do about these young intruders.

The first order of business was the litter box in the garage under the workbench. It had been Athena's litter box for a long time, and had all kinds of cat messages saying *this is where you do your business*. I picked up the sleepy babies, and walked out to the garage. Pulling the litter box out so I could see that correct actions were taking place, I put the kittens in the box. Athena came along to inspect the proceedings, and after a period of stretching the young critters began to dig as expected. Mission accomplished.

Athena's food dish was only a few feet from the box. I tapped the side of the dish and the kittens tumbled out of the litter box to investigate. Obviously, they already understood about crunchy catfood. They climbed into the dish and sat on the food while they ate. I would have to buy kitten food, but this would do for now.

While our guests were eating, I found an old comforter, folded it to a quarter of its size to make a fat cushion, and put the kittens on it. Little yarn ties that stuck out had to be sniffed, and pounced on viciously. Then they pounced on each other until finally falling asleep together in a heap on the cushion. The life of a kitten.

Conditions were good to leave the kittens in the garage and go do supper stuff in the kitchen. The kids would be home soon, and I had other responsibilities besides baby Siamese kittens.

It wasn't until we were sitting at the dining room table that my thoughts returned to the kittens. The period when the children come home from school, snacks get eaten, questions get answered, information gets passed on, supper gets prepared, and we finally sit down to eat, doesn't allow for much else. So, when John remarked conversationally, "There's a cat climbing up my leg, Mom." I had to think a moment what he was talking about.

For a few seconds we were busy capturing them. Gwen managed to grab them both. "Poor babies aren't allowed in people's dinner plates." She carried them off to the garage and shut the door. In answer to questions that followed, I explained my theory of how the kittens had entered the house, and my plan of finding their owner—mainly checking lost kitten notices on the grocery store bulletin board. The kids were excited by our animal guests, but Theo just looked at me. He knew it was likely we had just acquired two more in-house animals. I returned the look and shrugged my shoulders, pretty sure that if he had been home instead of me when the kittens appeared, things would have turned out much the same.

Over the next few days Jasper got climbed over by the marauding Siamese. This was worrying to him, because he knew that we never, never eat our friends. But, what does a dog do when used as a playground? Athena had no doubts about that issue. When a kitten got out of line, she just sharply whacked it with her paw. Mama cats didn't put up with any baloney, and Athena simply adjusted her personality to take on the chore of training young upstarts.

Theo also adjusted to the kittens, and became quite fond of them, even though they leapt on his stocking feet and bit his toes if he wiggled them. I'm sure he didn't do that on purpose just to watch them pounce. Of course not.

I had blocked in all of my new spectacular landscape themes and was slowly working with each painting. Fifteen canvases were really large and ten were of a more medium size. The medium ones were detail areas found on the big canvases and at a different time of day, which meant the colors would be altered. A bit like using the zoom on a camera lens, then turning the clock forwards or backwards. It would make an interesting Spring exhibit.

Not only was I busy painting, but my kitchen became a center for Christmas baking. The kids and their friends wanted to do favorite holiday cookie recipes or try out new ones. And, of course, as usual I was painting until a problem arose, at which point I would do a little laundry or go make something in the kitchen until I was ready to face painting again.

While in the kitchen I concentrated on rum balls and Hungarian poppy seed roll cakes, or alternately, ground walnut roll cakes. When Jody and I were little girls, a woman of Hungarian ancestry lived next door to our family home in Ohio, and she made these delicious pastries every Christmas. When Dad and Mom passed on, and we moved to Michigan to live with Grandma and Granddad, our former neighbor gave us her cake recipes as a going away gift. Jody and I got in the habit of making them as teenagers, and even now, our families still expect them every Christmas, just as we did when we were little girls.

Rosalie spent her creative efforts on Chocolate cupcakes with coconut sprinkled frosting, decorated with candies like snowman faces. She also made lots of fudge—plain milk chocolate, milk chocolate with pecans, dark chocolate with walnuts, peanut butter fudge, milk chocolate with coffee, dark chocolate with mint. Rosalie gets *into* fudge. She fixed many small tins of fudge assortments to give to friends and family.

There was a whole day when Gwen, John, Travis, Christina, and Tiffany took over most of my kitchen to make Christmas cookie cutter butter cookies. It was an ambitious undertaking that involved much making of dough and rolling it into several large balls, which were stored in plastic zip locks and refrigerated. One by one the balls were rolled out flat and pressed with cookie cutter shapes—pine trees, bells, half-moons, candy canes, stars, etc. These were baked and stored awaiting decoration.

The next day brought the really fun part: decorating. The dining room table was loaded with bowls of assorted colors of vanilla flavored frosting. Grouped in with them were containers of candy sprinkles, cinnamon hearts, candy sparkles, tiny chocolate chips, chocolate sprinkles, and assorted colors of sugars. In the center of the table was a platter of naked butter cookies. All the kids sat around the table for a serious session of cookie decorating.

"John, you're hogging all the green frosting."

"I'll trade you my candy sprinkles for your red sugar, Tiffany."

"Wow! That is a cool Christmas tree, Christina."

"Gwen, hurry up with the yellow frosting. I need it for my star."

"I like what Travis is doing on his cookie with the chocolate chips."

"Oh gosh, John, you've dumped over the blue sugar!"

Once the decorating was done, the kids divided the cookies into five large containers, and each took one home for his or her family. Since we always receive numerous cookie plates in return, it all evens out, and the kids love it. But, I had to watch myself. I could gain weight just sniffing the kitchen aromas at Christmastime.

The day after the cookie marathon, Rosalie was busy decorating the house with pine boughs brought in from the ranch. Ever since we had visited Carrington Ranch—now our ranch, but not as yet formally named—with the children, there had been a discussion about how to casually refer to Cornbread Mesa Ranch and Carrington Ranch without having to say the long names each time. We finally decided to say the *Big Ranch* when we meant the Carrington Ranch, and just *ranch* when we meant Cornbread Mesa Ranch. It saved a lot of time and confusion.

So, Rosalie was decorating the house with pine boughs from the *ranch*, filling the air with that fresh pine smell everyone appreciates at that time of year. We were getting ready for a caroling and eggnog party that the Girl Scout troop was to put on at our house. The Christmas tree in the living room was decorated. Candles were placed around the house and lit.

Just before the girls were to arrive, the doorbell rang and I went to answer it. When I opened the door, no one was there. But I noticed a brown package on the outside mat with my name on it. Since we were a little rushed for time, I decided to wait on opening it, and put it in the studio for later.

Walking into the kitchen a moment later, I could see that Gwen, Christina and Tiffany had everything ready to go. They'd put together a good assortment of sandwiches, and treats, and had made a large punchbowl of 7-Up, cranberry juice, and vanilla ice-cream, with maraschino cherries floating in the resulting pink swirl. And they had bought plenty of eggnog. All of this was arranged on the festively-decorated dining room table as the rest of the girls began to arrive.

Mona Henry and Katey Taggert came in the door carrying little booklets of carols made from copies that had been hole-punched and tied together with red ribbon. It was only four o'clock, but the sun was nearly down and temperatures were falling. Mona and Katey had brought warm coats and gloves for the caroling.

"Good grief, it's getting chilly out there." Katey put her coat on my bed with the others, and then joined the rest in the dining room to fuel up for the hours ahead. Since I had the beginnings of a cold, I had elected to stay home and tend the fire. Before long, a serious dent had been made in the edibles, punch and eggnog.

When everyone was bundled up again, Mona passed around caroling booklets and the girls quickly ran through a practice of *Deck the Halls*. As they went out the door, she said, "Stay together and don't shine your flashlights in people's faces."

John and Christian were out doing other holiday things with friends that evening, so Theo and I helped ourselves to sandwiches and sat waiting by the fire for the frozen carolers' eventual return.

"How are you liking having your office here in the house?" I hardly knew he worked out of the guest-room-turned-office because he was gone a lot during the day. The only time I saw him in the home office was when he had a special client appointment, and on evenings when he spent time catching up on paper work. This evening, for instance, he had stayed in the office working until the girls had gone out the door on their caroling mission.

"I like having my office down the hall from the bedroom. That way I can work late, and still be at home. No need to go out in the cold, lock the door, get in the truck and drive all the way back from Rancho Bernardo. That part is great." He bit into his sandwich.

As we talked and enjoyed the fire, two dark, triangular faces with wide blue eyes appeared over the arm of the sofa. I picked up the kittens and plopped them on my lap. They climbed up my chest with noisy meows offering to help me with the last bite of my sandwich. One tiny paw batted hesitantly at my mouth.

Theo got up to put more wood on the fire, stabbing at the burning logs with a poker, while sparks flew up the chimney. He sat back down beside me taking the darker kitten into the curve of one arm while he stroked the pale furry belly with his other hand.

The lighter kitten stuck its nose under my sweater, crawling between it and my shirt, to settle down for a nap. I had been watching the paper and local bulletin boards for inquiries about the lost Siamese pair, but nothing had turned up. We would continue to search, but as the weeks went by the chances of putting the owner together with these kittens became less likely. None of our neighbors had heard anything, and it was seeming more and more as though our kitty guests were permanent. In January, I would take them to the vet and see if they had any news, and if not, get the babies started with shots and any other necessary health care.

We had determined that one was male and the other female. Theo had been calling the female Cleopatra, because she was such an exotic creature with her slightly darker coat. And I had named the little guy under my sweater,

Bast, after the cat god of ancient Egypt. The names seemed to fit.

An hour later, the kittens had been removed to the garage, with the return of the girls and frozen leaders. The fireplace was popular for the girls to gather round, eat treats, and swill more punch and eggnog. Much joking and talk went on. The "band" members were discussing the timing of when a group should start thinking about "cutting a CD." Christina laughed, "Too many mistakes!"

Tiffany vigorously objected. "I disagree. We're getting better each time we play for someone."

"We do try harder when someone is listening to us," said Gwen. "But, we're going to have to try harder, longer, because we don't sound good enough, yet, to do anything recorded."

"Well, okay." Tiffany sounded reluctant. "But, we should start to *think* about making ourselves good enough. We're *lots* better than we were."

"A good name," said Christina, changing the subject. "We need a good name."

Gwen agreed. "You can't record stuff without a good name." In the next half hour several possible names were offered, but weren't considered cool enough by the girls. "Campfire

Cowgirls," "The Bronco-ettes," and "Torn Rose Petals" were a few that were rejected without much discussion. Being a wannabe country music sensation was tough.

I drifted over to Katey and asked how she was holding up, having band practice at her house two or three days a week. She had cup of punch in her hand. "It's kind of fun. Tiffany's never had many friends around before, and it's made a huge difference in how she feels about herself. Her whole mood has changed for the better. Bob and I figure the noise is a small price to pay."

I was glad they felt that way. The band might be around for a while. But I supposed if it got to be too much they could put in heavy-duty sound-proofing. Bob was a pretty good problem solver.

A few days before the end of the month, I thought about the pluses of this year's Christmas. Gram was healthy again. She had some limitations, but she was doing well. No terrible unresolved circumstance hung over our heads. The kids were all on track. I didn't have any current injuries. The Big Ranch was doing its regular ranch business and we didn't have to be involved there, as yet. We were good most everywhere. Should I now brace for something?

I wrote in my Journal: *On Christmas morning, when we gathered around the tree, we found both dogs and all three cats waiting there under the tree, as if they were the gifts. It was such a funny thing to come in with our cups of cocoa and coffee and see the sleeping animals. Christian looked at me as if it were a set-up, but it wasn't. He just thinks that way because he likes to play practical jokes, himself.*

We later found out that John had gotten up extra early, looked around to see if anyone else was up, let the dogs in, and then stumbled back to bed. Though, we still haven't figured out how the kittens manage to get through the cat door from the garage on their own. Learning John's part of the mystery didn't take away from the magic of the morning.

We had breakfast and opened our gifts, then drove up altitude to the ranch to see how much of the rain we had received in town had turned to snow up there during the night. A couple of inches blanketed the scene. Enough for John, Gwen, and Christian to make snow angels in the pasture. While they were making their angels, the horses and dogs—llamas are too conservative to get involved in a free-for-all like that—had to come over and see what was going on. So the angel impressions didn't last long. But everyone had a chance to feed his or her animals.

From the ranch we had all driven down to Lake Mirage to see Grandma and Granddad, and Aunt Myrtle. They had invited us for lunch. Gram had prepared fish roll-ups—a Swedish dish that involved delicious freshwater fish rolled into pinwheels with bread crumbs and herbs. They were held together with toothpicks and baked. Granddad had caught the fish and then helped her get it all together. When we arrived, we found our places around the normally round table, now turned oval, with Granddad adding the old extension piece to fit us all in.

After lunch we exchanged gifts, and then took our coffee and tea out in the yard to sit and watch the water birds—ducks and coots—cavorting on the lake while we reminisced about all the things that had happened over the past year. When the sun got red in the sky and the wind off the lake turned cold, we said goodbye, and packed ourselves into our vehicles to drive back home.

It had been a wonderful day to record in the Journal. A person needs days like that to read back over for times when things aren't going so well.

I looked around me and stretched. I was in the studio, and it was early afternoon. I needed to do something about the clutter that had gotten tossed on my drawing table over the holidays. I hadn't painted much the last couple weeks. Holidays tend to stifle concentrated effort in that direction. But, it was time to set things straight in order to focus on my art again. Time to get rid of the junk.

I got up from the comfortable blue chair and crossed to assess what all was piled on the drawing table. New art supplies for projects in the future, old supplies for things currently underway, resource books, sketch pads, photographs, matt color samples, and so on. I began to sort everything into stacks to put away. I was doing well until I noticed the brown paper wrapped package under a large sketch pad at the bottom of the pile.

Vaguely, I recalled picking that package up from the mat in front of our door, putting it in the studio, and planning to open it when I had a chance. The chance never came that evening, or the next day, and more things got put on top of it until it was completely forgotten.

Turning the package over, I saw my name, "Janna," printed in capital letters. No indication who it was from. Probably a note from the giver was inside. I ripped off the brown paper and found a white box with a lid. Still no note. Opening the lid revealed folded tissue. On top of the tissue was a typed note that read, *May your days be merry and bright.* In my mind I completed the rest of the stanza to the song "White Christmas"—*and may all your Christmases be white.* How nice.

I lifted the tissue to see what the gift was. Yuk. I knew right away something was wrong. Underneath the tissue paper were photographs of Dillon Cody in questionable situations that many people wouldn't want to even know about, let alone get a photo-gallery of. At the very bottom of the stack was another note that said: *Merry Christmas!* It was signed, *a Friend.*

I looked at my watch. It was a time of day when one might expect Bob Taggert to be at the Betty's Burgers, getting coffee and a snack. I wrapped the package back up, put on my coat, took the package out to the Highlander and drove to the fast food place. Sure enough, there was Bob's cruiser. I pulled in beside him, and he powered down the window. I could see Kyle Krupp in the passenger seat. Apparently, they had been talking over coffee.

"To what do I owe this pleasant interruption?" Bob asked and then spoiled it by turning to Kyle, saying, "See. I can talk like that, too." Apparently, Kyle had been giving him pointers on being more charming with ladies. I didn't know how that would work. On the whole, Bob's manners were fairly basic. He wasn't offensive, but he didn't mollycoddle people.

I said, "I received a package that you might want to look over. It's a little like, but not the same as, that other package I brought you many months ago." I was trying to inform him without saying anything crucial in case he didn't want to share this with Kyle.

However, Bob must not have minded about Kyle. He said, "Unless you have private reasons not to, I think you can show me what you have. Kyle and I are working together on the problem, if it's what I think it is." He looked questioningly at me.

I nodded. "How do you want to do this?"

"Let's go inside and get a corner table. The place is pretty empty right now."

A couple minutes later we carried drinks over to a table in the empty dining area. Before I handed Bob the package, I told them its history as far as I knew it. Bob slipped on some thin rubber gloves he had handy in a pocket, and reached for the box. "This looks a lot like that last package you handed me."

With raised eyebrows, he and Kyle looked through the photos. They examined the note and wrappings. And then they looked at me.

I shrugged my shoulders. "I don't have any idea why someone would give something like this to me." One photo showed Dillon video-taping through what appeared to be someone's bathroom window. Another showed him in a bedroom posing a nervous-looking, mostly undressed, school-aged girl for his camera. Still another showed Dillon climbing out of a window in someone's house. These were the photos on top. The captured scenes became more unsavory the further I had delved into the box.

"It's kinda like this person *knows* that Cody isn't one of your favorite people," said Bob. "This sort of evidence, showing a person who looks like Cody, who is possibly breaking several laws, and, depending on conviction, might mean doing serious time, is not meant to be a kindly act. It looks like this person hates Cody's guts."

"Yeah," said Kyle. "Maybe it's the same guy who pushed Cody in the creek a few weeks ago." He looked at me. "We've never gotten anything on that."

"It's a possibility," Bob agreed. "We'll have to take this to the lab to have it tested for fingerprints and possible DNA. These pictures were probably intended to cause serious discomfort for Cody. But, they aren't so much evidence of crimes as they are hints of his activities." He pointed to the images of Dillon. "None of these photos are perfect identifications of Cody. Mostly, they create an *impression* that this is Cody because of the kind of clothing he's wearing and the way he stands."

Bob turned the photos over and looked at the backs of each, searching for any additional information he could find. "Over all, this package makes me much more curious about the photographer than about Cody. Although, we will make sure to take a closer look at his business practices based on this little gallery." He placed the pictures back in the box. "It would be satisfying to find one clear fingerprint somewhere among these."

"My prints will be on them," I reminded him. "I didn't realize what it was until I opened it."

"That's okay. You can come in to the station tomorrow morning and let us take your prints for elimination purposes. Thanks for bringing this to us, Janna. It may be just what we need."

15

RANCHO VALLE DE LA TRUENO

January—February

A FEW DAYS AFTER THE TURN OF THE YEAR, I was stuffing whites into the washing machine and thinking about the general rhythm of life around me. People tend to begin new projects when a new year starts. It just seems like a good time to start fresh, or even to work a new slant on an old problem.

For example, Theo had been talking about making a second pasture out at the ranch in a small southeastern valley area. He'd figured out how to make a road back there, and how to clear a pasture area, keeping the major trees and characteristics of the land that make it beautiful. The project had been rattling around in his mind for months. He had planned what had to be done first, then second, and so on, but many other things had demanded his attention, and the project had been put off. Today, with the exuberance of January enthusiasm, Theo, Matt, and Hernando were finally going at it by clearing a road that wound past our campsite, and swung around the mountain-bearing south into the small, pasture-sized valley just beyond.

It was a project that Theo could work on as his schedule allowed, because there was no immediate push. As our animal population was growing, eventually we would need the space. Christian had been talking about getting a horse since he had been spending so much time at the ranch, and I was pretty sure that Hernando was saving his money for a horse of his own. In this area, horses are plentiful and easy to acquire at low prices.

With the new pasture, we'd be able to move the llamas to the new space and have more room for horses in the original fenced field by the manager's cabin. Or it could be we'd do it the other way around and the horses would go to the new pasture. However it ended up, it would alter things at the ranch, and could affect how the animals were handled. A January change.

Another person who was changing things was Christian's friend, Michelle. She had improved her health enough since the accident that she felt she could go on with her education plans. She was moving to Tucson, Arizona, to attend the winter-spring semester at the University of Arizona, working toward a degree in electrical engineering. It was wonderful that she had pulled herself back up, and was moving forward with her own new beginning. Now we would only see her at vacation times. She and Christian had been dating, but it was hard to tell if there was anything other than friendship there. Distance could cause re-evaluation.

At home, Gwen and her fellow band members had decided that they needed to concentrate more on their song-writing. The plan was to meet at our house on Sunday afternoons and think up new song themes. They would toss words around until they became stanzas, and hopefully a song would emerge with the addition of more stanzas. It seemed like good experience, no matter how it developed.

I settled down in the comfortable blue chair and opened my notebook on the children to the section I had set aside for Gwen. I would probably never have to be concerned about Gwen taking good advantage of educational opportunities. She was a natural executive. Those things were good. The problem was that having executive tendencies caused her to want to manage other people's lives for them. It was pretty weird having to remind myself, occasionally, that *Gwen* was the child and *I* was the mom—not the other way around. She had methods of guiding others in a direction she wanted them to go that were sometimes subtle. From time to time I had to shake myself to remember just who should be doing the leading here.

But, I had been Gwen's mom for a long time, and I understood her. She could see logical necessity, faster and more often, than the average person—though, obviously an eleven year old girl still had a lot to learn. And it upset her to see a friend moving on a path that could lead to trouble. Being very compassionate, she often tried to *fix* things for others. But, Gwen and I had talked about how people learn— through solving their own problems and mistakes—and how important it was to let friends do their own thinking.

I said, "Would you be able to do multiplication easily if you hadn't memorized the tables yourself, and then practiced the problems? No one else could have done that for you. Other things that people need to solve aren't much different than that. It comes down to this: The more you practice your skills and do your own thinking, the more able you are to handle the next problem that comes along."

She could understand that, but it was tough to mind her own concerns when she just *knew* that she could solve the other person's trouble with no difficulty. Fortunately, her friend, Christina had a very strong personality of her own. She insisted on equal standing with Gwen from day one of their friendship. Christina knew how to deal with Gwen.

But Tiffany didn't. Tiffany was still learning how to make friends, while keeping her own personality intact. I knew that Gwen was very tempted by her new friend's insecurity. Gwen's natural instinct was to try to make things okay for Tiffany. I would guess that a lot more than song writing would happen at our house on Sunday afternoons.

I wrote in the notebook: *Point out to Gwen her successes in her relationships, and how those were achieved.*

That evening Christian, John, and Travis had participated in the Winter Challenge at the

Main Street Dojo. Even though Michelle's dojo days were probably finished for now, Christian had become interested in sharpening old skills to be in better physical shape for his search and rescue work. So the boys all went together. Theo and Rosalie went with them to watch the testing and provide moral support.

The idea of the Challenge was a formalized testing of the students' current levels of skill in the martial art they were training for karate and judo. Sensei Jim Kowalski considered Challenge Testing as an important way to know what a student still needed to practice before attaining the next level.

Rosalie sat with me in the studio afterwards talking about the evening. She had changed to pajamas and was holding a cup of cocoa. "Travis is elated because he earned a yellow belt. He'd participated in two other Challenges, and finally made it up to the next level. You should have seen how happy his dad was."

"Important progress," I agreed. "How did John do? Did he pass his Challenge?"

"Yup. He was jumping all over the place on the way home, totally jazzed. His instructor tied his green belt on him, and John just grinned. Right away he started talking about the requirements for the red belt."

She went on to say, "I met a really interesting woman while I was there. Her name is Rebecca Kowalski, Sensei Jim's sister. I've seen her at school, because she's an accounting instructor, but, never had her as a teacher." She arranged herself more comfortably in the chair. "Anyway, I had a chance to talk with her before the Belt Ceremony. She's interested in fabric crafts, too, and specializes in quilts that are like photographs of a scene. I'm sure you've seen when they use all kinds of tiny patterned squares of fabric, and light and dark pieces—like pixels on a monitor screen—and then you stand back and can see it's the Eiffel Tower, or a portrait of George Washington."

I laughed, enjoying her description.

"Well, Rebecca does stuff like that. She says she programs information about her quilt idea into her computer—she's also great at computer stuff—and it figures out how she has to put the squares together to make the quilt picture. It's a painstaking thing, and she says she spends about a year on each quilt. It's how she relaxes." She tilted her head back to drink the rest of her cocoa.

On Friday morning the following week, Theo didn't have any appointments, so we decided to exercise our horses while riding out on the Big Ranch. A thousand yards down the road from where I had crawled through the barbed wire one fateful day last fall, was a gate. Theo dismounted to open the gate. I walked our horses through the opening, and Theo closed the gate behind us.

Beyond was a dirt truck trail, probably for doing fence repairs, putting out salt licks, checking cattle tanks for water, and other unending chores that I was beginning to understand were required maintenance on a cattle ranch. We rode along at a leisurely pace down the road for about an hour, looking over more acres of land we had never reached when we were inspecting the Big Ranch prior to the transfer of title.

The land rolled away endlessly, grasses rippled in waves of new green in the wind, almost like a tide coming in and going out. Every so often there would be a swale where trees would grow around a wet-season creek bed. At this time of year the streams all had a small amount of water in them, and their banks were muddy. Deep hoof prints sunk into the mud where cattle had come down to drink. And among the cattle tracks could be seen those of deer, lynx, mustang, coyote, and mountain lions.

On the way back to the pasture, where we dropped the horses off, Theo and I talked of Rosalie's plans for her business. Since their meeting at the Dojo, Rosalie had met Rebecca Kowalski for lunch a few times to discuss business possibilities. They both thought their personalities had clicked and that they might work well together as a partnership.

Rebecca was in her late twenties and had taught accounting at Rosalie's school for several years. She loved the sort of business Rosalie proposed to begin, and she also thought Rosalie's business plan was good. Rebecca's idea was that she would handle the books and other related portions of the business. She would kick in her half of the money for start up and continuing expenses of the business. But, she intended to keep teaching in the evenings as an income cushion for the first few years of business, and also because she just enjoyed teaching. She felt that this way she would have the best of both worlds.

I told Theo about this development, and he thought it sounded pretty good. "How about Rosalie's part in it? Has that been discussed?"

I said, "Based on a talk you and she had a while back. Rosalie says she has offered to contribute her own half to the business matching what Rebecca puts in. Her personal efforts would center around running the day to day business of the store, doing creative displays, and going on buying trips. Although, she said she wanted Rebecca along for her input on the buying. And Rosalie says she wants to continue taking business courses in the evenings, to fill in any places where she feels lacking."

Theo nodded. "Have they picked out where they want to set up shop?"

"They haven't actually started looking, yet. They've only just decided that they might make all of this work. But, Rosalie mentioned that they would probably rent a storefront in an older building on Main Street to keep their expenses manageable."

Theo looked thoughtful. "Sounds practical as far as it goes. If they have the right location, work really hard, and make the right buying decisions, they have a good chance of making a go of it. I'll have another talk with her about some solid plans."

"On another subject," I said, "Micah and Sonya have to return home at the end of the month."

"Time sure goes by fast," said Theo. "Seems like they just got here. Micah approved the changes in the plans he suggested for the caretaker cabin and museum beside the Mesa. That's another thing we have to get started at some point."

We directed our horses single file across a creek bed and back up the other side. "Has anything been done about Kolichiyaw, the skunk, or any other wild animals visiting the Mesa House?" I asked.

"I brought up the question to Jeb Hazard to get his opinion of what would be least damaging to the site. He's studying the question and will get back to me."

We rode back under the Cornbread Mesa Ranch sign and returned our mounts to their pasture. Waving to Matt, we climbed into the Ranger and headed for home. As Theo pulled into our driveway, his mind had turned to other subjects. "Have you noticed that Christian is dating other girls since Michelle left for school?"

I said, "I don't think he and Michelle put any conditions on their dating while living in different states. I know he's been making the acquaintance of girls in his Search and Rescue crew."

Theo looked amused. "He's been pretty bold since Michelle's been gone. I don't think he's ever dated anyone else before she left, has he?"

"No," I admitted. "He didn't need to do any dating in high school because of his readily available girl friendships at that time. And then he decided Michelle would be safe to date during the latter half of his senior year. But, now it has occurred to him that he likes to take girls out, and Michelle isn't around. So, he's been looking for girls he has something in common with. After all, how many girls can there be like Michelle, who can take apart a truck engine and put it back together with no left over parts?" We got out of the Ranger and walked to the front door.

Theo laughed and shook his head. "Christian's love life has always been a mystery to me. At least he isn't getting girls pregnant."

"Amen to that!" I said.

On the morning of the last Monday in January, Bob Taggert knocked on my door after the children were off to school. I invited him in for coffee and he followed me into the kitchen. I poured him a cup and put it at his usual place. He looked like he had been up all night and needed sustenance. I popped a couple bagels in the toaster.

As he sat there quietly drinking coffee, I asked, "You want to tell me what's on your mind? Or would you rather eat bagels and tell me later?"

Bob looked back at me with a tired expression. "The information won't improve with aging, and there's no way to soft-peddle it. So brace yourself ... Dillon Cody is dead."

I sat down with a thump and stared at him.

Bob stood, picked up the cup of tea I had forgotten on the counter, and put it in front of me. Then he pulled his bagels out of the toaster, put them on a plate, and buttered them. He brought the bagels and a refill of coffee over to the table and sat down again. "Loretta May says she knocked on his door all weekend and couldn't get him to come to the door. The car was in the drive, so she knew he was there. She got worried and called the landlord, who came and opened the door. Together they found Dillon in his bed, dead. There was a bottle of pills on his night table that might have done the job if he took enough of them. We don't have the medical examiner's report, yet, but it looks like suicide."

"Why?" I asked. I couldn't imagine anyone that I would less expect to commit suicide. Dillon was always so self-protective and self-centered. I drank some tea to put warmth back in my body. I felt cold and dismal. I wouldn't exactly miss Dillon. But, I didn't wish him dead, either. No matter who it is, it's always sad when someone dies, unnaturally. Until death, a person still has a chance to pull things together in his life and make it better. Death ends that chance.

Bob shook his head. "No note," he said. "Maybe he had a guilty conscience? Who knows why people do this."

I looked at him. "Do you really think he killed himself?"

"That's what the death scene looks like from the evidence, and that's probably how it will be recorded unless the medical examiner comes up with something else."

I drank some of my tea. Bob ate his bagel and drank more coffee.

Finally, he said, "I'm not gonna make waves, but I plan to keep my eyes and ears open, just in case there is another explanation. There have been a lot of unexplained deaths, and they have all been called suicides."

I nodded. "I figured you would."

The phone rang and I stepped across the counter to get it. It was Gram. "Janna, is Myrtle ... there? Can't find her. Didn't sleep ... in her bed ... last night. I'm worried."

"No, Gram." I said, feeling concern rise inside. "I haven't seen her. Are you sure she didn't go back to Florida?"

Gram said, "Her things are still ... in her bedroom ... in the cottage."

"And she couldn't go anywhere without her clothes," I finished the thought for her. "Listen Gram, I'll see if I can find her. I know some of her friends, and I'll call around to see if she spent the night with one of them. I'll call back in an hour to let you know if I find out anything." I hung up.

Bob lifted his eyebrows at me, and I said, "Aunt Myrtle is missing." I began to page through the little book of phone numbers we keep by the counter phone. As I was about to dial a number, the doorbell rang. I put the phone down to answer the door. Bob followed on my heels.

I opened the door to find Aunt Myrtle standing on the step, looking very wobbly. Bob and I both took an arm and led her to a chair in the family room.

"Oh, thank you my dears. You are so kind." And after saying that she put her head back against the chair and fell asleep. Completely out.

I called Gram and told her to call off the search. "Why is she there? And where was she … all night?"

I explained that Aunt Myrtle had fallen asleep before she could tell me anything. "I'll quiz her as soon as she wakes up, Gram. She looks exhausted, so I better let her sleep." When Gram agreed that that was best, I told her I'd bring Aunt Myrtle back home as soon as she seemed able to move around. "If necessary, we can keep her here for a while if she's sick. But don't worry. We'll take good care of her."

"Thank you, dear. Wonder what on earth … happened to her?"

"I'll call as soon as I have any information, Gram." She said she'd wait for my call, and hung up.

Bob and I went back to the kitchen and let my great aunt doze. "What do you think?" asked Bob.

I shrugged, bewildered. "I have no idea, and neither does Gram."

We drank more coffee and tea, waiting for Aunt Myrtle to resurface. Normally she took a nap or two each day. I was keeping my fingers crossed that the snoozing was something like that. She had just gotten extra tired and needed a nap. I spoke my thoughts out loud to Bob.

He said, "I would have thought that she may have been drugged. But, we can't jump to conclusions until we hear her story." I could tell that he didn't want to leave until the mystery got solved. It was an odd thing to happen during the same period of time that Dillon passed on. I had almost forgotten about that with the new concerns about Aunt Myrtle.

After a while we heard a cough from the family room and went immediately to check on my aunt. She was sitting with her eyes open, blinking. "Why, how did I get here?"

"That's what we were wondering, Aunt Myrtle," I said. "Don't you remember arriving at our front door?"

She sat and blinked some more. Bob sat with her while I went in the kitchen to get her a cup of tea. I handed her the tea, which she took eagerly. "Thank you, my dear. I am so thirsty." She drank it quickly and then looked over at me.

"Could you take me home now, dear? I think I need to get to my little bed and take a nap. This has been a very nice visit, but I'm quite tired."

Bob took her arm to help her up, and the three of us got into his police cruiser and headed toward Lakc Mirage. Bob had carefully settled Aunt Myrtle in the backseat, where she leaned her head back and promptly went to sleep again.

As Bob started the car, I said quietly, "I don't know what to think. She acts like she is exhausted. But, she doesn't seem to remember coming to my house. Is that drugs or old age catching up with her?"

Bob shook his head. "I'd like to suggest that she go to Pomerado Hospital for drug testing and general evaluation, but I don't want to upset her."

"I wouldn't want that, either. Perhaps, we can talk to Granddad and make sure he knows what has happened as far as we know it, so that he can gently find out anything she might recall later. Granddad doesn't like unanswered questions, either."

Bob agreed that was probably our best course. When we got to my grandparents driveway, Granddad was there and helped me wake Aunt Myrtle enough to get her into the cottage and into her bedroom. She laid down on the bed right away. I pulled up her comforter and we left the cottage.

The three of us talked in the drive for a few minutes, and I explained how confused Aunt Myrtle seemed to be. Granddad had already heard about the death of his next door neighbor, and I got the impression he, also, thought the coincidences were odd and uncomfortable. "I'll let you know if she has any information about where she's been or what happened to her," he said gravely. "In the meantime, the best thing is to let her rest." He gave me a warm hug, and left us to go into the house and talk to Grandma.

Bob drove me back home and dropped me off. Before he left, I promised I'd be in touch if I heard anything.

Later, in the wee hours of the morning, I found that I wasn't sleeping. I got up and went into the studio to write in my Journal. It was one of those nights. The kind of night that happens when too many unexplained things happen at once. My subconscious gets disturbed and wants me to wake up and figure it out. I had no idea what was going on, but it was necessary to calm my mind. So, I wrote everything I knew about Dillon's passing and about Aunt Myrtle's strange incident. Then I wrote: *I always think of January as a month of beginnings. I guess there are endings, as well.*

A couple days later it was February. Thunder rumbled in the clouds as I sat at the kitchen table eating a bowl of Manhattan-style clam chowder, while I was filling out a shopping list. I always did a major grocery shopping trip at the beginning of each month. That way, I had only to get a few items as the rest of the month progressed. Not that I was going to do any shopping that day.

February had come like a lion roaring, with unusual lightning zapping the sky, mountaintops, and any trees that dared stand too tall. Our backyard neighbors had one of their great oaks split down the middle by a powerful electric stroke that was so loud, everyone on the block thought there had been an explosion. In this area of the world there are few thunder storms, as compared with many other places. However, one of those rare crashing storms from the Gulf of Mexico had blown into San Diego County in the last couple days. The winds were high, blowing rain up under the umbrella and down one's neck. There was no way to stay dry when leaving shelter. Uncomfortable.

That morning I had driven the kids to school, as usual, on days like these. Christina Johnson had been a passenger, as well. Stacy and I had an arrangement when the weather was really bad. I took the kids to school and she picked them up. Now I was inside watching Mother Nature flash and crash.

My sweet husband—who had so thoughtfully made a fire before leaving that morning—had an appointment that couldn't be put off down in Escondido. He had let the dogs in to dry off by the fire. Soon they had fully cooked themselves on one side and turned around to do the other. Athena, the "momma cat" lay comfortably soaking up warmth between the dogs. The kittens snoozed with her until they got too warm, then moved to a position away from direct heat, and back again when they wanted to cook some more. Every so often I had to disturb them by adding another log.

I wasn't very interested in painting. Instead, I took advantage of the outside display of weather. Wandering from window to window all around the house, I directed my camera lens at the light show flickering across the ominous dark sky. Trees were bending, and whipping around in the wind. Light objects—papers, toys, leaves, twigs, garbage can lids—sailed past the window in the direction of the wind. I sketched impressions of the passage of the storm—dark shadows, the glistening street running with water. Many of our Texas umbrella tree branches were all over the front yard. Sudden flashes caused stark illumination in unexpected places. Birds hunkered down on branches with feathers fluffed out. The mood of the storm was gloomy, but exciting. Wonderful stuff for paintings, if it could it could be captured.

The energy and clash of the weather, reminded me of how fortunate we were to have warm, dry shelter. The roof over one's head doesn't have to be very good, at all, to appreciate its presence on such a day. Even caves must look pretty good when the weather becomes overbearing. It's the contrast that makes us value what we have.

After tiring of peering out at the storm, my energies turned to more cooking. Earlier I had made a big pot of clam chowder. And now a kettle of navy bean, onion and ham soup simmered on the stovetop. Good amounts of hot, satisfying food paid dividends of appreciation from my family in foul weather.

As the afternoon moved on, I made an apple cobbler for that evening's dessert. When the kids and their friends came in the door, I was cutting up celery and carrot sticks to set next to a bowl of oranges for snacking. "Take your wet things out to the laundry and hang them on the rack to drip," I said.

John peeled an orange as he glanced past the counter into the family room. The animals were still zonked out by the fire. He said, "This is a wet dog, day, I guess. I'm glad I'm not a wild animal today. There must be wet critters all over the place."

Gwen and Tiffany heard John's remark and looked at each other. "Wet dog day," repeated Gwen. "That sounds like the title of a song." They quickly conferred with Christina, grabbed their snacks and went into the dining room to sit around the table and compose lyrics. A lot of odd statements had become parts of songs in recent weeks.

John and Travis glanced at each other, shrugged, and didn't say anything. There was no understanding girls. "It's a good thing you have those three-sided shelters for the horses and llamas out at the ranch," said Travis.

John nodded, crunching on celery. "Yeah. The llamas all snuggle together on bad days. They're still going to be a little damp, though. The wind is blowing the rain from all sides today."

A bit later, I was taking cheese biscuits out of the oven—seemed a good accompaniment for soup—when Theo blew in the door. By the time I had tucked the biscuits in a napkin-covered basket, he had shed his wet outerwear and emerged from the bedroom in dry sweats.

Reaching to an upper shelf in the cupboard, he brought out two wine glasses and filled them with Chablis. He handed me a glass and pointed toward the studio. Theo likes to sit in the quiet corner of the studio with me on trying days, and wind down for a few minutes before supper. Since supper was basically ready, I had the luxury of relaxing with him while he told me about his day.

He took a long sip of wine. "You should be glad you weren't out in it today. Lot of trees down. Traffic is snarled by accidents. Many roads are flooded, not to mention whole areas of land. I was lucky to have made it home without problems."

"Were you able to do all that you planned, in spite of the rain?"

"For the most part. I met the client and showed him my estimate for the draining and treatment of soil and run-off from his mines. He liked the methods I recommended, and they fit his time frame."

He sipped more wine. "I've been thinking of finding a new name for the Big Ranch. Something more interesting than Carrington Ranch. The current name is merely the name of the last owner. So it's not even historical. It might be good to have a memorable name for advertising purposes, especially if we plan to attract tourists. What do you think?"

"A more appealing name would be better. Did you have any ideas?" I finished my wine.

"Nothing that sounds right. I think it should be related to what the land is used for or its location. A name that would be naturally associated with a large ranch."

I stretched my imagination out thinking of ways we had talked about using the land. The buffalo was a compelling and romantic mental picture, since we were thinking of possibly bringing in buffalo later on. Some name that would, maybe, bring to mind the free spirit of the buffalo of the old west. I mentioned some of these thoughts aloud.

Theo and I were still musing over the possibilities for a name when we all sat down to supper a short while later. He introduced the problem to the children to take advantage of any sudden inspirations they might have.

Christian offered, "Wild Buffalo Ranch. That's simple, though I suppose you couldn't call them wild, exactly."

"How about The Ranch of the White Buffalo," said Gwen. "Of course, I don't know if any of them would actually be white."

Christian said, "I think white buffaloes are extremely rare."

"It would be really cool if we got one, though," said John. "I think you just have to wait and see if any of your animals have an albino baby." John had been studying breeding since he had acquired his llamas.

Rosalie had been reading up on the importance of buffalo in historical Indian life ever since Theo had mentioned the possibility of grazing the animals on the Big Ranch. She commented, "A few books poetically mention, *'the thundering herds that covered the plains.'* Could we use that image somehow?"

"Thundering Herd Ranch ... Thundering Buffalo Ranch," said Theo as he tried out a few versions of Rosalie's idea.

"How about Thunder Valley Ranch?" I suggested. "The ranch is located in a wide valley. So that would also include a physical feature of the ranch in its name."

"And the first part of the name can mean thundering buffalo herds or thundering weather. It allows more latitude, but it's still an interesting name. I think I like it," said Theo. "In looking over the old maps when the Spanish were still here, I noticed it was called Rancho Valle de la Trueno. 'Trueno' means 'Thunder.' So, your idea of naming it Thunder Valley Ranch may even resemble its historical name.

We determined that everyone was to ruminate over the name, Thunder Valley Ranch, for a couple weeks, and maybe come up with something even better. But, I noticed the kids began to refer to it as Thunder Valley Ranch when they weren't using our nickname the *Big Ranch.* Probably, no name changes would happen officially until the Morales' were gone, in any case.

As I stood to offer dessert to anyone interested, I felt little claws in my leg. Reaching down, I pulled Bast's small furry body into my arms. "We have warm apple cobbler with ice cream for dessert," I announced, handing the kitten off to Rosalie. She gathered up Cleopatra, as well, and put them back in the garage. Athena went along to watch over her charges.

Later, when I checked the studio to retrieve the wine glasses, I found all three cats asleep in my favorite blue chair. I could still hear the rain on the roof and the wind blowing in sudden gusts, but the cats didn't pay it any heed. They were all safe and dry. Nobody does warm and cozy like a cat.

16

BREAK THROUGHS

March/April

THE WHOLE MONTH OF FEBRUARY had been wet, and the memorial service held for Dillon Cody had set the mood for the later part of the month. We had attended as a family, along with other long time members of the community. A duty to the deceased and to the living. Now the sun had come out again. Things that had come to a dead stop last month, now began to move again. Or maybe the return of the sunshine was such a relief that we just wanted to think everything was coming together.

But, some things were actually on track. After diligently checking for a few months, with no success, for notices posted about lost Siamese kittens, I finally made a vet appointment to put them through their little operations in March.

Another sign of things becoming unstuck: Rosalie had quietly given Matt his promise ring back, after realizing he had been casually seeing other girls. He hadn't precisely been dating them, but it had become obvious that he wasn't going to be happy with an arrangement with Rosalie where he wasn't the boss. So, he had been checking out the field.

When Matt discovered that there were girls who would be pleased with what many see as a more traditional way of life, he and Rosalie had a talk. The upshot was that they decided to just be friends. I think both of them were relieved when this painful decision was finally made. It was sad that things didn't work out, but now they could individually move on to whatever came next.

Rosalie was so busy with Rebecca in putting their new crafts business together, while continuing to work and go to school, that she didn't have a lot of time to mourn the lost relationship with Matt. In any case, she didn't seem to lack for interested males to take her out for a fun evening when she had one free. I noticed the Forest Service rep taking up some of Rosalie's time again, but she wasn't confining herself to any one person.

There was one thing that gave everyone a breather last month. Aunt Myrtle went back to stay with Violet again to continue saving Florida's fresh water. Although Aunt Myrtle never did remember what had happened to her before she appeared on our doorstep in that strange way in January, her health didn't seem to have suffered, and so she saw no reason why she shouldn't continue on with her re-education mission.

I continued to note, as I flipped the calendar pages, each month, that we hadn't seen or heard from Red Thunder for quite a while. He had warned me that it could be a long time before he resurfaced in Coyote Canyon from wherever he had gone for the DEA, but as the time lengthened my uneasiness grew.

I was sitting in the studio thinking all these thoughts and writing in my Journal one March evening, after supper, when Christian sat down in the other chair. I looked at him and smiled.

Every time I look at my oldest son I realize how much he is maturing, physically as well as mentally. He had lost a lot of his young teenage-boy look and was beginning to take on the appearance of a man. His blonde good looks had always been an asset for him, but as a mature man he was going to be a person who would be noticed. Fortunately, Christian didn't have an arrogant personality. He was too absorbed with figuring out how to do all the things he wanted to do without over-taxing himself. His lazy streak had made him an efficiency expert when it came to chores and amusements, alike. He was my laid back son.

"Mom, can Don Schneider and I live out at the ranch cabin this summer like we did last year? I mean, Matt will be up at that special buffalo ranch this summer, so I kind of figured maybe Don and I could live there and help Hernando with the chores and stuff."

We hadn't advertised around our purchase of the Big Ranch. But, Theo had told Matt, since he had a need to know as our ranch manager, and we might eventually have quite a lot of back and forth with animals and people. Part of the information Theo passed on was the possibility of our grazing buffalo at the Big Ranch. This idea captured Matt's imagination, and he was determined to learn about the handling of buffalo. After doing a little research, he asked Theo if he could take the summer off from Cornbread Mesa Ranch and work on the Denton Springs Buffalo Ranch north of us in Riverside

County. Apparently, they were willing to take agricultural students for the summer to help with their big buffalo herd, in exchange for a low wage, room and board, and experience working with the animals.

Matt aspired to be manager of our Big Ranch someday. Whether Matt would ever be experienced and knowledgeable enough to handle a job like that, we didn't know. But, it never hurts to get more experience and education toward your goals. So, Theo told him it was fine for him to go work with buffalo for the summer. However, Theo warned him that decisions for the future ranch manager position would depend on who was the best person to fill the job. That wouldn't necessarily be Matt.

I said to Christian, "I think your dad has it in mind for Hernando to be in charge as temporary manager for the summer. But, if you and Don want to stay out there to help out, I'm sure Hernando would be glad of your company. There are three bedrooms, so there's plenty of room." Christian actually got along better with Hernando than he did with Matt. Sometimes Christian and Matt rubbed each other the wrong way. But, Hernando had Christian's respect as soon as he realized how often Hernando had rescued me from threatening situations. As far as Christian was concerned, Hernando was *okay.*

"Cool. I'll tell Don. This'll be great." He remained in the chair and I understood that he had more to talk about. "So what do you think about men's baseball, Mom?"

"What are you asking?" I'm not much of a sports person, but I enjoy going to games where people I know are playing.

"I've been thinking about playing in the Men's Baseball League, but I don't know if I should take the time. My schedule is pretty full already."

"I think you should exercise your pitching arm. Hang around the baseball guys and watch them practice, and then see if it's something you want to do."

"Don plays on the team. I could go with him a couple times and meet the players." He nodded to himself. "Thanks Mom. I gotta go. I promised Ursula I'd meet her at the Pie Shop." He got up and left.

Ursula? Must be another girl from Search and Rescue.

Toward the end of March, Aunt Myrtle flew back into San Diego again. She was due to take some medical tests her doctor had scheduled, so she decided to stay for a couple weeks to enjoy the family. Of course, as usual, she wanted me to take her to see Loretta May DuBoise a couple days after she arrived.

Loretta May had begun catering pastry for restaurants and for people's parties since the last time we'd seen her. She had bounced back quickly after Dillon's death and opted to follow her dream of being a pastry chef. She was very glad to see us, and we were immediately seated at her little table facing another amazing spread of her delectable creations.

That day Loretta May was dressed in a shimmery beige-gold dress accessorized with a silky matching scarf tied in her hair trailing over her shoulder and down her arm. Around her waist was a spotless white eyelet lace apron.

Both Aunt Myrtle and I remarked on her creative presentation—pastries in the shape of little colorful birds and flowers—and the always memorable flavors and textures. Loretta May glowed as she we praised her pastry art. "I have a *special* peche flambé I've been experimenting with and you just *have* to test it for me."

She darted back into her small kitchen and returned with an elegant tower of puff pastry built over her homemade peach ice cream. Over the top of this gargantuan sweet treasure she drizzled a fine peach liqueur. Then, with a flourish, she lit the liqueur with a match and the tower blazed like the Fourth of July. Unfortunately, her attractive scarf trailed briefly in the flaming liquid. Instantly fire traveled up her scarf to her very flammable hair-sprayed locks.

Both Aunt Myrtle and I gasped with horror. Loretta May screamed, and instantly Aunt Myrtle was galvanized into action. She picked up the nearest cloth, which was the tablecloth and whipped it off the table, throwing it over Loretta May's head to smother the flames, while I dialed 911.

It was a sad fact that, although Loretta May was shielded from the more severe burns that might have happened, her lovely antique china, heirlooms from her mother and grandmother, crashed all over the floor and shattered in a hideous mess of pastry and fractured porcelain.

Aunt Myrtle and I did our best to clean up what we could while the paramedics took Loretta May away, but the room was going to take a professional cleaning. And nothing was ever going to restore the delicate china to its former glory.

I had a feeling that perhaps the incident spelled the end of Aunt Myrtle's friendship with Loretta May. The look Loretta May gave Aunt Myrtle as the paramedics took the injured woman away, was not one of love. I was guessing that Loretta May might hold Aunt Myrtle responsible for the loss of her china, even though the dear elderly lady may have saved her from much more serious injury. The problem with Aunt Myrtle was that her rescues often came at great cost to the recipient. It was, therefore, sometimes difficult for them to recall the benefits of Aunt Myrtle's aid. Most people eventually paid a price when they dealt with Aunt Myrtle.

On the last day of March, just before Aunt Myrtle left to go back to Florida following the medical tests, she had found a smashed crystal vase of flowers on the front step of her cottage and recognized it as one she'd sent to Loretta May. This did not bode well for their friendship.

On April Fool's Day, I went into the Indian Heritage Store for a couple sketch pads. Amanda was at the front counter effectively displaying the wares of her Indian jewelry artists in her usual way. But, something seemed a little different. I studied her for a moment to figure out what had changed.

It was the top she was wearing. It wasn't black and it was cut higher in the neckline than usual. Though still alluring, it no longer broadcast seduction. For heaven's sake! Amanda had become more *modest* in her costuming! The beautiful silver collar she wore—inlaid with coral, mother-of-pearl, and green turquoise—lay on a fitted sage green silk top. Her attractive figure was still apparent, but no lavish amount of skin was showing. Rather, the overall effect was rich and refined.

Refined. I looked around the store to see if anything else was affected by this change. Nope. Apparently a personal change had occurred. I decided I liked this new look much better. The old enticing black top could make a person forget that Amanda was a lot more than just a sexy woman. The way she now appeared didn't deny her appeal, but presented her as an attractive *person*. Definitely an improvement.

"Stop staring at me," said Amanda self-consciously. "Is my hair mussed?" She checked with her hand to make sure her abundant dark hair hadn't come loose from the worked silver barrette.

"Sorry," I said. "I was just stunned by your new image. You look great!"

"Thanks." She smiled and held out her left hand for me to inspect a handsome diamond engagement ring.

I hugged her warmly. "Congratulations!"

"Kyle gave it to me on Sunday, and then took me shopping for new clothes." She ran her hand over her new top. "He said it bothered him that my old black tops revealed so much. But, he didn't feel he had the right to request I make a change until I accepted his ring." She grinned happily at me. "He wants to keep me to himself, 'under wraps' he said. So, I have changed my display costume to please him, because he has certainly pleased me."

"It's a good change for you. You look prettier dressed this way." Which was saying something. "When do you plan to get married?"

"We thought October would be good. That way our families will be able to attend the wedding. Our relatives are scattered all over the United States and Mexico. Anyway, I like romantic autumn weddings." She hugged herself. "I can hardly believe it's real."

"I'm happy for you," I said, remembering the years that Amanda had searched for a man who would be a genuine partner in marriage. When I thought about my first sight of Kyle, ranting in poor Stevette Strike's driveway after his car had been rammed, I realized that you never really knew the potential of other people. I was glad that things had worked out so well for Amanda and Kyle.

"Me too," she laughed. "Neither of us has been married before, so everything's new. But we decided we want to get a house. Probably somewhere in town to be near the store and handy to the station." She shook her wrists and said, "I'm so happy I feel like I have champagne in my blood!"

We discussed other exciting aspects of Amanda and Kyle's plans, and then I collected the sketchpads I'd come in to get, paid for them, and left the store. As I got into the Highlander, I saw Hernando coming out of the Horse's Tale next door with a nice saddle in his arms. He threw it in the back of his truck and then headed down the road toward the ranch. It had been his dream to have his own horse, and it appeared he had bought one. Odd that he wouldn't use one of the extra saddles in the tack room. Guess he wanted something special. I pulled out of my parking place and drove toward home.

I was feeling really lifted after talking to Amanda, and my attention was caught by the beauty of the day. Thoughts of going home to paint didn't appeal. Instead, the mountains beckoned. April was one of the loveliest times of the year. Mother Nature was trying on her whole wardrobe this month. Every plant that had ever considered blooming strutted its stuff in April. The sun came out daily, sometimes interspersed with rain. Big puffy white clouds often towered in the sky just for show. Everything looked bright, clean and newly refurbished from the mountaintops to the valleys. Birds flitted everywhere calling and screeching at each other, answering the demands of hungry offspring. In southern California, Mother Nature had a busy April schedule.

I stopped home, ate a sandwich, and changed to sketching clothes. Grabbing my pack, I jumped into the Highlander. An idea that I had begun working on a couple years before had come back into my mind.

One day during the summer some time ago, when things had been really difficult and I seriously needed distraction, I had scaled a rare, easily-climbable tree from the stand of California Sycamores that line the wet-season creek running alongside the road by the ranch pasture. The idea had been to sit up in the tree and observe various views that could be seen through a framing of leaves. It now seemed an idea that could be taken further. I wasn't interested in sycamores that day, but was intrigued by the fresh new leaves that were coming out on many of the other trees. That spring-leaf color could be worth capturing as a frame around the landscape beyond.

At the ranch, I saddled up Lion and began searching for the right tree. The problem with trees, I realized, was that you couldn't count on any assistance from them. Many of the most beautiful trees were unwelcoming to the climber. In addition, when one takes into account the limitations of a fifty-one-year-old, somewhat arthritic, un-athletic woman, the difficulties in choosing a climbing tree begin to mount.

Nevertheless, I was determined to find one tree I could scale without an insurmountable risk. I had done it once before. It should be possible to do it again. Think positively.

Eventually, I ended up in the little meadow by the old house ruin. Big old Live Oaks shaded parts of the meadow there. But, no way could I walk up to the base of any of those trees and begin climbing. Some of the branches were sufficiently low, but they weren't regularly spaced enough to give the stepladder effect I needed. Yet, as I inspected the position of one of the oaks, the thought came, "Why *climb* it?"

I dismounted and left Lion, reins hanging down, to snack on the fresh green grasses all around. Carefully following my eye along the horizontal spread of oak branches, I noted that it nearly ran into the side of the mountain. This was a very convenient happenstance. I removed the pack from Lion's saddle and slipped it onto my back. Then, I turned to spy out the best place where branch met mountainside.

Carefully, I began my scrabble over rocks and boulders—keeping alert for rattlesnakes—staying with the easiest route, until I reached the thick oak branch. Boosting myself onto the branch, I proceeded to scoot sideways along it—sitting—until I was about halfway out from the trunk of the massive tree. The ground was then about twenty feet below me.

From inside the foliage of the tree, I peered through thousands of small, new green, prickly leaves amongst the older, dark green ones. The tree is called a *Live Oak* because it never loses all of its leaves at the same time. It sheds leaves year-round and regrows new ones constantly; however, the tree still has more new growth in the spring than at other times.

After removing my pack to sling it over a nearby branch, I looked around at holes in the leaf masses, revealing scenes in the meadow and beyond. Lion was visible grazing lazily on the grass a little distance away, next to a couple bushes of beautiful Mountain Lilac. I quickly snapped several photos at different focal lengths. Then I rapid-sketched color details of the scene with pastels. The holly-like leaves made a handsome frame. Just as I finished, Lion moved to another spot where he wasn't as visible.

Next, I looked to the west, and through the leaves saw Table Rock—a favorite boulder that had hosted many impromptu picnics—and the Big Ranch spreading out down in the valley. At this angle, several old bundles of acorns became part of the frame around the scene.

I continued taking photos and drawing details until I felt I had exhausted the potential of my perch in the tree. Time to ease my way back down the branch to the mountainside. Packing my stuff back into the pack, I slipped it on my back.

Now to get myself out of the tree. I heard a snort beneath the tree and realized that Lion was telling me to hurry up. I called to him, "Hold on, Lion. I'm coming down."

I leaned forward a bit to see if I could locate him through the leaves. Unfortunately, I had misjudged how far I could lean with a backpack strapped on, without undermining my position on the branch. As I leaned forward, the slight momentum carried me further than intended. I felt myself losing secure contact with my seat on the branch, and knew I was about to launch out into space. Frantically, I looked for another branch to grasp in the available split second before I was no longer supported by anything.

During the last possible instant of time before crashing to the ground twenty feet below, I managed to grab a much smaller and weaker branch. I clung to it as though wrapped around a pole pointing now at the ground. The small branch was in distress, having not been created to handle the weight of a woman and her backpack.

The dipping of the branch brought me beneath the canopy of leaves, so that I could clearly see the ground and Lion standing there with grass in his mouth, watching me. "Lion!" I gasped. "Come here, Lion." I clicked my tongue in the familiar way I used when I wanted him to get into position for me to mount him. Of course, things were a little different now. Normally I wasn't hanging from a frail tree limb. He continued to munch and look at me considering the problem. I could tell that he was wondering what he needed to do to get his carrot.

Horses don't normally do unique and complicated problems well. Lion loved me and would probably protect me if he saw me in clear danger. But, as far as he could see, hanging from a tree was something I had chosen to do.

"Come *on*, Lion." I emphasized my tone of distress. My horse tentatively moved a little closer as I heard the branch creak ominously. "Just a little further, boy. Come on now. I need your help."

Just as I felt the branch finally give way, Lion positioned himself underneath my feet. I dropped to the saddle, and was trying fairly successfully to balance so as to lower myself to a sitting position, when I felt hands grab me around the waist. Turning my head, I looked into the face of Red Thunder. My involuntary shout of surprise and relief at seeing him must have caused him to think I had damaged myself. He pulled me out of the saddle and put me on the grass, saying, "Are you hurt?"

"No. Not at all," I assured him. I threw my arms around him for a big hug. "I'm so *glad* you're home! We've been wondering and worrying about you."

He returned the hug, smiling, then sat back on the grass and shook his head. "Now I feel truly welcomed. It wouldn't be a normal home-coming if I didn't have to rescue you from something. I see you're hanging out in trees, again." He grinned. I was slowly getting the picture that some men really enjoy a rescue role, so I didn't argue with him.

"I see you've changed your look," I retorted. He had cut his hair short in a big city executive style and was wearing an expensive pearl gray dress shirt with dark slacks. No moccasins that day, but instead he was shod with polished wingtips that were very out of place in a mountain meadow. Because of his undercover work with the DEA, he often used clothing as camouflage. It was easy to see this last job had taken place in a big city and probably involved white collar and executive types.

On his previous job for the DEA, he had used his Indian background to blend into the Coyote Canyon area while tracking criminal activity at a meth-amphetamine lab. The Indian costuming may also have served him as another chance to try on his Native American identity. I've never known what he would wear if he were merely choosing clothes for personal style and comfort. Maybe he didn't know, either.

"Yeah," he said. "I was relieved to finish up that chore. It'll be good to wear jeans again. I haven't stopped at my apartment yet. I wanted to come directly here to breathe some sage and feel mountain air. But the first thing I saw after I parked the truck was your feet dangling from the tree, and Lion trying to figure out what to do. It was then that I realized things were back to normal." He laughed, his dark eyes lit with pleasure.

I glanced at the sun and realized it was nearly suppertime. "Come home and have dinner with us," I invited. "We are in need of your company after you've been gone so long."

He nodded agreement with a smile. "I haven't had a properly home-cooked meal since I left Coyote Canyon." He helped me back up on Lion.

I patted Lion's neck. "Good Boy. You get an *extra* carrot today." Red Thunder said he would be at the house in a short while. Lightly gathering up the reins, I rode out of the meadow and down the road. I took my time giving Lion his well-deserved treat, brushing him down while he munched, telling him what a splendid horse he was. He knew he was splendid, but he enjoyed the attention. He stuck his nose in my ear and snorted.

I got home before Red Thunder arrived, and stopped in the kitchen to tell Christian that we had company for dinner, then went into the bedroom to change. When I came out to the living room a half hour later dressed more presentably for dinner, Theo was talking to Red Thunder, and Christian announced that supper was ready.

Red Thunder had changed into what had always been his usual evening wear. Black jeans and a turquoise western shirt. Instead of wingtips he was wearing black moccasins. He looked more like we were used to seeing him. I wondered if he would keep his hair short or let it grow again.

As we sat down at the dining table, everyone welcomed him. We were all relieved that he had reappeared healthy and whole.

Rosalie came to the table late, since she had only returned minutes earlier from chores involving the new crafts store. She and Rebecca had spent the last week ordering inventory for their new business. When she rushed into the dining room, she hadn't noticed, at first, that Red Thunder had rejoined us. Her mind was far away on yarn qualities and colors. When he addressed a question to her about school, she looked stunned, obviously shocked at his sudden presence after months of nothing.

"Where have you been? Why didn't you *call* us and let us know you were okay?" she demanded.

Red Thunder looked at her, helpless with concern. "My job doesn't allow for any non-emergency communication with friends or family while I'm on a case. It has to do with the safety of everyone involved."

Rosalie looked away, and Theo eased the situation, saying, "You've missed a lot of changes around here." He went on to detail the creation of the new pasture for the llamas.

"Don't forget to tell him about the new ranch, Dad," said John, taking a large forkful of mashed potatoes. This was one of Christian's meatloaf and mashed potatoes nights as chef.

"New ranch?" A question formed in Red Thunder's eyes.

"Well," said Theo. "Do you remember that the Carrington Ranch next to Cornbread Mesa Ranch had been sitting for a while unofficially for sale? There didn't seem to be any takers, so Janna and I decided we'd sleep better if we made an offer, in lieu of some big developer coming along with an idea to turn all that wonderful pastureland into tiny lots with houses all jammed together."

I added, "We are still forming our plans for the property, but five hundred acres are going to the California College for Southwestern Agriculture, strictly limited to agricultural uses." I looked at Theo. "I suppose, for now, we'll leave the rest mostly as it is."

Theo nodded. "The Morales family—who manage the ranch—are staying a while longer, so we are merely continuing the former arrangement with them, until they retire to Mexico. After they're gone, we may try to develop a buffalo operation there."

"And there's the museum," said Christian. "Don't forget the cool Zorro house."

Theo told Red Thunder about tentative plans for the large Spanish house, and ended by saying, "But, none of it is going to happen very soon."

Red Thunder, obviously surprised, said, "It's beautiful land and I'm glad it won't be developed. Maybe you can find me a job there, since I just quit the DEA." We all exclaimed at his announcement, and he went on to say, "I had been thinking seriously about resigning before this last job, but didn't move quickly enough to avoid getting swept up in the operation just concluded. Now I'm a free agent, and ready to take a break. Maybe, just do sand paintings and jewelry for a month or two. Though, eventually, I'll have to figure out where I go from here with my career, such as it is."

Theo and I had known this was coming, because Red Thunder had talked to us, individually, in the past, while sorting out thoughts of whether or not he wanted to remain a DEA operative. It was nice to know he had finally made his decision. Much safer for his heath, and naturally, we liked being able to see him regularly at our dinner table. I had been missing our sketching trips out into the interior of the ranch, as well. Apparently, Rosalie had also missed him.

Theo said, "That's *good* news! We can discuss some ideas that have we developed after dinner, if you like." He was referring to the Mesa House Museum plans, and that he would be glad to get Red Thunder's input.

After dinner, Theo and I went with Red Thunder into Theo's office to talk. The room now looked like a geologist's office with its shelves of books about rocks, minerals, water, soils, fossils, and other related material. There were many different kinds of rock samples on bookcases and desk, and some piled on boxes off to the side. He had moved his heavy oak desk and leather upholstered office furniture up from the old Rancho Bernardo office, which was now closed. One whole wall of the home office was of glass and faced on the atrium. In the atrium, he had placed small potted trees—broad leaf pine, bottle brush—and various interesting, large rocks from the ranch, among which sat more mineral samples and fossils.

Red Thunder sat in one of the comfortable tan leather chairs facing toward the atrium, and waited to hear about the Mesa House.

Theo said, "We finally hammered out a good design for the Mesa House Museum with our architect. Our Hopi caretaker, Micah, agrees that it's better for someone to be right there, on the spot, in an apartment behind the museum. We were hoping that you might stay in the second apartment frequently enough to fill in the periods when Micah and Sonya can't be there."

Red Thunder said, "I have no objection to living out at the ranch by the mesa. I may decide to keep my town apartment, as well, but I'll see how things go." About an hour later, after Theo had shown him all the plans, and we had discussed the information dribbling in from the archeologist, Jed Hazard, pertaining to the Mesa House pottery and artifacts, Red Thunder thanked me for dinner and went back to his apartment.

Theo was occupied the remainder of the month consulting in his field on aquifers. This was for a client who represented a small water district near the village of Guatay. The client was concerned about over-burdening the level of the water table. So, Theo did a multiple well flow study of the aquifer with computer modeling for future supply. As a consequence, we didn't see each other much except at bedtime, and late at that.

One night we were lying in bed talking, when Theo brought up the subject of Rosalie's happiness. "Has she talked to you about what's on her mind these days?"

"Some," I said. "She's excited about the crafts store. She and Rebecca are still ordering inventory and delivering it to the storage shed." Theo and I had offered a large, secure storage shed at the ranch as a sort of temporary warehouse until the girls were ready to lease their retail space next month. "They've been drawing up their ideas for store displays and planning their expenditures for advertising. It's a pretty exciting time for them."

"I get that part," he said. "But when she's not talking about the store project, she doesn't look very happy."

I said, "I'm sure you understand that she may not be completely over the collapse of the relationship that she and Matt had. Both of them misread each other's goals and intentions. It was sad on both sides, and things like that take time to get past."

"Maybe," he said. "But, I know she goes out with other guys, now. She isn't just sitting at home."

"True. Perhaps she misses having a special relationship, even though the one with Matt didn't work out. There's something very nice about spending your free time with that one person you really care about." I snuggled closer to him.

Theo's arms tightened around me. "You're probably right. I wouldn't want to think what my life would be like without you in it." We both knew that happiness was something that had to be sought, cultivated, and then thoughtfully maintained.

17

OLEANDER TEA

May

ONE SUNNY MORNING IN MAY I decided to have my usual chamomile tea sitting at the back patio table. The wild flowers we encouraged to grow in our backyard, plus, all the flowering bushes lining the yard made the view a pleasant morning break from painting.

I slid open the back door and noticed Hernando's old truck parked back by the corral. Turning toward the table to set my tea down and investigate, I stopped. My employee and self-appointed protector, was slouched in a patio chair, his head on his chest, snoring.

I coughed loudly, but no effect. Hernando didn't even break a snore. Patting him on the shoulder only caused him to slouch sideways. In fact, he became more and more sideways, until I was afraid he was going to fall out of the chair.

"Come on, Hernando. Wake up!" I tried to shove him upright, pushing at his shoulders. His young body, densely packed with muscle, was very heavy to lift. Realizing the futility of my actions as his slide to the patio floor became more inevitable, I mentally pictured how to protect his head from the hard tiles.

Fortunately, I was able to prevent any harm to Hernando's head, which was good. But, as he slipped down to the tiles, I neglected to consider my own vulnerable position as I tried to cushion the blow. By the time I located the flaw in my reasoning, his flaccid body had pinned me to the floor.

I lay on the tiles with Hernando sprawled unconscious on top of me, and re-examined my situation. He weighed a ton, and nothing I had done to wake him had helped. I had tried yelling. Yelling hadn't helped. Punching him in the arm hadn't helped. He was dead to the world. Immovable. And something in his shirt pocket was painfully jabbing my stomach. I slowly squished my hand between his chest and my abdomen and to move the offending object. I was pleasantly surprised that it turned out to be a cell phone, so at least I could call for help.

I called Red Thunder's cell. He picked up. "Wolfe here."

"It's Janna. Would it be convenient for you come to my house around to the back and assist me?"

"I'll be there in five." He hung up. He never wasted time with questions, preferring to make his own analysis upon arrival.

Though it was handy to be able to call on a man used to dealing with emergencies, I could picture my sketching partner shaking his head in amusement over my present predicament. Hmm. It should be possible to slowly ease sideways and out from under, which could save me some embarrassment. Oozing out from under Hernando's unconscious weight wasn't comfortable, but with concentrated persistence, I was able to free my crunched body seconds before my friend came walking down the garden path.

I was just sitting next to Hernando on the patio tiles rearranging my clothing when Red Thunder arrived. Standing up, I limped over to my cold tea, and sat down in the chair Hernando had vacated to take a long drink. Hernando was no longer snoring, but was still asleep.

I had a bad feeling about this situation. I was thinking drugs, but was reasonably sure that Hernando wasn't a user. Aunt Myrtle and her, "emergency pills" were still in Florida, so no worries there. Something, however, was definitely amiss.

Red Thunder looked perplexed, glancing first at Hernando and then at me. Lowering himself into a chair, he sat waiting for an explanation.

"I found him sitting here, sleeping, when I came out to take a break from painting." I described my concern about how I couldn't wake Hernando, and then when he began to slide his body behaved like a large, super heavy, bag of mush. "Briefly, I was stuck under him, but found his cell phone. That's how I managed to call you."

My friend had been listening with that half-smile, but soon got serious. "He isn't just asleep. He's either sick or on drugs. Do you know this guy?"

It occurred to me, then, that Red Thunder had never met Hernando. Nor did he know the circumstances of Hernando's hiring. Bob Taggert must have kept the information to himself. You could always count on Bob to be discrete in a good cause. However, it was now necessary to reveal some background. I hesitated, trying to figure out where to start.

Red Thunder leaned back. Patient.

I quickly assured him. "It's okay. His name is Hernando Valdez. Bob Taggert has already run his identification through the police system and found no record. And he agrees that Hernando was just a good kid who was given bad information by someone who wanted to use him. Actually, Hernando was always harmless and saved my life more than once. We turned him around and now he's doing fine."

"Doing what?" Red Thunder looked at me intently. He'd apparently caught on that Hernando had been my "mysterious protector."

"He's working at the ranch now as Matt's assistant." I held up my hand to forestall any premature outrage. "Shortly after you and Bob gave me the special cell phone, I realized that Bob's Plan B wasn't going to work. So, I went with my own plan and set up a circumstance where Hernando and I could discuss things." I went on to tell about how naïve and clueless Hernando had been in working toward his goal of owning a horse and some land.

"So, you offered your stalker a job." Red Thunder looked a little dazed.

"Well, Hernando has come to my aid again since he's worked for us. And he's very good with horses and other animals. Theo and I have kind of adopted him. He's a good kid."

"Theo went along with this?"

"Well sure. It's not as though I could sneak him onto our ranch as an employee without Theo knowing about it. I told Theo immediately after Hernando and I had our little talk. Theo was a little hesitant when I first suggested giving him a job."

"I'll bet."

"But, as soon as Theo met Hernando and looked him over, he agreed to give Hernando a chance to prove himself. And he's working out well, so we think it *has* been a good decision."

Red Thunder sighed, rubbing his face. "It's not how most people solve their stalker problems. But, then why would I expect you to do anything normal? I'll have to have a talk with Taggert."

"It's good," I said. "You'll like Hernando."

My saying his name again must have finally penetrated Hernando's coma. Suddenly his eyes popped open and he stared around trying to figure out where he was. He noticed me and moved to sit up with a grunt.

I rushed around to him. "Just relax, Hernando. Don't try to get up, yet. Do you have a headache or feel anything strange?"

He ran his hands through dark hair that had been trimmed short and over his face. Clad, now, in a western shirt with sleeves rolled up, and jeans and boots, he looked a little pale as he made an attempt to stand up.

"Let me help you." I held out an arm to steady him. "Let's go in the house and I'll get you some coffee and something to eat."

Hernando docilely let me guide him into the house. Red Thunder followed closely behind, clearly not sure what to make of the situation. I placed Hernando at the kitchen table and poured cups of coffee for both men. Since it was now nearly lunchtime, I made turkey sandwiches, and put out some coleslaw, chips, and fruit.

We ate in silence for a few minutes. I could see that Hernando was trying to recall what he was doing here. Meanwhile, Red Thunder's eyes were going over the young man like a precision instrument sizing him up—remembering everything he knew about him.

Finally, Hernando said, "I'm sorry, Janna." He shook his head. "I don't remember coming here. I feel strange, and I just don't remember."

I patted his arm. "Take your time. It might help you to know that I think you've been drugged. You were asleep on the patio when I went out there this morning."

Red Thunder asked, "What's the last thing you remember before you woke up on the patio?"

Hernando looked at him as though he was seeing him for the first time. I said, "This is my very good friend, Thad Wolfe, Hernando. He's helped me many times when I've gotten into trouble. In fact, I immediately called him when I discovered you on the patio this morning."

Hernando apparently accepted my word at face value and began to strain his memory backward in time to answer Red Thunder's question. I could see that Red Thunder was relaxing after observing the young man for a while. It must have been obvious that there was only friendship between us. Hernando was no longer a dangerous mystery stalker. He was just a young guy trying to put one foot in front of the other, and at the moment it was hard going.

"I was at Lake Mirage yesterday. It was my day off and I wanted to make the final payment for my horse." He smiled at me wanly. "You'll love him. Lightning is like a king. All black like a night with no moon. I got him for a very good price because he had been in an accident while being trailered from Ramona. He got cut up and bruised in the crash and it took him a long time to regain his health, but now he's good enough for light riding. His value is much less because of his scars and some problems from the accident. But, I thought he would be good for breeding. Theo looked at him and agreed the stallion is a good buy because of the bloodlines. He will be delivered to the ranch next week."

I smiled at Hernando. "A dream come true. I'm glad for you, Hernando."

Red Thunder cleared his throat.

Back to business. "What's the last thing you remember after buying the horse?"

Hernando thought. "I was really happy after making the arrangements for Lightning's delivery. I walked back to my truck, and sat there thinking about the great saddle I bought for him. I want him to feel special, so I got him a nice saddle." He sat there eating his sandwich, trying to recall. "I'm sorry. Nothing else comes."

Red Thunder asked, "Was your truck locked while you were making your deal about the horse?"

"Nah. It was on this quiet lake road across the street from the lake properties, and the truck isn't what someone would steal. I even left my windows down because it was a nice day."

Red Thunder looked at me and then back at Hernando. "Did you have anything to drink in the truck?"

Hernando paused, then said, "I had a half-finished can of cream soda in the cup holder. Nothing else." An idea seemed to form. "I drank a sip of the soda, but it tasted off. I guess I fell asleep, because I don't remember anything after that. I must have awoke and drove here. Maybe I knew I needed help." He stared at me. "You think someone put something in my soda?"

"It's possible. My Aunt Myrtle had something like that happen to her a little while ago. She lives in Lake Mirage, too, if you'll recall. We lost track of her for a day and a night, and then she showed up in a daze. A little like you."

Red Thunder looked at me with curiosity.

I said to him, "Aunt Myrtle's in Florida right now, and she is supposed to be flying into San Diego tomorrow. It couldn't have been her. But it does seem like there might be someone who is occasionally doping folks in Lake Mirage. Do you have any idea how to go about finding out who's doing this?"

Red Thunder shook his head. "Not at the moment. I'll have to talk to Taggert. There may be other things that could relate to this incident. Everything a criminal does, thinking he won't be noticed, becomes an arrow pointing at him to the careful observer." He stood up. "Sadly, although it gets easier to catch perpetrators with each crime they commit, it's hard on the public."

Hernando stared at Red Thunder. "Why would someone spike my drink? Was it just a joke?"

Red Thunder looked at him with a serious expression. "I think you stepped into something you didn't understand when you started playing tricks on Cody."

Hernando flushed, but didn't say anything.

Red Thunder continued with the ghost of a smile, "Although a lot of us were laughing, there was someone who wasn't entertained. And that person is still out there. You need to watch your step. Probably would be a good idea to stay away from the Lake Mirage area for now."

He lifted an eyebrow at me. "I can always count on you to liven a dull day. Gotta go. Thanks for lunch." He nodded at Hernando and left through the backdoor."

I kept Hernando with me the rest of the day, watching to see that all was well with him. Beyond looking washed out, he seemed okay. The young have good powers of recuperation. I kept giving him liquids and food, which seemed to affect him like medicine. By the time Theo came home and we told the story to him, Hernando was much better. Of course he wasn't a ninety year old lady. That might have made a difference.

Aunt Myrtle arrived the next morning, and I made the trip to have lunch with my grandparents and aunt in honor of her visit. While I was there, I managed to accompany Aunt Myrtle back to her own cottage for a private chat.

I mentioned Hernando's sad experience without telling her his identity. Then I asked her about her thoughts on doping people. May as well get the facts, I thought grimly.

Aunt Myrtle blushed. "Well, my dear. I no longer carry my emergency pills with me. I'm not completely convinced anymore that they always have the positive result I'm seeking." She cleared her throat. "Last January, my sad experience of ending up on your front stoop, made me reevaluate the emergency pills." She said in confidential tones, "Somehow, I managed to take one of them by mistake, confusing it with my aspirin. Of course, after that I had to do some more thinking about those pills. Such a silly mistake to make, and I was fortunate that I didn't have more problems than I did. I'm sorry to have inconvenienced you, my dear."

I told her I was just glad she wasn't carrying them anymore.

She assured me, "Oh yes, those pills are gone now. Instead, I now use chamomile or valerian tea. Although the Seminole medicine man told me, and I sadly found out, that valerian can make people nauseous at times." She sighed. "I'm still experimenting with aids that soothe the stress of others. I really do think most of the bad things people do are rooted in personal stress and discomfort."

"But, Aunt Myrtle, one should never give things to people without their consent. It's illegal and," I added the clincher, "it's rude!"

"Oh my dear! I would *never* do that. Ever since I've stopped using my emergency pills, people always know what they're getting. My goodness, anyone knows what a cup of tea looks like. I just give them tea." She looked off into the distance, thinking. "Of course, they never ask what *kind* of tea it is. But there are so many kinds of herbal tea these days, I guess they assume it's mint or lemon or something soothing like that." She looked back at me. "So you see, the tea soothes them and nothing bad happens. Of course there is that little wrinkle about the valerian."

I asked her if she was still trying to re-educate real estate developers.

"Well, yes, it's so important that they relax properly while Violet and I help them to absorb the facts about Florida's need for fresh drinkable water." She shook her head sadly. "It's a long, slow, process to visit the owner of every construction company to convince them to think about the ecological benefits of halting construction in order to preserve the remaining fresh water in the state of Florida."

"I can see that it would be," I said.

She continued, "But, I'm proud of our successes thus far. A couple of gentlemen promised very sincerely that they would move to another state to forward the cause." Aunt Myrtle fairly glowed at this tale of sacrifice.

"That's nice," I said, remembering suddenly that Aunt Myrtle doesn't actually need drugs to make people want to do whatever is necessary to make her go away. I wondered if my aunt had started a stampede of builders fleeing Florida to escape her "help." It struck me that Aunt Myrtle was sort of like another force of nature—like a hurricane that wore little lace collars. I had to think about this before I talked further with my aunt.

Aunt Myrtle lay down for her nap, and I let myself out. On the road back home I decided to visit the Mesa House. I wanted to sit on top of it and stare into the national forest and beyond. The mesa top had become another place of quiet and reflection for me. I needed to still my mind and just think peaceful thoughts.

I drove on the dirt track crossing our ranch to Wildcat Lake, stopping at the place where the game trail comes out from the Mesa House. Using the "back door," as Micah called it, was a lot simpler than the entrance Red Thunder had originally discovered.

I followed the game trail on foot to where it goes by the cliff side. Along that path Live Oak scrub grew densely beside the rock wall. By carefully lifting branches away from the rock as I proceeded, I could make my way to the hidden steps that ascended to the Mesa House. Over the years, Micah had trimmed the scrub to make the passage somewhat easier than it might have been, but it was still a prickly way to go.

Arriving at the top of the steps, I moved to one side of a seemingly solid wall of rock and found the narrow slit just wide enough for a not-too-plump person to slip through. On the other side, I emerged into a small, dark room and continued into the larger room immediately next to it. It had a stone bench against the wall.

I sat on the stone bench to remove my backpack and get to my water bottle. As I leaned back against the wall to take a long drink, I felt something crawl into my lap. Putting my hand out without looking, I began to rub a soft, furry head as I drank. I'd become pretty blasé about petting Kolichiyaw. She knew I was a pushover for animals, even if they were a tad on the smelly side. But, Kolichiyaw's scent never seemed overly strong, considering that she was a skunk.

I stood up and set Kolichiyaw down, and was about to cross the floor to another section of the Mesa House, when Theo suddenly popped into the room. He must have seen the Highlander and came in search of me. As far as I knew, he hadn't ever been introduced to Kolichiyaw, as yet. At least the skunk wasn't behaving as though they were acquainted. She went very still, watching Theo from her position in the center of the room. Theo turned into a statue as soon as he saw her.

"Unh," he said.

"Not to worry," I told him. "She actually likes people. But she doesn't know you, so to make her acquaintance it would be good if you offered her something tasty to eat." I knew he always carried snacks on him. He was always hungry and kept energy bars in spare pockets for when he was desperate and not near food. "Slowly crouch down taking whatever snack you have out of your pocket and put it on the floor in front of you. Then you can let her sniff your hands."

He followed my directions. Kolichiyaw cautiously sniffed, then eagerly ate the peanuts he had placed before her. He held out his hands when she was done eating and let her sniff them. Then she pushed her face into his hand to be petted. It was a ritual she was used to, but Theo wasn't. I could tell he was startled.

I said, "Just think of her sort of like a cat."

He petted her head and stroked her back. She leaned into his touch and didn't seem alarmed when he slowly stood up. He looked at me. "Now what?"

"Now you're a pal," I informed him. "I think she has you classified under non-threatening pushover."

"So do I always have to show up with peanuts?" He watched the animal with curiosity.

"No, she'll cut you a lot of slack. The deal is if you happen to have food, you must share it. But, one doesn't always have food."

Theo said, "I think I'm in trouble. I almost always carry something on me, and I suppose she'll smell it and know."

"She'll accept what you give her."

"I can't believe we're discussing my relationship with a skunk." Theo watched Kolichiyaw as she investigated the dark shadows under the stone bench, and nosed around the room.

Theo turned to me. "The reason I hunted you down is because I have news. First, I've been offered a regular column in Science Views. The Editor wants me to address a large variety of geological subjects of current interest and answer questions that people write in on geology."

"Very neat! How often does your column show up in the magazine?"

"Once a month. And," he paused while pulling out a large envelope he had been carrying under his arm, "our architect, Todd Jergen, just delivered the completed plans for our new house. We can start the house as soon as we hire a builder, get the county to approve the plans, and get a building permit."

"Wow. I think we need to celebrate!" I threw my arms around his neck and gave him a kiss. I'd been wondering when we'd hear more about the house that Theo proposed to build up on the mountain.

He smiled. "Do you feel like eating Chinese?"

A couple hours later, after a shower and change of clothing, we were sitting at our favorite Chinese restaurant on Main Street eating eggrolls and sipping iced tea. We were discussing details of what we wanted in the building of the new house while we waited for our main course.

"It looks like Todd included everything we asked for." I examined the book of blue prints spread out on the table. "I like the way he's made space for a large pantry off the kitchen." I turned the page. "And the traffic pattern is very appealing the way it naturally flows through the house."

Theo dipped his eggroll in some hot mustard. "Did you see his solution for the outside? I suggested using stone on the bottom level of the house and logs on the upper level, so as to follow the Puebloan building styles." He pointed to the outside fireplace drawn on the wide front porch. "Here's where he's included the existing old stone fireplace."

I started to close up the folder of blueprints as our dinner arrived at the table. Looking past the woman serving our meal, I could see Aunt Myrtle being shown to a table across the room with Loretta May Duboise. That was a surprise. Apparently, they had renewed their friendship. Based on the recent history of pain and blame, I was amazed to see Loretta putting it all behind her to start anew with Aunt Myrtle. That just showed you could never really tell what was going on with other people.

Theo spooned Kung Pau Chicken over rice, saying, "That'll be a great place to gather around the fire in the evening after dinner and look out at the stars."

I noticed that Aunt Myrtle and Loretta May were being served tea and chips with dipping sauce while they waited for their food. They were deep in conversation.

I said, "We'll have to get some really comfortable outdoor furniture for that porch. We'll probably use it a lot."

Loretta May was gesturing broadly to Aunt Myrtle on some absorbing subject, her hand sweeping over the cups of tea, barely missing them.

Theo swallowed a bite of food. "It'll be great to be away from the town lights. We'll get a better view of the constellations from our new house site." Theo loved to watch the progress of the stars as they changed position through the months of the year. To him, it was like looking at a calendar in the deep country night sky.

My eye was caught by Aunt Myrtle's hand accidentally turning over the bowl of chips. As she tried to quickly tip it right-side-up again, her sleeve swiped Loretta May's tea cup and it dumped on the table, dripping into Loretta May's lap. I could hear the high pitched tones. "Oh! I'm so sorry, my dear." She pushed everything on the table to one side while she blotted up the tea with napkins. Their waitress came to assist the process of putting things right again. Another waitress brought a fresh cup of tea and more chips. The whole scene was business as usual with Aunt Myrtle.

"Did you see the balcony above the porch that comes off the master bedroom?" Originally, Theo had thought we would keep the second floor as bedrooms that could be shut off when we had no visitors. But, Todd had thought our purpose would be better served by keeping the whole *front* of the house—upstairs and down— for our regular use and close off the *back* of the house when only Theo and I were there.

Theo pointed to the blueprint. "We can sit out on the balcony Sunday mornings and drink coffee while we read the paper." He paused to add soy sauce. "And your studio will get great light from the sky lights on the second floor, across from the bedroom."

I skewered a peapod with my fork. "I'm looking forward to seeing it when it's finished. I thought I had a pretty good set-up at home, but Todd seems to have made some improvements in the studio storage areas, and, of course, I don't have that wonderful view to look out on at home in the garage."

I looked up to see Loretta May scoop up a substantial amount of hot mustard on a chip as she gestured and then shove the chip in her mouth. Her eyes grew big and she began to fan her mouth frantically. She must have distractedly put her chip in the wrong dip. With one hand wiping her eyes, she reached out with the other to grab a cup of tea, obviously with the idea of washing down the burning mustard. She took a big gulp and then downed the rest of the tea in an effort to soothe her distress.

But evidently, something was wrong. When Loretta May realized she had mistakenly picked up Aunt Myrtle's untouched cup to drown the hot mustard, she gasped loudly. "Oh my God!" And fell out of her chair onto the floor.

By this time, Theo, registering my look of dismay, turned around to scan the scene. One glance at Loretta May's unconscious body on the restaurant floor and he had his cell phone out, punching 911 for emergency help.

I got out my cell and called Bob Taggert. It seemed to me he might be interested in the contents of that tea cup. And I was pretty sure that Aunt Myrtle wasn't at fault for the medical emergency this time. As soon as I finished talking to Bob, I made my way across the room to be moral support for Aunt Myrtle, and to save her from the irate restaurant owner who had recent memories of a past disaster associated with my great aunt.

"I just don't understand it," said Aunt Myrtle, a very worried expression on her face. "She's had so much stress lately. Maybe it was too much for her. I hope it wasn't something I said."

I assured Aunt Myrtle that for once, it was unlikely that she had caused this calamity. I privately thought that Aunt Myrtle's happy, innocent demeanor had been too much for Loretta May's sense of personal justice. Bob appeared to agree with me. He had everything on the table left as is, and evidence samples were taken of all the food and drink for analysis.

Loretta May was hauled off to the hospital with a police woman as a companion.

The night was a long period of endurance for those affected. Statements had to be filled out, and questions had to be answered. But, Bob allowed us to remove Aunt Myrtle from the scene after he had questioned her sufficiently to fill in what he didn't know. We took my confused aunt home to her cottage, and tucked her into bed.

Early the next afternoon, following lunch, Bob appeared at my door and I offered him coffee. He looked disheveled, as though not having been to bed since the previous day. But a satisfied, almost happy, look was on his face. I asked how things had turned out with Loretta May.

"The tea cup she accidentally drank from was laced with homemade oleander concentrate. High strength and quick acting. Apparently the same drug that killed Dillon Cody and Gudrun Bohn. The publicly released cause of death was given out as prescription meds, but actually, we found oleander in the capsules. You may be surprised to learn that a jar of oleander concentrate was found hidden in Loretta May's cottage. Evidently, she had planned to do away with your Aunt Myrtle by using the same substance she employed for the other two, but during the process, got distracted and was careless. She ended up drinking the cup of tea that had been intended for Myrtle."

I felt sick and sad about the whole occurrence. "How could she do such terrible things? And why? What did she gain from any of it?"

"She readily confessed to it all on videotape, with her lawyer present. He tried to shut her up, but she said she just wanted to get it all off her 'conscience.' As a matter of fact, her conscience doesn't bother her very much, because she tends to blame your Aunt Myrtle for most of her current problems. She said she immediately felt better after confessing the crimes, and thought she might want to open her own pastry restaurant when she recovers from the rather serious damage left by the oleander concentrate. Even if she would be allowed to leave, she'll likely be under close medical care for a time. She was lucky to survive at all."

I must have looked incredulous, because Bob said immediately, "When she's well enough, a period of psychological testing will begin. There could even come a day when the experts have a better idea of what is happening inside her head. But, I gather her childhood contained certain painful incidents at impressionable times, and since her mental condition was never addressed back then—and she was good at hiding idiosyncrasies—she just kept getting more and more unstable."

"Did she say why she killed Gudrun?"

"As we had guessed a while back, she had had a hidden relationship with Gudrun. However, Gudrun didn't want to leave Stevette Strike to be with Loretta May. So Loretta May told me she had no choice but to kill Gudrun, and that she felt much better after that. I got the feeling that that's how she takes care of problem people in her life—she just makes them go away, permanently, so that she never has to worry about them thwarting her again." Bob took a long drink of coffee. "I heard probably more than you'd like to know about how Loretta May solved her problems. Although you may be relieved to know that it was she who drugged the soda can Hernando left in his truck that day you found him on your patio."

"Good heavens! Hernando didn't even know her."

"Well, Loretta May is pretty sly. She said she saw Hernando putting together one of his little jokes against Dillon Cody, and thought it was quite funny. But, then she got to worrying after Cody died, that Hernando could be spying on her. That problem of a guilty conscience, again. Plus, you remember he was buying that horse across the street from her cottage. She wasn't sure just what his true business was, so she decided to settle the question by drugging his soda. Fortunately, he didn't take more than a sip, and the smaller dose allowed him to wander away in a half-conscious state."

I had to ask this. "Did she have anything to do with the deaths of those three women in San Francisco?"

"It doesn't seem so. She isn't reticent at this point discussing details of what she calls "justified" actions. She gave me a blank look when I mentioned the San Francisco deaths. I also asked if she had drugged your Aunt Myrtle a few months ago. She didn't seem to know about that, either. But she has a diary we're going to go over very carefully. I'm almost afraid of what might be in that."

I shuddered. I had never been comfortable around Loretta May, but I never would have guessed she was so completely separated from reality. This seemed to be a woman who had never learned to deal with relationships at all. I wondered if the psychologists in the years ahead would be able to help her find a path back to the real world. One thing was for sure, she wouldn't be opening her pastry restaurant any time soon.

I knew Aunt Myrtle would be sad for Loretta May, and her victims, when she heard the news. But knowing my great aunt, she'd chalk it up to "stress" and resolve to work harder to help others relax.

That evening Theo and I were soaking in the Jacuzzi at the club, reviewing Bob's comments. I had filled Theo in on what Bob had told me, and he was shocked that so much could have been going on, and no one had ever noticed the problems with Loretta May's personality.

"Well, it was difficult to put your finger on just what *was* wrong," I told him. "I wasn't comfortable around her, but I thought it was because her lifestyle ideas are so different from mine. It never occurred to me that she was just out and out nuts. Maybe other people had that problem with her, too. I mean, who would ever have considered Loretta May as the person who pushed Dillon in the creek, that time when he almost drowned? She just didn't come naturally to mind as a person who would do that."

"I'll bet Bob is reevaluating some of his ideas about now," said Theo.

"Bob said he'd been keeping careful notes on Loretta May because she had been the person to push for discovery of the body. In police work, Bob tells me, you always have to give that person special thought because of the high potential of them being the guilty party. So, in just following investigative rules, he had his eyes on her. And of course, because she lived so close, she had a lot of opportunity to cause harm if she were so inclined. The problem was that her motives didn't seem that pressing for a normal person. One doesn't usually do away with people just because they don't cooperate, or because they make difficulties in your life. Most people would just get a different job—she didn't really have to work for Dillon. And her sex-capades could have been a bit embarrassing, if revealed, but they wouldn't have affected her livelihood. Anyway, few people would really care that she was bisexual these days."

"I'm glad I never got to know her," said Theo. "In fact, I'm not sure I've ever met her."

"You'd likely remember if you had," I said. "I noticed she has an undeniable effect on men."

Theo smiled. "You're the only woman who has any effect on me." My sweet husband knew just the right answer to turn conversation in a more pleasant direction. He climbed out of the Jacuzzi and helped me into my robe.

18

A CELEBRATION OF LIFE

June

AROUND MID-JUNE, Bob came by the house with a "thank you" note addressed to me from Loretta May Duboise. Loretta May had been touched by my past belief in her possibilities as a chef. She wrote: *"You've always been so kind to me in my sad, difficult life. And it is largely due to your inspiration that I have had the courage to think of opening my own pastry restaurant."*

"Have you read this?" I asked him. "Does she really think she's still going to open a restaurant?"

"Don't know. But, I know for certain that she's considered a danger to society and is going to remain under heavy security, probably for the rest of her life. Or, at least twenty years of it. The psychologists have a fancy name for her condition, which I don't recall."

A few days later, on a Saturday, Theo and I hosted a barbecue out at our family campsite. Most of our friends came, as well as Grandma and Granddad. Aunt Myrtle had returned to her mission in Florida and couldn't be with us. And Matt had gone off to the buffalo ranch in Riverside County to work and gain experience over the summer with the large shaggy animals. But, all of our children were there and their friends.

It was a lively occasion. Rosalie, Gwen and Christian applied their combined culinary skills to provide most of the side dishes to accompany the excellent beef ribs that were sent over from the Big Ranch. And Christian also made up quantities of his special barbecue sauce.

While we ate tender beef ribs, slaw, potato salad, fresh cut vegetables, assorted pickles, baked beans, chocolate cake, and homemade vanilla-bean ice cream. Gwen, Christina and Tiffany entertained us with their music. They made few errors in their delivery these days, and were now calling themselves "Sunset Rose." They had finally decided the name of one of my favorite rosebushes would be good for their band. It sounded western and cool country, as well as romantic. All important ingredients to adolescent girls.

Sunset Rose played several old favorites—Born Country, You're Easy on the Eyes, and Sunset Rider—and then Gwen sang a sweet song the group had written about true friendship. And Tiffany sang about troubles worked out and rewards gained in reaching high to attain goals. Bob was so proud of Tiffany that he could barely contain the emotion, and Katey held his hand while their daughter sang. It was the first time Tiffany had ever had been brave enough to sing solo in front of an audience. The girls' voices and instruments were gaining a more mature sound with practice and the passage of time. Everyone applauded for a lengthy standing ovation when the musicians finished their set.

I wrote later in my journal that the whole day amounted to a sort of celebration of life. The twins had survived another year of school and would be big seventh graders in the autumn. Christian had gotten through his freshman year of college, and acquired some experience with Search and Rescue. Grandma had survived a stroke and had come back from her illness with new attitudes about food. Aunt Myrtle had survived a friendship with a very dangerous friend. Rosalie had moved on from her relationship with Matt and was on the verge of a grand opening, with business partner Rebecca, at their new crafts store. Red Thunder had returned from his assignment unscathed, and finally resigned from the DEA. Protection of the hidden Cornbread Mesa House had taken encouraging steps forward. And Theo and I had rescued the Big Ranch from an uncertain future to one of shining possibilities.

All of these things were worth celebrating. Along with numerous other things that had happened during the previous many months indicating steps forward for loved ones. Then, there was the fact that in a year we would probably be saluting the completion of our new home up on the mountain. This was the last month the site would be just a mountain meadow with an old house ruin.

I yawned as I closed the Journal and set it aside. Athena and the kittens were asleep in a pile on the chair next to me. In cat fashion, they usually scorned their own special cushion. I left the chair to the cats, got up to turn out the studio lights, and walk through the house. Everyone else had gone to bed more than an hour before, so I turned off lights, and checked doors and windows. After a quiet hour of releasing my thoughts in the Journal, I was finally sleepy enough to nod off.

Already in pajamas, I crept silently into the bedroom and slid into bed next to Theo. His strong arm reached out pulling me against him. He nuzzled my neck, whispering, "Everything okay?"

"Yeah," I whispered back, enjoying the comfort of his presence. Everything was definitely okay.

CPSIA information can be obtained
at www.ICGtesting.com
Printed in the USA
FSOW01n2337191115
13599FS